JORDAN WRIGHT

The Mandala Chronicles

Alternate Timelines

First edition

ISBN: 978-0-6455405-3-6

This book was professionally typeset on Reedsy.
Find out more at reedsy.com

For my kids, may you continue to grow into amazing, magical people, and surprise me everyday.

Contents

Acknowledgement

I had so much fun writing this book! There are so many people who helped bring Noah, Nora and Layla back to life for their next adventure, and I am so grateful to everyone who played a part in the creation of their story.

Firstly, I would like to thank my editor, Kate, who leapt wholeheartedly into my request for feedback on the parts of the book she liked. Not only did she help turn this book into something for everyone to enjoy, she helped squash my imposter syndrome while she was at it.

I want to thank my kids for always pushing me to be better, do better and write better. The imagination's you have puts mine to shame!

I also want to thank everyone who has been on The Mandala Chronicles ride with me for the past few years. There has been so much growth, shift and change that we all have whiplash, but it is always worth it in the end.

And lastly, to my readers, this dream would not be possible without you, so thank you for trusting me enough to indulge in my stories. This would not be possible without you!

Chapter 1 - Nora

Nora's eyes snapped open as she lay in bed at the soft scraping sound approaching the dark room she was confined in. No one had been to see her since the duplicate she had sent to fight Noah and Layla had disappeared, so it disconcerted Nora that someone, or something, was coming for her now.

Slowly leaning up on one elbow, Nora squinted, trying to see what was making the noise. Her eyes struggled to adjust.

A shift in the air caused a shiver to run down her spine, and the red energy barrier locking her in the room slowly dissolved to reveal a shadowy figure in the doorway.

"Tick? What are you doing here?" Nora pushed herself up into a sitting position to better see the Shadow Being she had created when her Ego had been pulled out of her chest when she first arrived in the Realm.

Tick retracted her long, clawed fingers, which she had been scraping along the floor, and silence filled the room. Nora raised her palm and summoned a bright amber ball of energy. She held it up, keeping her expression blank as she looked upon Tick's furious face, now an inch away from her own.

Tick's jagged teeth snapped as she took a step back, her sharp, wispy features flickering in Nora's light. "Your little hair trick didn't work," she spat quietly. Tick knew better than to make too much noise while her master, Garvan, was recovering from his rebirth.

"Trick?" Nora replied innocently, tossing the amber energy ball in the air. She clicked her fingers, and it floated next to her head.

"You could have easily beaten your brother on your own, but you decided to stay here instead, hiding away in your room like a coward." Nora could feel Tick's simmering rage as the Shadow Being leant back and flicked her long hair behind her shoulder.

"I wasn't under any instructions to go on the mission *personally*. Why should I risk myself when my double did a fine job on its own?" Nora rebutted calmly.

Tick's teeth gnashed. "Fine job? *Fine job?* There's not a scrap of it left!"

"But I *did* find where Noah and Layla were hiding. We're playing the long game here, Tick. No need to rush." Nora absently inspected her fingernails, watching as Tick's shadows exploded around her in anger.

"Garvan should have sent me!" Tick screeched, all concerns about being too loud gone. "I wouldn't have let them go free!"

"Oh really?" Nora cooed. "Where's Aaron, then? Didn't you go in person to retrieve him? I don't see him here."

"He had help," Tick snarled, clenching and unclenching her fists.

"As did Noah." Nora lifted her chin defiantly as one of Tick's clawed fingers roughly stroked her cheek.

"You're getting too cocky. I'll be watching you," Tick whispered in her ear before floating backwards out the doorway, replacing the barrier behind her.

"I'll be sure to put on a show," Nora crooned in reply. The ball of light floated back down to her palm and she re-absorbed the energy into her body.

Once Tick was completely out of sight, Nora laid down again and sighed, resting her arm on her forehead.

She drew a circle in the air, and a small round mirror appeared in her hand, glinting as she looked into the glass. A gift from Aaron, although she'd been tempted to smash it into pieces when it had arrived three days prior.

There, on the other side, were Noah and Layla, resting after a long day of planning.

She ached to be with them, to jump through the glass and rejoin the mission she'd started, but she was stuck here. Aaron had rescued Noah instead, leaving her behind to fend for herself.

Nora ignored the burning sensation in her throat. She knew she could handle herself, but still, a small part of her wished she was the one being taken care of.

The mirror shimmered as her thoughts drifted to Aaron, and she was now looking at him, lying in his own bed, nursing a nasty scratch that ran down his chest.

Nora flinched at the sight of him and shook the mirror, trying to get it to show her Noah again, but the mirror ignored her.

Resigned, Nora couldn't help looking at the muscles rippling along Aaron's bare chest, rising and falling as he breathed deeply in his sleep.

Nora's cheeks grew warm as she tried to look away, but her treacherous eyes dragged themselves down to where his blanket lay loosely over his toned abdomen, ending just under the V of his hips.

"Enjoying the view?" Aaron purred from the other side of the mirror, one eye cracked open as if he could see her.

Nora's heart leapt out of her chest at being caught, but she gave a disgusted groan in response before throwing the mirror as hard as she could at the wall.

The last thing she heard before it disappeared into thin air was Aaron chuckling.

She drew the circle again, trying to bring the mirror back so she could check on Noah, but nothing happened. Aaron had clearly taken his gift away since she was determined to smash it.

Scoffing, Nora rolled onto her side on her rock-hard bed, pulling the flimsy sheet over her shoulder mumbling, "Who even needs that many muscles?"

She could have sworn she heard Aaron laugh.

* * *

The next morning, after a restless night's sleep, Nora dragged herself out of bed to find a bag of fresh clothes and towels tossed into the room.

Garvan wanted to see her, it seemed.

Picking the bag up, Nora was instantly frozen in place. She let out a noiseless scream as Tick appeared out of nowhere. The Shadow Being hauled Nora's rigid body over her shoulder with ease, speeding her to the bathing room and unceremoniously throwing her inside.

"Garvan's picked up some new tricks," Nora muttered to herself as she unfroze, rubbing her ribs where Tick had gripped her and held onto the wall to steady herself as her head reeled.

When she felt like she was able to stand without toppling over, she pulled off her filthy pants and top and turned on the hot water, watching the room fill up with steam before adding some cold water and stepping into the bath.

Sitting down, Nora ran her hands over her body and noticed a sensitive spot over her ankle. An old injury that hadn't properly healed. She called blue healing energy to her fingertips and gently pressed them to her skin, letting out a sigh of relief as the ache disappeared.

Keeping the healing energy activated, Nora ran her hands over the rest of her body, taking the time to mend anything else that ached. She then dunked her head under the water before scrubbing her body down with a floral-scented bar of soap, holding back a sigh of satisfaction as the grime coating her skin floated away.

She had forgotten what it felt like to be properly clean.

Sooner than she would have liked, someone banged loudly on the door, and the bath water magically disappeared, leaving Nora cold and wet as goosebumps pebbled her skin.

Exhaling loudly through her nose in frustration, Nora unwillingly pushed herself out of the empty tub before quickly drying herself. She pulled on a new pair of loose grey cotton pants and a matching shirt, which had been inside the bag she'd been given.

Strolling out of the bathing room barefoot, Nora was guided to Garvan's Throne Room by a see-through, floating Shadow Being. It looked old and frail as it wafted down the hallway.

Before Nora could ask its name, it pointed her towards a pair of golden doors, which flung open as she looked at them.

Nora stepped inside, and her heart leapt into her chest. "What are you doing here?"

Chapter 2 - Noah

Noah's eyelids fluttered as something tickled his nose. Trying to ignore it, he settled deeper into his pillow– which just made the tickle worse.

Groaning softly, his body not ready to wake up, he tried rolling over to his side, but another, smaller body was in his way.

Eyes snapping open, Noah looked down and found the source of the tickling. A few rogue strands of Layla's curly red hair.

The two of them had been up late the previous night, planning how they were going to get to Zion's. They must have fallen asleep together.

As softly as he could, Noah lifted his head off the top of Layla's, where it had been resting, but the lack of warmth caused Layla to stir and slowly open her eyes.

"What time is it?" she asked groggily.

"I don't know," Noah replied softly. "I just woke up."

"Did you sleep okay?" Layla asked, holding back a yawn and pushing herself upright.

"Yeah." Noah cracked his neck as he readjusted his body. Everything was still sore from battling the fake Nora those few days ago. "I'm still a bit stiff, though."

Layla nodded sleepily, and after a moment, she stood up and stretched her arms to the sky. "Me too. I'm going for a shower," she said, her voice groggy as she toppled off the bed and padded towards the bathroom.

Noah watched her disappear down the hallway before flopping onto the bed again, lost in thought. It had been days since he had come back from that alternate timeline, and while Aaron's tree-mansion was lovely, they were no closer to figuring out how to get in contact with Zion, and they were about to run out of rations.

The only food they had left were tins of beans, and the thought of forcing another mouthful of those down made Noah's stomach churn.

Inhaling deeply, Noah mentally ran through the plan for the day before hauling himself out of bed.

Garvan had already undergone his rebirth. He'd shifted into his new body while Noah was trapped in that alternate timeline, which meant it would only be a matter of time before he sent someone else to come and find them.

Grabbing some clean clothes and tossing his dirty ones on the growing pile in the corner, Noah walked out to the living room in a towel and waited for Layla to finish in the bathroom.

His mind wandered for a few minutes until Noah faintly heard the sound of the shower turning off and the soft patter of feet on the wooden floor.

"We—" Layla started to say but choked on her words as she stared at Noah standing in just his towel.

All his training had paid off. He was now quite toned and muscular, and his hair, since they hadn't had any chance for grooming, now almost reached his shoulders and often flopped into his face. He pushed said hair away and looked at Layla, waiting for her to finish what she was saying.

Layla's cheeks flushed, and she turned on her heel. "Weneedtodoaloadoflaundrytoday," she said in one breath as she sped down the hallway to her bedroom, slamming the door behind her.

Noah contemplated following her but decided against it and padded his way to the bathroom. He and Layla had spent so much time together lately that the air was thick with tension, but they hadn't even kissed since that night in the hut.

He turned on the shower and exhaled loudly. The fresh steam wafting around the bathroom was refreshing, and Noah rubbed the excess sleep from his eyes.

Opening the cupboard over the bathroom sink, Noah grabbed his razor and some shaving cream that Aaron had left behind, lathered his face and raised the razor to his cheeks.

Preemptively wincing, Noah prepared himself for the umpteenth time to nick himself while shaving.

A soft *pop* rang in his ears, but he thought nothing of it as he opened his eyes.

"AAARRRGGGGHH!!!" Noah flung himself backwards, and shaving cream flew in all directions.

Instead of seeing his reflection in the mirror, Aaron was staring back at him.

"Hello!" Aaron said cheerily, raising his hand in greeting before reaching out of the glass and pulling Noah through.

The sensation of travelling through the mirror made Noah feel like he was being pulled through a straw. Then he landed unsteadily on his feet.

Pulling the towel tighter around his waist, Noah looked at his surroundings and saw himself, Layla, and the bed she'd been sitting on had been transported somewhere completely new. "Aaron? Where are we?" Noah asked.

"Hello!" a booming voice called from behind him.

Noah screamed again, turning wildly to see Zion greeting them with a raised hand like Aaron had. While Zion and Aaron were brothers, the only physical similarities they had were their vivid blue eyes, although Zion's were sky blue while Aaron's were sapphire. Noah had met Zion once before while he was on Earth, but the father of the Guardians held an intimidating presence. Noah always felt like a bit of a hillbilly when he spoke as Zion was always so formal.

"Let me help clean you up," Zion said to Noah after taking in his appearance. He waved an enormous hand in his direction, and Noah felt a tingle flow over him. Zion handed him a mirror he'd conjured.

Noah was now clean, neatly shaven and dressed in a pair of jeans and a t-shirt, with new sneakers that felt snug and comfortable on his feet.

"That's a neat trick," Noah muttered to himself, rubbing his hands over his smooth cheeks, no pieces of bloody toilet paper falling off when he did so.

Aaron pulled Noah into a one-armed hug. "I taught him how to do it myself."

Noah gave Aaron a shaky grin before walking over to where Layla was sitting on the bed. "I guess our plan to find Zion just got easier," he murmured, looking at the new outfit Zion had chosen for her. It was the same outfit he'd given Noah; jeans, a t-shirt and a new pair of sneakers.

Layla nodded. Her eyes narrowed at Zion, then she stood up, pulled her shirt further down, and followed Zion into the hallway he had started to walk down.

Noah jogged up behind her, into a corridor of seemingly endless white walls and closed doors.

"Uh," he began, "this is your house, right Zion?"

"Palace," Zion replied ahead of him.

"Palace," Noah corrected himself. "Why isn't there anything in it?"

"Because this is where everything begins," Aaron replied for his brother, as if Noah should know what that meant.

"What do you mean this is where everything begins?" Layla interjected, and Noah was grateful he wasn't the only one who was confused.

"Everything that is created," Aaron explained. "It could be a book, a new piece of technology or a scientific breakthrough. Anything and everything is first created here. This place, Zion's palace, is a white canvas, ready for anything to come into being. Once it's perfected, we then share it with Earth. We give humans inspiration and co-create with them from what we have started here."

"But, what if the person you give the inspiration to doesn't follow through, or something happens to them?" Noah asked.

"Then we give the inspiration to someone else, and so on, until it becomes a reality," Zion answered.

"Oh." Noah had never wondered how new things were created before, and he'd never have believed this was how it happened. He supposed it made sense.

"Here we are," Zion said after a short walk, stepping aside, indicating for Noah and Layla to step into a large white office. It had a long white conference table with a whiteboard at the front. "Have a seat." Zion waved his hand, and two chairs pulled themselves out.

Taking the proffered seat , Noah dropped down next to

11

Layla and looked up at Zion silently standing at the front of the room, gazing calmly at Noah as if waiting for him to speak.

Layla got in first.

"We've been trying to reach you for days!" she fumed. "If it was as simple as transporting us here, why did it take so long? You must have heard us calling out to you."

"I did," Zion replied, his deep voice sounding grittier as if he was holding back a thought. "I tried to bring you here many times, but the Realm wouldn't allow me to reach you until Aaron was healed."

Noah noticed the grim look on Zion's face and could almost hear the frustration at his inability to help the two of them.

"But we were there alone!" Layla cried. "Garvan could have come for us!"

"No," said Zion. "He couldn't."

"Why not?"

"I have kept him occupied with other issues."

Zion didn't elaborate further.

Layla hesitated, partially placated by his response. "It was still a long time to wait," she said quietly.

"We are sorry." Aaron walked over to her and cuddled her, resting his head on top of hers. "We did not mean to worry you."

"You are here now, though, and we have work to do," Zion said to Noah and Layla. "Garvan has undergone his rebirth, and until we can find out what he looks like, you two need to be on alert."

"I thought we'd be training," Noah piped up.

"You will be training. Here. We need to strengthen your muscle memories."

"Our muscle memories?" Layla asked.

"Your body needs to know what it has to do without you thinking about it. It needs to become instinct," Zion replied.

"Take this, for example," Aaron added. "In the morning, you have a routine, yes? Wake up, bathroom, brush your teeth, get dressed, eat breakfast and start your day, or something similar. Now, how often do you *think* about those tasks that you're doing? How often do you need to concentrate on those tasks?"

Noah and Layla both shrugged.

"Never, am I right?"

Noah and Layla nodded.

"That is because they are embedded in your muscle memory. You have been doing the same thing over and over again for so long that you do not need to think about it anymore. It is completely instinctive."

"Okay," Noah replied, "but what exactly are we committing to memory?"

"I am so glad you asked." Aaron's sapphire blue eyes glinted mischievously.

Noah shifted uncomfortably in his chair. He got the feeling that the training Aaron had put them through at the hut was child's play compared to what was coming next.

"I hope you are ready to work harder than you ever have before," Zion said to Noah and Layla.

Layla gave a soft cough, and Noah just gulped. He thought he already *had* worked harder than he ever had before.

Noah braced himself to hear what Aaron or Zion had planned for them, but an iridescent blue orb popped into the room.

"*He has made an appearance.*" a female voice reverberated

throughout the room.

"Send me as much information as you can, as soon as you can," Zion answered back immediately.

"I will send through everything I know as soon as I know it," the orb replied.

There was a short pause.

"Send your new recruits to me when you can. I have something to show them."

Zion nodded, and the orb popped again, disappearing into thin air.

Aaron placed himself between Noah and Layla, resting a hand on each of their shoulders. "Best get your adventure pants on," he said to them. "Your new journey awaits."

Noah stared at Zion, who called Aaron over. They retreated to a corner of the room and began to talk in deep, hushed voices.

It took him a second to realise that Layla had scooted over beside him and had her eyes closed in concentration.

"What do you reckon we're going to be doing?" Noah whispered to her.

"Shh!" she replied sharply. "I can almost make out what they're saying."

Zipping his lips tight, Noah strained his ears to see if he too could hear what Zion and Aaron were whispering about, although, after a few minutes, he gave up. He couldn't make out a word.

Sitting back in his chair and resting his hands behind his head, Noah stretched his back until it cracked. He then pushed his fingers into his tight muscles.

Deep breath in through my nose and out through my mouth, he thought to himself, closing his eyes and willing his mind to slow down.

Layla tapped his knee. Noah reluctantly opened his eyes and sat up straight in his chair.

"You two are going to see Nora," Zion said to them as Noah adjusted his position.

"We're going to meet Nora?" Noah exclaimed, pushing forwards in his chair so fast his abs cramped.

"No," Zion replied, "you are going to *see* Nora."

"Is there a difference?" Layla asked.

"Yes, there is," Aaron said. "Marian will help."

"Who's Marian?" Noah asked.

"The orb you saw before," Aaron said.

"The orb has a name?" Layla questioned.

"The orb is one of my children," Zion replied.

Noah stared at him blankly.

"Garvan may be holding their bodies hostage, but their minds are able to roam free, now that they are no longer shielding Simmy, if they will them to," Zion explained.

"So... Marian... is one of the Guardians that have been petrified?" Noah asked.

"That is correct."

"And she's going to transport us to Nora?"

"Yes," Zion said patiently.

"Okay..." Noah said slowly, trying to wrap his mind around how this would work.

"Marian!" Aaron called to the seemingly empty space beside him.

Pop.

Instead of the iridescent orb, a copper-skinned woman, who looked no older than twenty years of age, with straight brown hair tied up in a high ponytail that reached down to

15

her waist, appeared in front of them through a portal. Noah could see the white wall behind her, and was about to ask why before her vivid blue eyes caught his attention. He realised where the orb got its colour.

"Noah, Layla, meet Marian," Zion said, looking at Marian fondly. "She will take good care of you."

"Are you ready to go?" Marian asked the two of them. "We do not have much time, and I have a lot to show you."

"Yes, we're ready," Layla said, standing abruptly.

"Er, okay," Noah rambled, stumbling to his feet.

Marian held her hands out, inviting each of them to take one, then closed her fingers around them. The sensation was surreal as Noah could only feel a whisper of her touch. "Close your eyes. Otherwise, you will get dizzy."

Noah did as he was told, and then he felt a rush of warm air blow through his hair.

"You can open them now," Marian said to them.

Noah opened his eyes. He tried to get his bearings for a second as a wave of vertigo swept through him.

"Whoa," he heard Layla say. "Look at our hands."

Steadying himself, Noah focused on his hands and reeled. He was see-through!

Looking wildly at Layla, his eyes widened as he saw her outline, but could clearly see the wall behind her as well.

"Why are we see-through?" he asked Marian as quietly as he could. She was holding a finger to her lips to silence him.

"Your physical bodies are still with Zion," she said. "We are astral projecting."

"Astral… projecting…" Noah repeated slowly.

"Out-of-body experience," Layla explained to him calmly.

"Why aren't you more freaked out?" Noah demanded.

"I've done this with Simmy once before," Layla shrugged. "It's not so bad the second time."

Noah opened his mouth to ask more questions, but Marian's "Shh!" stopped him in his place.

"Come with me," Marian whispered, crouching low and running towards a large pillar and hiding behind it.

It was only then that Noah realised they were in the Throne Room, where the Guardians of the Realm were being held.

It was a room he was quickly becoming acquainted with as he had seen the eleven Guardian Siblings in their petrified forms many times, both in his dreams and when he had first arrived in the Realm.

The three of them squeezed in together. Marian, who was only slightly shorter than Noah, ducked under his armpit, while Layla, who was significantly shorter than the two of them, crouched on the floor and peeked her head around the pillar. She had pulled her wild red hair into a messy bun on top of her head to keep it from getting in the way.

"How are we going to see Nora?" Noah asked. "Why didn't we bring Ray with us?"

Silently, Marian pulled Vajrayana, who they called Ray, out from under her dark robe. The mandala quivered in her hands.

"Aaron gave her a tune-up while you were talking to Zion and handed her to me just before we left," she said.

Noah took Ray from Marian and held her tightly in his hand. Ray gave a small shiver of reassurance, and the warmth that spread through Noah's fingers calmed him down.

Layla put her hand on Noah's calf, because she couldn't reach his shoulder, and gave it a squeeze. "Look," she whispered.

"Get down," Marian hissed, pulling Noah's arm and dropping to the floor.

"What's going on?" Noah asked, his face uncomfortably squashed between Marian's hand and the pillar.

"Tick," Layla said. Noah shifted his head so he could see her.

Tick sauntered down the hallway muttering to herself, and for a heart-stopping moment, Noah saw her gaze roam over their hiding spot before continuing to track around the room.

Holding their breath, the trio waited for her to leave before standing back up again and spreading out behind the pillar.

"Do you think Nora's still in there?" Noah asked Marian, pointing to the dark room that Tick had walked past on her way back out to the corridor.

Nora had shown the room to him in a vision before he had come to the Realm from Earth.

Marian didn't answer, looking from the doorway to the petrified forms of her and her siblings. "Stay here."

Noah watched as she lightly sprung across to where her physical body resided and disappeared into it.

"What do you think she's doing?" Noah whispered to Layla.

Layla shrugged, her eyes sweeping around, taking everything in.

"What do you see?" Marian asked her.

Noah held back a yelp as he jumped. "Where did you come from?!" he hissed quietly. Marian had reformed out of thin air.

"I came from my body," Marian said nonchalantly. "It is harder for me to communicate with my siblings in this form."

"What did they say?" Layla, who hadn't been at all shocked to see Marian reappear, asked.

"We think Garvan is actively trying to find a way to get stronger," Marian said, her blue eyes narrowing. "With Zion around, Garvan cannot claim to be the most powerful being in the Realm."

"So he's getting Nora and Tick to find Zion on his behalf?" Noah asked.

"Garvan believes we have been in contact with Zion and is keeping his plans to himself. We are not sure of Nora's role, but we are keeping a close eye on her regardless.

"Why is Garvan keeping her here?" Layla asked. "When we fought that thing who took her form, she was incredibly powerful. Does that have anything to do with it? Is Garvan trying to use her powers for himself?"

"We cannot be sure," Marian replied, "but we think that might be the reaso—"

Suddenly, the large double doors at the back of the Throne Room opened, and a strong gust of wind forced Noah to cover his eyes.

When he opened them again, he and Layla were back at Zion's palace, the bright white room stinging his eyes.

"What happened?!" he demanded. "Why are we back here?"

Zion, who was sitting in a large chair in the corner of the room, looked at Layla. "Did you discover anything?"

"We saw Tick hovering around Nora's room," Layla said. "They may be working together."

"There is no chance of that," Aaron dismissed, sauntering into the room while stirring a cup of coffee. "Tick hates Nora. Does not trust her." Aaron lifted the cup to his lips, gulping down the liquid.

Layla stared at Aaron as he drank before turning to Zion. "We must have been forced out. Marian disappeared just

19

before we did."

"Thank you, Layla," Zion said to her. "This is a start. I wish you had been able to physically see Nora, but that will have to happen another day. You two had best get some rest. You were in your astral projection form longer than you may have realised."

Looking outside, Noah could see the sun beginning to set and gaped. Last time he'd checked, it was still morning. They really were in their astral projection forms for a long time.

"Time flows differently when you are not in your body," Aaron told them, letting go of his empty coffee cup and watching it fall before waving his hand over it, causing it to disappear into thin air. "Come, I will walk you to your rooms."

Noah numbly followed him down the hall. His body felt like lead, and his head was reeling as more questions than answers swirled around it.

Neither he nor Layla said a word during the walk.

Chapter 3 - Layla

Once Layla was sure Noah had settled in his room, she stuck her head out of her own doorway and assessed her surroundings.

She needed to find Zion.

The power Noah had shared with her—the power he'd gotten from the other timeline—simmered in her veins, and she rubbed her elbows as she willed it to settle. She was still getting used to it, her own life energy trying to expand to accommodate it.

Wandering aimlessly down the endless white halls, Layla turned another corner to find more pristine white walls in front of her. Sighing, she ran her hands over her face. "Zion!" she called, tired of going around in circles.

"Yes?"

Layla's head whipped around as Zion's deep voice answered, and she saw him standing behind her, having appeared out of thin air.

"You could have called to me from your bedroom."

Layla narrowed her eyes. "If you knew I was searching for you, why didn't you come to me instead of letting me get lost in these halls that all look the same?" She finished her sentence in one breath, unsuccessfully taming her frustration.

Zion's blue eyes sparkled with humour, but he didn't respond.

Taking a deep breath, Layla stepped towards him. "Anyway, I need to talk to you about something."

"I know you are upset with me for not coming to collect the two of you earlier, but I could not. I was unable to leave the Palace," Zion explained, raising his palms in defence.

"No, that's not what I—wait. The Realm is restricting your movements?"

"It is not important." Zion waved her off. "What did you wish to discuss with me?"

Layla paused, contemplating interrogating him further, but decided against it. Zion wouldn't share anything with her he didn't feel she needed to know. "You know about Noah's trip to that other timeline, right?" Layla asked.

"I do."

"Did he also tell you about the power boost he got from the Simmy over there?"

Zion paused. "He did not tell me, but I could feel it. He shared it with you too." It wasn't a question.

Layla lifted her arm in response, and Zion tentatively took it in his fingers, the power collecting where they lingered on her skin.

"You're not compatible with this energy."

Layla flinched at the words.

"If it was gifted to *you*, you would have been," Zion said gently, "but it was given to Noah. It is also from another timeline you have not been exposed to, which is why your body is rejecting it."

Layla let out a hum in response and waited until Zion had finished his inspection, his eyes meeting hers.

"May I?" he asked.

"Sure," Layla replied, not entirely sure what she was agreeing to.

Pins and needles immediately shot through the arm Zion was holding, and she winced as she saw the smoky tendrils of Simmy's red energy escape from her pores, swirling together as Zion caught them in his other hand.

"I will give it back to the Realm to look after," Zion said once the last of it pulled free. It dissolved into thin air as Zion released it from his grasp.

Layla's head cleared as soon as the energy left. It was like a fog had been lifted. Layla shook the arm that Zion had gently dropped to her side and looked around. She hadn't realised how sluggish she had been feeling with the foreign energy coursing through her.

"Is there anything else I can help you with?" Zion asked, tentatively turning on his heel.

"No," Layla replied slowly, and Zion half vanished. "Wait! Yes!"

Zion reappeared.

"When we were fighting Nora the second time, the fake Nora," Layla clarified, "Noah pulled off something he shouldn't have been able to. Aaron and Simmy never taught us, and I'm sure he didn't learn it in that alternate timeline."

Zion nodded for her to continue.

"He took a drop of his blood and smeared it on the spear he used to impale her. He said if it was the real Nora, it wouldn't have hurt her, but because it wasn't, he killed it. I'm worried about where that type of technique came from. All he said was that he had a gut feeling about how to do it."

Zion paused, a thoughtful expression on his face, before looking at Nora. "Noah has gone through a great deal of trauma. Both physically, with the awakening of his powers, and mentally, with losing his sister and leaving his family. It is to be expected that some part of him is drawn towards darker magic, but regardless, I must ask you to keep an eye on him to see if he dabbles in it any further."

"Do you want me to say anything to him? Maybe try and find out more about it?"

"Not yet," Zion replied. "Let me find out what I can first. The Realm is working in mysterious ways right now, and I cannot risk the two of you becoming tangled up in it."

"You mean it's becoming unstable," Layla said flatly.

Zion didn't reply, but his silence was confirmation enough for Layla. "I'll make sure to keep a close watch."

"Please do." Zion's eyes dulled, and Layla repressed the urge to pat him on the arm, not sure if it would be received as the comforting gesture she intended.

"Is there anything else?" Zion asked again.

"No."

Zion raised a golden eyebrow.

"I mean it this time," Layla reassured him.

"You are sure?"

"I am."

Zion gently rested a hand on Layla's head before turning around and disappearing.

Sighing, Layla ran her hands over her face before turning in the opposite direction and facing the endless white hall.

"Crap," she murmured to herself. "I should have asked him to take me back to my room."

A low chuckle filled her ears, and Layla was suddenly

dropped unceremoniously onto her bed.

Rubbing her tailbone where she landed, Layla grumbled a rough "Thanks" to the empty space around her.

The lights flickered in response.

Rolling onto her side, Layla rested her head on her hand and contemplated everything she had just learnt.

Noah was somehow being guided towards darker magic, and the Realm was becoming unstable.

What did that mean for their mission of keeping the Realm out of Garvan's grasp?

Chapter 4 - Noah

Noah placed the palm of his hand on the sensor pad that opened the door to his room and waited while it scanned. His brain felt foggy as he tried to come to terms with everything that had happened since Nora disappeared.

"You okay?"

Noah turned and saw Layla had peered out of her own room and was now looking towards him. "Yeah. Just trying to figure out what's going on with Nora."

"It feels like everyone has something going on at the moment," Layla replied, stepping out of her bedroom and letting herself into Noah's. Noah had been planning to get a snack from the kitchen, but it could wait. He hadn't had a chance to chat to Layla properly today.

"Do you reckon Zion will let Marian take us to Garvan's temple again? We might be able to catch a glimpse of him next time," Noah asked, folding himself down onto the squishy white leather couch in the middle of his bedroom.

"I doubt it," Layla replied, walking around the massive room, running her index finger along the white wall from the bedroom door to the en-suite. Finally, she came and sat down next to Noah.

An awkward silence passed between the two of them before Noah placed a tentative arm around Layla, nudging her to rest her head on his shoulder.

It took a moment for her to settle in, but when she did, Noah began stroking her curly red hair absent-mindedly. "We really need to start focusing on training again. We still don't know how to use our energy to its full potential, both on our own and with Ray. I mean, I know it's important to be able to shield and stuff, but surely there's more to it than that."

"Yeah," Layla replied slowly, her eyes closed, as Noah continued stroking her hair. "Plus, Zion and Aaron haven't exactly been forthcoming about what our roles as Guardians are going to be."

"Which is why we need to be training more," Noah repeated, dropping his hand and resting his cheek on the top of Layla's head, a few rogue strands of dirty blond hair falling into his eyes. "We can't become Guardians if we can barely defend ourselves, let alone the Realm.

"Mmm," Layla hummed in agreement, snuggling into Noah's warmth.

The two of them cuddled contentedly, enjoying the moment while they could, letting time lazily slip away, until finally, just as Noah was beginning to doze off, Layla pushed herself up with her hands and kissed Noah on the forehead.

Dazed, Noah watched as Layla got up from the couch and stretched her arms to the ceiling. She held her hand out and helped Noah up as well.

"I need to go," she said, her emerald green eyes slightly glazed as Noah met them with his amber ones.

"Do you have to?" Noah noticed Layla's cheeks flush, and he wrapped an arm around her waist, pulling her closer to him.

"As much as I would love to spend the day here with you, I need to find Aaron. There's something I have to chat with him about," Layla's muffled voice replied.

Letting her pull away slightly, Noah raised his eyebrow at her.

"About Simmy's mission," Layla clarified, but Noah noticed she averted her eyes.

Knowing better than to push her, Noah let Layla gently pull out of his arms and walk backwards towards the door, shooting him a cheeky grin as her back pressed against it. "Another time. I promise."

Noah just waved as she opened the door with the sensor and disappeared.

Suddenly exhausted, Noah staggered over to the bed and flopped down onto it face first. The second he closed his eyes, he fell asleep.

* * *

He was woken up the next morning by Layla gently nudging his shoulder. "Time to get up."

Groaning, Noah rubbed his eyes. "I'm awake," he said, although he really didn't want to get out of bed.

Huffing a laugh, Layla gave him a final nudge before leaving him to his own devices. He had a quick shower, brushed his teeth and dressed in a new pair of jeans, a white t-shirt and some comfortable white sneakers.

As soon as he was done dressing, Noah walked out into the hallway to see Layla waiting patiently for him. He grabbed her hand, and they went searching for their mentors.

Rounding a corner, Noah stopped as he heard muffled talking.

"Wait," he whispered to Layla, pulling her into him. "Can you hear that?"

Layla focused her ears and listened. "Three people?"

"Sounds like it."

As quietly as they could, in case they weren't supposed to hear what was going on, the two of them tiptoed towards the voices coming from the kitchen.

Layla reached the room first, and Noah let out a gasp when she suddenly knocked the wind out of him by elbowing him in the chest. She pushed herself out of his grasp with a scream of "Simmy!"

"Stay back!" Aaron called to her, thrusting his palm in her direction and wrapping her in a cocoon of sapphire-blue energy, forcing her to stop.

Layla froze mid-run, arms outstretched.

Aaron turned back to Simmy, the cocoon he'd wrapped Layla in slowly dissolving when he was sure she wouldn't move.

Hesitantly walking up behind Layla, Noah placed his hand on her shoulder. "Is Simmy alright?" he asked Aaron.

"She could not make it to the Realm on her own, so we had to transport her here ourselves. We could not risk Garvan finding her, and the energetic transition from Earth was too much for her to handle," he replied.

Zion was positioned behind Simmy, who hadn't appeared to have noticed Noah and Layla standing in front of her, pulsing sheets of golden energy into her.

Noah shuddered at the dull look in Simmy's brown eyes. Her usually thick auburn hair was hanging limply to her shoulders.

"What's wrong with her?" Layla asked, gently pulling out of Noah's grip to get a better look.

"She has been away from the Realm for too long," Aaron said to them. "She has been holding the position of Primary Guardian for longer than should have been possible, and she has not undergone a rebirth, even though she has completed all her life lessons for this body. All of this has put a strain on her body and mind, meaning right now, we need to help her undergo a transition in the safest way possible, to give her a break from being the Primary Guardian without giving that power to Garvan. When the two of you were transported here the other week and she was not able to travel here after you, she spent too much of what little power she had remaining trying to get to you."

Layla let out a whimper, and Noah squeezed her ribs in a small attempt to comfort her.

"What's happening to her now?" Noah asked. Simmy's form flickered in front of them as if she was going to disappear.

"We are replacing the negative energies that attached to her while she was on Earth with healing Realm energy," Aaron replied. "We are doing everything we can to help, but she was there for such a long time."

There were a hundred questions running through his head, but Noah held his tongue, leaving Aaron to focus on helping Zion heal Simmy.

"I thought Simmy was supposed to come here not long after we arrived," Layla whispered to Noah.

Noah shrugged in response. He'd forgotten about that.

"She tried to get here but was forced to stay on Earth. She was planning to arrive the same day we fought Tick and that fake Nora," Aaron, who had heard them, replied.

"This is going to take a while," Zion said, his voice strained with concentration. "Aaron, I do not need you here for this part. Take those two."

Nodding, Aaron lifted his hands from Simmy's back and took the unmoving Noah and Layla by the wrist. "Come, you two. There is a lot that needs to be done."

Not wanting to leave Simmy, Layla hesitated, but Noah grabbed her other hand and gently tugged her towards the door. "C'mon," he said softly, "we can't do anything for her here."

Reluctantly, casting one more glance at Simmy, Layla gripped Noah's hand tightly and let him and Aaron lead her away. "She'll be okay, won't she?" she asked Aaron.

"She will be fine," Aaron reassured her, but Noah didn't think he sounded convinced. "We need to take care of some things first, though."

"What things?" Noah asked.

"You two need to become fully-fledged Guardians. Today."

Noah tripped. "What?"

"It is the only way to pass over the Primary Guardianship without giving it to Garvan," Aaron said.

Noah hesitated, but Layla was nodding. "We'll do it."

"We will?" Noah asked.

"Noah, Simmy raised me. I'm not losing her when there's something I can do to help."

Noah gripped Layla's chin with his thumb and forefinger and searched her eyes for any hint of hesitation but was only met with fierce determination. "Okay, but wouldn't some extra training be beneficial first?"

The three of them began walking again. Noah stumbled

after Layla and Aaron as Aaron led them to a doorway at the corner of the palace, far away from the kitchen.

They walked into the middle of the room, and Noah saw Layla run her palms along her jeans, the only indication she was nervous. "We need to do this before Simmy's condition gets worse," she said, her voice breathy.

Noah's gut was churning. This didn't feel like the right time for him. Not yet. But they needed to take on the Primary Guardianship before Garvan could get hold of Simmy.

"Okay."

"Thank you," Layla said to him, squeezing his hand with hers.

Noah's heart skipped a beat as he squeezed her hand back.

Aaron watched them to make sure they were both on board before handing Noah and Layla a large mandala, which was embedded with deep blue sapphires. He closed his eyes, took a deep breath in, and exhaled, life energy exuding from his body.

Noah's hand that gripped the mandala started to grow warmer, then the rest of his body followed suit.

Heat radiated through him as the sapphire energy ran through his veins, burning Noah from the inside. It was like the mandala was pouring the life force of the Realm into him, changing his DNA from human to Guardian.

Chapter 5 - Noah

Noah's skin tingled as the pure Realm energy zapped through his bloodstream, but other than that, he didn't feel any different. It burned, but only for a few minutes, then Noah felt Aaron's energy fade away. As the energy from the transition settled into his veins, Noah flexed his fingers and looked at his palm.

It still looked like a normal hand.

"—for now, we need to focus on passing the Primary Guardianship from Simmy to the two of you." Realising Aaron was speaking, Noah snapped to attention. "We do not have much time. Garvan will have realised Simmy is losing grip, so we need to hurry."

Noah and Layla ran with Aaron back to Simmy and Zion, where Zion was still pulsing his golden energy into Simmy's hunched-over body.

"Stand around Simmy with me," Zion instructed Noah and Layla when they arrived, pointing them into position with a glowing golden finger.

Moving to where Zion guided them, Noah and Layla created a triangle around Simmy with Zion on either side of them before touching palms, an iridescent bubble forming around the three of them.

Once the bubble sealed, Aaron flung his mandala into the air above Simmy, flicking his wrist so it spun quickly enough to create a vortex. A high-pitched screech, which Noah thought sounded like water draining out of a bath, rang around the room as the excess energy from Simmy had carried with her from the Earth was absorbed. Noah managed to glance upwards and saw Simmy's red energy, tinged with black spots, swirl above their heads. Noah only had a chance to glance at it for a moment, before the influx of power which was pulled from Simmy was purified by Aaron's mandala and rammed into his own body.

Noah felt his skin tighten and prickle with goosebumps, and Layla's hand clenched harder around his as the new energy slammed into her as well.

Slowly, Zion released his palms from Noah and Layla's and guided them to close the seal around Simmy, just the two of them.

Without Zion there to buffer the energy, Noah had to dig his heels into the floor to stop himself from being pulled forwards. The vortex spun faster and faster, his body taking in more and more of the Primary Guardian energy.

How had Simmy been living on Earth, keeping this energy at bay all those years?

Noah felt Layla's hands trembling as she forced herself to keep the seal closed with him. The two of them now had sweat beading their foreheads, the energy seemingly never-ending.

Finally, when Noah felt his knees buckle and his palms begin to slip from Layla's, the energy pouring out of Simmy slowed to a stop, and an infinitely bright beam of light shone down on the two of them.

It took everything Noah had not to close his eyes and pull

away, but he pushed the urge down as the Realm's energy flowed through his veins.

He accepted it. He wanted this. This was his mission.

Something that had been laying stagnant, hidden within him sparked to life, and the same gut feeling he'd felt when fighting the fake Nora stirred awake.

Taking a deep breath in, expanding his lungs to their fullest, Noah felt invincible.

Noah exhaled, and the light dimmed. Layla's palm slipped from his, and Noah lowered his stiff arms, healing energy automatically flowing through them, relieving the tension.

He and Layla were Primary Guardians.

Noah's entire body felt electric, but he stumbled as he tried to move. His vision kept switching between Layla in front of him and the Earth.

"Come and sit down," a faint, gentle voice said to him, and he felt a firm hand grip his shoulders and guide him towards a white padded chair at the kitchen table.

Noah rested his elbows on the table and put his face in his hands, closing his eyes to try to stop his head from spinning.

The same firm hand then placed itself on top of his head, and the sensation of a raw egg dripping over him made Noah shiver as a cold, slimy energy oozed down him.

Once the sensation reached his toes, the visions slowed to a stop. Noah lifted his head, blinking white spots out of his eyes.

Through the haze, he saw Layla sitting on a chair at the head of the table, with her face in her hands like Noah's had been.

Zion lifted his hand from Noah and walked over to Layla, repeating the process with her.

Noah saw her shiver as the sensation ran over her body, and shortly afterwards, she lifted her head.

"What was that?" Noah asked.

"I calmed your nervous system," Zion explained. "You have just absorbed an extraordinary amount of pure energy from the Realm. Your bodies needed some help to adjust. The energy I dripped down you coated your bodies in a protective shield which will stay with you until your bodies become accustomed to its new DNA composition."

"How do you two feel?" Aaron asked, stepping out from behind Zion.

"Fine, now," replied Layla.

"Was that Earth we were seeing in those visions?" Noah asked, flexing his hands as the energy tried to settle beneath his skin.

"Yes, it was," Simmy said, her voice shaky as she tried to stand.

A rush of air hit Noah in the face as Layla bounded past him and jumped into her aunt's arms.

Smiling softly, Simmy patted Layla's hair as her niece nuzzled her nose into Simmy's cheek. "I am fine, Layla, just a little tired. I am glad you two are okay, and I am sorry. This is not the way I wanted the two of you to become Guardians."

Noah brushed off her apology with a wave of his hand. "For you, we would have walked into the middle of Garvan's lair."

Simmy's smile grew, and she nodded her thanks as she continued to pat Layla's wild red hair, brushing a few stray strands behind her ear.

Noah watched the two of them for a moment before looking at Aaron and Zion, his eyebrow raised in a silent question of what to do next.

"You need to learn how to control your new powers, and quickly. Simmy and her siblings were specifically born for this role. You two have been thrust into it in the midst of war," Aaron answered. "There is a very real chance this could blow up in our faces."

"So what do we need to do?" Noah asked. His new energy began coursing through him, eager for action after having been forced to lay dormant for so long within Simmy.

"It is time to start training again." A small blue energy ball formed at the tip of Aaron's index finger and, with a whistle, he let it fly through the room.

The small hairs on the back of Noah's neck stood on end as he tried to focus on the ball until a small blue speck caught his eye. He shot a bolt of amber electricity at it, causing it to explode into thousands of tiny sapphire pieces.

"No," Simmy interjected, glaring at Aaron.

Aaron sighed at her, lowering his finger, the remnants of his energy flying back to him and reabsorbing into his skin.

"Well, yes. But first, you two need to learn how to watch the Earth. It is important you know how to make sure it is safe and healthy, and then you can practise fighting." She said the last part with a pointed look at Aaron.

"Fine, fine. Party pooper."

Noah laughed at the exchange.

"Simmy is right," Zion said, stepping forward. "Noah and Layla need to learn how to pick up on any strange movements."

"What kind of strange movements?" Layla asked.

"Movements that suggest Garvan is infiltrating the Earth, manipulating the humans so that when they pass over to this side, they won't think twice about the Realm he is planning to create."

"I thought Garvan was looking to become a mighty ruler of the Realm, to control humans from here," Noah replied.

"He is," Zion said. "Or, that is what we believe his plan is. But it will be a long process, an ancestral journey, so he will need to start planting seeds on Earth soon, if he has not already started to do so. The Shadow Beings–" Zion shook his head, trailing off.

"That's going to take a long time," Noah said when Zion showed no sign of finishing his thought.

"Garvan is a patient man," Zion replied.

"And"—Aaron chipped in—"we believe he is now planning to use Nora to speed things up."

Noah saw Simmy avert her gaze to the floor.

"Do you think this too, Simmy?" he asked her. "That Garvan's going to use Nora?"

"We always knew she was brought here for a reason," Simmy said to him, but she didn't elaborate any further. Noah didn't push the subject. His stomach suddenly felt queasy.

"What's our next move?" Layla changed the subject quickly. "We're Primary Guardians now. We can't just focus on watching the Earth. We need to learn to control the energies in our bodies– learn to fight with them."

"That is the fun part, because fighting and defending will come to you naturally now," Aaron said, turning to leave the kitchen. "Let us take you back to the Earth room first, though."

"Earth room?" Noah asked.

"Where I took you to transition you into Guardians. You are able to see Earth in all of its entirety there," Aaron said, waving for Noah and Layla to follow him while Zion gently helped Simmy walk close behind.

As they got closer to the Earth room, Noah's body began to buzz, and he felt his new Guardian energies become alive. *We need Ray,* he thought to himself, and he instantly felt her warmth in his hand.

Layla, who had been slightly ahead of him, paused to fall into step with Noah, grasping Ray's other side when he held her out.

A crackle of amber and emerald energy sparked from Ray's largest sunstone as the two of them joined forces.

Yes. This felt right.

Taking the last two steps at a jump, Noah and Layla strolled into the Earth room and immediately doubled over as they were inundated with visions of people from all over the planet.

Noah heard Zion walk up behind them and felt him place a large hand on his back. *"Focus,"* Noah faintly heard him say.

Still holding onto Ray, Noah felt Layla's emerald energy reach out for him, and he replied with an amber spark of his own, the two energies combining in the middle of the mandala.

The visions stopped, and Noah was now looking at the planet as a whole.

"What are you looking for?" Zion's voice shot through Noah's mind. He knew Layla was hearing it too when she jerked Ray towards her in surprise.

"Places Garvan could have infiltrated," Noah replied.

Images flashed before his eyes once again, but this time they had a purpose. This time, Noah was searching for something.

Small pockets of dark energy caught Noah's attention, but there was nothing that signified to him that Garvan was taking over the place, so he kept searching.

"Garvan's either very good at hiding his energy signature, or he hasn't infiltrated Earth yet," Layla said after a few more minutes of searching. "What are we looking for, specifically?"

Simmy started an explanation, but Zion put a hand up to stop her. "No. You need to go into the chamber. Now."

"I cannot!" Simmy exclaimed.

"Aaron and I are very capable of training Guardians. We have been doing it for a long time now," Zion said to her, his voice firm. "You need to go."

"Go?" Layla questioned. "Go where?"

"She needs to become reborn," Aaron replied to her quietly. "She is back in the Realm and has learnt all her life lessons for this body. If she pushes it any further, she will fade out of existence."

Layla gaped at Aaron before, ripping her hand away from Ray, turning on her heel and stalking to her aunt. "Go!" Layla instructed, pointing her finger to the corner of the room towards a door that Zion had gestured to earlier.

Opening her mouth to protest, Simmy tried to step forwards, but Zion's arm blocked her path. "We will take care of them. Go to the chamber. Now."

With that last word ringing in everyone's ears, Simmy silently turned and stalked away.

"There are thirteen chambers within that room," Aaron said to Noah and Layla, as they watched Simmy disappear behind the door. "One for each Guardian, including Garvan, when he was still here."

"Didn't you all live at the temple where Garvan is now?" Noah asked.

"Most of the time, yes," Aaron replied. "But they would

come here to be reborn away from the action, where they could clear their minds and start afresh without distractions."

"Will Simmy be okay with us here?" Layla asked.

"She will be fine," Zion said. "Now, let us tune into your new powers, and I will show you how to use them to guide Earth back to its healthy state."

Eyes lingering on the door that Simmy had disappeared behind for a second, Noah turned and followed Zion to a large window that spanned the entire wall of the room, curving like it was following the shape of the Earth.

Zion waved his hand in front of him, and it lit up. Half was lit by the sun, the other the moon, speckled with stars.

Noah and Layla gaped in awe. It was the most beautiful thing Noah had ever seen.

Allowing them their moment, Zion rocked on his heels before Aaron walked over to him, pointed at a section and muttered in a low voice to Zion.

Nodding, Zion waved his hand over the globe once more, diminishing the lights.

Noah and Layla blinked and turned to Zion.

"That is the Earth," he said to them, "which I am sure you already know."

Neither Noah nor Layla said anything, so he continued.

"Your job as Primary Guardians is to keep watch over this globe and check for irregularities, signs that the humans are no longer in control of their lives. We have had to sit back and watch terrible things happen on Earth—plagues, natural disasters and even manmade disasters—but that is the way of life. Tragedies happen. The Earth purges, resets, and the cycle begins again."

Both Noah and Layla nodded.

"This is why it is imperative that Guardians must put the Earth before themselves. Sitting here, watching the Earth purge, especially if people you love were involved, could be too much for you, and you would try to stop it. Your input would not be impartial, and it needs to be. The Earth does what it needs to flourish. You cannot change that."

Again, Noah and Layla just nodded.

Zion gave them a second to ask questions, but neither of them did, so he continued once more. "Your job is to watch where the Realm and Earth connect, making sure that guidance is given to those who are asking for it and ensuring that those who pass over to this side are released of all karma and Earthly ties, so they can watch over their loved ones in peace."

Aaron stepped forward and lit up the globe once more with a wave of his hand. "Look at the globe and tell me what you see," he said to Noah and Layla.

They turned to the small Earth in front of them, focusing intently on it, their eyes scouring the planet for anything that seemed out of the ordinary.

"There," Layla said, pointing. "Near our home. It's shadowed."

"Correct," Aaron replied. "And what does that mean?"

"That Garvan is interfering there," Noah said.

"That is right," Aaron said again. "Now, again, it is important for you two to ensure the Earth is your primary concern. Nothing else. I know we are repeating ourselves, but this rule must be followed. If your family, Noah, or your friends, Layla, were in danger, and you had to make a decision between what was right for the Realm and saving your loved one, what would you choose?"

Neither of them replied, but Noah felt a churn in his gut.

"Exactly," Aaron said. "It is an impossible choice. As Primary Guardians, you both have the Realm in your core now. The Realm is a part of you. But a decision like that, it is cruel to ask you to knowingly make it, so the Realm will physically stop you from doing anything to jeopardise what needs to happen."

"Was Garvan targeting our home town to get to Nora?" Layla asked. "Do you think he's still trying to work an angle there?"

"You tell me," Aaron said to her.

Walking closer to the globe, Noah and Layla each gripped Ray in a hand and concentrated on their little town.

The globe automatically zoomed in on where they were focusing, allowing them to have a better look.

"There's probably a Shadow Being there," Noah muttered to Layla.

"Mmm," Layla hummed in reply, concentrating on something.

"Look," she said to him after a while, pointing at an area on the globe.

Noah's gaze followed where she was pointing, and he saw that she was looking at their school.

There, in the midst of hundreds of silver orbs—"They represent human souls," Aaron had said—was a darker orb, flickering between silver and black.

"Aaron! Zion!" Layla called.

Zion, who had been standing back, allowing the two of them to work between themselves, stepped forward to see what was going on.

"What's that?" She asked them.

Both Aaron and Zion paused for a moment, taking their time to fully understand what they were seeing.

"He could not," Aaron said.

"He must have," Zion replied.

"Has he really gone this far?"

"It seems so."

"What's going on?" Noah asked them.

Zion rubbed the bridge of his nose with his thumb and forefinger. "It looks like Garvan is infiltrating someone in your town. He is trying to take over their thoughts."

"What does that mean?" Layla asked.

"Humans have negative emotions which can be linked to their Ego, which you know is what turns into a Shadow Being in the Realm when they cross over without being cleansed from their human lives. This is what has been happening since the Guardian siblings have been petrified," Aaron explained, "but if Garvan is taking someone who does not have any experience with the Realm and feeding them information, twisting their thoughts to follow his plan and providing them with enough answers to keep them curious and wanting to know more, he will be able to control that person and have them do his bidding."

"What!?" Noah exclaimed. "He's creating an army on Earth already?"

"It seems like he is testing his ability to do just that," Aaron replied.

"This is more dire than we realised," Zion said. "We cannot allow this to happen. That person has no control over how they act, and the more they are exposed to Garvan... the more that dark power of the Realm engulfs them... the more they will completely lose sight of the person they once were. When

Garvan is finished with them, the power they began to rely on so much will vanish… and they will die."

Chapter 6 - Nora

"*Who do you think I am?*"

Nora cringed and pulled her pillow tighter over her head as she lay face down on her bed, the curious arched eyebrow and mocking smile haunting her.

He looked like Aaron.

So much so that, for a split second, she thought she was getting out of here.

But no. It was Garvan, back from his rebirth. And, thinking back on it, if she'd bothered to look long enough before running her mouth, she'd have been able to tell the difference immediately.

Sure, the height, sapphire blue eyes, black hair and crooked smile were similar, but Garvan's eyes were dead inside, his smile was cruel, and his build was nowhere near as muscular as Aaron's—whose toned frame she was going to pummel the next time she saw it for leaving her in this situation.

Releasing the pillow from her head, Nora rolled onto her back and threw it at the far wall. If she was being honest with herself, even if it had been Aaron coming to get her, she wouldn't have gone. As much as she wanted to escape—to see Noah and Layla—she was their best shot at getting inside information about Garvan and his plans. She just needed to keep playing her cards right.

Turning to roll over once more, Nora stopped as a small sound pricked her ears. There had been a few unusual sounds lately, ever since Garvan had gotten back from his rebirth. Nora was sure they were coming from the eleven Guardian siblings that stood petrified in the room outside her bedroom.

Pushing herself up, Nora stood and walked over to the red energy barrier and tried to see if anything outside had made that noise.

Not that she could see much. The barrier swirled and crackled, hurting her eyes as she squinted, trying to focus on the petrified siblings.

There was nothing to see, though. Everything looked exactly the same as the last time she'd tried to look out.

Although, in all fairness, the Throne Room could have been completely rearranged, and she'd be none the wiser. For all she knew, Garvan had placed an illusion over the barrier to make her see what he wanted.

That was the frustrating thing about being here. Even though she was slowly gaining Garvan's trust, she was still a prisoner.

Rubbing her sore eyes and waiting for them to readjust to the dimness of her room, Nora stomped over to her bed and plopped onto it roughly, used to the dull ache that shot through her tailbone as she hit the hard surface.

Raising her right hand, Nora called for her amber energy, the same colour as her eyes, to flow to her fingertips. Smiling, she created a small ball with it and playfully rolled it over her fingers.

Another sound, a closer one this time, caught her attention as she concentrated on her ball, and her smile turned into a scowl. She didn't look up, pretending she hadn't heard the barrier dissolve, and instead crushed the ball in her hand, shooting amber sparks into the room.

"Passing the time by splattering little balls, are we?"

"I can do the same to yours if you'd like."

Nora looked up just in time to see a flicker of dark amusement flash in Garvan's eyes and deepened her scowl.

This sadist would probably enjoy it. Nora suppressed a shudder.

Garvan gave her a cocky grin as if he knew exactly where Nora's train of thought had gone.

Holding back a gag, Nora reminded herself that this was the man who had kidnapped her and invaded her personal space every chance he'd gotten, even back when he was still in his decrepit form. The memory of his wiry beard tickling her ear still made Nora's skin crawl.

Looking at the reborn Garvan in front of her, even though he was more pleasing to the eye, she couldn't get past that instinctive revulsion she felt every time she saw him.

Thankfully, she no longer needed to hide her powers from Garvan.

When he'd called her to him before, after the initial shock had passed of seeing how much he looked like Aaron, he crooked his finger at her, an instruction for her to walk up to him, and placed his forehead against hers.

Thinking he was going to try to find Noah again, Nora had slammed her mental shields up so hard that even Garvan had flinched a little. But, at the slightest nudge from him, they crumbled. Instead of invading her mind, she felt something shatter instead.

The blocks he had placed on her when she first arrived

were gone.

If he'd noticed that there were fewer blocks than he'd initially placed, he didn't say anything, but Nora's heart still pounded.

Back in the current moment, Garvan lazily strolled up to her and wrapped a strand of Nora's wavy, dirty blonde hair around his index finger, his dull sapphire eyes boring into her amber ones. "I have need of you."

"You can keep those needs to yourself." Nora's upper lip curled in disgust as she tried not to show how much his presence creeped her out.

Garvan let out a dry laugh, letting the strand of hair fall back to Nora's shoulder before he stroked a finger down her cheek. "Not that kind of need, but I will be sure to keep you in mind should the desire present itself."

Nora's skin crawled, but she didn't react, knowing if she retaliated, then he would just find more reasons to touch her. So, she let him stare her down for a minute, a silent challenge being shot as he raised his shapely black eyebrow before letting out a half grin and taking a step back. "I am going to assume it was my sister who taught you all your Realm knowledge?"

Confused, Nora didn't reply straight away. "Your sister?"

"Simone. Did she not tell you about me?" He placed a hand over his heart in mock hurt.

"She never mentioned you at all, actually."

"Well, now I really am hurt. I have spent all these years looking for her, and she never even bothered to tell you about me."

Nora didn't reply. Her mind was racing.

"No matter," Garvan continued, "it is not like she is of any use to me anymore. The Primary Guardianship has changed hands. I was *this* close to snatching it away from her too." He held his thumb and forefinger a mere millimetre apart in front of his face. "Zion had his shield around them too tightly."

"Who's Zion?"

Garvan cocked his head, both of his eyebrows raising this time. "You really do not know what is going on? What your brother and friend are currently doing? Why my uncle Aaron was here? What your unique gift is? The gift that is the basis behind your powers in the Realm?"

A hot stickiness settled into Nora's stomach. She didn't know any of those things. Of course she didn't. She'd been stuck here the entire time.

She hadn't realised she'd spoken out loud until she heard Garvan's low chuckle. "This is true, but I thought at least my uncle had attempted to keep in touch with you after the… *friendship*… the two of you struck up."

The stickiness turned to liquid as Nora felt her face flame. "I have no idea what you're talking about."

"Sure you do. Scratch came to me time and time again, trying to find out why you were here and what I wanted with you. He even tried to convince me to let you go." Garvan gave a cold laugh, and Nora's skin turned to ice. "He could not let you know that, though. You would never have plucked up the courage to take care of yourself if you knew he was trying to help. Such a shame your brother and your friend came here earlier than expected. The two of you would have had more time to… get to know each other better."

Nora had heard enough. Raising her finger, she shot an electric bolt of amber energy at Garvan so fast it was a mere inch from his face before he managed to stop it.

Letting out a loud laugh, Garvan waved his hand and the energy ball dissolved into thin air. "Yes," Garvan said in a hiss. "This is the girl I have been waiting for. Come, we have much to get through. I thought, first, we should train you on how to actually use your powers. How are you going to be a proper asset to me if you are here tossing measly sparks around everywhere?"

Scowling, Nora stayed planted on the spot.

Already halfway out the door, Garvan turned his head back slightly. "Unless you would rather rot away in here?"

Nora scrunched up her nose, annoyed that she had no choice but to follow Garvan, because no, she didn't want to be stuck in this room any longer.

She followed him out the door, not looking back.

It was time she found out what was really going on. She was sure the *them* Garvan had referred to when he mentioned the Primary Guardianship were Noah and Layla. Maybe this meant Simmy was back in the Realm now too.

She had to find a way to communicate with them.

Her stomach gave another uncomfortable lurch as she thought of the mirror Aaron had gifted her and wondered if she could get it back.

If she kept Garvan happy, she might get a chance to reach Noah.

Chapter 7 - Noah

Noah and Layla stared at the map in front of them, trying to see if Garvan was manipulating more people, but they could only find the one.

"I don't think it's a coincidence that Garvan has chosen someone at our uni, where Simmy was," Layla said.

"Neither do I," replied Aaron. He was now lying on a white sofa in the corner of the room, throwing a small blue energy ball up in the air and catching it.

"How would Garvan have known Simmy was there? Wasn't she being hidden by the other Guardians?" Noah asked.

"I am not completely certain. I can only speculate that, with Simmy's body deteriorating, so too were the protections around her," Zion replied. He sat on the armrest of the sofa Aaron was lying on, running his fingers through his long golden hair in thought. "That would explain how he found Nora. If he had come down to find Simmy and found Nora instead, he would not have hesitated to take her."

Noah vaguely noticed Aaron pause tossing his ball briefly before Ray shuddered in his hand.

Noah let go of her, and she floated over to Zion, who held his palm open for her to sit on.

Once she landed, a large image of Simmy in her science

classroom appeared before them.

Simmy, wearing a red floral dress with her thick auburn hair tied into a bun at the nape of her neck, was being bombarded with questions by a brunette girl who had a long braid reaching down her back.

"What happens when you've completely let go of your Ego? Do we get to decide our fate? If thoughts become things, what happens when we think bad thoughts?"

"Abigail?" Layla whispered. "She's the one who Garvan's manipulating?"

Ray's images disappeared, and she floated back over to Noah.

Noah's mind raced. "Those images, they were all from when we were learning about the science of the mind in class earlier this year."

He looked over to Aaron, who caught his eye, and Zion, who was preoccupied with an iridescent orb that had appeared beside him.

"Marian!" Noah exclaimed, rushing over to her.

"Quick!" she whispered urgently, her human form appearing on the face of the orb, her brown hair loose and wild. "Come with me."

She reached through the orb, grabbed Noah's wrist and pulled him through to the temple's Throne Room.

He heard the soft thud of Layla's feet landing next to him as she was pulled through as well.

"Hide," Marian hissed to them.

Noah and Layla quickly and quietly ran behind the pillar in the corner, giving them an almost full view of the room in front of them.

With a small *pop*, the iridescent orb disappeared, and Noah saw a shimmer of energy absorb into Marian's petrified Guardian statue.

A sharp jab in his ribs brought him back to the task at hand, and, with his eyes watering, Noah rubbed the sensitive area and hissed, "Ouch."

"Shh," Layla hushed him in reply, brushing off his complaint. "Look."

The large, intricately engraved wooden double doors at the entrance of the room opened with a loud bang, and a sturdy young man was silhouetted in the doorway.

"Garvan," Noah whispered as the man stepped forwards, his features becoming clear.

No longer was Garvan a decrepit old man. Now, he looked no older than twenty-five, with cropped black hair, blue eyes and a formal outfit consisting of black dress pants, a black button-up shirt with the sleeves rolled up to his elbows and shiny black shoes, which clacked on the floor as he walked.

Noah started at the sight. He bore a shocking resemblance to Aaron.

If it wasn't for the silver rings on all ten of Garvan's fingers and the stony expression on his face, Noah would have a hard time telling them apart.

Layla gripped Noah's arm, and he looked down to see her pointing at Tick in the corner, who was keeping a watchful eye on the room.

They had to go before she found them.

Ray let out a low whistle, and Marian's portal popped back next to them. "Quick," she whispered.

Noah helped Layla through before silently following her, landing with a thud back in the Earth room with Zion and Aaron.

"Did you see him?" Zion asked.

"He looks like… Aaron!" Noah forced out, unsure of what their reaction would be.

Zion and Aaron glanced at each other.

"That is not surprising," Zion said.

Aaron threw the energy ball he had been playing with against a wall, and it exploded into thousands of tiny specks.

"You did train him," Zion continued.

"That little… eugh!" Aaron exclaimed, running his hands through his dark hair, leaving it sticking up in places. "I should never have taken him on as an apprentice!"

"You did not teach him *everything* you know," Zion reassured him. "He is not at your level, he just likes to think he is."

"What did you teach him?" Noah asked.

Standing up, Aaron paced around the room. "*Almost* everything I know," he said. "He was my most talented student. The energy he could bring to life… I had never seen anything like it."

"You did not teach him how to make relics," Zion said placated Aaron, his golden hair slipping over his shoulder as he eyed his brother. "That skill remains solely with you."

"And thank Realm for that!" Aaron exclaimed. "Imagine if I had shared that with him. The number of dark artefacts he could have created by now…"

"Thankfully, Nora did not have her half of Ray with her when she was captured," Zion mused. "Ray is extremely powerful. She holds an untold amount of energy, and in the wrong hands, the entire Earth could be damaged beyond repair in an instant, not to mention what he could do to the Realm."

Noah gripped Ray tightly in his hand, and she let out a crackle of amber energy in response.

Layla gripped Ray's other side, and her emerald energy ran over Noah's fingers. "What are we going to do about Garvan now?" Noah asked.

"You are going to have to learn how to master the new energy flowing through you, so you can use it to your advantage," Aaron replied.

"Together, you two will become almost unstoppable," Zion told Noah and Layla, "but you are both still so inexperienced that, right now, you would not stand a chance against Garvan,"—he walked over to the two of them and put a heavy hand on each of their shoulders—"which is why I am going to train you myself."

"I can train them—" Aaron began to object, but Zion held up a palm to stop him.

"You need to be here when Simone has finished her rebirth, so you can tune her mandala to connect with her new body. She is going to need you since she has been unable to use her mandala to its full potential for a long time."

Aaron let out a frustrated huff of breath and flopped back down onto the couch.

"Come with me, you two," Zion said to Noah and Layla, gesturing for them to follow him.

"Will Aaron be okay?" Layla asked after they'd walked out of the room.

"He will be fine. He is uncertain how things are going to pan out from here. He and Garvan were very close in Garvan's first few lifetimes, and now that Garvan has come back as an image of Aaron, he is feeling like Garvan is making a mockery of him, that he is Aaron's protégé no longer."

"Wouldn't Aaron feel better training us then?" Noah asked. "If Aaron knows exactly how Garvan's going to fight, then wouldn't he be better off teaching us?"

"The very fact that Aaron knows Garvan's every move is exactly why he cannot train you. His fighting style is unique, so you would wind up being taught the same way he taught Garvan. If that happened, you would be unprepared. Garvan has learnt too much since he has been gone," Zion told them. "Also, I was being honest when I said Simone will need him there when she comes out of her rebirth. Her mandala needs to become reacquainted with the Realm's energy, which is something only Aaron can do, as he is the one who created it."

Neither Noah nor Layla asked any more questions as they followed Zion towards a large green pasture out the back of his palace.

It was the size of a football field, and the sun made the blades of grass shimmer.

"Tell me," Zion said, turning to them as they took in the training field, "what did you learn while you were still humans?"

Noah had no idea how to answer that question, but thankfully Layla jumped right in.

"We learnt how to control our breathing, how to clear our minds and how to create a weapon using our unique skills. Noah's skill set is earth, and mine is fire. We've learnt how to act in sync, to envision the outcome we desire and how to put it into action."

"Fantastic," Zion said, waving his hand in the direction of the field. A large square fighting ring began to build itself in the middle. "I am glad you have some basic knowledge."

"Basic... knowledge?" Noah repeated slowly, turning incredulously to Layla, whose mouth now hung a little slack. "It took us ages to learn all of that!"

Zion smiled down at the two of them. "You are both still novices at the very beginning of your training journey. And you are Guardians now, so your training as a human will work on a minute scale compared to what you are capable of with your new powers. You need to expand on everything you have learnt in order to allow yourself to achieve things you never imagined possible. Can you do that? It is important for the two of you to have complete and utter faith in yourselves."

"We can do it," Layla said to him after a pause.

Noah, even though he wasn't sure about what he else could expand on, nodded. "We're going to become the best Guardians you've ever trained."

"I never doubted it for a second."

"Where do we start?" Noah asked.

"It is time for you to focus on your physical training. While it is important to become mentally strong, your physical health is directly correlated to your mental health, and the more physically active you are, the healthier you will become as a whole," Zion explained, and a thrill ran through Noah at the thought of finally doing some active training.

He looked over at Layla, who had a grin on her face too.

"If the two of you will head over to the fighting ring on the field, I will guide you through what you need to do," Zion instructed. "I will take Ray for the time being, Noah, so there are no unfair advantages."

Ray disappeared from Noah's hand and magically appeared in Zion's. Layla was wearing a shit-eating grin. "I can take him even without Ray's help," she purred, eyeing Noah.

Noah scoffed but grinned back. "You wish."

The two of them reached the ring and climbed in, with Zion strolling slowly after them.

"With the Primary Guardianship, your bodies have shifted, and you are now in peak physical condition. You will be able to fight better and wield much higher levels of life energy. But, as you are not used to it, you are going to have to take it slowly at first so your bodies do not overexert themselves," Zion explained as Noah stretched his muscles and Layla tied her hair back into a high ponytail.

"The only rule is that you stop if one of you is overwhelmed by your new life energy. Then, you will simply reset and start again."

Noah cracked his neck. "I'll try not to beat you too badly."

Layla let out a laugh, her emerald eyes glinting. "You couldn't even if you wanted to."

"I will leave the two of you to your own devices," Zion said after encasing the ring in a protective barrier to prevent any wayward energy from escaping their fight.

"Wait! How do we know if we're doing it right?" Noah called out.

Zion had already started walking away. "There is no right or wrong," he replied as he strolled back towards the palace.

"Let's just get straight into it," Layla said as she pulled her hair up into a high ponytail and crouched into a fighting stance.

Noah's body seemed to move on its own as he cracked his neck again and set his feet to keep himself balanced. It was a stance that Noah had never shifted into before. It was true, then. His body just naturally knew what to do.

Grinning, Noah let out a breath and surrendered all mental

control to his new instincts. He would have to trust that it wouldn't lead him astray.

"Let's start with physical blows first and leave the energetic fighting for later," Layla suggested.

"Sounds good to m—"

Before Noah could finish his sentence, Layla had launched herself at him and punched him in the side of his head.

Pain shot through Noah's temple, but Layla was already pulsing healing blue energy through him, and the pain subsided as quickly as it had arrived.

"Ouch!" Noah hissed, but Layla just laughed.

"Round two?"

Noah didn't give her a chance to reset her stance, quickly knocking her hand away from his head and pushing her back with a palm to her chest before stepping forward and aiming a punch for her nose. Layla blocked it by swiping her forearm upwards and retaliated with a knee to Noah's stomach as he lost his balance and tipped forwards.

Launching himself to the side so Layla's knee only grazed him, Noah swiped away a strand of hair which had fallen into his eyes, his pulse thrumming in his veins.

Layla crouched down in front of him, her right palm keeping her balanced while an emerald energy ball sparked in her left.

"I thought we were focusing on physical fighting first?" Noah questioned, but a thrill ran through him at the thought of testing his new powers out.

"We did," Layla replied. "Now we can focus on something more fun."

With a flick of her wrist, Layla's energy ball came flying at Noah's stomach, burning a hole in his shirt as he barely managed to dodge it in time.

Grinning, Noah dropped to his hands and knees and slammed his palms into the fighting ring, expelling a pulse of energy inside it and pulling a thin spear out of the ground with him as he stood.

Layla was standing opposite him, small red flames dancing across all five fingertips. She tipped her head backwards, a silent challenge for him to charge at her.

They sparred well into the afternoon, with no clear winner as they had both knocked each other into the ground more times than Noah could count.

He was puffing, and Layla wiped dirt and sweat off her forehead with her arm before Zion appeared before them. With a clap of his hands, their energy weapons dissolved, along with the fighting ring.

"Fantastic," he said. "That is enough for today."

Looking up from the ground, where he had unceremoniously landed as the ring disappeared beneath his feet, Noah realised the sun had begun to set.

"We weren't finished," Layla said. She had managed to stay upright.

"You have managed to tap into both your physical and your magical powers, so now it is time for a good meal and a restful night's sleep."

Noah stood and looked forlornly at the empty space where the ring had been.

"So you are not tempted to come out here and try again tonight," Zion said, winking at the two of them.

Layla threw him a sheepish look, and Noah coughed a guilty laugh.

"Come. There is someone I want you to meet."

Chapter 8 - Noah

Noah rubbed his aching shoulders as he followed Zion back into the palace. He hadn't realised how much energy he'd used. It had felt effortless at the time, but now everything hurt.

Walking silently, he and Layla followed Zion back to the Earth room, where Aaron was still waiting for Simmy to come out of her chamber.

Seeing that Layla was about to ask, Aaron shook his head. "She spent a long time on Earth. It is going to take a while for her to undergo a proper transition."

Layla nodded at him, gave a small smile and continued to follow Zion. He led them to the far corner of the Earth room, brightening the lights slightly with a wave of his hand.

A familiar *pop* sounded, and Marian's orb came into view in the middle of the room.

"Garvan has left for now," she said to Zion. "I have not been able to get a good read on him, which means he is cloaking his powers. He does not want us to know what he is capable of. From what I have been able to gather, he remembers everything from his past life. I believe that is why he took three days to undergo the transition, so he would not lose any memories."

"I thought as such," Zion replied. "Thank you, Marian. Send him in."

Marian nodded, disappearing from view.

Not a second later, the transparent figure of an older man, with smooth, dark skin and long salt-and-pepper dreadlocks that were loosely tied back, took her place.

"It has been a long time," the man said to Zion, his translucent form stepping out of Marian's orb and walking over to him.

"Much too long, Arel," Zion replied, clasping Arel's hands in his and bending his forehead to touch them. "We are in need of your help. Garvan is manipulating the mind of a young girl on Earth, someone who went to university with Noah and Layla. We believe he discovered Simone was there at around the same time he captured Nora."

"That type of energy cannot be on Earth for long," Arel stated, touching his own forehead to Zion's hands after he spoke. "It will begin to infect others if it is not dealt with."

"This is your area of expertise. We need your help."

"These are the two new Guardians?" Arel asked, looking at Noah and Layla, who each gave a half wave.

"This is them, yes. They are still in training, but I believe they are exactly what the Realm needs," Zion said, smiling warmly at the two of them.

"Why is energy manipulation your area of expertise, Arel?" Layla asked, bowing her head slightly to mimic what Zion had done.

Arel lowered his head in return. "I was once spending time on Earth to reconnect with its people, and I stumbled across a situation that got out of hand."

"Stumbled across a situation?" Noah asked, one eyebrow

raised.

Arel gave a wry smile. "I was most likely guided there by the Realm."

Noah gave a tight smile back. That sounded more like it.

"What happened?" Layla asked, moving closer to Noah, who placed an arm around her shoulders.

"I watched from a distance for a while, and the person, a male, was trying to bring people into a new religion he was starting. One where people didn't need to worry about their life's path, as they would have one chosen for them."

"That sounds familiar," Noah muttered, and Layla hummed in agreement.

"When I had seen enough, I showed myself to the man to learn the more intricate details of how this religion worked. He began to scream, and before I could do anything, he crumpled to the floor, turned to ash."

Noah stared at Arel. "What?"

"That's not where I thought the story was heading," Layla said. "I thought you would have found Garvan."

"We did not know what Garvan was planning that long ago," Arel answered, his mouth a tight line. "I believe Garvan saw me through the man's eyes and decided to kill him before I got a chance to find out he was behind the scheme. This was—well, I hope it was—his first attempt at energy manipulation. It seems as if he has refined his craft over the years."

"Is Garvan controlling Abigail as fully as he did that man? Will she die too" Layla asked. Her fingers grabbed onto Noah's shirt, and he gave her shoulders a quick squeeze.

"Did Abigail seem out of the ordinary when you last saw her?"

Layla shook her head.

"The three of you—" Zion started.

"Four of us," Aaron interrupted. "I am helping too." He looked at Zion fiercely. Zion's mouth tightened, but he didn't object.

"The four of you," Zion corrected himself, "will need to take this information and figure out a way to help Abigail without harming her. But first, you need to have a good rest."

"I will be seeing more of you both soon," Arel said to them, bowing his head.

Noah and Layla bowed their heads back in response.

The familiar *pop* of Marian's portal sounded, and Arel climbed through it, back to the temple with his siblings.

"*Will* we be able to help Abigail without hurting her?" Layla asked Zion.

Zion didn't look at her. "I cannot be sure. But we will try."

Layla gently touched Ray, who Zion had laid on a table next to her, inhaling a ragged breath, fighting back tears before asking Aaron, "Is the food already in our rooms?"

"Food fit for a queen," he assured her.

"I'll see you all tomorrow, then," she said, and she walked out of the Earth room towards her suite.

"When do you think Simmy will come out of the rebirthing chamber?" Noah asked Aaron.

"Normally, I would expect it to be a couple of days at least," Aaron replied, "but knowing Simmy and her desire to help you two as much as possible, I wouldn't be surprised if she fast-tracked everything."

"It would be good for her to join us while we trained," Noah pondered aloud. "Hopefully, we'll get to see her soon."

"You will," Zion said to him. "Now go, eat, rest. You are

going to need all of your energy for this task."

"See you both tomorrow, then," Noah said to Zion and Aaron, before following the same path Layla had taken, heading to his own suite.

It had been a long day, and his muscles ached. He just wanted to eat and then have a long, hot shower.

Noah reached his door and placed his palm on the sensor, watching as the door opened with a hiss.

"Hi."

Noah turned to the voice that came from his couch and saw Layla sitting on it.

"I brought my dinner over. Thought we could eat together."

Noah kicked off his shoes and walked over to the couch, sitting down next to Layla and taking the lid off the dinner that had been left for him on a tray.

"Chicken and veggies. Pretty standard fuel food," Layla grimaced, poking at hers with a fork.

"I could have gone for a burger, but sure," Noah replied, picking up a piece of broccoli and munching on it.

Layla breathed out a laugh, doing the same.

They sat in silence for a while, both picking at their meals, neither one knowing quite what to say.

Once their plates were almost empty, Layla shuffled on her seat and turned to face Noah.

"I want to try something," she said.

"Try what?" Noah asked, not sure what she had in mind.

"Close your eyes."

Noah did as he was told.

A few seconds passed, and just as he was about to open his eyes to see whether she was still there, he felt a warm pressure on his lips.

Layla's soft kiss sent tingles throughout his body, and before he could think about it, his hands gripped her waist, bringing her closer to him.

The two of them melted into each other, breathless gasps escaping from them both.

Noah lost himself in the moment, sinking deeper and deeper into the electricity running through him. There didn't seem to be an end to it, and the closer he got to Layla, the more he felt like he was pulling her into him.

"Noah." Layla sounded breathless, distant, but Noah ignored her, trying to recapture her lips which had escaped his.

"Noah!" Layla said more forcefully this time, placing a shaky hand on his chest and pushing him away.

Finally opening his eyes, Noah started as he saw they were encircled by a globe of amber and emerald energy.

Well, there was significantly more amber than emerald. It was almost as if Noah had sucked Layla's life energy right out of her.

Gasping, Noah pushed himself away from Layla completely, toppling to the floor and knocking over his tray of leftover dinner at the same time.

Trying not to squash any half-eaten vegetables into the plush white carpet of his room, Noah scrambled back, trying to get as much distance between him and Layla as possible in an attempt to stop pulling out Layla's life energy.

Stop! Noah thought desperately to himself, and slowly, he saw his energy unwillingly settle and flow back inside of him, releasing small bits of emerald energy, which quickly flew to Layla and reabsorbed into her body.

Running a shaky hand over his face and wiping sweat off

his top lip, Noah stared wide-eyed at Layla. She was pale. Much paler than usual.

"I am so sorry."

Layla let out a shaky breath and stared at her palms. "I think you only took a little bit."

"I didn't want it." Leaning toward her, Noah gently placed a hand on her back, rubbing it in soothing circles. "I really am sorry."

"Don't be. We've always had an energetic connection whenever we've kissed. I was expecting something to happen." Layla rose on trembling legs and picked up the rest of her, thankfully unscathed, tray of dinner. The steel cutlery rattled as her arms shook. "I might go eat in my room now, though. I just need some time…" Layla trailed off.

Guilt spreading through his chest, Noah merely nodded and watched as Layla walked towards the door, pressed her hand to the scanner and disappeared down the hallway.

Life energy crackling at his fingertips, Noah lifted them to his face and watched as amber and emerald electricity sparked between his fingers.

Chapter 9 - Layla

Exhaustion hit Layla as she stumbled to her bedroom. Slumping against the white wall, she pressed her palm to the sensor and waited for the door to hiss open.

Grasping her tray of food to her chest, so she didn't drop it, Layla slid to the floor as soon as she got inside. She placed the tray gingerly on the ground before crawling on her hands and knees towards the bed.

It felt like Noah had sucked her powers dry.

Groaning, she pushed herself up off the floor and fell back onto her soft white bedspread. She brought a hand in front of her face and tried calling her emerald energy to her fingertips.

A feeble crackle sparked, and Layla exhaled loudly, letting her hand fall onto her face. Her body felt like lead.

Hopefully, it'll just take a good night's rest for my energy to replenish, she thought to herself.

Stiffly rolling over, so she was face down on her bed, Layla let out a small whimper when she heard a soft knock at her door.

"It's open." Her voice was muffled by the doona, so she wasn't sure if the person outside had heard her, but she heard the familiar sound of the door opening. She lifted her head slightly to see Aaron walking towards her with a dark eyebrow raised.

"I cannot imagine that is very comfortable," he said, gesturing to her arms, which were bent at an awkward angle as she tried to keep her head lifted enough for him to see her.

Layla spat a strand of her wild red hair from her mouth. "I don't know what you mean. I'm incredibly comfortable."

At the wheeze she gave when she tried to roll onto her back again, both Aaron's eyebrows raised. "Noah run you ragged, did he?"

Layla flung her pillow at him as hard as she could, which wasn't very hard at all, and she saw Aaron cover a smirk as it bounced harmlessly off his stomach. She forced herself to sit up and glared at him. "Not in the way you're thinking."

"What way was I thinking?" Aaron purred, leaning in, his sapphire blue eyes glinting mischievously.

"I'm not answering that." Layla rolled her eyes, her cheeks growing warm. "But, in answer to your question, yes, Noah is the reason I'm as agile as a corpse right now."

The glint in Aaron's eyes dimmed, and his expression became concerned. "What happened?"

Layla opened her mouth to explain but figured it would be easier to show him. She raised her hand in front of her face to try and bring her life energy to the surface, but, again, only a feeble flicker sparked before fizzling away into nothing.

"May I?" Aaron gestured to the bed, and Layla nodded. Her side of the bed lifted slightly as Aaron sat beside her. "I am going to have a feel, if that is alright with you?"

Layla just nodded again, holding her hand out for him to examine.

Aaron closed his eyes, his own sapphire blue energy covering his hands, and Layla felt it tentatively explore her own. When he didn't feel any resistance from her, he began a full energetic body examination. Goosebumps raised the hairs on Layla's skin as Aaron explored her, his power trying to ignite hers.

Aaron was always so playful that it was easy to forget that he was thousands of years old and incredibly powerful.

After a few minutes, Aaron's energy receded into his own body, and he passed Layla's hand back to her, letting it rest on her thigh.

"Noah took your energy?"

"Yeah."

"You were... tuning Ray again?" Aaron looked away innocently, and Layla felt her cheeks flame.

"Yeah," she mumbled.

"Zion mentioned you said something about Noah dabbling in dark energetic magic when you fought that duplicate of Nora," Aaron pressed, all teasing gone from his voice. "This is another dark magic that Noah seems to be dabbling in."

"He's not dabbling... He doesn't even seem aware of it!" Layla insisted, "And he was so apologetic when he realised what he'd done."

Aaron placed a gentle hand on Layla's shoulder. "I am not saying he did it on purpose. It is just dangerous for this side of him to be projecting, especially since he is a Primary Guardian. Garvan used to dabble in dark energetic magic too."

"Noah's not like Garvan!"

"No, he is not," Aaron agreed, "but let us keep an eye on him regardless."

Layla sighed, flexing her hand, which was now prickling with pins and needles. "Okay, I'll make sure to let you know if anything else happens. Is that what you came here for?"

Aaron grinned, his hand squeezing her shoulder. "No. I came to tell you that Ray wanted to thank you for the good feed earlier."

Aaron jumped up and dodged another pillow that Layla swung at him, with much more force than the first one, and let out a laugh as he skipped to the door.

"Asshole," Layla murmured to herself once he disappeared, but she couldn't help but smile.

Chapter 10 - Noah

I t was a restless night.

Whenever Noah closed his eyes, the energies in his body, both human and Realm, felt like they were at war. Plus, the energy he'd taken from Layla was coursing through him, trying to find a place to settle. His body was buzzing, and he was exhausted.

By the time the sun rose, Noah had already been awake for hours, testing out his new abilities in order to keep his body occupied, so he didn't self-destruct.

It had taken a while to perfect, but he was now able to replicate the tiny energy ball Aaron would blast from the tip of his finger.

Standing in the middle of the room, guiding the pinhead-sized ball of amber energy around him with his fingers, Noah concentrated on making intricate patterns in the air and tried not to impale any of the furniture.

A knock on his door broke his concentration, and he narrowly missed burning a hole through the centre of the couch. Quickly, Noah stopped and guided the amber energy back to the tip of his finger, where it was absorbed back inside his body.

"Coming!" he called, wiping away a bead of sweat from his

brow, and he opened the door with a touch of the sensor.

Aaron greeted him, lazily leaning on the wall with a grin on his face. "Morning."

"Uhh... morning?" Noah replied.

Aaron let himself into the room, and Noah moved out of the way as he walked inside. "I was cleansing Ray last night."

Noah felt his palms tingle but replied nonchalantly, "Oh?"

Aaron stared at him for a second before producing his own tiny blue energy ball at the tip of his finger, flicking it so it flew around the room. "She seemed to enjoy the extra energy she received."

Noah walked over to the couch and flopped himself down, his legs over the armrest, letting the back of his hand land on his forehead. "I wish I had enjoyed it as much as she did," he said.

Aaron's energy ball disappeared. "What do you mean?"

"This new power we have," Noah waved his hand vaguely over his body. "I don't know what's going on with me, but somehow I sucked some of Layla's life energy out of her. She didn't say anything, but I know she was rattled. And now I don't know if that's going to happen every time we..."—he looked awkwardly at Aaron—"tune Ray."

Aaron's raised eyebrows and wide grin made Noah wish the cushions would swallow him whole.

Gaining his composure, Aaron forced the smile off his face and pushed Noah's legs off the arm of the couch so he could sit down. "Layla was in rough shape last night."

Noah sat up. "You saw her?"

Aaron nodded.

"I didn't mean to," Noah mumbled, running his hands over his face.

Noah felt Aaron's hand rest on his shoulder. "I know that. Layla knows that. But what you need to focus on right now is whether you can control these new powers or whether you are going to let them control you. There is no reason for you to be afraid of… tuning Ray."

Noah groaned.

"And, if the energy Ray received last night was anything to go by, Layla will not be turned off any future tunings," Aaron laughed and ducked as Noah pegged a couch cushion at him. "Alright, time for breakfast and training. You have got a lot to learn in a short amount of time."

Noah stretched his arms above his head, enjoying the pull of his tight muscles, before standing and following Aaron out the door.

"You are going to enjoy training today," Aaron said to him as they walked.

Noah looked at him quizzically. Aaron just gave him a conspiratorial smile and didn't elaborate any further.

As they made their way towards the kitchen, Noah began to hear a loud conversation between two other people. He recognised one of the voices as Layla's, but he couldn't put a finger on the other one.

Waking through the kitchen door, Noah saw Layla sitting with her back facing him, chatting animatedly with a young girl.

"Noah!" the young girl exclaimed, running up to him and wrapping her arms around his waist.

"Erm…" Noah paused awkwardly, looking to Layla for help, but she just laughed.

Noah looked down at the girl. She had long auburn hair that was pulled back in a braid and deep brown eyes.

It was the eyes that caught Noah's attention. They looked so familiar. "Simmy?" he asked hesitantly, pushing her an arm's length away and crouching down to her level so he could get a better look.

"Yup!" the young Simmy exclaimed. "I finished my rebirth, and I kept my old name too!"

"Why are you so young?" Noah asked incredulously. "I thought you guys came back as adults?"

"That depends on the lessons they have to learn," Zion said, walking over and placing a large hand on Simmy's head. Noah, who hadn't seen him in the kitchen when he arrived, jumped up and moved to stand next to Layla, giving them some space.

"I was on Earth for a very long time, so I have a lot of lessons to catch up on, but the quicker I go through them, the quicker I will grow. Although, I must admit, it is nice to be in this smaller body. It is so nimble!" Simmy laughed and jumped around the room.

"Alright," Zion said, smiling as he threw Noah an apple, "we do not have any time to waste. The three of you need to go outside and begin today's training."

"You're coming with us?" Noah asked Simmy.

"Sure am!"

"I told you you would enjoy today," Aaron said, winking at him.

"I've got Ray," Layla said, not quite meeting Noah's eye. Noah felt his skin prickle as he remembered the night before.

"Okay, cool," he replied as naturally as possible. "Let's go then."

Following the two women outside, Noah could feel Aaron's knowing stare boring into the back of his head and hurried his steps, not wanting to answer any questions he may have.

Once they reached the yard, Zion waved his hand over the field, and the fighting ring reappeared before them. "Same as yesterday. You are to test out your body's new abilities, but this time you will be fighting Aaron and Simone."

Zion took Ray from Layla, and both she and Noah walked up to the ring while Simmy and Aaron grinned at them from their spot next to Zion.

"We will let you two warm up first," Aaron said, cocking his head to the side. He gestured for them to begin.

Noah saw Layla roll her eyes at Aaron as she turned to face Noah, then she crouched down into her fighting stance.

Instead of the jeans and sneakers she had been wearing yesterday, Layla was wearing loose cotton pants and was barefoot, which gave her plenty of room to move and feel any energetic vibrations coming her way.

Noah wished he'd thought of that. He already felt restricted in his jeans.

Without giving him a chance to attack first, Layla pushed forward and tapped her index finger against Noah's forehead. Emerald sparks shot into his face, causing spots to jump in front of his eyes.

Disorientated, Noah stumbled back a step before pulling Layla's errant energy into his own body by waving his fingers over his face, just in time to see her drop to the floor and swing her leg in an attempt to knock him down.

Noah quickly jumped out of the way and flung Layla's own energy back at her, sending a zap of emerald electricity mixed with his own amber energy, which Layla caught and weaved into a small ball in the palm of her hand.

"That will do for now," Zion called to them. "Simone, Aaron, would you join them up there, please?"

Aaron waved his hand over his own jeans and t-shirt, transforming them into tan fighting leathers and boots that clung to him tightly, while Simmy shifted from a flowery dress into the same type of loose cotton outfit that Layla was wearing.

"Simone, you are with Noah. Aaron, you are paired with Layla," Zion instructed from the grass, Ray hovering above his shoulder.

Simmy walked over to Noah, her head not even reaching his shoulder, and he squirmed. She was just a little girl.

As if knowing exactly what he was thinking, Simmy shot a bolt of red electricity at Noah's feet, causing him to jump. "Do not go easy on me. Just because I look small, that does not mean I cannot beat you."

Noah let out a surprised laugh before squatting into a fighting stance. "I hope you're ready, then."

From the corner of his eye, Noah saw Aaron and Layla drop into their own defensive stances, waiting for Zion's signal to start.

"Ready?" Zion boomed.

Everyone nodded.

"Excellent. Go!"

The ring exploded in colour as amber, emerald, red and sapphire energy shot in all directions.

Noah's ear burned as Simmy's blast grazed past him. He dodged her attack, firing his own energy ball at her feet.

Dust clouded his eyes as the fighting ring became a mess of wayward energy, and Noah used this chance to pulse some of his energy into the floor of the ring with his hand and transform it into a spear which, by the time he had fully pulled it out of the ground, was as tall as him.

Someone, Noah wasn't sure who, blew all the dust away from the ring, leaving everyone in the open. A flash of movement behind him caught him by surprise as he saw Simmy, her hand covered in swirling red flames, running at him and aim a punch for Noah's head.

Twisting so hard his back cracked, Noah blocked the attack with his spear. Simmy's flame turned into a knife, and the two of them parried back and forth until Zion called time.

Panting, Noah glanced over at Layla. She was covered in dust, an emerald shield glinting off her skin as Aaron's tiny energy ball absorbed back into the top of his index finger.

"I am very impressed you both managed to hold your own against Aaron and Simone," Zion said to Noah and Layla. "There is still much to learn, but this is an excellent start."

Simmy held out her fist for Noah to bump. "You keep training like that, and Garvan will not stand a chance. We will have Nora back in no time."

Aaron and Layla walked over to them, Layla rubbing her side while Aaron shared some blue healing energy with her. "If training's going to be like that every day, I hope the Primary Guardianship comes with nine lives," she panted.

Chapter 11 - Nora

Garvan was playing games with her.

One minute she'd be getting ready to train, and the next, she'd be locked in her room without any warning.

Right now, she was locked in her room. She could hear Tick muttering profanities outside the red barrier about Garvan sticking her with Nora and how she should be travelling with him instead.

Her interest sparked, Nora had tried to coax more information out of Tick. The fact that Garvan was travelling so soon after his rebirth was unusual, so she wanted to find out as much as possible.

But Tick, the cow, was giving her nothing.

She resigned herself to pissing Tick off by pegging balls of energy at the barrier to make the wall Tick was leaning against shake. Nora smiled to herself when she heard Tick call out 'Master' and created an energy ball double the size.

As soon as she heard the first sizzle of the barrier coming down, Nora tossed the ball in the air and flip kicked it at Garvan's face. He caught it in the palm of his hand and absorbed the amber energy into his body. "Delicious."

Nora retched, throwing herself backwards on the bed,

resting her hands behind her head.

"You have learnt some new tricks. I have not seen that one before," Garvan said silkily as he sauntered right into her bubble of personal space, lazily slipping his hands into the pockets of his black leather pants.

"I needed to do something to keep myself occupied. First you offer to train me, and then you just shove me back in here. You're giving me whiplash."

"Please accept my sincerest apologies," Garvan drawled, and Nora rolled her eyes, pushing herself up to rest on her elbows, so she was a mere inch from Garvan's face. His blue eyes were void of light while his mouth tilted up in a thin smile. "It seems your brother has been wreaking havoc with the Realm's energies. I was trying to find out what caused such a surge. To no avail," he added at Nora's questioning look.

Nora sighed and looked at her fingernails in a bored fashion. "And here I was expecting you to actually be of some use."

Garvan gave a cold laugh and tilted her face up to look at his, his thumb and forefinger gripping her chin tightly. "I can make use of you if you would like."

Nora's eyes narrowed, her amber eyes flashing as she tugged her chin out of his grip. "I could take a knife and stab you in the eye."

Letting out a low chuckle, Garvan leaned forward, so his breath tickled Nora's ear. "Do not threaten me with a good time."

"Eugh!" Nora gagged and tried to pull away, but Garvan had leant across the bed so much she was now backed up against the wall.

"Are you two finished?" Tick furiously tapped her clawed

fingers against the doorway, and Garvan moved back just far enough for Nora to see Tick's shadows flaring behind her in rage. "I believe we have work to do."

Garvan smirked, and Nora's scowl deepened. She was tempted to push him away from her, but she didn't want to give him the satisfaction of touching him. So she just waited, holding his eyes in an icy glare as he roamed his own over her body.

"You need to bathe."

"No shit," Nora gritted out, trying not to sag in relief when Garvan finally took a step back from her.

As soon as there was some space between them, Tick was there, bathing bag in hand, gripping Nora's wrist in a bone-crushing grip.

Nora heard Garvan chuckle again. "Would you like some help?"

Before Nora could open her mouth to list the million reasons why no one would ever want that, Tick had pulled Nora into her. Roughly holding the back of her neck in her shadowy claw, she ran them to the bathing chamber as fast as she could.

Which was very fast.

As soon as Tick let go of her, Nora fell to her hands and knees, retching for an entirely different reason.

Before she'd had a chance to fully recover, Tick grabbed her by the collar of her tattered shirt and slammed her against the wall.

Gasping as the wind was knocked out of her, Nora cried out in pain and then again in anger. Wrapping her hands in her amber energy, she gripped Tick's wrist with one hand and her shadowy face with the other and blasted a vibrant white light.

Screaming, Tick let go of Nora immediately and clawed at the hole in her face with her remaining hand. "You bitch!"

Nora, who had dropped to the ground when Tick let her go, stood up and glared at Tick's face, which was slowly repairing itself. How she had been able to talk with half her mouth gone, Nora didn't know. "You slammed me against the wall! What did you think I was going to do?"

Tick ignored her. "Someone needs to keep you in your place. Master doesn't seem to want to do it, so I will."

Nora gave Tick an incredulous look. "He's holding me captive here! How is that not keeping me in my place?"

"You were all over him just now."

"Eugh! Ew, gross. He was all up in my personal space, and I can tell you right now that no one wants that."

Tick just continued to glare at her, and Nora felt herself grow restless. This was cutting into her washing time.

"Look, I'm not going to argue with you over this. If you want Garvan in your space, that's between you and him. Although, I'm guessing you've already put that offer on the table, and he's turned it down, since you're so worked up right now." Nora began to strip off her clothes as she spoke, pulling her ripped t-shirt over her head and undoing the knot in her loose pants.

"What are you doing?" Tick demanded, ignoring Nora's last statement.

"I'm here to wash, so that's what I'm going to do. If you don't want to see it, leave." Nora opened the wash bag and rummaged around until she pulled out a flimsy brown towel and much smaller washcloth. "I'm filthy, and you're cutting into my limited bathing time. It's not my problem you're pining over someone who doesn't want you."

Tick let out a hiss of anger, but Nora just turned and glared at her, her gaze full of ice. "I'm. Not. Arguing. This. With. You," she repeated, emphasising each word. "Now, if you want to stay and watch me bathe, I can't stop you, but you need to take a good look at your fetishes. They're a little creepy."

Tick opened her mouth furiously, then closed it before stalking out of the washroom, not bothering to close the door behind her.

Sighing as the hot water ran over her head and shoulders, Nora sank into the tub. With a cascade of water raining down above her, she took a deep breath, then smiled.

* * *

Garvan was waiting for her when she walked out of the bathing chamber half an hour later. She'd been tempted to stay there for longer, but the thought of Garvan coming in to collect her quickly inspired her to clean herself as fast as she could.

Even though there had been grime all over her body, she'd managed to lather enough of the flowery-scented soap over herself that she'd be smelling like it for days.

Thankfully, Garvan didn't mention it as she drew closer, instead opting to roam his eyes over her new all-leather outfit of tight black pants, an equally tight vest and combat boots that buckled all the way up to her knees.

Nora groaned when she'd first seen it, wondering how the hell she was supposed to move around with it on, but it was surprisingly comfortable and fit her like a glove.

"My little angel of death," Garvan purred appreciatively.

"Don't call me that. Ever," Nora shot, holding back a retch.

Garvan let out his usual low chuckle before holding his elbow out for Nora to take.

She ignored it, but Garvan pulled her back by her wrist as she walked past him. "Where are your manners?"

Not bothering to answer him, Nora just halted and stared at the hand gripping her wrist, her lip curled in disgust.

Taking his sweet-ass time, Garvan took a slow step towards her and placed her hand on the crook of his elbow. "Is this not better?"

"I thought you were supposed to be more agile in this new form? Why are you using me as a walking stick?" Nora replied blandly, trying not to pull her hand back, even though the intimacy of their position made her insides curl.

Garvan let out a short laugh. "You are so feisty."

Nora growled in response, but Garvan began to walk, towing her along with him.

If Nora wasn't so desperate to train, she would have shot an energy ball straight through his head, but, unfortunately for her, there was a lot she had to learn. So, she had to be on her best behaviour. For now, at least.

"I am surprised Aaron did not try and train you while he was here," Garvan mused out loud, and Nora saw his eyes shoot to her briefly as the fingers resting on his arm tightened. "He was the one who trained me, after all. Mostly, anyway."

Again, Nora didn't respond. Aaron clearly had priorities more important than her.

"Did you know that he taught your brother and your red-haired friend how they could use their unique Realm gifts almost as soon as he met them? Yet, he had known you for much longer and did not deem it important to teach you. I

85

wonder why that is?"

Nora resisted the urge to slam Garvan's smug face into the next pillar they walked past and instead just smiled sweetly at him. "He was probably worried I'd beat his ass."

Garvan turned to her, his lips tilted upwards mockingly. "Maybe."

The two of them walked in silence until they reached a room engulfed in sunlight.

"Are you sure you won't burst into flames as soon as the sun touches you?" Nora asked drily, lifting her free hand to shield her eyes from the brightness.

"If you have a vampire fetish, all you had to do was say so. I would gladly nibble your neck for you."

Letting out a disgusted groan, Nora ripped her hand out of Garvan's grasp and stomped into the room. Then, she paused.

The room led out to a huge balcony, bigger than her living room back on Earth. The huge glass double doors, adorned with intricate golden spirals, opened by themselves as she got close to them, and a soft gasp left her lips.

The temple floated. In the sky. So far up, she could barely see the ground beneath them. But that wasn't the breathtaking part. All around them, cascading down the side of the temple, were rainbow waterfalls, the soft tinkling of the water disappearing captured her ears as she stared.

Nora jogged to the golden fence that surrounded the balcony, decorated in the same intricate design as the glass doors, and looked around. These balconies in the sky were all over the temple, and waterfalls cascaded from them all.

She couldn't peel her eyes away. They were beautiful.

"Stunning, yes?"

Nora hadn't heard Garvan approach, and she jumped

slightly when she heard him breathe into her ear. "They're gorgeous. Why haven't you torn them to the ground?"

Garvan didn't smile. "I do not hate things of beauty."

Nora stared at him and gestured to the Realm below them. "I find that hard to believe."

"The Realm needs to be cleansed if it is going to be reborn. It is an unfortunate truth, but a truth nonetheless."

Nora's skin prickled at the intensity on Garvan's face, and she found she couldn't look away from him. Even when he took the chance to step closer, well into her personal space, she held her ground, searching his eyes for a lie.

The two of them silently stared at each other until Garvan broke away, his eyes going sharp as he looked towards something in the distance.

"What's wrong?" Nora found herself asking.

Garvan turned to her and gave her a tight smile. "Your brother is a pain in my ass."

Nora's whole body jerked at the mention of Noah, and she shifted in the tight leather as she turned sharply to where Garvan had been looking, but she couldn't see anything.

"Feel free to train here for as long as you wish. There is a bedroom inside as well. It is now yours. I will be back soon to begin your real training."

Before Nora could say anything, Garvan opened a black energy portal, stepped through it, and disappeared.

Chapter 12 - Noah

An iridescent orb caught Noah's attention as he walked back into the palace with the others.

"Hey, Marian," Noah said as she came into view.

Marian's image waved to him and opened a portal, which Arel stepped through, his long, salt and pepper dreadlocks tied back at the nape of his neck.

"What's going on?" Noah asked.

"The next stage of your training," Zion said to him. "You are unable to learn everything here, so I am sending you, Layla and Arel to Earth to help Abigail."

"And me," Aaron said.

"Me too," Simmy piped up.

"No," Zion said to them. "You two need to stay here and watch the Realm."

Zion's words were met with furious objections from both Aaron and Simmy, and Noah secretly hoped Zion would give in. He would feel more at ease with the two of them coming along.

"No!" Zion boomed, stopping the argument. "It will be too easy for Garvan to capture you if you all go together!"

Aaron and Simmy both huffed in annoyance but didn't push the subject any further.

"Now, Noah, Layla, you are going to have to work fast to cleanse your friend of Garvan's manipulations. Arel," Zion turned to his son, "you have the most knowledge when it comes to this, so you are here to guide the children. Make sure you provide the knowledge on how to perform the cleansing, but allow them to make all other decisions they believe to be right. This is their training, after all."

"Of course," Arel agreed. "I will do everything in my power to guide them."

Zion gripped Arel's hand in thanks and turned back to Noah and Layla. "It is imperative you cleanse your friend and get back here as soon as you can. If Garvan notices what you are up to before you finish the job, it will not end well for her, I am afraid."

"We've got this," Noah said, more confidently than he felt. He grabbed Ray, who had floated over to him from Zion.

"We'll be back with Abigail," Layla said, grabbing hold of Ray as well.

"Good luck, the three of you," Zion said to them. "Marian, please create a portal."

Marian drew a circle in mid-air, and a silver portal appeared in front of them. "Be quick. Portals to Earth are hard to maintain," she said.

"We'll be back soon," Layla said to the others, giving an apologetic smile to Simmy and Aaron, who were still fuming.

"Come," Arel said, grabbing Noah and Layla's hands and stepping through the portal. "There is no time to waste."

"Stay alert," Zion called out as they disappeared.

Noah landed roughly on a patch of grass with a thud, and Layla landed just as awkwardly next to him.

"Not as easy as walking through a portal in the Realm," Arel said as the two of them regained their composure. His astral projected form was completely unruffled.

Noah brushed some stray strands of grass and a few dead leaves from his clothes.

A familiar building caught his attention from the corner of his eye, and his heart gave a lurch as he took in their location. They were back at their university.

"We need to move swiftly and quietly," Arel said, rolling a thick golden ring with a large opal around his fingers before putting it on the middle finger of his right hand.

"Is that your relic?" Noah asked. "You don't have a mandala?"

"I like having use of both my hands when I am working," Arel replied. "Marian does not have a mandala either, you know."

Noah thought back to the times he had seen Marian and realised he'd never seen her use a mandala either. "I never noticed."

"She uses a lapis lazuli necklace," Layla told Noah. "Now that the Guardians aren't using all their energy to keep Simmy hidden, they're able to tap into their powers more, which means they can use their relics too. Even in their astral projected form." She nodded at Arel, and Noah noticed Arel's body was translucent. He didn't want to seem rude and ask, so he assumed Arel was astral projecting from his body back in the Throne Room.

"The girl is heading towards a lavatory," Arel said to them, breaking Noah's attention away from Layla and towards where Arel was pointing.

Arel closed his eyes and placed his pointer and middle fingers on his forehead. After a moment, his ring began to glow and shoot out vibrant rainbow colours. "The opal allows me to see visions of people I am looking for," he said, answering Noah and Layla's unasked question.

"That will come in handy. What's the plan?" Layla asked.

"We're going to need to make sure she's alone," Noah chipped in.

"And that she is not in contact with Garvan," Arel added. "If he finds out you are here, then everyone in this vicinity will be in danger. You two are the Primary Guardians. If you die, then Garvan is going to take that power for himself."

Noah's heart gave a small lurch, and he gripped Ray tightly in his hand, his fingers tingling as she sent out amber sparks of encouragement.

"Okay," Noah said, taking the lead. "Layla, you're going to have to go in after her and make sure there's no one else in there with her. If there is, get them out as soon as you can. Once the coast is clear, Arel and I will go in and seal Abigail inside the building with Ray. I'm hoping to use the shield Aaron taught us, but on an external source." He turned to Arel for confirmation that his plan would work, and the older Guardian gave him a curt nod.

"I think it will be better to take her back to the Realm with us and purge her of Garvan's influence before he can manipulate her any further," Layla added.

Noah nodded at her. "That will help reduce any casualties."

"We could probably use the rebirthing chamber to do that," Layla continued, rubbing her hands on her cotton pants.

"You two are in charge," Arel said to them. "I will show you what to do wherever you decide to do it."

"Arel," Noah said, "I'm going to need you to help seal Abigail with me. You have the most experience with this type of situation, and we only have one shot."

"Of course," Arel replied. "If I was in my full Guardian form, it would be easy, but since I am only a projection, I do not know what the limits of my powers are, so I will do what I can to assist you."

"We're going to have to take the risk," Layla said. "We need to get back to the Realm as quickly as possible so Marian doesn't become drained holding this portal for us. We'll also need to find out what Abigail knows about Garvan's plans, so we can try and get a step ahead of him."

"Alright," Noah said, determined. "Layla, you know Abigail the best. You lead the way."

Without waiting for the boys to be ready, Layla ran through the university to Abigail, leaving Noah and Arel sprinting to catch up with her.

"C'mon!" Noah yelled, turning to make sure Arel could keep up with them, but the older man rushed past him with shocking speed.

"Come, child!" Arel called to him as he raced next to Layla. "We need to keep together."

Grasping Ray tightly in his hand, Noah pushed his legs harder as he tried to catch up with them, a mixture of excitement and fear coursing through his body.

Even though he felt much stronger, Noah was still puffing profusely as he caught up to Arel, who was hiding and waiting as Layla tiptoed into the girls' bathroom.

Squatting behind a hedge and making sure he could see the doorway Layla had disappeared through, Noah took a few deep breaths to steady his heart rate as he waited for Layla's signal.

Sure enough, not long after she'd gone inside, Layla's hand

shot out through the door, beckoning them to come in.

Noah and Arel glanced at each other, and Arel held up three fingers. Noah nodded, understanding that they would both enter the building on the third count.

Arel lifted one finger and Noah pulled Ray to his chest.

Arel's second finger lifted and Noah noticed that Ray felt colder than normal, but he dismissed it. He was nervous. Ray was just mimicking his nerves.

Arel's third finger lifted, and the two of them stormed through the door.

Noah's eyes widened in horror at what stood before him.

Noah dropped Ray to the floor, but before she hit it, she disappeared into thin air.

"I'll be taking that," Abigail's distorted voice sneered.

Abigail looked terrifying. Her hazel eyes were cold, and she emanated a dark, shadowy aura while she held Layla by her hair and dug a long, sharp, shadowy claw into her neck.

"Tick warned me I might be having guests, but I didn't think it would be so soon. Luckily, I was prepared," Abigail said chillingly, her eyes boring into Noah's.

"Let. Her. Go," Noah said, his voice thick and gravelly.

"Or what?" Abigail laughed. "You're going to attack me? Risk hurting your little girlfriend? You don't even have your precious mandala."

Noah grit his teeth as Abigail removed the claw from Layla's neck and showed him Ray, who was trapped in a dark ball of energy hovering next to Abigail's head, the light from her sunstones had dimmed.

Arel stepped forward, his hands out in front of him. "Give us the girl and the mandala, and no one will get hurt."

Abigail rolled her eyes. "Who's going to hurt me, old man?

You? Where's your walker? Don't make me laugh."

Arel's mouth tightened at her words, and Noah saw his eyes flicker with impatience.

"Very well," Arel said, lowering his hands. "I stand down."

Abigail scoffed. "Like you had a choice." She raised a clawed hand to pull him closer, but Arel took advantage of her overconfidence and shot a beam of opalescent energy right into her face.

Screaming, Abigail pushed Layla to the floor and covered her eyes as the energy burned and blistered her skin. The shadow surrounding her bubbled as it began to disappear.

Without hesitating, Layla grabbed Ray from her prison, hissing as the shadows burned her hand, and pulled the relic free.

"Go!" Arel called to them, forcing the bathroom door open with a blast of energy.

Noah grabbed Layla by the shoulders and led her outside.

"I don't think so," a familiar voice cackled. "You're not getting away this time."

Noah stopped and held Layla close as Tick appeared, her shadows writhing around her as if they were trying to reach for the two of them.

"Now, give me that mandala, and come with me," Tick said, holding out her clawed hand.

Chapter 13 - Aaron

"Zion, you cannot possibly expect me to just sit here while the kids are down there by themselves," Aaron vented to his brother, who was restlessly tapping his finger against the glass screen showing the Earth.

Instead of replying, Zion used his large thumb and forefinger to zoom in on Noah, Layla and Arel's location, his mouth forming a tight line.

"Zion!" Aaron demanded. "We cannot stay here and do nothing. What if Garvan notices they are there? He will take the Primary Guardianship from them, and we will have no chance of healing the Realm."

"The Realm—"

"The Realm is unstable! It is not going to do a damn thing," Aaron cut him off, slamming his palms down on the screen in front of them, forcing Zion to look at him. "Simmy has already gone off to learn as many lessons as she can today, to try and help the kids in a more developed form. I cannot do that, but I *am* able to go to Earth and help them right now. I have always trusted your judgement, but now, I am wondering if I should just go without your consent."

Rubbing the bridge of his nose with his thumb and forefinger, Zion let out a growl. "The Realm used to guide me towards the best path..but now... I cannot get a grasp on what is right anymore, on what is best for the Realm. I do not think even the Realm itself knows."

Aaron looked at his brother expectantly. Their eyes met, Aaron's sapphire and Zion's sky blue, and Aaron refused to look away. He'd already been forced to abandon Nora. He wasn't going to make the same mistake with Noah and Layla.

Zion blinked and turned back to the Earth on the glass, hesitating for just a moment. "Let us go."

Not giving his brother a chance to change his mind, Aaron gripped him by the wrist, opened a portal to Earth and threw the two of them through it.

Chapter 14 - Noah

Noah pulled Layla closer to him, shielding her from Tick.

He could feel Ray burning white-hot in Layla's hands, which were pressed against his abdomen, ready to go on the offensive, but Noah inwardly hushed the relic.

Tick sneered at the two of them and gave a loud, scratching laugh as Arel pushed through the door, rushing outside to help.

"She will be fine," Arel said to Layla, who had shot the Guardian a questioning glance as he'd emerged from the bathroom without Abigail. "Right now, we need to worry about this one." He gestured towards Tick.

"*We* aren't doing anything," Tick said mockingly. "Shouldn't you be sitting in stone somewhere?"

A shocked look flitted across Arel's face as Tick flicked a small square of black energy at him, holding him in place. Noah just stood there, unsure how to help, as he watched the energy expand until it engulfed Arel completely.

"No!" Layla screamed, ripping herself out of Noah's grip. She forced Ray into his hands and launched herself towards Arel, trying to grab hold of him before he could disappear.

"Too late," Tick sing-songed, looking at her long, clawed

fingernails as if she was bored. "He's just gone back to where he belongs. Garvan's trophy room."

Noah's head swam as he watched the last of Arel's dreadlocks fall into the portal while Layla was flung back by an invisible barrier. The heat Ray was emitting caused Noah's hands to blister, but he held onto her even more tightly, forcing himself to keep a clear head.

In through the nose, out through the mouth, he mentally coached himself, trying to calm his heightened senses, which were screaming at him to blast Tick apart.

Layla dropped to her hands and knees, searching the floor for any trace of energy she could find to bring Arel back, but there was nothing. She turned furiously towards Tick, still kneeling on the ground, a large emerald energy ball forming in her hand as she raised it above her head. The electricity crackled through it, snapping and popping as it grew bigger, smoking loose strands of hair which were blown into it by the breeze.

"Uh-uh," Tick tutted, shaking a clawed finger at her. "Don't get too carried away, my dear. I don't want to hurt you before the guest of honour arrives, but I'll be willing to claim self-defence if it comes down to it."

"As if you could—" Layla began, but Noah cut her off.

"Guest of honour?" He stepped towards Layla, pulling her up to her feet and keeping a tight grip on her shoulders, ignoring the small sting of the energy that was still crackling in her hand.

Tick gave a shrieking laugh and stepped aside as a black portal opened behind her.

Noah gripped Layla's shoulder even tighter. A black-booted foot stepped out, followed by a familiar golden staff.

"Garvan," he hissed, the heat from Ray exploding in his hand. Layla reabsorbed her energy ball into her palm and grabbed Ray's other side.

Garvan's blue eyes flashed dangerously, and a condescending smile graced his lips. His cropped back hair shone in the sunlight, accenting the black pants and silky black dress shirt he wore. He took a casual step forward, sinking his free hand into his pocket.

Noah tried to keep his expression neutral, but his heart was running at a hundred miles a minute. They hadn't planned on meeting Garvan here! They weren't ready!

"Concentrate. We're Primary Guardians now," Layla whispered to him, even though her voice cracked as she spoke.

Nodding to her, Noah gripped Ray so tightly his fingernails dug into his palm and started channelling his energy through her, connecting with Layla's own channelled energy.

"Hand me that mandala, and I will spare your lives," Garvan said lazily, calmly watching the two of them while Tick cackled behind him.

"Why do you want her?" Layla called, stepping forward to put herself between Garvan and Ray.

Garvan raised his eyebrows at her. "Did my father not tell you?"

Noah tensed.

"That mandala is the original relic." Ignoring the shocked reaction from the two in front of him, Garvan continued, "There is no limit to the power it can wield as long as the wielder is strong enough." He ended with a cold laugh, slowly looking the two of them up and down. Noah's skin prickled uncomfortably as Garvan's eyes took in every inch of him. "My... they really are scraping the bottom of the barrel here.

99

How old are you two, twelve?"

Noah opened his mouth to respond but was cut off by Tick cackling even harder, holding her stomach as she doubled over.

"Tick!" Garvan called, snapping his fingers.

"Yes, Master!" she replied instantly, all traces of laughter gone.

"Take Abigail back to the temple. I am not yet done with her."

"Yes, Master," Tick repeated, and in an instant, she had sped into the bathroom, collected Abigail and brought her outside. Tick opened a portal and stepped into it, tugging Abigail in behind her.

Noah caught a glimpse of Abigail's face as she was pulled through, and his stomach churned at how pale it had become. How she kept her eyes downcast.

"No!" Layla screamed again, blasting her signature green energy ball from her free hand in the direction of Tick and Abigail, but she was too late. The two of them disappeared, and Layla's energy, instead, burned a hole into the side of the building.

"What do you need Abigail for?" Layla demanded, turning furiously to Garvan and pulling Noah forward as she tugged Ray along with her.

Noah could feel Layla's furious energy pulsating through Ray, and he knew he needed to match it if they were going to stand a chance of surviving this encounter. He took a deep breath and allowed this whole experience to wash over him. Nora, the Realm, becoming a Guardian, blaming Garvan for it all.

"That is my business," Garvan replied in a low voice as he

looked at Layla. "Why not hand me that mandala now, and you won't suffer the same fate."

"That's not going to happen."

Garvan sighed and pinched the bridge of his nose. "I am afraid this is where you die then. Such a pity. I could have used the set." He eyed Noah from head to toe once more. "It just was not meant to be."

He tapped his staff on the floor. The pulse of energy it created knocked Noah and Layla off their feet, sending them sliding across the ground on their backs.

Noah grunted as the wind was knocked out of him, losing with it the energy he'd been storing.

White spots popped in his eyes, and he tried to reach out to Layla telepathically, but as soon as he opened his mind, he was met with a wave of anger. Then, he was pulled to his feet by a furious redhead.

"You disgusting, vile, sorry excuse for a Guardian," Layla screamed at Garvan, taking a heavy step forward with each word, the ground around her shaking. "Someone like you could *never* rule the Realm! You don't have the brains, nor the power!"

Garvan's eyes flashed dangerously. "No?" he asked, lightly tapping his staff on the ground once more.

Noah and Layla were flung backwards again, and Noah let out a heaving moan as, for the second time, the wind was knocked out of him.

Quicker than Noah could blink, Garvan launched himself forwards and pinned the two of them down by their chests with his staff. "I will be taking that mandala now," he hissed quietly, his lips close to their ears as he knelt between them.

Noah tried to hold on to Ray as tightly as he could, but the heat she was producing continued to make his skin blister. He could hear her angry rejections as Garvan reached for her, but the second Garvan wrapped his long fingers around her, he let out a cry and jumped away.

The spots finally receding, Noah saw Garvan's hand was red and blistered where he had grabbed Ray, and he was furious. "What did you do to my hand?" he demanded, black energy wrapping itself around his scalded fingers.

Noah didn't know, but Ray's angry hisses turned into a loud screech, piercing his ears.

Layla raised Ray into the air and shouted something that Noah couldn't hear. He could feel his energy being pulled out of him, moulding to Layla's will, shaping itself to assist her attack. He surrendered to her, giving her all the energy he could spare.

Thousands of tiny amber and emerald needles shot out of Ray towards Garvan, piercing his skin and clothes.

Garvan waved his uninjured hand in front of him, producing a shimmering black shield, which the needles bounced uselessly off as he studied his injured hand.

Layla's furious scream tugged at Noah's life energy, and she poured more of it into Ray. The needles were replaced with a solid energy blast, her emerald energy and Noah's amber energy mixing together.

Noah continued to permit Layla to pull as much energy out of him as she needed, but he had a sinking suspicion Garvan would be left with barely a scratch.

Letting out a cry, Layla pushed Ray forwards, firing a blast directly at Garvan's chest.

"You are really starting to annoy me, girl!" Garvan growled at Layla as he waved his now-healed hand in front of him, removing the shield while white smoke from the attack wafted behind him.

He absorbed the energy that had just been fired at him into his hand. Emerald and amber light reignited out of thin air, and he flipped the blast back at them while stomping his foot on the ground, causing the earth beneath them to shake, knocking both Noah and Layla to the ground once more.

"Noah!" a familiar voice screamed.

It was only then that Noah realised their fight had drawn a crowd. It was Ash who had called out to him. Her dark eyes looked at him worriedly, but Noah didn't let himself linger on her.

Noah briefly glanced at the people watching. His stomach lurched. It looked like most of the campus had gathered, although it appeared they all thought it was some sort of show, as they were laughing and cheering for their favourite to win.

"Get out of here!" Layla called to the crowd as she and Noah scrambled to their feet. "Go! Quickly!"

Garvan sneered as he watched Noah and Layla fruitlessly try to get their peers to leave, but the crowd just continued to watch. Not a single person moved.

"Idiot humans," Garvan drawled, and Noah swivelled, pulling Layla around with him. "What is the harm in thinning a few of them out now? It will save me time later on." Garvan turned to face the crowd directly and pointed his finger in their direction, a tiny black energy ball appearing at the tip. "Goodbye."

"NO!" Noah screamed, letting go of Ray and sprinting towards Garvan, putting himself in between his peers and the energy ball.

Layla followed closely behind him, using Ray to cast a shield over the crowd, trying to protect as many people as she could.

BOOM!

Brilliant gold light blinded Noah, forcing him to stop in his tracks and shield his eyes with his elbow.

"Garvan," Zion's deep voice rumbled. "Enough."

Before Garvan could protest, Zion extended a large hand in his direction and closed his fist, driving Garvan's arms and legs to his sides and forcing him to drop his staff.

Noah saw Garvan struggle against the invisible bindings, glaring angrily at Zion.

"Sleep," Noah heard another voice whisper, and he turned to see Aaron projecting his sapphire blue energy on the students surrounding them, his magic enticing them to softly curl up on the floor and fall asleep.

Relief flooding through him, Noah turned back to see that Garvan was still struggling violently against Zion's constriction, his staff trying to jump back into his hands. Zion refused to release him, although he looked like he was straining to keep hold of him.

"Aaron," Zion called in a strained voice. "Now."

Aaron flew past Noah towards Garvan with a furious look on his face and touched one thumb to Garvan's third eye, the space in the middle of his forehead, and his other thumb to the middle of his chest. "Release!"

For a minute, a blinding blue light surrounded the university, forcing Noah to shield his eyes again and reach for Layla, who had stumbled beside him, grabbing her hand.

But as soon as their hands touched, a turbulent wave of black energy forced the two of them apart again.

"Layla!"

"Noah!"

Thump

A hard body knocked into Noah, and he instinctively grabbed hold of it, trying to catch his breath as gale-force winds replaced the onslaught of black energy.

"This isn't over," Noah heard Garvan call from behind the veil of energy. "Until then, enjoy your new adventure."

Noah heard a roar escape from the person he was clinging to and felt himself being sucked into a vacuum.

Chapter 15 - Noah

H e was going to be sick.

Noah's stomach churned as everything around him spun.

Faint screams of *'No!'* and *'Stay back!'* rang through his ears as he spiralled through the air, but his eyes were so tightly clenched he couldn't see where the voices were coming from. He blindly held the other person as close to him as he could so they wouldn't be separated.

With the other person gripping him back just as tightly, Noah concentrated on projecting his energies to get a reading of where Layla could be, but the longer he fell, the further away her energy became.

Soon, he couldn't feel her at all.

As Noah pulled his energy back within himself, he felt his feet roughly hit solid ground. His knees buckled, and he fell to them. He threw his hands out to help catch his fall, letting go of the person he'd been clinging to.

"You alright?" he heard Aaron ask breathlessly. "That was the world's longest cuddle."

Despite feeling like he was about to throw up, Noah cracked a tiny smile. "I'm fine. You?"

"Yeah," Aaron replied.

Noah waited until his head stopped spinning, then opened his eyes to see Aaron lying on the grass next to him, rubbing his face with his hands. "You are not supposed to be here. Garvan meant to only send me away. Sorry, mate."

Shakily standing up, bracing with his hands on his knees, Noah tried to shrug. "Well, we're here now…" He lifted his head, which felt like it was made of lead, and looked around. "Wherever here is."

A sudden rustle in the bushes behind them made Noah jump, and he turned his head so fast his neck cracked.

Digging his fingers into his sore muscles, Noah squinted at the figure while Aaron, who had also jumped up at the sound, moved in front to shield him from whoever was coming.

"You two, get in here, quick!" a feminine voice whispered harshly.

Noah stretched his neck and placed a hand on Aaron's arm to see past him. "Simmy?"

"Yes! Now come this way," the older, plumper Simmy said to them, waving her hand behind her, beckoning them to follow.

Aaron shrugged at Noah. "I do not feel any negative energy from her."

"I think…" Noah said slowly, his eyes widening at the brash Simmy in front of them, with her thick auburn hair looking slightly matted, "I think I've been here before."

"Now is not the time to ponder!" Simmy exclaimed, walking back towards them, frustrated. "Come. With. Me!"

"Alright, alright!" Aaron said, raising his hands in defence. "Sheesh, she is a bossy one."

Noah nodded slowly, following the brash Simmy back to her house.

Once they were inside, Simmy closed the door behind her and made sure that all the old, flowery printed curtains were drawn before turning to Noah, her hands on her hips. "What are you doing back here?"

"Uhhh…" Noah started.

"Do not get your mandala in a knot," Aaron chided Simmy. "He did not have a choice. Garvan sent him here against his will."

"And what are *you* doing here? You should be in the Realm!" Simmy walked over to Aaron and roughly poked her finger into his chest.

"I did not have a choice either!" he exclaimed loudly, rubbing the spot she had poked and moving her finger away from his chest with one of his own. "It all happened so fast."

"I hope the others are okay," Noah said to no one in particular.

"I see you are in your own body this time," Simmy said to him, eyeing him up and down. She grabbed three dusty teacups from a glass cabinet behind her and tried to rub them clean with a filthy cloth that had been sitting on top of it. "What? I have not had visitors for a while," she said defensively in response to Aaron's look of horror.

Aaron clicked his tongue and shook his head, then flicked his wrist above his head. All the dust, grime and dirt that had accumulated over time lifted from all the furniture and disappeared.

"Oh," Simmy said, placing the towel back on top of the cabinet. "Thank you."

"I… uhh… yeah, I guess I am in my own body this time," Noah replied, answering Simmy's question from earlier. "So this *is* the same place that duplicate of Nora sent me, then?"

"Yes, it is," Simmy replied. "A world not too unlike your own but changing rapidly. Also, I do not think that you were sent here by accident."

"What do you mean?" Noah asked, following Aaron as he walked into Simmy's living room and made himself comfortable in a squishy armchair and crossing his legs.

"I got a visit from your Nora," Simmy said. "You are not a Guardian in this timeline as I lost my powers much more quickly than the Simmy in your timeline did, even before I gave you the last dregs of it. Garvan was able to find me, capture Zion and begin his takeover of this world. That is, before your Nora showed up."

"Nora's been here?" Noah exclaimed.

Even Aaron looked shocked. "What do you mean she *showed up*?" he demanded.

"Not long before you two arrived she astral projected herself here and provided me with another mandala to help keep things in balance," Simmy replied impatiently. "I am *technically* a Guardian here, so I still have some sway in the Realm. Your Nora said it was her job to stop Garvan."

Aaron looked sceptical. "Show me this new mandala she provided you with."

"I would gladly allow you to tune it up for me," Simmy said, pulling a mandala, slightly larger than her hand with brilliant blue sapphires embedded in it, from her dress pocket. "Sapphires, to help bring protection and good fortune to this timeline."

Aaron turned it over in his hands, weighing it, then began to tune it by expelling some of his own energy to flow through it. "Looks the same as mine. Did the me from this timeline create this?"

"I would imagine so," Simmy replied. "I do not know anyone else who could create a relic this unique and powerful."

With a look of unease still across his face, Aaron began to whistle. A tiny blue ball of energy began to weave its way through the mandala, mixing with the sapphires, causing them to glint in the light the energy projected onto them. "It does seem like my style," he said, handing it back to her. "It is in near-new condition and seems to be happy working with you."

A wide smile spreading across her face, Simmy took the mandala back from Aaron. She held it in both hands, closed her eyes and took a deep breath in through her nose and out through her mouth.

The mandala began to glow and crackle with Simmy's red energy. A screen appeared in front of them, and images of this timeline began to play.

They watched Simmy escaping the Realm before Garvan could petrify her and arriving on Earth, many years later than the Simmy from Noah's own timeline. Both he and Nora were already born.

Layla and her parents dying in a car crash.

Simmy struggling to maintain her hold on the Realm with no one to pass the Primary Guardianship off to.

Zion coming to Earth to help stabilise Simmy's powers, and Garvan using this chance to find her.

Zion giving himself up to hide Simmy from Garvan once more, imprisoned in his temple.

Aaron stuck as Scratch, needing to keep an eye on Garvan and do his dirty work.

Nora, her flickering form finding the Aaron of this timeline and asking him to make this new mandala for Simmy.

Nora bringing the mandala to Simmy, telling her to take good care of it.

Simmy reconnecting to the Realm with her new mandala and using her slowly replenishing powers to draw Aaron and Noah here after, what looked like Garvan attempting to dispel them completely into limbo.

The screen dissolved, and Noah turned to Simmy. "We're here for a reason, aren't we? But last time I was here, you told me this timeline had nothing to do with me. That I needed to focus on my own timeline."

"That is still true," Simmy said, "but we are now intertwined. There are forces at play that will affect both our timelines."

"Garvan must have created these timelines," Aaron said slowly, realisation dawning on his face. "He must be trying to ensure his victory, at least once."

"What do you mean?"

"Well, Zion, the original twelve Guardians, Garvan and I are eternal beings, the only ones in existence that I'm aware of. Regardless of time and space differences, there should only be one group of us. Having more could be catastrophic, as our powers could potentially clash and create or destroy realities. The same applies to the Realm. One Realm, regardless of how many timelines. The fact that the Zion from this timeline has been captured and the Simmy standing here in front of us has not undergone the rebirthing process means that this is a fabricated timeline. Garvan must have been creating these for quite some time now," Aaron explained.

"Does that mean you and I could be from a fabricated timeline?" Noah asked. "Could we be a figment of Garvan's creation?"

"We could be..." Aaron hesitated, thinking. "There is a way

111

to find out." He turned to Simmy. "Use that mandala, and hit me with your strongest blast."

"What?!" she exclaimed.

"The Aaron that created that mandala was created based on the original Aaron's DNA. If I am the original Aaron, the mandala will not be able to hurt me, but if I am a duplicate, then there is a chance I will die from the impact."

"Aaron! You can't do that!" Noah exclaimed, his eyes going wide. "It's way too risky!"

"I would rather die than be used as a pawn in one of Garvan's games," Aaron replied bluntly. "If I *am* a duplicate, then my death might be able to slow down his plans."

Noah turned to Simmy, who, to his horror, was holding the mandala in front of her with both hands, channelling her shaky energy into it. "You can't seriously be considering doing that?"

"He has a point, Noah," Simmy said to him, "and we don't have time to be figuring out alternative methods right now."

"But—"

BOOM!

Red energy hit Aaron's body with full force, and a bright blue cloud of smoke erupted where Aaron had been standing.

"Aaron?" Noah called, looking from the cloud of smoke to Simmy, who had gone deathly pale. "AARON!"

"Wait," Simmy said to Noah, placing a hand on his arm to restrain him. Noah tried to pull free, but her grip was vice-like. She was much stronger than she looked.

Noah's heart pounded. Minutes passed, and there was no sign of Aaron as smoke billowed around the room.

Finally, someone coughed, and Noah let out a breath of relief.

"You did not really think I would leave you here all by yourself?" Aaron wheezed, appearing out of the cloud and coughing into his elbow from the acrid smoke.

Noah pulled out of Simmy's loosening grip. "Well, you did just agree to be blown up."

"True," Aaron agreed, walking over to Simmy and pulling her shaking body into a tight embrace.

"Let me heal you," Simmy said to him, raising her hand, which was already radiating with blue healing energy.

"No need. I am totally fine," Aaron said, lowering her hands with his own. "Anyway, you are going to need as much energy as you can muster for our next task. That mandala is quite the relic," Aaron continued, rubbing his shoulders. "What is her name?"

"Tashi," Simmy replied. "It means 'good fortune'."

"I like it." Aaron held out his hand for her. "Alright, Tashi, you are going to need to work with me here."

Tashi shivered in response, recognising Aaron's energy signature as that of the person who created her.

"Good girl," Aaron said. "Simmy, come here and place a hand on Tashi. Noah, you are going to need to take my free hand."

Both of them moved forward and did as they were told.

Aaron closed his eyes and gripped Tashi tightly with one hand, his other hand pulling some of Noah's amber life energy from his body and entwining it with his own sapphire energy.

Everything was still for a moment, then Tashi began to glow. She grew brighter and brighter, forcing Noah to close his eyes as well.

Once the light had reached its peak, Tashi expelled a pulse of energy, blowing hot air onto Noah's face with such force he could feel his eyebrow hairs shift. Everything returned to normal.

Noah's eyes readjusted to the dim lighting of Simmy's house. He paused. Instead of just one Tashi in front of them, there were two identical mandalas.

Aaron had split the relic in half.

Aaron passed him one of the mandalas, and he could feel his energy melding with Tashi's as she warmed in his hand.

"Fit for a Guardian," Aaron said, winking.

Chapter 16 - Nora

The soft pillow under her head did nothing to settle Nora's jitters. If anything, she preferred the rock-hard one she'd been forced to sleep on before because it took her mind off everything that was happening.

If she had something to complain about, she wouldn't have time to focus on any of the thousand terrible questions swirling around her head.

Garvan had been gone for almost a day now, and Nora hadn't slept a wink.

She reasoned that it must be because she was still regulating her sleep cycle from the mess it had been in her old room, but deep down, she knew better.

Nora was absolutely terrified that Garvan would find out what she'd been up to.

She'd astral projected to another timeline because, some-how, the Nora she'd created from a strand of her hair, the one she'd sent to fight Noah and Layla while Garvan underwent his rebirth, had managed to send Noah to an alternate timeline.

If Tick hadn't mentioned it in one of her ramblings while she was on guard, Nora would never have known about it. But, she had realised, if a strand of her hair had the ability to send someone else there, surely she would be able to send *herself* there.

It had taken a long time. Many failed attempts left her more battered and bruised than usual, and it drained her energy so quickly she barely had any left to heal herself afterwards.

Thankfully, no one ever questioned why she looked like absolute shit all the time.

One of the perks of being a prisoner, Nora supposed.

She'd hurt herself so badly one time that she almost gave up. That was when she got the idea to send an astral projection of herself instead of trying to send her physical self.

When she actually thought about it, considering she couldn't even leave her room, there was no chance of her being able to escape to a whole other timeline.

And, of course, the first time she'd tried it, her astral projected form was deposited directly into the living room of that timeline's Simmy.

What Nora found had horrified her, and she knew she couldn't leave the timeline in the state it was in, even though seeing that timeline's Aaron had sent her heart racing so fast she thought it was going to thrum its way out of her chest.

She had wanted to stay longer and help, but Nora returned to her body as soon as she'd given Simmy the sapphire mandala.

The sound of the glass patio door sliding open sent a jolt through Nora, and she quickly pushed herself up onto her elbows.

One look outside told her it was still night-time, the waning moon shining brightly in the sky.

It could be Tick doing her rounds, but the lack of cursing and muttering made her suspect otherwise.

Quietly sliding her hand under the pillow, hiding the dagger she had created out of amber energy, Nora didn't blink as a flash of movement caught her eye.

"You are awake."

The growled statement came from directly next to Nora's ear, and she reacted instinctively, gripping the shadow's shirt tightly, pulling it down and flipping them both, so the shadowy figure was trapped underneath her. She held her energy dagger directly against its throat as she pinned its arms down with her knees.

A low chuckle came from it. "If you wanted to roll around in the sheets, all you had to do was ask."

The figure clicked its fingers, and a ball of black energy floated above them, fluorescent enough to faintly outline Garvan, and the cocky grin on his face, completely unfazed by the knife pointed at his jugular.

Nora narrowed her eyes, pressing the blade against him even harder. "Did you hurt them?"

Garvan didn't pretend to misunderstand. "As far as I am aware, they are fine."

Nora raised an eyebrow. "As far as you're aware?"

"My father took the redhead back with him as soon as I sent you brother and my uncle… elsewhere."

"Elsewhere?" Nora questioned. "Where's *elsewhere*?"

Garvan merely shrugged, blowing lightly at the dagger in Nora's hand and watching it disappear before quickly pushing his feet into the bed and lifting himself up.

His hard chest hit Nora's, causing her to cough out a breath as the wind was knocked out of her, and before she knew it, she was now the one pinned.

"About that tangle…" he purred in her ear, flicking his

117

tongue out to taste the shell of it.

Nora's skin crawled, and she tried to wriggle free, but Garvan merely cocked an eyebrow at the movement, and Nora flushed as she realised what it must have felt like against him, stilling immediately. "I would rather lick Tick's hairy armpit."

"I do not believe Tick grows hair," Garvan mused, his face still mere millimetres from Nora's, "but if that is a particular kink of yours, I am sure it can be arranged."

Nora let out a growl of disgust, fighting the urge to squirm.

Garvan held her to him for a long moment before lifting himself off and standing next to the bed. "Get some rest. We are training tomorrow. Distraction-free. I am going to see what you are capable of."

He turned on his heel and stalked out of the room, leaving Nora flustered and frustrated.

Sleep was a long time coming.

* * *

Garvan hadn't been lying when he said he wanted to see what Nora could do.

Without even giving her a chance to change out of the strappy white silk nightgown she'd found and worn to bed the night before, Garvan had stormed into her room and woken her up with a lazy flick of his wrist, sending a black energy ball into the pillow next to her, making it explode.

Nora's eyes had snapped open to find white feathers falling softly down on her face and had immediately pushed herself up and rolled onto the floor, missing Garvan's next blast by mere millimetres as it hit the pillow where Nora's head had just been.

Then it had been blast after blast after blast for hours.

The nightgown was now ripped and bloody, but Nora didn't dare bring any attention to it lest Garvan find out that she didn't have anything on underneath.

Thankfully, it reached her calves, so she was still able to run and dodge without worrying about it riding up too far.

Garvan's crooked smirk gave her the impression he was enjoying the view, though, which just made Nora push herself harder. She wasn't going to show any discomfort in front of him.

Blast. Dodge. Blast. Shield. Blast. Knock back. Shoot a blast of her own, which Garvan would dissolve with a wave of his hand the second it left Nora's.

Finally, Garvan gestured for Nora to stop.

Instead of collapsing to the ground like she wanted to, Nora held her back ramrod straight, looking daggers at Garvan for his stupid training.

She was starving, dehydrated, and practically naked. If the next words out of his mouth weren't telling her to go and have a nice long shower and a hot meal, Nora was going to blast Garvan's head off his shoulders.

"You really know nothing, do you?"

BAM!

The blast Nora shot at his face hit the wall as Garvan knocked it to the side without even blinking, his stupid, smug mouth uptilted in a smirk as if he'd known exactly where her train of thought had been going.

Panting, Nora glared at him, which just made him chuckle as he stalked towards her from his perch near the glass double doors.

119

With a wave of his hand, the room repaired itself, including Nora's nightgown and the pillows he'd destroyed earlier.

"You are free to eat and shower, but you are pathetically undertrained, so do not waste your time taking too long," Garvan said. He then slid his hands into the pockets of his tight black pants and sauntered out of the room without closing the door behind him.

Storming over to the door, Nora slammed it shut. She stomped her way back to the bed, grabbing the fighting leathers Garvan had left for her and then trudged to the shower.

Not bothering to wash her hair, since she would just be getting filthy again, Nora tied her now shoulder-blade length dirty blonde hair up into a messy bun before turning the hot water on as high as it would go, letting the steam fill the room.

She needed her muscles as limber as possible. She just *knew* what Garvan had in store for her next was going to hurt like a bitch.

Chapter 17 - Nora

"It is not surprising that my sister and uncle have not told you anything about your power's potential before," was Garvan's greeting as Nora padded into his makeshift Throne Room after her shower, her black fighting leathers clinging to her as she moved.

Nora forced down a grimace at his words, instead opting to look around the room. She'd only been in here a few times, and the tacky gold and red drapings covering the walls and obscenely large black throne that Garvan lazily draped himself over always made her skin crawl.

"There is a power within you that may even rival my own," Garvan continued, brushing over the fact that Nora hadn't replied.

Finally turning her head towards him, Nora cocked an eyebrow. "Why wouldn't they tell me about that? It sounds to me like it would have been an advantage for them."

"They may have just been incompetent enough to not realise your full potential," Garvan went on, and Nora clenched her jaw as she waited for him to finish his monologue.

"It appears as if they have hooked into your brother, though. They are not ones to make the same mistake twice. I will give them that."

Nora fought down a scowl as Garvan's blue eyes flicked from inspecting his fingernails to boring into her own amber eyes, a strand of his black hair falling into his face from the slight shift of position.

The two of them stared at each other, sizing each other up before Nora placed both her hands on her hips and flicked her high ponytail behind her shoulders. "Have you finished talking to yourself, or do I need to wait even longer for you to tell me about this power you've been hinting at?"

Garvan's mouth lifted into a crooked smirk as he pushed himself forward in his throne, resting his elbows on his knees and his chin in his hands. "I can let you stew on it longer if that is what you would prefer."

"*Tell me*," Nora hissed, tired of pretending she didn't care that she'd been left in the dark this whole time. Whether Simmy and Aaron knew what Garvan was talking about or not, *she* was the one Simmy had been training to become the new Guardian. They had to have had an inkling about it all. And Noah had these powers too, it seemed, if Garvan was to be trusted. Which, in all honesty, he probably wasn't. But, seeing as he wanted to use her for his own personal gain, she doubted he was telling her too many untruths.

Nora made a mental note to remember that. She had a slight upper hand if push came to shove. Garvan needed her. Not the other way around.

"I could sense some Realm energy coming from you when I found you on Earth," Garvan drawled. "I originally assumed it was because you had been in contact with my sister, which is why I took you to act as leverage so she would come out of hiding to find you. Which she did not do."

Nora's heart lurched. She knew Simmy couldn't travel to

the Realm when she'd been captured, yet it still hurt that she'd been left to fend for herself.

Refusing to let Garvan see he'd hit a nerve, Nora lazily waved her hand at Garvan to continue.

"Imagine my surprise when you were able to get out of the cuffs I placed on you that first night."

Nora's wrists ached at the memory, and she resisted the urge to rub them.

"I had to place energetic blocks on you while you slept. You were too unstable to train then. You still hoped someone was going to come and rescue you."

"And now you think I'm just going to sit back and let you use me to remake the Realm in your twisted image?" Nora asked, rolling her eyes.

"I believe you are open to seeing things from my perspective," Garvan replied, finally pushing himself up from his throne and stalking towards her, waving a hand over himself and shifting his formal outfit into black fighting leathers which shuffled softly as he walked.

Nora narrowed her eyes. "I haven't seen any evidence that your perspective is one worth investigating."

"You have seen less than a fraction of the Realm, so you really do not have any opinions worth voicing," Garvan drawled back, his eyes flickering as Nora's jaw clenched. "Everyone's powers are linked to something they have a talent or passion for or a personality trait. Unfortunately, *snide bitch* is not very useful in a battle, so you are going to have to think of something else."

Nora almost snorted at the remark, but she covered it with a cough instead.

"A talent or passion," Nora mused, quickly moving the

conversation along.

"If you need a reminder of what passion feels like, I would be more than happy to assist," Garvan crooned as he finally reached her.

"The only thing I'm passionate about is causing you immeasurable amounts of pain." Nora ignored his arm as it lightly brushed against hers.

"Promises, promises," Garvan leant forwards and whispered into her hair, inhaling deeply.

Flexing and unflexing her hand, Nora held her ground, absolutely refusing to give Garvan the satisfaction of knowing he made her skin crawl. *What am I good at?* she thought to herself.

The only obvious answer that came to her was swimming. She loved being in water. She wasn't the best of the best, but jumping into a pool and punching out a few laps always recharged her battery.

Plus, Simmy had told her the first answer that pops into your head, before you overthink things, is usually the correct one.

"I'm a good swimmer," Nora said slowly, and Garvan, whose face was still brushed up against her, paused.

"Swimming," he mused, taking a step back and looking her over. His eyes leisurely drifted from her face to her toes.

"I enjoy being in water. It energises me," Nora continued, fighting off the urge to shove her thumbs into Garvan's retinas.

"Water. Hmm." Garvan mussed up his hair as he thought, and Nora's eyes flew to watch the movement, her cheeks warming against her will.

"Did your brain stay geriatric during your rebirth, or have

you always been this slow to process information?" Nora deadpanned as she willed her heart rate to slow down.

Garvan's eyes slid back to her, his lips tilting upwards. "I was merely putting the pieces together."

"What pieces?"

"You were in water when I first took you."

"Glad to see you admitting your abduction."

Garvan cocked his head to the side, but he didn't deign to respond. "There was no plausible reason for you to have been able to conduct an energy blast as powerful as you did back on Earth, let alone one that could damage me. As small as that damage was," he added at Nora's gleeful smile. "If you truly have an affinity with water, and it recharges you, as you have mentioned, then you would have been able to subconsciously tap into the energy within the water you were submerged in to create that blast."

"Okay," Nora said, drawing the word out, "so what does that mean? That I need to lug around a blow-up pool with me everywhere I go?"

Garvan gave out a chuckle. "You should be a lot more pissed off about how little you have been taught. There is water in *everything*. You can learn to tap into the water already flowing around you."

Chapter 18 - Noah

Tashi's power complimented Noah's perfectly.

Noah pulsed his life energy through the relic, revelling in how easy it was to use her.

After a few minutes of tuning Tashi and testing what their limits were together, Noah turned to Simmy. "What do we do now?" he asked.

"Nora said that our main objective was to stop the Garvan of this timeline from becoming stronger," Simmy explained, grabbing the dusty old book from her back room. Noah remembered that this book was where all the times and dates of the Guardians' rebirths were recorded. "You said that the Garvan in your timeline had undergone his rebirthing already, yes?"

"That's right."

Simmy nodded as if she had expected this. "He would need to be a step ahead of his duplicates. It looks like Garvan from this timeline has not undergone his transformation yet. That means we need to get to him while we still have an advantage. We need to free Zion, too, so he can lock this Garvan up instead of letting your Garvan absorb his energy. It may only be a small win, but the less power the Garvan from your timeline can absorb from his duplicates, the better chance we have of stabilising the Realm."

"I can lock this Garvan up," Aaron said, cracking his neck as he spoke.

Simmy stared at him for a second. "Are you sure? It is going to take a lot of energy, and Zion has an untapped amount. When was the last time you tapped into your full potential? You feel like you have been capped-"

"I am not going to hold him forever," Aaron cut in, ignoring Noah's questioning glance. "I can trap him until we are able to free Zion from his cell, and then *he* can hold him."

"Okay," Noah said, rubbing his thumb over the large sapphire in the middle of Tashi, "that sounds about as easy as everything else we've ever attempted. What's the plan?"

"You're going to need to wait until Garvan heads into the rebirthing chamber."

Noah, Aaron and Simmy's heads spun towards the new voice.

"I can't stay here for long, but I want to help you guys as much as I can."

"Nora?" Noah croaked, taking a step towards the translucent image of his sister. "Where are you projecting from?"

"I'm still in Garvan's temple." Nora smiled warmly at him, extending her hand, but when Noah tried to take hold of it, her fingers flickered, and his slipped right through. "Tick called him away on urgent business, so I have a small window of time." She turned to Simmy. "It's good to see you again. I'm glad you've been able to use the mandala I gave you."

"It has been a big help," Simmy replied, gripping her half of Tashi tightly in her hands.

"Wait a minute," Aaron said abruptly. "Hold on. We had just decided that taking Garvan on now, while he is in his older form, would be the best idea."

"This Garvan is a tiny bit slower than the Garvan in our timeline but by no means weaker," Nora replied sharply, turning to him and placing her hands on her hips. "You have as much of a chance defeating this Garvan as you had of defeating ours. You need to wait until he goes into the rebirthing chamber before you attack. He's vulnerable there. His body needs to regenerate, and he'll be unable to protect himself."

"I am well aware of how the rebirthing process works, thank you." Aaron narrowed his eyes at Nora, but Noah could see a hint of a smile. Yet, when he turned to see Nora's reaction, her amber eyes were ice cold.

"Then why didn't you come up with this plan yourself?"

"Won't there be guards?" Noah asked, trying to defuse the situation.

"Yes." Nora looked at him, now completely ignoring Aaron. "But you should be able to beat them, and Tashi will protect you."

"How will we know when he has gone into the rebirthing chamber?" Simmy asked.

"I'll give you a sign. In the meantime, train. Help Noah reach his full potential as a Guardian, and don't leave out any important information." Nora grit these last words out, and Noah raised a confused eyebrow while next to him, Aaron shuffled uncomfortably on his feet.

"How am I supposed to reach my full potential without Layla?" Noah asked his sister, still trying to grasp the whole situation. "This whole time, we've been training to become the Primary Guardians as a team. Am I supposed to just forget everything I've learnt so far?"

"No," Nora said gently to him, taking on the voice she always used when Noah felt lost. "Of course not. But she's with Zion and the Simmy in your timeline, training the same way you are and honing her skills as an individual so that when you eventually come back together, you'll be even stronger."

"We will guide him," Simmy said, walking over to Noah and wrapping an arm around his elbows. She was too short to reach his shoulders.

Aaron stayed silent, staring intently at Nora.

"Yes, Aaron? Can I help you?"

"You seem to know an awful lot about Garvan and his weaknesses," he said to her. "Why?"

"You're going to have to figure that one out for yourself."

Suddenly, Nora turned swiftly to look behind her, seemingly seeing something the others couldn't. She whispered, "I'm out of time. Good luck!"

And then, she was gone.

Noah's hands clasped at thin air, his heart lurching. He'd been so close to her, and she was gone *again*.

Simmy squeezed his elbows in reassurance and turned to Aaron, whose own hand was half reached out to where Nora had been.

Seeing that Noah and Simmy were looking at him, Aaron lowered his hand back down and rubbed it awkwardly on his tan leather pants. "Are we *really* going to wait until Garvan's rebirth before we attack? Can we trust her information?"

Simmy pondered for a second before answering. "She has some valid points. You were not any closer to defeating Garvan in your own timeline before he underwent his rebirth. Why would it be any different here?"

129

"I trust her," Noah said. "She wouldn't lead us astray."

Aaron sighed and ran his hands through his dark hair. "She has been through a lot since you last saw her, Noah."

"She wouldn't lead us astray," Noah repeated firmly.

"You are the Primary Guardian. It is your call," Aaron replied, but Noah could see he was still hesitant.

Noah absently ran his thumb over Tashi's smooth sapphire's again and looked from Simmy to Aaron. "What do we do now? What training do I need? I'm used to training with Layla. I'm going to have to learn a whole new process if I'm going to fight by myself."

"Relax," Simmy hushed him. "It is the same process. You are just going to be relying on your own powers instead of relying on someone else."

"What do you mean?"

"I will show you," Aaron said, walking to stand next to Simmy. "Simmy, come and demonstrate with me. We will do a simple shield."

Noah stepped back a couple of paces to give them some room, but the backs of his legs hit the three-seater lounge chair, and he ended up sitting down.

"Right," Aaron said as Noah got comfortable, "this time when you are working with Tashi, you are going to need to be able to create a shield, keep it in place and also attack your opponent by yourself."

Noah's voice raised an octave. "Oh, is that all?"

"Watch. This is how your energy flowed before." Aaron and Simmy both held on to Tashi, facing each other.

"Shield!" they called, and a shimmering sapphire forcefield appeared around them.

"Attack me, Noah," Aaron said.

Standing up again, Noah created a bow and arrow, taking the wood from one of the window frames. He focused his energy on bringing it to life and duplicating it until twenty amber arrows were floating in front of him. "Yah!" he called, shooting arrow after arrow at Aaron.

They hit the forcefield head-on but were effortlessly deflected, disappearing into amber sparks as they hit the floor.

"Okay, now watch what happens when you work by yourself." Aaron let go of Simmy's mandala and took out his own, shifting his energy in the process. Tashi was now brimming with Simmy's red power, while Aaron's own mandala began to sparkle and crack with sapphire energy.

Aaron lifted his index finger, and a tiny blue ball of energy appeared. He began to whistle, and Noah dropped to the floor to dodge the attack flying towards him.

Ball after ball flew at him as Aaron's relentless energy kept coming back while Noah ducked and weaved away from it.

"Protect yourself!" Simmy called from her spot beside Aaron.

"Shield!" Noah shouted as he jumped over the lounge chair, holding Tashi above his head. His energy sparked from the relic, and a small iridescent bubble formed around him, allowing him to move and be shielded at the same time.

"Excellent," Aaron cheered as he fired more attacks at Noah. "Now what are you going to do?"

Noah lifted his index finger, and his own little ball of amber energy appeared atop it.

"Oh, I see how it is," Aaron laughed. "Alright, alright. Bring it on."

Noah grinned and called, "Yah!" directing the ball where to fly with his index and middle finger.

Aaron created his own shield to protect himself while also keeping up his onslaught of attacks.

Neither one of them backed down. Ten, fifteen and twenty minutes passed, and neither Noah nor Aaron had managed to land a single blow on the other, but Noah had reached his limit.

Taking one last dramatic jump into the air, Noah flicked a final energy ball at Aaron before landing face-first onto the three-seater couch. He made a T in the air with his hands to signal a timeout.

Both Noah's shield and his energy ball disappeared—Aaron had flicked them away effortlessly—and Tashi was tucked safely under his chest.

"Enough," Noah panted, "enough."

Aaron, who hadn't even worked up a sweat, laughed. "You did well. Although, if we were having a proper fight, you would not have lasted a minute."

Noah groaned and showed him a gesture that would horrify his mum, making Aaron roar with laughter.

Simmy, shaking her head at the two of them, walked over, exhaustion etched on her face. It had been a long time since she'd used a relic. "It looks like I am going to need some extra training myself," she said, sitting down on the soft armchair. "I am very much out of practice."

"We will not have much time to rest," Aaron said, tucking his mandala away in his pocket. "Nora could send us her signal at any time. We need to be ready. Recharge quickly, and then we will need to get back to training."

Noah groaned again and rolled off the couch onto the floor. "I'm going to go for a walk," he said, pushing himself to his knees and crawling to the front door.

Simmy shook her head at him while Aaron laughed. "So dramatic," Simmy sighed tiredly.

"While you are walking, make sure to stay out of sight," Aaron called to him, "and set yourself a challenge to practise your energy control."

Noah waved at them in acknowledgement as he crawled out the door, closing it softly behind him. *Practise my energy control,* he thought to himself. *I should head to the gardens.*

Chapter 19 - Noah

The botanical gardens were one of his favourite places in the entire neighbourhood. He'd spent many weekends there with his parents and Nora, learning about all the different plants and their unique needs.

It wasn't too far from Simmy's house either, just a couple of blocks.

Noah walked the familiar path on autopilot, thinking about how young and carefree he and his friends all used to be and how he, Nora, Ashlee, Mia, Max and Josh used to hang out, taking turns wreaking havoc at each other's houses.

It felt like a lifetime ago.

As his mind sifted through the memories, Noah reached the gardens and began walking the paths, looking at all the plants in bloom.

The temperature had hinted it was spring, but the gardens confirmed it. There were flowers blooming in every colour imaginable.

Soft perfumes wafted around him, and Noah took a deep breath in, inhaling the different scents.

He felt completely at home. He'd forgotten how much he needed this exposure, how much being in the garden was a part of him.

His eyes fell on a hibiscus plant, which had soft pink flowers, and he noticed one of the buds was late to blossom.

Walking over to it, Noah gently laced his fingers around the closed petals and encouraged his life energy to flow through it, his power coursing all the way down to the plant's roots.

Before his eyes, the bud began to bloom, but instead of the pale pink of its neighbours, this flower was dyed with amber.

A surprised smile lit up Noah's face, and he sat in front of the hibiscus for a while, soaking up the sun, before deciding to test his powers out on some other plants.

A white rose bush caught his eye, so Noah wandered over to it, finding another late bloomer. He cupped his fingers around it like he had done with the hibiscus.

Allowing his energy to course through the flower, it too opened before his eyes. Like the hibiscus bud, the rose was also tinged with his amber energy.

Noah decided to try again. More buds that were late to blossom were given a kickstart, and all were dyed with amber.

A blissful hour passed, and Noah stood back and looked at his craftsmanship. Speckled throughout the gardens were his works of art. Bright, blossoming flowers, all sporting his energy signature.

Noah looked at them with pride, his fingers tingling as energy crackled through them.

As he turned to move onto another section of the garden, Noah heard a twig snap and a girl giggling.

Crap! he thought to himself, wildly looking for a place to hide.

Noah quickly dived behind the hedge that trimmed the garden and ducked, peeking his head out just enough to see who was coming towards him. To his horror, he saw that it was the Ash and Noah of this timeline who, by the looks of things, had reconciled since Noah had been here last.

They were holding hands, laughing and chatting. Then, the other Noah pulled Ash in for a deep kiss, one of his hands gripping her long dark hair, which hung loosely down her back, while the other cupped her cheek.

Noah saw Ash quickly glance around to make sure no one could see them before enthusiastically kissing him back. Noah knew the reason Ash had checked they were alone was because her family is very strict. Her parents had always said they wanted her to end up with a nice Indian boy from their community. They had told her so in front of him and Nora one day after finding out Noah and Ash had kissed playing a game of spin the bottle when they were ten.

It felt weird watching them, but Noah couldn't look away either. He needed to make sure they didn't spot him.

That wasn't a conversation he needed to have today. *'Oh, hi! Yes, I am you, but not you. Get it?'*

Noah slapped his forehead. He should have known the gardens would be his favourite place in this timeline, too!

Now he had to figure out how he was going to get out of here.

The other Noah and Ash pulled apart and began walking towards one of the park benches, and Noah let out a sigh, ducking his head even lower behind the bush. The hedge he was hiding behind was in the middle of a circular walkway, and if he jumped out, they were guaranteed to spot him.

Pulling Tashi from his pocket, Noah rested his forehead on her. "What can I do?" he whispered.

Tashi shivered and warmed in response, her sapphires lighting up.

The next second, Noah felt himself lurching forward. Tashi was pulling him through a portal.

Pop

Noah awkwardly landed back in Simmy's living room.

Both Aaron and Simmy barely glanced up from their cup of tea at Noah, who was piled awkwardly, feet-over-head, on the living room floor.

"Hello," he said, his voice muffled by the carpet.

"Hello," Simmy replied, taking another sip of tea. "Go for an adventure, did we?"

"Something like that," Noah said, untangling himself and sitting cross-legged.

"You have time for a quick cup of tea and a snack before we start training," Aaron said, handing Noah a teacup and an apple.

"Thanks," Noah said gratefully as his stomach grumbled. He hadn't realised how hungry he was.

"Using your powers by yourself is incredibly draining," Aaron said, watching Noah devour the apple in a few bites, "but you will get used to it."

Noah nodded at him, chewing vigorously before replying. "It feels completely different. It's like trying to ride a bike without training wheels for the first time. I'm not used to pedalling without support."

"Practice, practice, practice," Simmy instructed, taking a bite of a Monte Carlo biscuit. "You have been relying on Layla since you began this journey, but it is time to stand on your own two feet, so when you both come back together, you will be stronger than ever. Now that you have finished your apple, you are going to need to re-centre. Close your eyes and breathe deeply. Visualise the task at hand and work your way

137

through it. What needs to happen? What is the end result? How are we going to accomplish this task?"

Noah took a deep breath, in through his nose and out through his mouth, closing his eyes as he did so, his cup of tea and apple core sitting next to him on the floor.

Deep breath in through the nose for five.

Deep breath out through the mouth for five.

Repeat.

As he drifted deeper into his meditation, all the noise around him began to disappear. Noah opened his eyes to bring himself back, but when he did, he could no longer see Simmy's living room. Instead, he was in a dark void with nothing surrounding him. There was only just enough light for him to see his hands.

"Hello?" he called.

No reply.

Forcing his eyes closed again so he didn't freak out, Noah stretched his tight neck muscles and tried to focus his thoughts. "What's the next step?" he asked himself. "What do we need to do?"

"Noah?"

His eyes snapped back open.

Layla now stood before him, a surprised smile on her face. "I'm so glad you're alright!"

Noah bounced up off the ground and leapt towards her, pulling her into a tight embrace.

"I've been so worried about you. Are you okay?" he said.

"I'm fine," Layla replied, pulling away and cupping his face with her hands. "I'm with Zion and Simmy. We're working towards a solution to rescue Abigail and hopefully put a stop to Garvan manipulating any more humans."

"How are you going to do that?"

"I'm not sure yet. Zion's been acting strangely ever since you guys got pulled through that portal. I think it has something to do with his energies that are connected to the Realm, but Simmy and I haven't been able to get a straight answer out of him."

"Has Nora been in contact with you? Is she helping you?"

"No…" Layla replied slowly. "Why? Has she been in contact with you?"

"Yeah!" Noah replied excitedly. "I'm in the timeline I was sent to when we fought that fake Nora. There's another Garvan here."

"There's another Garvan?"

"It's a long story, but before I can come back to you, we need to seal him. I'm with Aaron and the Simmy from this timeline. We're going to do it together."

"Be careful," Layla warned, her green eyes becoming worried. "You're stronger than you were before, but we're still learning. We're not even close to reaching our full potential yet."

"I know," Noah said, covering Layla's hand with his own, "but we don't have a choice. We need to seal him so Garvan can't gain any power from this timeline."

"Take this," Layla said, handing Noah Arel's opal ring. "Arel asked Marian to give it to Zion after he was forced from our fight. It might be able to guide you."

"Won't you need it to rescue Abigail?"

"We'll need it eventually, but we're not using it right now. You need it more than we do."

"Thank you," Noah said gratefully, taking the ring.

As soon as he closed his hand around the cold metal, the

room around them began to dissolve. Noah gripped Layla's arms.

"Be safe. I'll be back with you as soon as I can," he said, giving her a quick kiss on the lips.

Layla rubbed his cheek with her thumb. "Come back safe."

Noah blinked. Layla and the room had disappeared, and he was once again in Simmy's living room, the opal ring safely clasped in his hand.

Standing up, Noah looked around but couldn't find Aaron or Simmy anywhere.

He walked over to the front door, which was open a crack, and could hear Simmy's muffled voice.

Thinking she was talking to Aaron, he walked out the front. "Simmy?" he called, "Aaro—"

He cut off mid-sentence.

Simmy hadn't been talking to Aaron.

Standing in her front yard were Max, Mia, Josh, Ashlee, Nora and the Noah of this timeline.

"Hello, Noah," Simmy said, smiling tightly while Aaron stood next to her with his face in his hands. "We have guests."

Chapter 20 - Layla

"Layla, hello? Layla!"

Simmy snapped her fingers in front of Layla's face, pulling her back to reality.

"Where did you drift off to?" Simmy asked, throwing her long auburn hair, which was tied up in a high ponytail, over her shoulder.

"I connected with Noah. He's in another timeline, working with you and Aaron to stop one of Garvan's plans," Layla replied, rubbing her eyes as a wave of exhaustion washed over her.

"Another timeline?" Simmy frowned. "I should not be in any other timelines."

Layla shrugged. "He's been there with you before. He was trapped there after a fight with a Nora lookalike not long after we met Aaron."

Simmy's eyebrows all but disappeared into her hairline. "He has been there *before*? And a *Nora lookalike*? There is clearly a lot I need to be caught up on."

Layla gave her small aunt a smile. "Yeah, a lot happened after we left you on Earth, but we'll need to catch up on everything later. What can we do about Abigail?"

Simmy frowned. Her flowery summer dress swished as she

paced in thought. "Even if we do get her back, I am afraid she won't be able to stay in the Realm for very long, which makes me think she is being held on Earth. She does not have any Realm energy flowing through her. The only reason you, Noah and Nora have been able to stay here unscathed for so long is because you had been in contact with a relic, which had embedded you with the Realm energy you needed to sustain yourselves here. Humans are usually overwhelmed by the rawness of the Realm's energy. Do you remember how you felt the first time you met Zion back on Earth?"

Layla nodded. The feeling of every nerve being on fire wasn't something she was going to forget anytime soon.

"Well, that is what it feels like for humans in the Realm. The only thing is…" Simmy trailed off thoughtfully.

"The only thing is?" Layla prompted after a short silence.

"The only thing is, maybe, because Abigail has been exposed to Garvan's energy, she might be able to sustain herself here long enough for us to help her without causing her too much damage."

Layla hummed in response. "Well, that would be great, but we still need to find her first. Everything we've tried so far hasn't worked, and she's not showing up on the map in the Earth room like she was before."

"They must have made an effort to keep her off the radar," Simmy murmured. "If only I was at my full strength! I would be able to find help out more."

Layla took a step closer to her aunt and wrapped an arm around her slightly shorter frame, "Don't think like that. We're here and working together right now because of everything you sacrificed and accomplished. The Realm is still in one piece because of you. When your body readjusts to being in the Realm, it will all flow easily again, but you can't expect to come back here after—what, forty years?—and immediately slip back into your old routine."

Simmy leaned into Layla's hug and sighed. "I know, but I still wish I was more useful. After being at half strength for so long, I was looking forward to flexing my magical muscles."

Layla laughed and let Simmy go. "You'll have plenty of time for that, but let's take another look at that map first and see if anything's changed. Then we can spar again. I still need to work on using my powers without Noah."

Simmy created a playful red energy ball, which she flicked lightly at Layla, who squealed as it tickled her ribs. "It is on."

Chapter 21 - Noah

Noah stood awkwardly on the doorstep of Simmy's house, unsure of where to look.

His eyes glazed over Simmy, who was fussing with her thick auburn hair and flattening the floral dress covering her plump body, and came to a rest on Aaron, who was still standing with his face in his hands, shaking his head.

No one said anything while they sized each other up until Simmy finally said, "Shall we go inside, then?" She turned on her heel and stalked inside without waiting for an answer, pushing past Noah.

Everyone else shuffled awkwardly before following her into the house.

Noah had almost made it to the living room when the Nora of this timeline grabbed hold of his sleeve and pulled him aside. "You're my brother in your own timeline too, aren't you?" she asked.

"That's right," Noah replied slowly. "How did you know about the other timeline?"

"Can we trust the other Nora?" Nora asked, ignoring Noah's question.

Noah stared blankly at her. "You've met my Nora?"

Nora nodded. "Yeah, she's the one who told me to come

here today and bring everyone with me."

Noah felt a lump grow in his throat. What was Nora planning? "You can trust her," he replied croakily.

"She's not safe where she is, though, is she?"

Noah shook his head. "No, she's not. My friends and I from my timeline are working on a plan to get her back."

Nora nodded once before joining the others, who were waiting in the living room.

To Noah's surprise, she walked straight over to Josh, sat on his lap and gave his freckled cheek an absent-minded kiss, like the act was so second nature she barely registered she was doing it.

Josh's cheeks turned pink, highlighting his red hair, and a boyish grin spread across his face, which made Noah grin himself. *I'm glad this Nora has seen how awesome Josh is,* Noah thought to himself.

Then, to his surprise again, everyone turned to look at him expectantly. Noah's mouth went dry as he looked at Aaron, who nodded and gestured for him to speak. *Oh, right. Primary Guardian,* Noah reminded himself.

He cleared his throat and addressed the room. "From what Nora here has just told me, it appears as if my sister Nora, my twin, brought you here today because we need you to help us in our mission to capture Garvan." From the silence that followed his statement, Noah was sure they had no idea what he was talking about.

No one asked for an explanation, though, so he continued. "We're going to go after him as soon as he starts his rebirth. We'll capture him, then Aaron and I will take him back to our timeline with us."

A bead of sweat trickled down Noah's neck. None of this

sounded convincing to him, not after how much trouble they'd already had with Garvan. "Nora, my sister, will be sending us a signal when it's time for us to go to the Realm," he finished unconvincingly.

"Yeah, Nora filled us in about what was going on, but *what* exactly will we be doing?" Max asked, raising his hand and gesturing towards himself and the rest of the group.

"I… uhh… I don't know *exactly*," replied Noah, looking awkwardly at Simmy and Aaron, trying to telepathically encourage one of them to step in for him.

Simmy stepped forward. "As my students, I really wish you would all leave and keep yourselves out of danger." Her statement was met with silence and stillness. "But, since I can see that is not going to happen, we need to provide you with some form of protection. A weapon," she continued. "Aaron?"

Aaron looked at the group in front of him in exasperation. "This is going to be messy," he said but walked over to them nonetheless. "I need something of yours. Something you keep on you at all times."

Mia handed over a ring.

Max passed over his sunglasses.

Josh his watch.

Nora a necklace, which Noah recognised as the same one that their mum had given to his Nora as well.

The Noah of this timeline handed over his belt.

And Ashlee handed over one of her earrings.

Aaron took the pieces the group offered and channelled his life energy into them until they were engulfed in an electric sapphire light.

Tashi burned hot in Noah's pocket, and he grabbed hold of her, leading her to where Aaron was working. He placed her over the top of Aaron's hands and watched as his amber energy melded with Aaron's, creating new relics for the group to use.

"These are only partial relics," Aaron said when they were finished. "You have both Noah's and my energy within them, a Celestial and a Primary Guardian. They will help protect you while we are here, but once we have gone back to our own timeline, they will lose their powers."

Aaron walked around the room and handed the partial relics back to their owners, who accepted them gratefully, if a little hesitantly.

"They're so warm," Ashlee said, tucking her long brown hair behind her ear and clipping her earring back into place.

"They are designed to protect you," Aaron said. "Once the warmth wears out, you will know they have lost their powers."

"What powers do they have?" Max asked. His hair was long enough that it was standing in a small afro, which held his sunglasses in place. "Can I shoot, like, laser beams from my eyes?"

"Yes," Aaron replied.

"Really?" Max asked, a wide grin spreading across his face as he pulled his glasses off his head and turned them over slowly in his hands.

"Yes," Aaron repeated. "Do not try it now!" he called frantically as Max put his glasses on and screwed up his face in concentration.

Mia punched him in the arm. Her ring was already placed back on her index finger. "Stop trying to kill us all."

Max took the glasses off and sheepishly placed them back on top of his head. "Sorry."

The others laughed.

Noah felt a twinge in his gut as he watched the exchange. He'd never gotten the chance to tell his friends about the Realm, and watching the others in front of him really made him wish he had.

"Your powers are loosely related to the item that you gave me," Aaron said to the group. "Your ring creates an incredibly sharp blade from the gem on top that can cut through anything," he said to Mia. "Your sunglasses can be used to shoot energy beams at your targets, as you know," he said to Max. "Yours," he turned to Josh, "can be used to slow down time for a short period."

"Cool!" Josh said, taking a closer look at his watch.

"Your necklace can be turned into an unbreakable chain," Aaron said to Nora. "Your belt, when linked, can become a portal for transportation," he said to Noah. "And your earring," he turned to Ashlee, "can be used to hear anything from a distance."

The group all began to talk over one another in excitement, asking to have a look at each other's relics.

Noah, Simmy and Aaron left them to it while they re-grouped in the corner.

"Are we really taking them with us?" Simmy asked, worried. "They could get hurt."

"Nora sent them to us for a reason," Noah said, trying to convince himself it was a good plan. He really didn't want to see his friends get hurt.

"We do not have time to be arguing about this," Aaron interjected. "We do not know when Nora's signal will be, and we cannot send them in like this. We need to prepare them as much as possib—"

CRASH!

The three of them jumped apart to see Simmy's cabinet of fine china lying in a pile on the floor, a dust cloud floating above it.

Max slowly lifted his sunglasses back onto his head. "Sorry," he said weakly.

The rest of the group quickly scrambled to find their seats again and sat quietly, waiting for Noah, Aaron and Simmy to join them.

"Erm," said Noah, addressing the group once the dust had settled, "how many of you know what's actually going on?"

Nora raised her hand, and Noah pointed at her to give her the floor.

"Well, when the other Nora came to visit me, she told me that there was a guy who was trying to take over this place called the 'Realm of Intention', and if he did, then this timeline and all the other timelines would be in danger," she began.

"She also told me that our timeline was created by Garvan, and if we didn't want to completely disappear from existence, then we needed to help you capture the Garvan here and keep him locked away, so your Garvan can't absorb his powers. Oh, and also, we need to free a guy named Zion, who is the only one strong enough to keep Garvan captive."

The group stared at her.

"I know you told us this on the way here, but it still sounds super confusing," Mia said. The others nodded.

"Let us break it down," Simmy said, stepping in, and Noah saw her teacher instincts take over. "We need to free Zion, capture Garvan, take him back to Zion's palace so he can hold him there, and not get ourselves killed by Garvan's guards."

"That sounds about right," Aaron said, nodding along and checking each task off his fingers. "Simple enough."

The group looked at him incredulously.

"Would it be easier if we split into two teams?" Noah asked. "One to free Zion, and the other to capture Garvan. We'll be pretty conspicuous otherwise, nine of us wandering around the temple."

"That is a good idea," Simmy said. "We will have to split up depending on the relics."

"Zion is probably tied up wherever he is," Aaron said, "which means Mia, you need to be in the group that goes to rescue him. Your ring can cut through any bindings and can help get him free."

"One free Zion, coming your way," Mia replied, saluting him.

"Ashlee, you are going to have to be in the group that is capturing Garvan. You will be able to hear what is happening in the chamber itself, and you will also be able to tell us what the guards are doing."

"Got it," Ash said, nodding at Aaron.

"Max, you are going to need to be with the group going after Garvan as well. Your sunglasses will make for a powerful attack against the guards."

"Damn straight!" Max said, tapping the glasses on his head with his finger. Everyone else jumped away in case they decided to detonate again.

"Josh, you are going to need to be with the group rescuing Zion. You will be able to slow down time long enough for Mia to cut Zion free. If you hold onto Mia while you are using your relic, both you and she will be unaffected by its power."

"Okay, I'll help in any way I can," Josh said. Nora smiled warmly and kissed him on the cheek once more.

"Nora, your relic will be of best use in the Garvan team. You will be able to tie Garvan up after we have got to him, so he can't escape when we meet up with Zion."

"Gotcha!" she replied.

"And Noah," Aaron nodded at the Noah from this timeline, "you can be with either team, but I think it is best if you go with the group rescuing Zion. Once you have rescued him, you can use your belt to transport everyone to the other team, so we can all escape the temple together."

"Sounds like a plan," the other Noah replied.

"Simmy, you go with the Zion team as well. I am sure a friendly face would be welcomed right now. Who knows what the Aaron of this timeline has been subjected to? I may not be someone Zion wants to see right now."

"I think so too," Simmy agreed.

"Noah, you and I will go with the team capturing Garvan. I suspect there is going to be more of a fight, and we will need as much attack power as we can get."

"Okay," Noah replied. "Should we try to rescue the other Guardians too? They'll still be petrified in the Throne Room."

"It is best to leave them there for now," Simmy answered for Aaron. "Once we rescue Zion and capture Garvan, we will be able to go in and save them, but if we try and do too much at once, we are going to become overwhelmed."

"Okay, they're your siblings. You know what's best for them." He stepped over to Simmy and gave her shoulders a reassuring squeeze, which she responded to by patting his hand.

"Alright," Aaron said, "let us split into our groups and begin training. You all need to learn how to use your relics before we go charging head-first against one of the most powerful beings alive."

Mia, Josh, the Noah from this timeline and Simmy branched off and headed for the backyard, where they could practise without risking any more of Simmy's fine china.

Ashlee, Max, Nora, Noah and Aaron all headed out the front for the same reason.

Noah watched as the couples, which had all been split into different groups, reassured each other as they went with their respective teams. Mia's cheeks turned pink as Max kissed her on the top of her head, Josh pressed his forehead to Nora's after brushing his lips against it, and Ashlee pulled the other Noah into a deep kiss, which made his own cheeks burn red.

He turned away from the sight. Noah's heart twinged, and he wished Layla was with him right now. He missed her, and he knew if she were here, there was no way they would fail this mission.

"Come on," Aaron said to him, quietly pulling him by the elbow. "The others will meet us outside."

Noah followed him, wrapping his fingers around Tashi and willing her to send Layla a message for him. She let out a blue spark to confirm the message could be sent, and Noah voiced a quick note on their mission and let her know he wished she were here with them.

Once he was done, he watched as Aaron sat lotus-style on the grass, then followed suit.

"We are going to have to teach these kids to clear their minds first," Aaron said. "It is the number one tactic they need to learn in order to control their relics properly."

Noah nodded in agreement, straightened his back, placed his hands on his knees and closed his eyes. He inhaled deeply for five seconds and exhaled slowly for five seconds, focusing on the space between his eyebrows and allowing any stray thoughts to flow through, not giving them any attention.

He enjoyed clearing his mind now. There was always so much happening at any given moment that taking the time to sit and breathe was quickly becoming one of Noah's favourite things to do, so he took a few more deep breaths in and out, enjoying the small moment of peace.

A rustle next to him broke him from his trance, and he wiggled his toes to get the blood flowing through his body again.

Ashlee, Max and Nora had joined them. They sat down lotus-style with Noah and Aaron, following their example, and closed their eyes, taking deep breaths.

Aaron began speaking, but it sounded far away to Noah, who had slipped back into his trance as everyone had settled down around him. The deep breaths fueled his body, preparing him for what was about to happen.

Breathe in, two, three, four, five.

Breathe out, two, three, four, five.

Noah's head began to feel fuzzy. The hairs on his arms stood on end, and a daunting feeling settled into the pit of his stomach.

His eyes flew open. They were all in danger.

Chapter 22 - Nora

It hurt to blink.

Everything in Nora's body ached. She'd used up far too much energy, but she hadn't had a choice.

Astral projecting had become second nature to her now, and she'd even managed to project herself back to that alternate timeline to give Noah some extra help.

But she'd stayed there longer than she should have—it had been too long since she'd seen Noah—and had almost been caught by Garvan as he arrived back. Garvan had been furious at Tick that her urgent business was only about the other Shadow Beings in the temple becoming restless, so Garvan had sent Tick off to deal with them.

Which brought Nora to why she was in so much pain. Garvan was frustrated at being dragged away for something so useless, so he was training her to the bone.

He also wasn't joking when he said there was water in everything, and he expected her to be able to extract every last drop and turn it into something she could use to her advantage.

Nora rubbed one of her aching shoulders and stretched her neck. It was almost time to begin again. Even when Garvan wasn't training her, he expected her to train without him.

She'd tested his limits the other day when she'd gone and dipped her feet in one of the pools surrounding the waterfalls instead of training. She'd woken up the next morning back in her original room.

Panic had set in immediately, and she'd pounded at the red barrier sealing her inside, banging her fists on it until they were raw.

It was only when Garvan had sauntered down to find her hours later and she'd launched herself at him with a crackling energy blade, that she realised just how much she needed to be in open space.

There wasn't a hint of a smirk on Garvan's face as threatened to take away her newfound freedom if she wasn't going to use it to train.

Nora hadn't tested him since.

Inhaling in through her nose, holding it for a count of five and slowly exhaling through her mouth, Nora embraced the sweet flowery scent that washed over her, both from the blooming gardens surrounding her and the scented soaps she now lathered herself in every night.

Even her black fighting leathers were being washed with some soft, flowery fragrance..

Not that she knew who washed anything. Apart from that one Shadow Being who had guided her to Garvan's Throne Room, she hadn't seen anyone else around besides herself, Tick and Garvan. Even Aaron, when he'd been here as Scratch, hadn't mentioned anyone else being in the temple.

But there must be plenty more. Who else would be picking up her discarded clothing every night after she'd fallen asleep and washing them? And she certainly wasn't making her bed every morning, but it was always made when she came back to her room in the evening.

Nora knew it wasn't Garvan. Aside from the obvious, that he thought such chores were beneath him, she also knew he would probably keep her discarded underwear for his own personal uses.

The sick bastard.

She ran through her basic stretches and warmed up her muscles, then lightly stepped over to the pool at the edge of the balcony, crouching down and dipping her fingertips into the water, allowing it to merge with her amber life energy. It crackled on the surface as droplets of water began running up her palms, over her arms, and eventually covering her whole body, hardening as she turned them into an invisible shield.

Next, she walked over to the middle of the balcony and placed her arms in front of her, palms facing upwards.

The air around her rippled as she called as much water to her as she could without killing everything in close proximity.

That hadn't been a fun lesson to learn the first time she'd tried this. Not only had she massively overexerted herself energetically, Garvan also had to pull the energy she'd taken out of her and place it back into everything she'd sucked it out of. All the plants had withered, and even the wood holding the balcony together had started to crumble while she'd been standing on it.

Garvan had, naturally, found it hilarious, cracking a snarkier grin than usual as he fixed her mistake.

The thought of him needing to help her made her determined to master her powers as quickly as possible. It would be pointless to try to take him down while he was standing behind her, correcting her every move.

Her fingers tingled as she felt the objects she'd connected

with reach their limit, and she stopped pulling from them.

A small, shimmering ball of water floated formlessly to her hand, and she played around with its shape for a while before splitting it into hundreds of tiny needles.

"You started early, I see."

Nora only slightly tensed as Garvan approached her.

She hadn't heard him come outside.

Turning her body around, moving her hand with the water needles behind her back, Nora gave a cutesy smile and lowered her lashes. "I was wondering when you'd get here," she purred.

Garvan stopped barely a foot in front of her and leaned in to tuck a strand of loose wavy hair behind her ear. Nora quickly lowered the shield around that side of her face.

He didn't know she was able to create shields, and she planned to keep it that way.

"Today, we will be focusing on energy control while fighting. You need to be able to stay in control under any and all circumstances, no matter whom you may be fighting against."

"Sounds interesting." Nora raised her shield back up as Garvan's fingers drifted away. "You should show me how it works."

Flexing her hand, the hundreds of water needles shot out from behind Nora's back, around her body, and straight into Garvan's chest and arms.

The slight widening of his eyes was the only indication that Garvan hadn't seen the attack coming, but, infuriatingly, he lazily waved his hand, and the needles became water droplets once more, falling uselessly to the floor.

With a wave of her own hand, Nora called the droplets back to her palm, absently rolling its formless shape around her fingers, and looked at Garvan through her lashes, an innocent smile on her face.

"And here I was thinking I had finally won you over." Garvan's eyes narrowed, but there was a hint of a smile on his face that told Nora he wasn't displeased with her efforts. "I will be out for a little while today. Continue to practise. I am enjoying these sharp surprises you are throwing at me."

"I bet you are," Nora mumbled, and Garvan's smile widened.

"Do not miss me too much."

Nora scoffed.

After he had turned on his heel and stalked away, Nora ran through some mobility exercises on autopilot before sending out an energetic call throughout the temple to make sure Garvan was truly gone.

Not daring to relax, so Garvan wouldn't be able to accuse her of slacking, Nora astral projected a part of herself to the alternate timeline where Noah and Aaron were. "Time for that signal."

Chapter 23 - Noah

Quickly standing up, Noah called out, asking if Aaron could feel the same dark presence he could, but before Aaron could reply, a strong gust of wind forced him to shield his head behind his arms.

Noah dropped to his hands and knees and crawled his way to the others, who were all clinging to each other on the ground. He yelled at them to go inside, his leg muscles straining as he forced himself to stand up. His body was hunched over to keep him balanced, and his hair was flying wildly into his face.

As he watched the group of friends grab each other's wrists and try to stand, Noah saw Aaron throw a sapphire ball of energy at them, which turned into a spherical shield, giving them enough cover from the gale to be able to run to the house and slam the door behind them.

Noah forced his way over to Aaron and reached out to him. The two of them linked their hands in a monkey grip, so they wouldn't slip and become separated. Once he was anchored, Noah grabbed Tashi out of his pocket.

"SHIELD!" Noah shouted, hoping to create some sort of barrier between them and the winds, which were now threatening to rip trees out of the ground. "WHAT'S GOING

ON?" he yelled to Aaron.

"IT SEEMS LIKE OUR PLAN TO INVADE GARVAN'S TEMPLE HAS BEEN PUT ON HOLD," was the reply he got.

"NO KIDDING!" Noah called back sarcastically. "I WAS ACTUALLY REFERRING TO THE WIND."

Aaron opened his mouth to reply, but mid-sentence some-one behind Noah slipped their hand through the shield and yanked him backwards by his hair, which, reaching down to his shoulders now, was an easy target. The skin on his arm stretched painfully as Aaron gripped him even tighter to stop him from being dragged away.

"Grab a Parker twin," Tick's venomous voice whispered menacingly in his ear. "Garvan will be pleased when I come back with the brother."

"LET! HIM! GO!" Aaron called over the still-roaring winds as he yanked Noah towards him with each word. The shield had done nothing to protect them from the noise.

"No." Tick snapped her fingers to create a black bubble around the three of them. "Shan't. Grab a twin. Those were my orders, so I'm going to take the boy back with me and enjoy watching this pathetic little timeline go up in flames."

"We're not going to let that happen," Noah grit out. The pain from Tick pulling his hair was making his voice hoarse.

"And what are you going to do about it?" Tick sneered softly in his ear.

Tashi was burning hot in his grip, but Noah ignored the pain. All he knew was that all the people in this timeline, his friends and everyone else, deserved to live, and he wasn't going to let Tick take that away from them.

Noah released some of his energy, feeling it flow through Tashi, and he willed it to create a razor-sharp amber blade around her. He held his palm flat as Tashi hovered a few centimetres above it, her sapphires beginning to glow. He shot a look at Aaron, silently telling him to create a distraction. Noah watched as he created his signature energy ball at the top of his finger and whistled, shooting the ball right through Tick's forehead.

"ARGH!" she screamed, poking a clawed, shadowy finger through the hole the ball created. "My head! You're going to pay for that!"

She pulled Noah's hair backwards so forcefully that he lost his balance and hit the ground heavily. His tailbone throbbed in pain from the impact. Eyes watering, Noah watched as Tick's long, shadowy fingers became knives, stretching quickly towards Aaron, who barely managed to dodge out of the way as she sliced at him. One of her nails grazed his cheek, causing a thin gash.

Tick's laugh of triumph caused her to take her eyes off Noah for a split second, and he took the opening, throwing Tashi like a frisbee at the Shadow Being, amber energy blades cutting through her wispy body like butter.

The laugh of triumph turned into a scream of shock as she was cut in two.

Noah caught Tashi as she flew back to him. Before Tick had a chance to retaliate, he threw the mandala again, this time slicing through her arms.

He continued to frisbee Tashi again and again, each time cutting Tick's shadowy figure into smaller chunks, not giving her time to regenerate.

Preparing to throw Tashi one last time, Noah stopped as he saw this timeline's Nora forcing her way towards him through the winds, stretching out her arm for Aaron to pull her into the bubble.

"I'll trap her," she said as Aaron tugged her through, taking off her necklace and watching it expand at her touch. She ran over to where Tick was frantically trying to regenerate and wrapped her necklace around each individual piece before tying them together, the unbreakable chain glinting.

As quickly as they had started, the winds stopped, and Noah breathed a sigh of relief.

His sigh quickly turned to a gasp as a static *pop* sounded, and suddenly, standing behind Aaron, was Garvan. Noah knew it was the Garvan from this timeline as his long grey beard was as wiry as ever, and his veiny, translucent skin was pulled tightly over the hand that gripped his golden staff.

The staff he was holding against Aaron's throat.

"Master," Tick called weakly from her chains. "You came for me."

Garvan scoffed at her in disgust. "You had the simple task of bringing me one mortal, and you failed. I have no time for someone as useless as you."

Tick's cry of despair pierced even Noah's heart, and he turned to Garvan angrily. "What do you want?"

"I need a twin from this timeline," Garvan said, slowly looking him up and down.

"I'm not—" Noah began, but the look Aaron shot him stopped him in his tracks.

"Not what, boy?"

"Not going to go without a fight!" Noah corrected himself, raising Tashi once more.

Garvan gave a cold laugh. "I could finish you in a second, but I think you *are* going to come with me. Willingly."

"Why would I do that?"

"I know there is a house full of people over there with nowhere to run. An easy target, no?"

Garvan gestured towards Simmy's house with his head, and Noah's blood ran cold. He was right. The others needed to be kept safe, and if Garvan really needed a twin from *this* timeline, then this could be his chance to thwart Garvan's plan.

Noah hung his head in mock resignation. "If you leave the others alone, I'll go with you."

"I thought you might." Garvan clicked his fingers, and a heavy gold chain pulled Noah's hands together and wrapped itself around his wrists. Garvan removed his staff from Aaron's neck, and Aaron immediately rushed over to Nora.

"What about me?" Tick, whose body was trying to regenerate through Nora's bindings, called out. "I won't fail you again, Master. Please, don't leave me here."

Garvan didn't give any inclination he'd heard Tick's plea as he roughly grabbed Noah by his shoulder and opened a black portal to the Realm.

Noah looked behind him as far as he could and saw Nora crouching next to a distraught Tick. Aaron was looking at him, a mixture of anguish and determination on his face.

Turning back to Garvan, Noah stepped through the portal, closing his eyes against the deep darkness that caused him to see spots. Garvan's black energy prickled his skin uncomfortably, and when he opened his eyes again he was in the Throne Room. The familiar setting gave him an unsettling sense of security.

Looking at the eleven petrified Guardians, he wondered if Marian and Arel were watching him and whether they knew their counterparts' spirits had broken free of their confinement.

A hard shove from Garvan forced a strained 'oof' out of Noah, and he resigned himself to being guided to the small hideaway at the back of the Throne Room, which Nora occupied in his own timeline.

It looked dusty and unused. There was a single bed pushed into the corner, with a pillow that looked as soft as granite and a thin blanket that appeared as if it would disintegrate at the lightest touch.

"Get comfortable," Garvan said, shoving him onto the rock-hard mattress. "You are going to be here for a while." He turned on his heel, exiting the room.

"Aren't you going to unchain me?" Noah demanded.

Garvan didn't even look back at him as he paused mid-step. "No," he said, and walked away, locking the door behind him as he left.

A single flickering candle was the only light Noah had, and it took several minutes for his eyes to adjust to the darkness.

The chains binding his wrists were beginning to rub and hurt, and he cursed Garvan under his breath as he wriggled his hands, trying to slip free. It was no use. The more he struggled, the tighter the chains bound him.

He should have known Garvan had enchanted them.

Noah's eyes prickled as tears began to well, and he furiously shook his head. *No*, he thought to himself. He wasn't going to give Garvan the satisfaction of making him cry.

Flopping down onto the pillow, Noah winced. He'd been right in assuming that it was as hard as a rock.

Closing his eyes and taking a deep, shaky breath, Noah willed himself to think of something—anything—other than being trapped here.

"It took me a few tries to get out of those chains, too."

Noah's eyes flew open, and he felt like he ripped his abdominals with how quickly he sat up. "Nora?"

"Shhh!" she hissed, raising a flickering finger to her lips as her astral projected form became more prominent. "Do you want him to come back?"

"Oh, sorry," Noah whispered. "What are you doing here?"

"I'm here to rescue you, of course."

Chapter 24 - Noah

"You're here to rescue me?" Noah hesitated as Nora tried to jiggle the chains to get a feel for how tightly he was locked in. Her translucent hands dropped them every few tries though, so the chains kept tightening around Noah's wrists.

"Yup," Nora replied, giving up trying to touch the chains with her hands and creating a small energy blade with her index finger instead. Poking her tongue out of the side of her mouth in concentration, Nora began to cut through the bindings, sparks flying as the chain stubbornly resisted Nora's ministrations.

Noah flinched as the sparks flew into his face but kept as still as possible while Nora worked, her blade flickering along with her astral projected form.

After Nora had almost nicked him with her blade for the tenth time, the chain finally snapped, and, rubbing his sore wrists, Noah looked at his sister. "You don't seem surprised I'm in this room."

"I'm not," Nora replied, not meeting Noah's eyes.

A moment of silence stretched between the two of them, and then Noah jumped off the bed furiously. "*This* was your plan?! *This was your sign?!*" he exclaimed.

A flicker of guilt crossed Nora's face. "It was the only way to make sure this Garvan didn't get his hands on one of the other twins. If he did..." She shook her head.

Noah snorted angrily. "You could have told us what you were planning."

"No, I couldn't," Nora replied earnestly. "Garvan would have been suspicious if you agreed to go with him straight away."

Noah stiffly lowered himself back onto the hard bed and leaned against the wall, glaring at his sister. But, after a few minutes, he sighed and extended his arms. "C'mere."

Nora raced over and accepted her brother's hug.

Even though Noah felt like he was hugging a sheet, Noah relaxed into it, enjoying Nora's familiarity. After a while, he let her go and looked her in the eyes with his identical, narrowed ones. "Why is Garvan trying to get a hold of one of the twins from this timeline?"

Nora shivered. "I'm still figuring out what it is about us that's so important to Garvan's plans myself. He hasn't been overly forthcoming, but he's obsessed with training me. Look, it's only a hunch, to be honest, but it can't be a coincidence that he's kept me alive for so long, and you're now a Primary Guardian."

"Mum mentioned that Simmy was looking for us when she first came to Earth," Noah murmured.

Nora paused. "Mum knew Simmy?"

"Didn't Simmy tell you? I thought you knew."

"No, Simmy only told me I needed to become a Guardian because the Realm was in danger."

Noah and Nora stared at each other for a moment before Nora shook her head, her mouth forming a tight line. "Anyway, from what I've been able to gather from listening to Tick, Garvan's created five alternate timelines, so his duplicates in them can absorb our life energy. The original Garvan then plans to merge with his doubles to make himself stronger."

Noah gaped. "He's planning on absorbing us in every timeline? Like, eating us?"

Nora shrugged. "I don't know how it works, but it doesn't sound pleasant."

Noah placed his hands on Nora's arms. "How are you still alive then? Why hasn't he absorbed your life energy yet?"

"I think he wants to make me stronger," Nora replied. "I can only assume he wants to absorb the other Garvan's first to see how much more powerful they make him, and then I'll be the last surge of energy. One that will make him unbeatable. Plus, I'm keeping him entertained."

Noah's eyes narrowed again. "What are you doing?"

Nora shrugged, but her eyes drifted to the floor.

"Nora…"

"Look, he's teaching me how to fight and how to use my life energy to its full potential. Which, I might add, is more than Simmy or Aaron ever taught me."

"How do you know Aaron?"

"He was one of my jailers, but that's not important right now."

The speed with which Nora changed the subject made Noah want to press for more information, but Nora waved her hand in dismissal. "I'm not doing anything brash. He has peeked into my head a few times. That was how he found out you were going to become the next Guardian."

"He's been inside your head? *That's* how he found out? Do you know how much trouble that caused us?"

"I'm sorry!" Nora exclaimed. "I didn't have a choice! Aaron was the one who put him up to it."

Noah recoiled. "What?"

"Well, sort of. Maybe not that time, but in other ways, Aaron was the reason Garvan was able to cause you so much trouble. He just used me to get to you." Nora paused and then sighed. "Aaron probably didn't have a choice either. Not that I've forgiven him, the asshat, but he had a mission too—"

"I won't say anything to Aaron if you don't want me to," Noah interrupted. Nora had a habit of going on tangents when she was frustrated. "What now? What do we need to do to stop the Garvan here in this timeline?"

"I sent a message to Asshat– Aaron just before I got here, so he and the rest of the group should be going along with their plan as we speak," Nora replied, checking over her shoulder as if she could hear the others.

"They're here?" Noah exclaimed, jumping up from the bed. "We need to help them!"

"You're forgetting that you're a prisoner," Nora said, calmly pushing him back down by his shoulder. "No one can know you're free."

Noah groaned, rubbing his face with his hands. "I can't just sit here and do nothing." He pulled Arel's ring out of his pocket and played with it, running it between his fingers.

Suddenly, the opal began to glow, and broken images began flickering in front of them.

Nora moved to sit next to him at the same moment that Noah saw a familiar flash of wild red hair.

And again.

And again.

Each time, the image became clearer. It looked as if Layla

was coming closer.

Noah blinked and hit the wall as Layla jumped out of the light and into his arms.

Grinning at his shocked expression, Layla planted a soft kiss on his lips in greeting.

Noah felt his cheeks turn red, and he looked awkwardly at Nora.

"That's, uh, a new development," Nora said with a raised eyebrow.

Layla gave a squeal and jumped off Noah, running towards Nora and attempting to pull her into a tight hug. "Oh, I've missed you so much."

"I've missed you too." Nora returned Layla's hug with as much vigour as she could in her astral projected form. "But there's no time to waste. Now you're here, you can help Noah. Do you have your mandala?"

Layla, who was wearing Ray on an energy chain around her neck, gave her to Nora.

"You have your half of the other mandala, don't you, Noah?" Nora asked, holding her hand out.

"Other mandala?" Layla asked.

Noah pulled Tashi from his pocket and handed her to Nora. "Aaron split a mandala created in this timeline into two pieces. He gave one to me to help me learn how to master using energies on my own."

"She's beautiful," Layla replied, looking into her deep sapphires.

Tashi let out a blue spark of appreciation.

"I'm going to merge them," Nora said.

Noah and Layla stared at her.

"Merge them?" Noah asked.

"The only way to beat Garvan is to keep getting stronger ourselves," Nora said. "Ray and Tashi are powerful relics, but they will be even more powerful together."

Nora held the two mandalas on her palms and asked them, "Are you okay with that?"

Both Ray and Tashi shot out a spark of approval.

"Alright then."

Closing her eyes, Nora pressed her palms together, resting Ray and Tashi against each other. Ray's sunstone energy and Tashi's sapphire energy exploded, and the room filled with their light, orange and blue covering the walls as the mandalas merged.

Noah shielded his eyes with his hand and reached for Layla's fingers, which were brushing against his knee, gripping them tightly as they waited for the energy dancing around the room to slowly dim.

Before them, instead of two relics, Nora held onto one mandala. Ray's sunstones were still in place, but the fifth stone embedded around the outside was now a deep, sparkling sapphire. Tashi dissolved after Ray absorbed her power, and Noah shivered as small balls of pure Realm energy floated to the ceiling before disappearing.

Levitating off Nora's hand, the mandala floated towards Noah and Layla, and the two of them took hold of it.

An energy like nothing Noah had felt before surged through him. He could feel every hair on his body stand on end.

He heard Layla gasp as the sensation ran through her as well.

"We might actually have a shot now that Tashi and Ray are merged," she said. Noah gently reached over and squeezed Layla's fingers, a grin spreading across his face.

Chapter 25 - Aaron

"I was really hoping by this age I would be guarding cocktails by the beach," Aaron muttered as he stood on alert in Garvan's temple, waving the group of friends through the corridor one at a time so they wouldn't be discovered. "But no," he said, drawing the word out, "I am here playing chaperone for a bunch of fight-crazed Earth teens instead."

"Do not forget, I am here too," Simmy chipped in beside him. Her long auburn hair was pulled back into a high ponytail at the back of her head, which meant Aaron could see the sly grin on her face.

"You were always up for a crazy plan, though."

Simmy let out a low chuckle. "I have not had much time for that lately."

"Who has?"

After waving Ashlee, the last of the teens, down the hallway and into another small room, Aaron and Simmy quietly followed after them, keeping an eye on each other's blind spots.

When Nora had briefly shown herself to him back on Earth, he wasn't sure what he expected, but telling them all to get to the Realm and Garvan's temple as soon as they could wasn't it.

Naturally, the friends had all jumped at the chance for some action, and with a click of her fingers, Nora had created a portal for them all to step through.

Aaron had tried not to imagine what Garvan had been doing with her for her to be able to create a portal strong enough for six humans and two Realm beings to jump through, all while in her astral projected form, but he couldn't deny he was impressed.

Even if he wasn't sure these powers were for the best, as Garvan always had ulterior motives.

But, seeing as he, Aaron, was the reason she was still stuck with Garvan, he should be glad all her limbs were still attached, and she hadn't aimed those powers at him. Yet.

He had tried to talk to her, but before he could ask anything about where she was or how he could help her, she had gone. Disappeared before his eyes.

Clenching his jaw in frustration, Aaron stayed on task, trying to find Zion. With Noah gone, the plan to split up had been briefly put on hiatus, and the group had decided to work together as a team.

He wasn't under any illusion that it was a solid plan, but there was only so much he could do with everything they had working against them. He just had to have faith that they would all come out of this alive.

Especially Nora.

"Aaron, we have a problem."

Looking up, Aaron saw three of the teens jump through Noah's belt-portal and disappear. Simmy shot Aaron a lot before creating her own portal and jumping through, trying to find where the teens had gone.

"Shit."

Chapter 26 - Noah

"So, I need to stay here? Garvan can't know I've escaped, right?" Noah asked reluctantly.

"Technically, you should be here, yes, but we also need you out there so we can all escape together," Nora said. "Take Ray and create a projection of yourself. You're going to need to make it realistic, which means it needs to move around, breathe and sleep. That way, if someone comes and checks on you, it won't look suspicious."

"Oh sure, yeah, no worries at all," Noah replied sarcastically.

Nora and Layla both cracked a grin.

"You'll be fine," Nora said. "If you don't get it right the first time, you can just try again."

"Okay." Noah exhaled loudly and shook his arms and legs, hyping himself up. "Let's give this a shot." He closed his eyes, concentrated on the image of himself he wanted to create, and willed Ray to craft the projection in front of him.

At the sound of muffled laughter, Noah opened his eyes.

The projection he'd created was very... well, it didn't look like Noah, to say the least.

A blobfish would be a more accurate description.

"I'm... err... I'll try again, shall I?"

"That's probably a good idea," Nora said behind her hand

while Layla tried to stifle more laughter.

Exhaling again, Noah focused harder on not only what he wanted the projection to look like but also what he wanted it to do. How he wanted it to react when someone came to the room. How he wanted the projection to sound.

He felt Ray heat up as their energies weaved together, and he opened his eyes again.

It was almost like looking in a mirror.

Smiling at him was a near-perfect double of himself.

Noah smiled back. "Hello."

"Hello," his double repeated.

Noah tentatively held out his hand, reaching out a finger. His duplicate did the same, and as their fingers met in the middle, a small amber spark zapped between them.

Quickly pulling his hand away, Noah rubbed his stinging finger on his jeans and explained the situation. "I need you to stay here and pretend to sleep while I help our friends with a mission. If someone comes to check on you, make sure you answer, but don't say anything else."

"Okay," the double replied.

"Oh," Noah added, remembering something. "Sorry, but you're going to have to wear these." He picked up the discarded chains from the floor and locked them in place.

The double shook his arms, making the chains clang on his wrists. "Heavy."

"Sorry," Noah apologised again. "We'll be as quick as we can. If you get into trouble, just... *poof*... back inside me, okay?"

"Okay," his projection agreed and laid down on the bed. "*Poof.*"

"He's so cute," Layla said, and Noah's heart gave a twinge of guilt at leaving him alone. Although, if he re-absorbed into

Noah, then it would be a helpful sign they'd need to hurry. *So really, it's a good thing we're leaving him here*, Noah justified to himself.

"We need to go. Now," Nora said, waving Noah and Layla to the door. "We have to see what the others are up to. Here, I'm going to use Arel's ring," she said to Noah, holding her hand out for it.

Noah gave it to her. Nora slid it onto her index finger and whispered, "Show us our friends."

Simmy, Mia, Noah and Josh were in their own group and had reached the part of the palace where Zion must have been kept, but they were battling a Shadow Being who wouldn't allow them to progress any further.

Simmy was knocking back blow after blow of the Shadow Being's attacks, pulling the others behind her while Josh was holding up his watch and pressing his finger to the face of it. It took a couple of tries, as he had to keep making sure the rest of the group were touching him as he worked his relic.

On the third try, the watch glowed a bright yellow, and Nora, Layla and Noah watched as the Shadow Being's movements slowed to a snail's pace.

"We need to go help them," Layla said, tugging on Noah's sleeve.

"What about the others?" Noah asked. "They could be in more trouble than these guys."

"You two go and help this group out," Nora said, waving her hand over the projection to make it disappear. "I'll find the others and give them a hand."

Noah opened his mouth to object, but Nora held her hand up before he could say anything. "I'm more than capable of handling myself. Now go."

177

Noah clenched his jaw but didn't object. Grabbing Layla's wrist with one hand and gripping Ray tightly with the other, he turned to his sister. "We *will* see you soon."

Nora kissed his cheek before tightening her wavy ponytail. "I'll be waiting for you. Both of you." She squeezed Layla's hand.

Noah felt Layla place her other hand over his, and he turned to her. "Let's go."

"Oh, wait! Here!" Nora handed over Arel's ring, which Noah took and slipped on his index finger. He then watched as his sister opened a portal without any relic to help her.

"Let's go!" Layla urged, holding tightly onto Ray alongside Noah. Ray's gemstones glowed brightly, and the two of them stepped into the portal, taking them to Simmy and the others.

Noah heard Josh yelp in surprise as they appeared before him, but as soon as Noah and Layla's feet touched the ground, the effects of Josh's watch took hold and they began moving at the same slow speed as the Shadow Being.

"What do we do?" the other Noah yelled to Simmy, who was waiting for the Shadow Being's next attack to reach them.

"We are going to have to release the effects of Josh's relic and include them in the circle before Josh uses it again," she said, turning to look at him. "Do you have the strength to keep this up?"

Josh was pale, his forehead dripping with sweat, but he said breathily, "For as long as you need."

Simmy gave him a concerned look but nodded, squeezing his elbow in support.

"Okay," Simmy said. "On the count of three. One."

The group edged closer to Noah and Layla.

"Two."

Another step closer.

"Three!"

Josh released his watch, and Simmy repelled the Shadow Being's attack with her half of Tashi while the others sprinted towards Noah and Layla.

Josh grabbed hold of them, along with everyone else, and activated his relic once more, doubling over as the strain of supporting so many people began to take its toll.

"We do not have much time," Simmy said, looking at Josh, her brow creasing with worry. "Noah, Layla, Zion is in the room behind the Shadow Being. We have not been able to reach it, but I can imagine his powers are being completely suppressed. I need the two of you to create a portal and get over there with Ray to free him."

Noah and Layla nodded.

"Mia, I need you to go with them and help cut any bindings that Zion may be held in."

"Got it," she replied, sliding over closer to Noah and Layla.

"Noah," Simmy said, looking at the Noah from this timeline.

"Yes," he replied.

"I need you to create a portal and get Josh out of here. He needs rest."

"Where can I take him?"

"You can take him to where I'm being held captive," Noah replied and elaborated at the other Noah's questioning glance. "There's a projection of me in the room I was confined in when Garvan brought me here. As long as the two of you are quiet and keep out of sight, you should have no worries laying low there for a little while. It's a small chamber off the side of the Throne Room."

The other Noah nodded, unlooped his belt and visualised

the location while Noah described it.

A small amber portal appeared before them, and Noah took a peek inside to make sure it was the right place.

Seeing his projection lying down on the bed, Noah nodded and gave a thumbs-up.

Looking through his portal, the other Noah grabbed hold of Josh, supporting him under his arms.

"Are you ready?" Simmy asked. "I am going to keep this one occupied while you all go to work." She pointed in the direction of the Shadow Being.

"Ready," the group replied in unison.

"Okay. One. Two. Three. NOW!"

Josh released his relic and slumped into the other Noah for support as he stepped them into the dark bedroom, the relic closing them inside once they were through.

Layla and Mia gripped tightly to Ray while Noah used her to create a portal to the room where Zion was being held, and the three of them jumped inside.

Before everything went dark, Noah caught a glimpse of Simmy repelling more attacks from the Shadow Being, then firing her own onslaught of red energy balls.

Noah watched until the portal closed behind them, and he let out a breath as his feet touched the ground in the dark room.

"Who's there?" a faraway voice called out.

"Noah Parker," Noah replied, holding an arm out to stop Layla and Mia from moving any further.

"From this timeline?"

Noah hesitated to answer, and he gripped one of the girls' hands tightly, willing Ray to provide them with some light as he held her in his other hand.

Obliging, Ray's gemstones glowed just bright enough for Noah to see his immediate surroundings.

The hand he was gripping was Mia's, and he let it go, hastily mouthing an apology to her, which she waved off.

Layla was standing on the other side of Ray, trying to see further into the darkness.

"I think we need to go this way," she said, walking to the right.

Noah and Mia followed her, and Noah held Ray out to see where they were going.

The room seemed endless.

"We're not getting anywhere," Mia said.

"I'm sure I can sense a presence this way," Layla insisted.

"The room's been enchanted," Noah said in realisation, and he stopped abruptly. "Garvan couldn't let just anyone come in here and find Zion."

"Well, what do we do then?" Mia asked.

Noah crossed his arms and tapped a finger on his elbow. "You have my back?" he murmured to Ray, and she let out an orange spark of acknowledgement.

Noah cleared his throat loudly. "Can you repeat the question, please?" he called into the darkness.

"Are you the Noah Parker of this timeline?" the voice repeated.

"Yes," Noah replied, purposely ignoring Layla and Mia's shocked reactions at his response.

The room roared as it became engulfed by the same winds that had been at Simmy's house back on Earth.

Noah quickly pulled Layla and Mia together and forced Ray into Layla's hands.

"What—" she began to ask, but Noah raised a finger to his

lips.

"Trust me," he said.

Nodding hesitantly, Layla whispered, "Shield," and a barrier appeared, protecting her and Mia from the gale.

Noah gave her a thumbs-up, then turned his back and walked into the thick winds. "What do you want from me?"

A ball of white light appeared in front of Noah and floated toward his face.

Noah held out his hand and clasped his fingers around it as it landed on his palm.

The second his fist closed, he was roughly teleported to a new room.

He landed heavily on his back, the wind knocked out of him. Noah grunted as he tried to gather his bearings, but his eyes were watering too much, and his body ached from the quick transportation.

"Stay still," the voice said to him softly.

Noah did as he was told and laid his head on the cool floor.

A few minutes passed as Noah caught his breath. As his vision began to clear, he started as he started at a pure white room, exactly the same style as Zion's palace back in his own Realm.

"You lied," the voice said. "You are not the Noah of this timeline."

"No, I'm not," Noah replied. "Where are you?"

The room appeared to be empty.

With a small *pop*, the Zion he had come to rescue appeared before him, unchained and unharmed.

Chapter 27 - Layla

T he room was still pitch black, apart from the small glow coming from Ray's gemstones.

Mia shuffled beside her, and Layla reached out to grip her hand. "Are you alright?"

"This is completely surreal," Mia replied, squeezing Layla's fingers with one hand and toying nervously with her short, platinum-blonde hair with the other. "I'm guessing you're from that other timeline too? I've never seen you around before."

"I was told the Layla Forrest of this timeline died when she was an infant, in a car crash with her parents."

Mia stilled. "I'm so sorry to hear that."

Layla shrugged. "My parents died the same way in my own timeline. I just managed to survive somehow. Simmy raised me instead."

"How is it that there can be so many similarities between our two timelines, yet so many differences?"

"I haven't had a chance to think it all through properly, but Garvan probably needed to create as many different scenarios as he could in order for there to be a reasonable rate of success for the duplicates of himself he created to absorb one of the twins. What I've been wondering is when these timelines were actually created. Everyone here has lived full, whole lives. How could that have happened if these timelines haven't been around as long as our original one?" Layla murmured, keeping Ray in front of her so she could see if anything changed in their surroundings.

"Maybe…" Mia paused.

"Maybe?" Layla pressed.

"Maybe the timelines have always existed, and the only thing Garvan's done is recreate the Realm and the people there. I don't think Nora or Noah here have any special powers. Maybe the timelines existed, but the separate Realm's didn't."

Layla paused, then turned to Mia. "You might be onto something, actually. I have been told before that there should only be one Realm. I bet that *is* what Garvan did."

"I don't understand how that would be possible, though." Mia clenched Layla's fingers and swerved as a light clang sounded behind them. Layla shone Ray's light in the direction it came from, but nothing was there.

"I don't know. I know he's crazy powerful, but that type of creation seems like something that only a Celestial could do," Layla replied, turning back around.

"What's a Celestial?"

"Aaron's one, and so is his brother Zion, who Noah's gone to rescue. They were the first beings created for Realm, and Zion then created Simmy and her siblings to help guide the people of Earth. When the human population began to grow too big and become more complex, Zion created Garvan to help the siblings out."

"Is there any chance that this Garvan guy is a Celestial?"

Layla paused. It had never crossed her mind before. Could

Garvan be a Celestial? Zion would surely have the power to create one, or at least, he and Aaron together would have the power. "There could be a chance…" Layla trailed off, her mind whirring.

Mia pulled Layla closer to her as another muffled sound rang in the distance. "Well, if we get out of here, I'll help you figure it out."

Layla swallowed deeply and nodded. "If Garvan is a Celestial, then we're in more trouble than we realised."

Chapter 28 - Noah

"Uhh... you look like you're okay," Noah pointed out, slowly looking over the Zion who stood as a free man before him.

Zion gave a tired laugh, his tied-back blond hair blowing in a wind Noah couldn't feel. His white robe rustled as he took a step forwards, the golden chains on his toga glinting in the light. "Garvan may be strong, but not strong enough to fully contain me, even if I am a mere duplicate."

"You know you're a duplicate?"

"Yes, I am aware of Garvan's plan to use these timelines to make himself more powerful by absorbing your or Nora's life energy. A coward's way of gaining strength, if I do say so myself."

"A coward's way?" Noah asked meekly. "I mean, I suppose. I don't know about you, but I'm not overly keen on having my life energy sucked out of me."

Zion created a small golden energy ball and began to play with it absently, watching as it rolled over his fingers. "I do not blame you, but there are other ways to get stronger. Garvan just refuses to put in the work. He wants immediate results, an easy way out, which will not be sustainable."

"Do you know why Garvan is after Nora and me?" Noah

asked. "Surely we can't be the only people in the entire world for Garvan to choose from."

"Actually," Zion replied, "you are."

Noah paused.

"What?"

"We have rules in the Realm," Zion explained. "We cannot use our powers to alter the course of mortal lives. You all have your journeys and your lessons to learn, and everything that happens, whether good or bad, happens for a reason."

Noah nodded that he understood.

"Your grandparents—your mother's parents—tried desperately for years to have a child, to no avail. Year after year, your grandma was unable to fall pregnant, until it became too much, and they resigned themselves to being childless."

"I didn't know that," Noah said quietly.

"One day, your grandfather stumbled across a tale that told of magical beings who lived amongst humans, granting them wishes. Now, this wasn't true as such, but my children would often come down to Earth to recharge after their Guiding months. How the humans became aware that my children were capable of magical feats, I can only speculate, but nonetheless, someone would always seek them out while they were down there."

"Grandpa met one of the Guardians?" Noah asked.

"Yes. He met your Simmy. Your grandparents trekked for months, following the tales, until they came to the middle of the country where an old, spiritual rock resided. You may know it," Zion said pointedly to Noah, who nodded. "Simmy loved Uluru and the connection she felt with the Earth near it. She was there when your grandparents arrived. They found her and begged her to gift them a baby and told her their story of how they had been trying for years to fall pregnant."

"Is Simmy the reason Mum's alive?" Noah whispered.

"Simmy was hesitant at first. As I mentioned, we are unable to alter the paths of humans and their journeys throughout their lives, but the Realm allowed her to grant your grandparents their wish."

"Why?"

Zion lowered himself to the ground, folding his legs lotus-style, and gestured for Noah to do the same. "The Realm must have been able to feel that there would come a time when it would need the humans it helped create. You have a natural connection with the Realm. Did you know that, Noah?"

"When I was first introduced to it, Simmy said that Nora and I had a natural ability to wield the powers of the Realm. I didn't know what she meant by it, though…" Noah trailed off.

"Your mum was born thanks to the Realm, and those powers trickled down to Nora and yourself."

"So, Mum could be a Guardian too? Is that why Simmy looked for her when Garvan had petrified all the other Guardians?"

"Yes, your mother could become a Guardian as well. But, since she chose not to expose herself to the Realm, the role fell to you and Nora."

"She chose not to? Mum told me when Simmy found her, she'd asked where her twins were straight away."

Zion paused. "Your mum had a hard choice to make. She was so young when Simmy found her. She chose not to become a Guardian."

Noah stiffened.

Zion gently gripped Noah's chin with his large thumb and

forefinger and turned his head, so Noah was looking him in the eye. "Not a day goes past where she does not regret putting you in this position."

"But Nora and I grew up the same as all our friends. There was nothing special about us until we started working with Simmy, and even then, we couldn't do much unless we were in the Realm. Well, I couldn't anyway."

"Children have an innate ability to connect with the Realm, but it is something that, sadly, becomes stamped out of them as they begin to fit in with society," Zion said, a look of disdain on his face. "If people were allowed to live their lives how they pleased, the Realm would not be fighting a losing battle trying to stay connected to them. The Realm is as connected to the people of Earth as they are with it. The fact that it has become so unstable means part of its connection to Earth has become fractured."

Frazzled, Noah pulled his chin out of Zion's grip. "But Nora isn't a Guardian. Layla is."

"Circumstances allowed Layla to be exposed to the Realm from a young age, thanks to her being raised by Simone. Being exposed to a Primary Guardian for so long allowed her to subconsciously wield the Realm's energies with ease," Zion said.

"Whoa," Noah breathed. "That's a lot to take in."

"It is," Zion agreed, "but, as you are not the Noah of this timeline, I need you to take it in quickly, so we can find him and Nora and keep Garvan away from them."

"Oh," Noah said, avoiding Zion's piercing blue eyes, which were staring holes through him. "Right, yeah, well, I know where they are. We need to pick up the friends I left when I came to you, and then I can take you to them."

Zion stood, pulled a golden hourglass out from his white robe and held it in the palm of his hand. "Grab hold."

Noah pushed himself to his feet as well and gripped the handle of the hourglass. A gentle floating sensation washed over him, and with a *pop*, they were transported back to the pitch-black room.

"Is that you, Noah?" he heard Layla call out.

"It's me. I've got Zion with me, too," Noah replied, letting go of the hourglass.

"Hold on," Zion's voice rumbled through the dark room. He clapped his hands once, and the room lit up brilliantly.

Noah looked over at Mia and Layla, who were shielding their eyes against the sudden white light, and ran over to them. "Sorry guys, no time to adjust. We need to get to the others." He grabbed each of them by the wrist and pulled them over to Zion, who held out the hourglass once again.

"Where to now?" Zion asked.

"The Noah from this timeline is hiding in a small chamber near the Throne Room with another friend of ours. The Nora from my timeline, the Nora from this timeline, Simmy– who I can only imagine has turned the Shadow Being guarding you to dust by now– Aaron from my timeline and the rest of our friends are going after Garvan," Noah explained, trying not to get tongue-tied.

Zion rubbed his chin in thought. "Noah from here and his friend will be fine for now. We need to meet up with the rest of your group. Hold on tight."

Noah guided Layla and Mia's fingers to the hourglass and then grabbed hold of it himself. The same gentle sensation engulfed him, and with the same soft *pop*, they reached a room Noah hadn't seen before.

"This is where Garvan is?" Noah asked.

"This is my old chamber," Zion growled. "It is only fitting he took it for himself when he had the chance."

"Are the others here?" Mia asked. The tone of her voice told Noah she was eager to make sure Max and her friends were okay.

Zion nodded, pressed his finger to his lips and beckoned to the trio to follow him.

Noah, Layla and Mia followed closely behind him, trying to see past his enormous body.

CRASH!

The loud noise caused Noah to jump, and he felt Layla grip his arm tightly.

"What was that?" Mia exclaimed, pushing past Noah and Layla to see what was happening.

"Quickly!" Zion called to them, taking off in large strides towards the chamber ahead.

They sprinted after him, although, even at their fastest, they were trailing far behind.

Panting, they reached the chamber. Chaos greeted them.

Garvan had begun his rebirth, and twenty Shadow Beings were battling the rest of the crew.

Chapter 29 - Noah

Simmy and Aaron were back to back, firing blasts of energy from their mandalas, trying to keep ten of the Shadow Beings from advancing.

The Noah from this timeline jumped through a portal to their right and started creating portals for Ashlee and the Nora from this timeline to pass through, where they could then take Nora's necklace and bind a Shadow Being with it.

"We got caught," he panted as he caught Noah's eye. As he said it, Noah felt a tugging sensation in the pit of his stomach and knew his double had *poofed* back inside of him.

Josh, who had come through the portal with Noah, grabbed hold of Max and slowed the room down around them just enough for Max to fire a few extra rounds from his sunglasses at the advancing Shadow Beings. Mia ran over to them once Josh had restarted time, her ring blade at the ready, slashing at the Shadow Beings, who hadn't been deterred by the blasts.

Nora's astral projected form flickered feebly as she ran, panting, to Noah, Layla and Zion. "Garvan's gone into the chamber," she puffed. "This started off as one Shadow Being, but every time we attack it, it keeps duplicating. Aaron managed to blast one to dust completely, but if we don't get it all in one go, it just regenerates and multiplies."

Suddenly, a Shadow Being crept up behind Nora, its long thin fingers reaching for her shoulder.

"Nora, watch out!" Noah yelled, trying to pull her behind him, an amber energy ball forming in the palm of his hand.

Nora turned and saw Tick reaching for her. "Stop!" she called to Noah, holding her hand out. "It's okay. She's on our side now."

"What?!" Noah exclaimed.

"Can we trust her?" Layla asked, Ray sparking with emerald electricity in her hand.

"Nora from this timeline brought Tick with her when she and the others came here. She was completely broken after Garvan left her for dead, and she's been a big help, telling us where to find Garvan and taking us to the chamber."

Noah narrowed his eyes. He wasn't fully convinced, but there wasn't any time to argue. "What do we need to do to beat this Shadow Being?" he asked Tick.

"You need to create a big enough blast to destroy all of its duplicates and the original in one go," Tick replied, looking to Nora, who nodded her support.

Noah turned to Zion and Layla. "We're going to have to do this together," he said before looking at Nora. "Aaron and Simmy need to keep the Shadow Being occupied while we charge up a big enough blast, Nora, can you...Nora?"

A giant hole had appeared through Nora's chest, and she gasped in pain. "It looks like my time here's up," she wheezed. "I'll be fine," she added, trying to reassure Noah and Layla on seeing their horrified expressions. "I've just spent too long in this projected form. You can do this without me. Just focu—!"

She disappeared in a flurry of amber energy.

Noah squeezed his eyes shut and clenched his fist. Nora

was gone. Again.

"She'll be fine," Layla said to him, trying to keep him on track even though her jaw was ticking. "We don't have time to worry about her right now. We need to stop this Shadow Being." She turned to Zion. "Can you help us?"

"I am already charging a blast," Zion replied, holding up a golden globe of energy the size of his massive hand. "I am going to need you two to contribute, so we can manipulate it to affect only the Shadow Being and not hurt your friends."

"Can we do that?" Noah asked, furiously swiping away a tear that had spilled down his cheek.

"You are going to need to create an energetic shield to protect the humans and Guardians," Zion said to him. "Layla, you are going to have to create a barrier to stop the Shadow Being from escaping into the cracks of the walls. We need to make sure we get all of it."

Noah and Layla nodded, holding onto Ray and weaving their own individual energies through her in sync with one other.

Sweat dripped down Noah's brow as he concentrated on visualising the Shadow Being disintegrating while his friends remained unharmed.

Every time he felt he was getting close, his gut told him it wasn't quite right, and he had to tweak his barrier. More than once he questioned whether he should just settle for good enough, but each time the image of his friends being blasted into nothingness would slam into his mind, so he'd let out a deep breath and continue working.

The shimmering gold orb in Zion's hand grew bigger and bigger, soon pushing Noah and Layla back to the edge of the room as they watched Simmy, Aaron and the others battle the ever-growing number of Shadow Beings.

"Are you two ready yet?" Zion called to them. His voice sounded strained, and Noah quickly glanced in his direction and saw sweat beading on his forehead.

"Almost!" Noah replied.

"Yes!" Layla called.

"Layla, help Noah," Zion instructed.

Layla grabbed hold of Noah's hand and matched her energy frequency with his, finding the friends he hadn't yet been able to protect.

"Are you done?" Zion asked again, his voice breaking as he held onto the enormous ball of energy.

"Ready!" The two of them called out together, weaving the energies they crafted through Zion's.

"Grab hold of something, kids," Zion said, pulling himself up to his full height while his eyes darted around the room, taking in the battle in front of them.

Noah saw Aaron and Simmy stop firing at the Shadow Being when they heard Zion's warning, which also tipped off the Shadow Being, who screeched and ran, diving for the nearest crack to escape through.

"Layla!" Zion called.

Noah and Layla channelled their life energy through Ray to block every exit in the room. Their amber and emerald power forced all of the Shadow Being's fragments to come flying back into the one Being, flickering angrily.

Zion's body shook, and Noah pulled Layla under his arm, shielding her from the brunt of Zion's blast as the Celestial closed his fist.

His power exploded around the room, engulfing it in a brilliant golden light, the force of it pushing Noah and Layla hard against the wall.

Noah felt, more than heard, Layla call out to the others, but he couldn't see if they were alright. Not when Zion's energy blast was nearly blinding him, even with his eyes closed and hidden behind his elbow.

The Shadow Being screeched as Zion's power intensified, having pinpointed its target.

Noah took a shaky breath, praying to the Realm that he had been able to protect everyone.

Skin tingling, Noah pulled Layla tighter to his side, more to anchor himself than anything. His arm hairs stood on end, and a shiver ran through his spine. Instead of deflecting Zion's energy, it felt like his body was trying to absorb it.

He'd never dreamed so much energy could come from one being.

Finally, Zion's power began to subside, and Noah gently released Layla from his embrace, rubbing his eyes as spots danced in front of them.

Out of his hazy vision, Noah saw Zion hold his palms out in front of himself. His golden life energy began to retract inside of him, pulling what little Noah had absorbed back out as well, leaving Noah feeling like a cold breeze had swept over him.

It was only when he felt Layla completely leave his side that Noah realised he was swaying slightly. Shaking his head, Noah snapped himself out of his reverie and jogged over to meet Layla and the others, pulling Aaron and Simmy into a tight hug, making sure they were okay.

"We are fine," Aaron said, his voice muffled against Noah's shirt. When Noah pulled away, Aaron was smiling.

"Where's Nora?" Simmy asked, looking at Layla, but Layla

just shot her a sad look and shook her head.

"She was pulled back to our timeline," Noah said. "But, if you can, I need you to get a message to her for me when we get back to your place. I need you to tell her the reason Garvan is coming after the two of us. I'll give you the memory now, and you can pass it on to her in case anything else happens while we're here."

Simmy nodded and held out her hand as Noah placed his index finger to his forehead, pulling out a shimmering amber ribbon. "This is the memory of Zion telling me everything. Make sure this gets to her."

"You have my word," Simmy said, placing the memory within one of Tashi's sapphires.

Zion, who had finished retracting his energy, walked over to the group. "We need to hurry and find Garvan. If we leave it too late, he will finish the rebirth process before we can act, and you are all too tired to face him fully regenerated."

Noah grabbed Layla's hand and they ran towards the room the Shadow Being had been guarding. "He must be in here."

The rest of the group began to follow him, but Noah stopped as he felt Zion's hand on his shoulder. "Both Noah and Nora from this timeline need to go back to Earth," he said. "If Garvan becomes desperate, he will absorb them right here and now, and his power will become unimaginable."

Noah's skin pricked uncomfortably where Zion touched him, but he forced himself to ignore it. "You're right," he said, over the furious cries of *'We can take him!'* and *'Let us fight!'*

He turned to the twins of this timeline and gave an apologetic grimace. "We can't risk losing you two. This timeline is going to need you more than ever once we capture Garvan."

The twins argued, but when even their friends wouldn't

back them up, they reluctantly agreed to head back to Earth.

"Thank you," Noah said to them. "Simmy, can you take them back to your house?"

"I can," Simmy replied, "but do you not need me here?"

"You can come back once you know they're safe. It's more important to get them out of here right now," Noah said before addressing the rest of the group. "Anyone else who would like to go back with Noah and Nora can leave as well. We're not going to keep you here against your will. If you want to leave, just raise your hand."

The group looked at each other and then back at Noah, who felt a sudden pang of longing for his own friends. Not a single one of them had raised their hand.

"We don't know what we're going to face here"—he wrung his hands together—"so we need to have each other's backs. Nora, before you go, can you please give Layla your relic? We'll need it to bind Garvan."

"Take care of it," Nora said, unclasping her necklace and giving it to Layla.

"I won't let it out of my sight," Layla promised.

"Alright, you two," Simmy said, taking Noah and Nora's hands. "Let us go."

"Be safe, everyone," Nora said.

"We'll see you soon," said the Noah from this timeline, looking pointedly at the group as if they would argue that they wouldn't.

When none of them did, the other Noah nodded and stepped towards Simmy, who used Tashi to open a portal back to Earth. With a *pop*, they were gone.

"Alright," Zion said, walking in front of the others, "stay behind me. Aaron, I will need you by my side."

Aaron clapped him on the shoulder. "As always."

With Zion and Aaron leading, the rest of the group followed behind and waited as Zion removed the barriers protecting the room. Once the door was open, they tentatively walked inside.

"Hello, brother." A figure stepped into the light.

A low growl escaped Zion's lips. "I was wondering where you went."

Noah peered out from behind Zion, his mouth dropping open. Standing before them was the Aaron of this timeline.

Chapter 30 - Nora

S itting with her feet dangling over the waterfall, Nora rested her head against the golden railing trimming the balcony.

Garvan hadn't returned yet, but her body was spent. He'd know she hadn't been training, but Nora was beyond caring at this point.

A moment ago, she'd received a sapphire through a small portal from the alternate timeline she'd just left, and Nora was fuming.

Why had no one told her about herself and Noah? How had her mum kept this from them? She'd *chosen* not to help the Realm!

There had been plenty of opportunities for Simmy to tell her why she, Nora, was the one Simmy had chosen to train to become the next Guardian, but she hadn't.

Did Layla know too?

No, she couldn't have. Layla couldn't lie to save herself. If she'd known, it would have been the first thing she'd told Nora.

She must have been drawn to Nora when they'd met because of her sensitivity to the Realm's energies which were embedded in the core of Nora's being... apparently.

Knocking her head lightly against the gold railing, Nora's gut churned. If Layla had felt that connection with Nora, maybe she'd felt it with Noah too. Maybe whatever's going on between them is based on Layla's sensitivity to the Realm energy running through Noah.

Nora shook her head. Now wasn't the time to fall down a rabbit hole about her brother's love life.

They'd been lied to. Or, at the very least, they had been purposefully left in the dark about their roles in this mission.

Zion, Simmy, and even Aaron had left out vital information. Information that she and Noah deserved to know.

Nora stiffened as she heard soft footsteps padding towards her. She quickly tucked the sapphire into her bra and drew her water shield around her.

"Where were you?"

Garvan's whisper in her ear caused Nora to jump. She whirled, finding him crouched down next to her, his head tilted to one side, no sign of the usual arrogant smirk on his face.

"What do you mean?" Nora's chest tightened in panic. There was no way he could know she'd astral projected to the other timeline. She'd used every protection she could think of to make sure he'd never find out.

"Just now. I have been standing here for five minutes, and you did not notice."

Resisting the urge to grab for the sapphire she'd hidden, Nora forced herself to shoot Garvan a hooded look. "I was thinking about changing things up tonight if you're interested."

Garvan's blue eyes flashed. He grabbed the hand Nora had begun extending towards his chest and pulled her roughly

201

towards him. "Do not lie to me."

Ripping her hand out of his grip, Nora pushed herself to her feet, ignoring the protests her body screamed from the movement. "Don't lie? *Don't lie?!* That's rich coming from you. All you people *do* is lie! Why am I here, Garvan? Why have you kept me alive? Why are you training me? And don't feed me some bullshit story about wanting to show me the deeper meaning behind your sadistic schemes."

Nora's pointer finger throbbed, and she realised she'd been jabbing Garvan in the chest as she spoke. His black dress shirt had an indentation where it had been poking him.

There was a pause as Garvan's cold eyes searched Nora's.

"I need your power," Garvan said finally. He took a step towards Nora, and when she didn't back away, he took another one. "You are special, as I am sure you are aware. I need to become as powerful as possible in order to change the Realm."

"And making me super strong and then killing me is the way to do it?" Nora spat.

"Kill you? I do not think I could kill you, even if I wanted to. I need your power, not your life."

"What does that even mean?" Nora threw her arms in the air, exasperated. "I'm tired, Garvan. I'm tired of being spoken to in riddles, I'm tired of being given half a story, and I'm tired of being used as a pawn in other people's games. What do you want from me?"

Garvan closed the rest of the distance between them, this time taking a longer stride so he was pressed flush against her, and lifted Nora's chin with his thumb and forefinger, tilting her head back so she couldn't look away.

Slowly, giving her time to push him backwards, Garvan

lowered his face towards hers, his grip tightening on her chin the closer he got as if he was restraining himself.

Nora stood frozen. Part of her wanted to throw Garvan off the side of the balcony, while the other part wanted to rise onto her tiptoes to meet him.

Garvan's lips were a hair's breadth away from hers when he paused, giving Nora one last chance to pull away. She didn't, so he lightly brushed them against hers in a featherlight touch.

Nora's knees went weak.

When she didn't object, Garvan pressed his lips fully to hers, opening them and licking her bottom lip, making Nora lightheaded.

Her brain felt sluggish, slow, so it took a moment for Nora to realise what was happening. When she did, she gasped, ripping her face out of Garvan's grip and shoving him away from her as hard as she could.

But she had become so weak that her push didn't even rock Garvan, and instead, he caught and steadied her as she stumbled backwards.

Nora's eyes widened as she saw her amber life energy running down the veins in Garvan's throat before disappearing underneath his collar.

"I want your power," Garvan said quietly, deeply, his blue eyes looking brighter than they had earlier. Nora didn't know whether it was from the kiss or from her life energy he had just absorbed. "But I do not want you dead."

Nora opened her mouth to reply, but Garvan turned on his heel and walked out of the room, leaving her holding onto the railing for balance, staring after him.

Chapter 31 - Noah

Z ion's chamber was dark as the group stared at Aaron's duplicate blocking their way into the room. "It is nice to see you too," he sneered at Zion. "Got out of your chains, I see. I suppose these infants helped you?" he said, gesturing towards Noah and the others. "And you have brought the original me with you as well. How thoughtful. Now I can get rid of him."

Aaron's double lifted his arm above his head and slashed it down diagonally in front of him, shimmering black energy erupting from his fingertips.

Before Noah could blink, the original Aaron created a barrier around them and whistled a small blue ball of energy into existence, holding it on top of his finger. As he stared the other Aaron down, he pushed his way to the front of the group, forcing everyone, including Zion, behind him.

"That energy looks like Garvan's," Layla whispered, looking wide-eyed at the other Aaron. He was now swinging a black energy blade around in front of him, not taking his eyes off the group.

"It is," Zion growled, taking over Aaron's shield as his brother prepared to attack his double. "Garvan infected him with a portion of his personal energy in an attempt to control him."

"It looks like it worked," Noah muttered, watching as the two Aaron's began to battle in front of them, their powers evenly matched. "It must have been some power. It wouldn't have been easy to get Aaron under his control."

"I was already confined by the time Garvan got his hands on my brother," Zion replied, "but from what I could feel, the sheer amount of chaotic energy forced into Aaron nearly killed him."

"What do we do?" Layla asked. "We can't just sit here and wait for these two to finish each other off."

"We need to keep moving forward with our mission. If we capture Garvan, then any control he has over the people in this dimension will become obsolete." Zion watched the two Aarons as they fought, his fingers twitching as if he wanted to separate them, but he forced himself to look at the group instead.

"We'll need to move quickly before one of these two slips up and gets themselves killed. We'll follow your lead," Noah said while the rest of the group nodded in agreement.

"Grab hold of each other," Zion instructed. "Make sure not to get separated."

Layla gripped one of the golden chains hanging off Zion's robe with one hand and grasped Mia with the other, who grabbed onto Max. Noah did the same on Zion's other side, holding onto Ashlee and Josh.

Ashlee's deep brown eyes caught his for a brief moment, and Noah felt his cheeks warm as the vision of her and the other Noah kissing in the botanical gardens jumped to the forefront of his mind.

"Concentrate!" Zion growled. "The energy in here is

designed to distract you."

Shaking away the thought, Noah turned and walked with Zion, pulling the others along with him.

"Stay close," Zion instructed as a black energy ball bounced off the barrier protecting them.

The group huddled closer together. Noah cast a glance at Layla and saw her clench her jaw as determination crossed her features. Gritting his teeth, Noah gripped Ashlee's hand tighter and pulled her and Josh forwards, refusing to allow himself to get distracted as energy blasts bounced off the shield with more fervour than before.

"Where do you think *you* are going?" the other Aaron called out. Noah felt the air shift around him before the barrier shook.

Noah began to turn around, but the other Aaron yelped suddenly, and the barrier became sturdy once more. Noah glanced back to see a trickle of blood dripping down the other Aaron's temple as a tiny sapphire ball quickly flew away. "I am your target," Aaron said, absorbing the ball back into the palm of his hand and creating his own energy blade.

Touching the gash on his face, the other Aaron growled furiously. "You are going to pay for that."

Aaron swung his blade and flicked blast after blast of black energy away from himself. They hit the walls of the room surrounding them, creating small craters where they landed. "Go!" he called to Zion as an energy blast missed his nose by millimetres.

Not needing to be told twice, Zion raised his palms to the sky. The forcefield around them turned into an iridescent bubble, which lifted them towards the room where Garvan was undergoing his rebirth.

The group instinctively ducked as a beam of black energy came barrelling towards them, but Zion turned and back-handed it away, tossing it back towards its owner.

Slamming the door open, Zion threw the group inside and sealed the entryway behind him with his golden energy. "We need to find Garvan quickly," he instructed the group. "Pair up and search the room."

"I... don't think we need to split up, mate," Max said, pointing to the middle of the room.

Noah squinted. The lights were dim. Zion summoned a ball of light, which floated to the ceiling and lit up the room in a warm glow.

There, in the centre lying in the glass rebirthing chamber, was Garvan.

Noah gasped as he watched Garvan's body shifting and changing before his eyes, the long grey hair shortening until it became neatly cut and black, the wrinkled old hands becoming smooth and young, and the skinny, veiny arms becoming tough and muscular.

"Quickly!" Zion called, smashing the glass and pulling Garvan out by his hair.

Garvan's eyes, one wrinkled and grey, one clear and blue, snapped open. "What are you—?" he croaked but was cut off abruptly by Layla, who had unclasped Nora's necklace. She tied Garvan's hands and feet together, so he was in an awkward backbend, while Zion held him in place.

"Max," Zion called, "destroy the chamber with your sunglasses."

"On it, boss." Max saluted, nodding his head, so his sunglasses dropped onto his nose, then blasted the chamber.

Zion threw the constricted Garvan over his shoulder and

looked down at the group. "We need to get him back to my palace as soon as possible before his body begins to revert, and he can use his powers again."

"Why can't he use his powers now?" Mia asked, running to keep up with Zion's large steps. He'd turned and begun running back out the door they'd come through, his energetic barrier shattering with a flick of his hand.

"Garvan's life energy is split between his new body and his old body," Zion explained. "They are too unstable for him to use right now, as he would risk serious damage to himself. Since he has not fully undergone the rebirthing process, his body can revert to his older self, stabilising his powers again. Which is why we need to hurry and get him back to my palace, where I can lock him up."

"I'll help you," a hesitant voice called to them as they passed the fighting Aarons and entered the hallway.

"Tick!" Ashlee exclaimed. She pulled her hand out of Noah's grip, ran over to the Shadow Being and gave her a hug. "Where did you go?"

"I've been here, keeping out of sight until you needed me. Noah, you can use Arel's ring to create a portal that all of you can travel through," Tick said, pointing at the ring on Noah's finger.

Twisting the ring around with his thumb, Noah looked at her, debating whether he could trust her.

"The other Aaron is slowing down now that Garvan has been confined," Tick continued, "but if you don't hurry, Garvan's energy will take over him again."

"We will have to bring him with us," Zion said, turning around to find Aaron now carrying the other Aaron, looking worse-for-wear, under his shoulders towards the group.

Noah ran over to them and supported the other Aaron by pulling his dangling arm over his shoulders, taking some of the strain off his exhausted friend.

"He stumbled, so I got him right in the chest," Aaron explained as Noah raised an eyebrow at the abrupt ending to their fight.

"We need to go," Zion said, nodding at Noah. He twisted Arel's ring around his index finger with his thumb once more before creating a portal for the group to travel through.

The familiar *pop* rang in his ears, and, with a thud, the group landed on the soft green lawn of Zion's yard.

Chapter 32 - Noah

Without waiting for the others, Zion rushed inside, Garvan still over his shoulder.

Aaron pulled Noah inside after him, coating each of his fingers in healing blue energy as they carried the other Aaron between them.

"Are we going to follow them?" Noah heard Ashlee ask as he stumbled through the doorway.

"Yes, we are," Layla replied, the sound of quickly shuffling feet following her response.

Noah gently placed the other Aaron on a white kitchen chair in the corner of the room and took a step back. Aaron knelt before his slumped duplicate, gently pressing blue-coated fingers on the injuries dotting his chest and stomach, syphoning out the infecting energy Garvan had placed within him.

"Where's Garvan?" Ashlee whispered, softly walking over to stand next to Noah.

"I think Zion took him to the rebirthing chamber," Noah replied absently, watching Aaron work.

Everyone fell silent as Aaron pulled strand after strand of dark energy out of his duplicate's body and cleansed it with his own before watching the other Aaron to reabsorb it.

"Is he going to be okay?" Mia asked, walking over to them.

"He should be," Aaron replied. "Thankfully, not all of his life energy was tainted, just the energy surrounding his heart."

A soft *pop* caused everyone to look to the corner of the room, and Ashlee and Josh gave a small yelp of delight before dashing over to the Noah and Nora of this timeline, and running their hands over them to make sure they were all alright. Simmy and Tick, who were standing behind them, moved away to give the couples some space.

"I went and got them after you guys left," Tick explained under Noah's glare. "I thought they'd want to be here."

"She was right," Simmy said, stepping between them and giving Noah a stern look before heading in the direction of the Earth room.

Nodding stiffly, Noah turned to Layla, who placed a gentle hand on his arm. "She did help us when we were fighting the Shadow Being."

Placing his hand over Layla's, Noah looked at the group surrounding them. Ashlee was cuddled into the other Noah's chest, Josh had lifted Nora up and was spinning her around as she laughed, cradling his head, and Max and Mia were holding hands while they watched Aaron working in the corner.

"I hope these guys can all live peacefully after this," he said to Layla, pulling her into him and kissing the top of her head.

"Me too," Layla replied, her voice muffled by his shirt. She shifted, so she was facing him. "It'll all depend on whether we can get to the other timelines in time."

"We'll have to head back to our own timeline as soon as Garvan here has been fully contained," Noah said. "Also, I need to speak to our Zion."

Layla gave him a questioning look. "Is everything alright?"

211

"Zion here told me why Garvan has been after Nora and me," Noah replied, clenching his jaw. "I want to know why he didn't tell me himself."

"When would he have had the chance to?"

"He could have told me at any time!" Noah exploded. "I have a right to know why my life got turned on its head all of a sudden!"

"Of course you do," Layla replied, more sharply than Noah was expecting, which made him look down at her, "but Zion wouldn't have kept it from you for no reason, so don't go jumping to conclusions."

Noah clenched and unclenched his jaw and took a deep breath in through his nose. "You're probably right," he said on the exhale. "I'd still like to talk to him, though."

"And you will," Layla said, "but we need to finish our job here first." She pushed some wayward red hair away from her face and grabbed his hand. "Let's go check on Simmy and Zion and see if they need our help."

Without replying, Noah let her lead him away, ignoring the looks he got from Aaron at his outburst.

Tapping on the door, Layla let go of Noah's hand and opened it a crack. "May we come in?"

"Of course," Simmy called to them.

Layla held the door open for Noah, gesturing for him to enter first.

"Thanks," he murmured, reaching out and giving her hand a squeeze before walking over to Zion's giant body in the centre of the room.

Bright golden light exuded from his being, making the rest of the room look exceptionally dark in comparison.

Garvan was still in his chains and was now confined inside

a large gold sphere, which hovered in the air above an open rebirthing chamber.

"What's he doing?" Noah asked quietly.

"Making sure that Garvan stays in his current form. No reverting back to his old body, no transforming to his new body, his powers stuck in limbo," Simmy replied.

"What will that do?" Layla asked.

"It will make sure that everyone who has been manipulated in any way by Garvan will be able to revert back to their old selves and that Noah and Nora here in this timeline will have no need to be worried that he will come after them again," Simmy explained.

"Does that mean your siblings will all become free now?" Layla asked, excited.

Simmy beamed at her. "Yes, it does, and I will also be able to return to the Realm."

"It is just the beginning," Zion said to them as he walked over. Garvan was floating behind him, his eyes, one old and one young, closed. "But we are a lot further along than we were before, so thank you."

Noah's expression softened. "I'm glad we were able to help."

"You are going to have to get back to your timeline now. There is a lot you need to do. We are all grateful for everything you have done for us," Zion said, holding out his arm.

Noah gripped Zion's forearm tightly and bowed his head.

"Do you need anything before we go?" Layla asked Simmy as she pulled her into a hug.

"I have my family back," Simmy replied, pulling her head back to see Layla. "What more could I ask for?"

At the sound of feet approaching, Noah turned to the doorway to see the others all standing there, including Tick and the two Aaron's.

"We're going to stay and help rebuild the Realm. We want to make sure Earth isn't affected too badly by what's happened here," the other Noah said.

"And I will train them," Aaron's duplicate chipped in, leaning on Max for support.

Noah walked over to Aaron and Layla who had congregated together and watched as Zion approached them and held out his hourglass. "I will transport you back to your timeline," he said.

Noah, Layla and Aaron all touched their index fingers to the cold metal holding the hourglass together, a golden portal opening as they did so.

"One," Zion counted, "two, three."

Noah felt his body give a soft jolt, and with a *pop*, he was back in the kitchen of Zion's palace, a teenage Simmy staring at him in surprise.

With a yelp, she ran at Noah and threw her arms and legs around him. "You are back!" she cried.

Layla and Aaron stepped through the portal, and Simmy cried out just as excitedly, jumping off Noah and pulling them into a tight hug.

Noah gave a small laugh, his tired body begging him to sit down.

"You need rest," Simmy said to him, letting go of the others and looking at them in concern. "You all do. Go. I will send some food to your rooms. Zion is working on a project right now, but I will tell him you are back, and you can see him tomorrow."

Nodding gratefully, Noah took Layla's hand, and they walked slowly to their rooms. Aaron stayed behind to talk to

Simmy.

"Let's go to your room," Layla said, and Noah looked at her in surprise.

A deep blush graced Layla's cheeks. "I was separated from you for too long. I missed you."

Noah felt his cheeks turning red too but was about to decline. He was exhausted. After a glance at Layla, though, he saw that she looked just as tired as him, so he followed her to his room. When they arrived, he flopped face-first onto the bed, falling asleep the second his head hit the pillow.

Chapter 33 - Layla

L ayla's body had never felt as stiff as when she woke up the next morning.

Her eyelids fluttered open, and her fingers twitched as she remembered where she was. She was lying face-down on top of the doona, and she could feel some of her hair sticking to the drool that had dried on the side of her mouth.

Groaning, Layla lifted her heavy head and dragged her hand down her face, sluggishly wiping the drool and hair away. She needed a shower. Badly.

Flopping her head back down into the doona, she wriggled her toes and fingers, stiffening as her pinky brushed against something warm.

Wha—? Oh, right. I'm in Noah's room, she thought, before shuffling over to give herself some more space to stretch on the enormous bed they'd shared.

Both of them had been so exhausted after coming back from the other timeline that they hadn't even said goodnight to one another before sleep claimed them. Well, that's how it had been for her, anyway.

Once her blood was circulating enough for her to function, Layla pushed herself onto her forearms and rested her head on her shoulder, looking at Noah.

His hair, which had grown so much longer and messier than it had been on Earth, was pushed up at the front where he'd been lying on it, and she was glad to see she wasn't the only one who had been drooling.

Breathing out a small laugh, she lightly brushed a few stray strands of hair out of his face, then leaned over and kissed him on the forehead.

When he didn't stir, she gently sat up and stretched her arms above her head, her back cracking as she twisted it.

There was a lot to talk about with the others.

Wriggling her toes in the soft carpet when she stood, Layla shot Noah one last look before padding her way to the door, opening it with the sensor and walking the small distance to her own room.

As she walked inside, she found a fresh pair of denim shorts, a red singlet, a matching bra and underwear set and a pair of red sneakers waiting for her on her untouched bed.

"Yes." Layla breathed the word, drawing out the s through her teeth. She ripped off her dirty outfit and threw it in a pile on the floor.

Walking as fast as her stiff legs would carry her, Layla raced to the shower and turned on the hot water. She watched the room fill up with steam before adding just a fraction of cold water and stepping under the heavy stream.

Closing her eyes and releasing a deep sigh, Layla tilted her head back and let the water flow over her tired body, letting the heat work its magic on her sore muscles. She stayed there, enjoying the warmth until her fingers became pruned.

She grabbed a bottle of musk-scented body scrub from a shelf in the shower and lathered herself with it, making sure that everything down to her toes was squeaky clean.

Finally, after she had washed, rinsed and detangled her hair as best she could, Layla turned off the comforting stream of water and stepped into the steaming bathroom, grabbing two towels. She wrapped one around her hair and the other around her torso.

She knew before she had even stepped into her carpeted bedroom that Simmy would be waiting for her. They hadn't had a chance to catch up since she had returned, and she knew it hadn't been Zion who had laid out the perfect outfit for her to wear.

"Are you hurt?!"

Simmy was on her before Layla had the chance to utter a greeting, springing up from the bed and launching herself at Layla, lifting her arms above her head to check for any bruises. One at a time, thankfully, as Layla needed to hold the towel in place.

"I'm fine."

Simmy's sceptical look forced Layla's lips to tilt upwards into a smile, and she gently pulled her arm out of her aunt's grasp.

"Truly, I'm fine. Aaron is the one who did the hard battling. You should be checking on him."

"I already have. He is on bed rest until I have decided otherwise."

Layla looked at Simmy incredulously. "As if he's not already walking around the palace, looking for more danger."

Simmy laughed. "Well, I got a decent meal into him anyway. He has a lot on his mind."

"A lot has happened. I don't blame him," Layla replied, gesturing for Simmy to turn around so she could get dressed. "I need to talk to him, actually. About Garvan."

"What about Garvan?"

Layla could hear the frown in Simmy's voice and hesitated before replying. "He was created to be more powerful than you and your siblings, right?"

"Right," Simmy drew out the word.

"But he was still meant to be just a Guardian?"

"*Just* a Guardian?" Simmy emphasised.

"Yeah. So, you wouldn't be able to create another Realm, would you?"

"There is only one Realm, Layla. Regardless of what timelines Garvan creates."

"Actually, there's not. That's the thing. What if Garvan didn't create those timelines specifically, but the Realm's attached to them?"

"I am not sure I understand."

"Everyone in the timeline we came from has lived a full life. A full life they remember, from what I've been told, anyway. But the Realm seemed... off. New. The Simmy in that timeline struggled with her powers until Nora astral projected and guided her. It was like she hadn't had the same amount of experience you had. Even the Zion over there was calling himself a duplicate. If there's only supposed to be one Realm, they shouldn't exist. So, Garvan had to have created them."

Layla finished dressing and spun Simmy around by her shoulder. "Garvan's a Celestial."

"That cannot be."

"Why not?"

"Because," Simmy paused, "well, because..."

"Because?" Layla drew the question out.

"Because he is just a Guardian!"

219

"Okay, okay. That's what I want to chat to Aaron about, anyway. He might be able to shed some light on the situation."

"You need to eat something first," Simmy snapped before rubbing her eyes with her fists and leaning forward, resting her head on Layla's shoulder. "Sorry," she said, sinking into Layla as she wrapped her arms around her. "I am still getting used to these teenage hormones. I had forgotten how difficult it can be to go through puberty. Next time, I will definitely come back older."

Layla let out a small laugh, squeezing Simmy's shoulders.

"I was really worried about you," Simmy mumbled into Layla's shirt.

"I'm back now."

Simmy nodded before sniffling and righting herself.

"I hope you didn't get any boogers on my new shirt," Layla joked, forcing a grimace on her face.

Letting out a thick laugh, Simmy shook her head. "Not in a place you can see, anyway."

At Layla's disgusted look, Simmy turned her back and walked towards the bedroom door, which opened with a soft *hiss* as she placed her hand on the sensor pad. "Aaron is usually in the kitchen. Let us look for him there."

Grumbling about having to wear a crusty shirt, Layla followed, her stomach rumbling. Even if they didn't find Aaron, Simmy was right. She definitely needed something to eat.

Chapter 34 - Aaron

runch.

The salty tang of the chips Aaron was eating hit the back of his throat as he shoved another handful into his mouth. The packet crinkled as he immediately reached in for more.

He stared at the blank white wall in front of him as he tried, again, to contact Nora.

The longer she was held captive by Garvan, the less he was able to connect with her, and it was starting to scare him.

He had hoped when she'd astral projected into the alternate timeline with them that they would have had a chance to talk, for him to explain what had happened. But she had shut him out.

And he was afraid she was doing it again.

A part of him actually hoped she was, because if she wasn't, that meant he couldn't connect with her because Garva—

"For the love of the Realm, if you try to force yourself into my thoughts one more time, I'm going to melt your brain."

Aaron almost sagged with relief but clung to the thread for dear life. "I have been worrie—"

"Don't you dare lie to me. Or do, since that's all you seem to have ever done."

Aaron blanched. "What are you talking abo—?"

"*GET. OUT. OF. MY. HEAD.*"

"Just tell me what is going on."

"*Like you'd even care. I'm not going to be a pawn in your games anymore.*"

The sound of crunching foil filled the kitchen as Aaron clenched his fist around the chip packet. "What lies has Garvan been feeding you?"

"*None, surprisingly, which is more than I can say for you.*"

"I have never lied to you!"

"*Omitting the truth is just as bad.*"

Aaron's heart lurched. "What do you me—?"

"*I don't need to explain myself to you.*"

"Would you stop cutting me off and answer the damn quest—!"

"*Leave me alone, Aaron. I don't need you.*"

"WAIT!"

The connection severed. Aaron threw the crumpled chip packet on the kitchen floor before roughly pushing himself to his feet. The white bar stool he'd been sitting on clanged to the ground loudly.

"When I told you to eat some vegetables, I did not mean deep-fried potato."

Aaron whirled around to find Simmy and Layla shooting cautious glances at each other and then at him.

"You should be more specific next time," he muttered, squatting to pick up the discarded packet and cleaning the crumbs away with a wave of his hand.

"What happened?" Simmy asked as she walked over to right the fallen stool.

Aaron didn't reply. He didn't want to get their hopes up

by saying he had been in contact with Nora. Not when he wasn't sure he would be able to do so again. After a pause where the two of them continued to look at him expectantly, Aaron said, "There has just been a lot going on."

"I've got more to add to your plate, unfortunately," Layla chipped in, perching herself on the kitchen counter and banging the heels of her sneakers against the bench.

Aaron rubbed the bridge of his nose. "I am not sure I can take any more, but what the heck. Hit me."

"Garvan's a Celestial."

Aaron's hand flew from his face, and he turned to Layla so fast his neck twinged. "What?!"

"We *think* he is a Celestial," Simmy added, trying to placate her uncle, seeing the wild look in his eyes. "Well, Layla thinks he is a Celestial. I think she is wrong, but she thought we should come to you and check."

Layla shot Simmy a look, which Simmy replied to with a guilty grimace and a shrug.

"That is not possible," Aaron said, brushing off the claim before dread settled in the pit of his stomach. "Is it?"

He paced over to the fridge, pulling out a bottle of water and downing half of it in two gulps. "Is it possible? No, it cannot be possible. But could it be? It must be. We were just in another *Realm*. There should not be another Realm. IS IT POSSIBLE?!" Aaron shouted the last question, and he saw Simmy and Layla jump at the unexpected noise.

"I am afraid it is entirely possible," came the voice of his brother as he stepped through the wall Aaron had been staring at. "We did purposely share more power with Garvan in order for him to guide his siblings."

"We?" Simmy pitched in from the kitchen counter, where

she'd sat next to Layla. "I thought you were the one to create us, Father."

"I did create you and your siblings, but I enlisted Aaron's help with Garvan. I thought by combining our life energies, Garvan would become as powerful as we needed him to be in order to support you all throughout the year."

"So you *did* create another Celestial?" Layla confirmed. "And he created the other Realm then, not the timeline?"

"It appears that way." Zion looked tired. Aaron knew he had been pushing himself to his limit, trying to keep the Realm from collapsing entirely, and he also knew they didn't have much time until Zion reached his breaking point. They really couldn't be worrying about this right now. If Garvan truly was a Celestial and was creating other Realms—which he had suspected but stupidly ignored while they were there—then this opened up a whole new problem.

"Girls, give us a moment, will you?" Aaron gestured for Layla and Simmy to leave the kitchen. He waited until they had disappeared down the hallway before running his hand through his dark hair and letting out a deep breath. "This changes things."

Zion didn't answer, but Aaron wasn't going to give him the satisfaction of walking away from him this time.

"Zion."

Still no reply.

"Zion!" Aaron said more forcibly. "Did you know about this?"

Finally, Zion turned to him, looking wearier than Aaron had ever seen him. "I had begun to suspect it when the Realm started to become unstable. The only way that could have happened was if it had been split."

Aaron ran his hand down his face. "The other Realm in that timeline is a fragment of this Realm? Garvan is splitting the Realm apart? Has he done it more than once? My duplicate in the timeline we just came from told me he was one of five created. Does that mean Garvan has split the Realm five times?"

"It appears that way."

"Why did you not tell me? We should be doing something!"

"What do you think I have been doing?!" Zion boomed, and Aaron's eyes widened slightly. It was unlike his brother to lose control.

"I have been working painstakingly to keep the Realm in balance, holding the seams of it together with my own hands! Do you not think I wish I could be out there fighting this battle with you? Do you not think I notice how capped yours and my children's powers have become? Do you not think I am trying to remove the restrictions that have been placed on me so I can protect our home?" Zion's voice grew louder, his hands gesticulating wildly with every statement. "Garvan has too much influence over the Realm. When he split it, he embedded a part of himself within it, so whenever we oppose him, the Realm will be forced to block us in any way possible." Zion's hands touched his heart and then created a sweeping arc "Garvan is a creation of ours, and while I find no joy in removing him from this world, I understand it is a necessity. Yet, I am unable to step any closer to him than I currently am. The Realm is blocking me from doing so." Zion frowned, then sighed at his brother. "So yes, Aaron, I had become suspicious, but while you are still free to roam wherever you want and help the children, I needed to keep this job myself, so you did not feel obliged to assist me instead of them. An endeavour I

225

now see was pointless."

Aaron clenched his jaw. "You do not need to shield me. I am very capable of making my own decisions."

"I am awar—"

"Are you?" Aaron pressed. "Are you really? Because it seems like I am here acting as a babysitter while you are taking on the brunt of everything else."

Zion paused, looking through him, and Aaron wished he hadn't said anything.

"If this is about Nora—"

"This is not about Nora," Aaron grit out, cutting Zion off again, "not in the way you are thinking, but it is dangerous that she has been left to fend for herself with him. He could corrupt her mind, body and soul, and if he gets his hands on her power, we are all in danger."

Zion's eyes continued to bore into Aaron's own until, finally, Aaron averted his gaze.

"I will begin to include you in my plans from now on." Zion's voice was gentler than it had been previously, and Aaron inhaled deeply in an attempt to curb his frustration.

"You better." With that, Aaron stormed out of the room while Zion disappeared in a flash of bright light, leaving the kitchen empty.

Chapter 35 - Nora

"You are learning more control, but you are still as weak as a lamb."

Rolling her eyes, Nora flung an amber energy dagger at Garvan's chest, which he dissolved with a flick of his finger.

They had been training every day, and while Nora could feel her life energy returning, she was still weaker than she had been before.

Garvan hadn't mentioned why Nora was playing catch up, but she'd kept her distance nonetheless.

Well, as much distance as she could, with Garvan popping in unannounced whenever he felt like it.

"Gee, I wonder why," Nora muttered to herself. If Garvan wanted to ignore that he'd stolen her power, he could, but she had never enjoyed walking on eggshells.

She saw Garvan's eyes flicker. Blue, now with a small speck of amber. "If you are going to master your powers, you are going to need to become physically stronger."

Nora had kept up with her physical training since she'd been here, and she knew she'd be able to hold her own in hand-to-hand combat, but she wouldn't tell Garvan that. The less he knew about what she could do, the better.

"Where's Tick?" Nora said, changing the subject, crafting more daggers that floated above the tips of her fingers while dodging the small black energy balls Garvan effortlessly tossed her way.

"She is busy with other duties around the temple, but if you miss her, I would be happy to put her back on guard duty."

"I would rather pluck out my own eyeballs," Nora replied nonchalantly, but her mind reeled. *What could be so important that Garvan has her working on it full-time?*

"I advise you not to snoop around," Garvan continued, throwing a larger energy ball in Nora's direction. It disappeared as she went to dodge it before reappearing behind her and exploding on her shoulder.

Gasping in pain, Nora stumbled forwards. She hadn't had enough energy to wear her water shield today, so her skin burned and sizzled from the blast.

Glaring at Garvan, Nora tentatively touched her raw flesh, wincing as red-hot pain shot through her.

"Let me," Garvan said, starting towards her with his hand held out.

She flinched away from him, and her shoulder screamed in pain from the sudden movement. "No!"

Garvan halted.

"I can do it myself." Nora half turned away from him and side-stepped over to the pond on her balcony, kneeling down next to it and dipping the fingers of her sore arm into the water.

Immediately, the water tickling her fingertips began to glow a healing blue before trickling its way up her arm and wrapping itself around her injury.

Sighing in relief, Nora sank fully onto the ground, calling

for her healing energy to embed itself in the water, which began patching up her torn, blackened skin.

If she hadn't been so aware of Garvan's presence, she wouldn't have heard him softly pad his way over to her, but as it was, she tensed up as he crouched down beside her.

"You do not want me touching you."

"I've never wanted you touching me," Nora bit back.

"You did not back away from me before."

"A moment of insanity. One that won't happen again."

"I was merely trying to show you what I meant about only wanting your energy."

"My *life* energy, Garvan. You only want my *life* energy."

Nora saw Garvan's mouth tighten, but he didn't say anything more as he watched her water work its magic.

"You need to start using your water more when we fight. Maybe next time, you will not be caught off guard."

Nora merely hummed in response, peeling back the burnt leather from her wound so her water could properly cleanse it.

A moment of silence passed between them before Garvan stood and turned on his heel. "I will have a new pair of leathers sent in for you. We will resume training as soon as your shoulder has healed."

Not bothering to reply, Nora tilted her head upwards, her mouth pulled into a grimace. She has started to become too comfortable here. It was time for her to figure out what Tick was doing and where Garvan was always disappearing to. She wouldn't be able to astral project and help Noah again, but this was more important. Stopping Garvan from the inside was the only way for her to escape.

He wasn't going to get another *drop* of her life energy.

Chapter 36 - Noah

"Noah? Noah? NOAH!"

Groaning, Noah rolled from his front to his back. His body was stiff, and his neck protested as he tried to turn towards the voice calling his name.

Forcing his eyelids open, Noah squinted against the bright light, his eyes dry. "Yeah?" he mumbled groggily. He wanted to go back to sleep.

"Zion has called everyone to the Earth room," the voice said, and Noah felt a small hand jiggling his shoulder.

"Simmy?" Noah asked, resting the back of his hand on his forehead and closing his eyes once more.

"It is me," Simmy answered, and he could feel her head nodding through the hand on his shoulder

"Where's Layla?"

"She is with the others. Zion asked me to come and get you. Are you alright?"

"Yeah," Noah said, pushing himself up onto his elbows. His head, heavy, rolled back, so he was staring at the ceiling. "Just... tired. Really tired."

Simmy looked at him in concern. "You can barely keep your eyes open."

Noah, whose head had now dropped back onto the bed, his

back arched, hummed at her in response. His body felt like lead.

"Stay here," Simmy instructed him, turning and rushing towards the door. "Although, it doesn't look like you could go anywhere, even if you wanted to," she added as an afterthought as she disappeared into the hall. Noah's bedroom door shut with a hiss behind her, the noise ringing in his ears.

With a groan, Noah let his body flop backwards, blindly grabbing for a pillow and covering his face with it to block the light, which was making his eyes water.

He wasn't sure how much time had passed, but sooner than he would have liked, someone was gently shaking his shoulders again.

"Wake up," they called to him. "Time to wake up, Noah."

Noah forced his eyes open again, his eyelids resisting the movement.

"What's wrong with him?" he heard Layla ask. Her cool hands felt nice against his hot cheeks as she gently scooped up his face in her hands.

"It could be a few things," Aaron replied slowly.

Even though Noah's eyes were fuzzy, he could see the faint shine of Aaron's healing blue energy, which was the only indication Noah got that Aaron was trying to heal him, as he didn't feel any better.

"I am going to get Zion," Aaron said after he had checked Noah over from head to toe. The blue glow disappeared.

Noah barely registered the sound of retreating footsteps and the hissing of the door as he snuggled into Layla's hands.

"I've got you," she said to him softly, lifting his head, laying it on her lap and stroking his hair.

"He will be okay," Simmy said to her. "Zion and Aaron will

231

figure out what is going on."

Noah felt himself drift between consciousness and unconsciousness until the sound of two sets of feet hurrying into the room forced Noah back to reality. Soon, he felt Zion's large hand gently cover his forehead.

"Take a deep breath in for me, Noah," Zion instructed.

He went to fill his lungs with as much air as he could, but felt it go down the wrong hole and coughed it all back out again.

Through his closed eyelids, Noah saw Zion's hand glow with his golden life energy, and Noah felt his body grow warmer as pins and needles prickled through him.

The sensation lasted a few minutes, and when Zion lifted his hand from Noah's forehead, his body felt lighter, more rested.

"I have transferred some of my own life energy to you," Zion explained once Noah pulled himself into a sitting position. "You should feel well enough to travel to the next timeline now. I am afraid we do not have time to catch up before you leave. Layla told me you wanted to talk. Please remember, your body is not used to the pure energy of the Realm flowing through it. It did not have any time to adjust before you were forced into the other timeline, and that excess stress has taken a large toll on you. Layla, having been exposed to these energies since she was a child, is used to what pure Realm energy feels like, so her body is not reacting as negatively as yours. The life energy I have transferred to you will help keep you alert while also helping your body to adjust more quickly from now on. Now, you need to get to the next timeline quickly. There is a disturbance occurring there that cannot wait."

"Wait…" Noah began. While his body felt stronger, his head was spinning. Zion's energy melding with his own was making him queasy.

"You must go!" Zion said, holding out his hourglass to transport Noah, Layla and Aaron to the next timeline.

"I am going too!" Simmy interjected, stepping in front of Zion, her expression showing there would be no room for argument.

Zion hesitated for a second before nodding once. "There will be no stopping you?"

"No, there will not."

"Very well. You all need to be touching this hourglass before I can transport you."

Layla took Noah's hand, and they put their index fingers to the hourglass together.

Aaron placed a steadying arm around Noah's shoulder and touched the hourglass with the other. "We will be back as soon as we can," he said to his brother.

"Be careful," Zion replied, his hand glowing gold. And, with a *pop,* they were transported.

Chapter 37 - Noah

I t was night when they arrived. And silent.
Eerily silent.

No people, no cars rumbling in the background, not even the sound of crickets chirping.

As soon as his feet touched the ground, Noah dropped to his knees and held his face in his hands, shaking as his body tried to adjust to Zion's life energy. Travelling through the portal had shaken the power coursing within him, making him even more nauseous than before.

Layla knelt next to him and handed him Ray. "Take her and use her to help the process," she said softly.

Noah took Ray gratefully and sighed in relief as the mandala warmed in his grip, settling some of the turmoil running through him.

"Where is everyone?" Simmy asked the group. Noah lifted his head enough to see her looking around at the empty street. "There does not seem to be any sign of life here."

"That cannot be good," Aaron replied, taking in the scenery. "I do not want to imagine what Garvan must have done to make it so lifeless."

"What about this timeline's Noah and Nora?" Noah questioned, taking Layla's offered hand. She helped him stand back up. "Do you think we were training to become Guardians here? Maybe Garvan has already captured them and has absorbed their power. Maybe he's already taken over this Realm, and our Garvan has already absorbed his power."

"Calm down. You and Nora weren't Guardians in the other timeline," Layla reminded him. "The first time they'd heard of the Realm was when our Nora encouraged the other Nora to go and see Simmy."

"I do not feel a connection to anyone here," Noah heard Simmy say as she pulled out her moonstone mandala and placed it over her heart. The stones glowed softly. "Surely if there was someone here who had been created from me, I would feel some sort of connection." She looked at Layla.

"I'm not sure," Layla replied. "I was dead in the last timeline. Plus, I was still human, so I doubt I would have felt anything."

"I felt something," Aaron said. "I did not know what it was at first, but as I got closer to my counterpart, it became stronger. Did you feel anything?" he asked Noah.

"I... don't think so," Noah replied, gripping Ray more tightly as he tried to remember. "I don't really know. There was so much going on."

"Well, do you feel anything now?" Simmy asked him. "Can you feel whether the Noah of this timeline has been taken?"

Noah closed his eyes and took a deep breath to clear his head. There was something calling to him. It was faint, but it was there. "I can sense something," he said slowly, "but I can't be sure whether it's my counterpart or not."

"We should check it out," Aaron said. He pulled out his sapphire mandala, beginning to create a portal for the group to step through, when Ray began to shiver in Noah's hands.

"Wait!" he called to the others. "Ray's sensing something."

Layla stepped closer to him and went to grab hold of Ray as well.

"No!" Noah said brashly, pulling Ray away from her. "I mean," he added hastily, looking at Layla's hurt and confused expression, "Ray's infused with some of Zion's life energy at the moment. We need you at full capacity, we can't risk you becoming as unstable as me."

Layla nodded slowly as she lowered her hand but said nothing, eyeing him cautiously.

"What is Ray reacting to?" Simmy asked, walking over and putting an arm around Layla.

"I think there's another mandala around here," Noah replied. "I feel like we need to find it."

"But what about Garvan? We have to make sure he hasn't gotten hold of the twins here," Layla rebutted.

A flicker of irritation sparked in Noah. "We will need to be as strong as possible when we meet Garvan, and another mandala can help us." His gaze shifted between Simmy and Aaron, who were looking at him, keeping their faces as neutral as possible.

"We have to do this!" Noah insisted, causing Ray to buzz loudly in his grip.

"Alright," Simmy said gently, releasing Layla and taking a tentative step towards him, "if you are sure, lead the way."

"I'm sure," Noah said, determined. "Thank you." He shot Simmy a grateful look, a small smile on his lips.

"Where do we need to go?" Layla asked him, placing a soft hand on his shoulder.

Noah hadn't noticed Layla move back to his side, and he flinched as her touch sent unpleasant shivers down his spine, the energy coursing through him thrown off balance again.

Noah shrugged his shoulder away from her. "Let me find it," he said, purposely looking in the other direction.

Ignoring Layla's attempt to grab hold of him, he sat on the ground, crossed his legs and closed his eyes, gripping Ray tightly with both hands. "Where is the mandala?" he whispered to her.

Ray shuddered under his touch and projected flashes of objects through his mind until resting on an image of his parents huddled away inside their house, his mum gripping a mandala with amethysts embedded within it.

Gripping Ray tighter, Noah tried to squeeze some more information out of her, but instead, the image flickered and began to fade.

Once the image was gone completely, Noah released the relic, then stood and turned to the others. "I know where we have to go."

Aaron, Simmy and Layla stepped over to him, and Layla held out her hand for Ray.

"What?" Noah asked her.

"I was going to take Ray, so I can transport us where we need to go," Layla replied, her tone flat.

"Oh," Noah said, rubbing his thumb along Ray's smooth edge. "Actually, I thought that *I* could create the portal for us."

"Are you in a state to do that?"

Noah flinched. He did feel weird, but the thought of anyone else touching Ray made his arm hairs stand on end. "I'm fine."

Out of the corner of his eye, Noah saw Aaron throw Simmy a furtive glance as Layla stepped back towards them.

Taking a steadying breath, Noah held onto Ray with both hands and tried his best to focus, picturing the four of them arriving at his parent's house. After three failed attempts, Aaron walked over to him and gently laid a finger on one of Ray's sunstones, sending a jolt of blue energy through her, trying to connect with her tune. But as soon as that jolt escaped his finger, Zion's life energy, which Noah had weaved through Ray, zapped Aaron in return, and he winced. Noah gave him a fevered glance as Aaron sucked on his burnt index finger.

"What happened there?" Aaron asked, his voice muffled by his finger.

Noah ignored it and ground his teeth. "I'll try again," he said, taking three deep breaths in and out.

The powerful energies within him warred, the pure Primary Guardian energy and Zion's Celestial energy both trying to reign supreme, but Noah refused to let them distract him and yelped in triumph as he managed to create a crackly portal. "Quickly!" he instructed the others, ushering them through the amber and gold energies that the portal was sparking with.

The others shot sceptical glances at Noah, but Noah grabbed each of their hands and pulled them through, not giving them a chance to voice their concerns, before quickly following after them.

The portal stung as the energies tried to absorb back into him, but when he landed, Noah was pleasantly surprised to see himself and the others had arrived safely on his parents' front lawn.

The surprised looks on the others' faces told him they hadn't expected to come out the other side unscathed either.

"The mandala's in there," Noah announced, puffing out his chest and pointing to the house. He moved towards the front door.

Noah turned to see if the others were following him and caught them all glancing nervously at each other.

"Will he be okay?" Noah heard Layla whisper from behind, and he kept his head turned to see the response.

Aaron pressed a finger to his lips, indicating that Noah could hear them, and continued to walk in silence.

As he turned back to the door, Noah felt Zion's energy coursing through his veins like a bolt of electricity, yet he could also feel it beginning to meld with his own. He held a hand out in front of him and watched as amber electricity crackled between his fingers while golden sparks flew out alongside it.

Clenching his fist, stopping the flow of energy, Noah dropped his hand to his side. He frowned as he saw that the front door of his house was unlocked and had been left open by a crack. He waved the others forward. "Someone's here," he whispered, pushing the door open with a creak and peering inside.

The entrance was dark. Not a single light was switched on, and the house felt empty, yet Noah was sure he'd seen his parents here. This *had* to be where the mandala was.

He stepped inside, and something moved in the darkness. "HAH!"

A large shadow jumped out from behind the cabinet, and the end of a broom swung towards Noah's face.

Before Aaron had a chance to wave the broom safely away, Noah spun around and shot an enormous amber energy beam towards the culprit, hitting them head-on and sending them flying into the wall of the next room over.

"Paul? *Paul!* Are you okay?"

Another figure, a smaller one, ran towards the crumpled mess on the floor, pulling it into their arms.

The lights were quickly flicked on by Layla, who had shoved Noah out of the way as she ran over to Jen and Paul Parker in the living room.

Noah gaped, covering his mouth, horrified at the bleeding gash on his father's forehead. The broom was lying forgotten next to his limp hand, while the amethyst mandala was clenched tightly in the other.

"Out of the way," Aaron said, pulling Noah to the side as he rushed forwards, healing blue energy already rippling on his fingertips.

He placed his hand on Paul's chest and listened closely for a heartbeat. "It is steady," he announced to the room before beginning to heal the damage Noah had caused.

"I… I… I didn't…" Noah began, his eyes wide as he took in the scene before him, pulling Ray up to his chest. His knuckles were white from clenching her so hard.

Simmy walked up to him and placed an arm around his waist. "We know," she said, "but Noah…" She trailed off.

He knew what she was going to say. Zion's life energy was too much for him to control. He didn't know how to use it. It was making him unstable.

Simmy held out her hand, and Noah reluctantly passed Ray over to her, the turmoil within him rising again. He forced his arms to his side to keep from trying to snatch Ray back.

"Just for the time being," Simmy said to him, wrapping her smaller hand around one of his. "You need to face the turmoil head-on to come out the other side of it."

Nodding, Noah patted her hand and then let it go, walking stiffly over to where the others were working on Paul.

"Here," he said, gently prying the amethyst mandala out of Paul's hand and giving it to Simmy. "It'll be best if you merge this."

Simmy took it from him and walked into the kitchen, placing the two mandalas on the table next to each other.

Noah watched as the three bright lights of the mandalas from the different timelines lit the room magnificently. Orange, blue and purple energy weaved together as Simmy's skilled hands worked their magic, melding the two mandalas into one.

When she came back, Ray shone even brighter, her new sapphire and amethyst shimmering happily next to her sunstones.

"Here," Simmy said, taking Noah's hand and placing it on one of the amethysts. "Amethysts help bring peace against turmoil and increase your intuition. It will help you clear your head and accept Zion's life energy."

She was right. As soon as Noah's finger brushed against the amethyst, it was like a pathway opened in his mind. Zion's energy was no longer fighting within him. Instead, it found a steady flow.

Sighing in relief, Noah leant towards her and planted a light kiss on her forehead. "Thank you."

Simmy smiled but waved him off, pointing him in the direction of his parents.

Noah walked over to them, knelt down and placed an arm around Layla. "Sorry," he mumbled to her.

She squeezed his knee in return, acknowledging his apology.

"How is he?" Noah asked Aaron, who was still healing Paul.

"He will be weak for a while," Aaron replied, looking at

241

Noah sternly. "That was quite a blast you hit him with."

Noah nodded guiltily.

"But he will be fine as long as he rests," Aaron continued. "I am going to work on him for a little while longer. You should head into the kitchen."

Noah nodded again, then stood up, offering Layla a hand, which she gratefully accepted. He turned to his mother, who was staring at him with a questioning look on her face. Noah offered her a hand as well, which she tentatively took.

"You look just like my son..." she said to him slowly, turning her head from side to side to look at him from different angles.

Noah chuckled. "I am your son," he replied, "just not from this timeline."

Jen lifted an eyebrow but didn't question his response. She allowed him to pull her towards the kitchen, where Layla had flicked on the kettle to make them all a cup of tea.

"Mummy?"

Noah turned and saw a young girl half-hiding behind the doorway, looking from Noah to her mother, unsure whether it was safe to come closer.

Jen jumped up from the stool she was resting on and scooped the girl up in her arms. "It's okay, Nora. I think we can trust these people, even if there was a little accident earlier," she said pointedly to Noah, who responded with a grimace.

"He looks like Noah," Nora said, pointing at him.

"Hi," Noah said, walking over to her and holding out his hand. "I am a Noah, just not *your* Noah. Is your brother here?"

Nora took Noah's hand and shook it. "I'm Nora," she said as she puffed out her chest importantly. "I'm eight years old.

And no, he's not here."

"Nice to meet you," Noah said, casting a concerned glance at Layla.

Layla walked over to them, the whistling kettle forgotten. "Can you tell us the last time you saw your brother?" she asked.

"It was a few days ago—" Jen began, but Nora placed a small hand over her mum's mouth.

"They asked me!" she scolded Jen, a frown on her face.

Jen pulled Nora's hand away, putting her hands up in surrender. "Go on then," she said to her daughter calmly, "you tell them."

"Thank you," Nora said to her mum, then turned back to Noah and Layla. "He disappeared from here a few days ago. A man with black hair and blue eyes took him so mum and dad have been hiding out in the front room every night so they could beat him if he came back. He won't though. Noah's come to see me a few times while I've been sleeping and he said the man won't come for me," Nora explained.

"What?" exclaimed Jen. "Why didn't you tell me?"

Nora looked at her mum in confusion. "You never asked."

Noah grasped one of Nora's hands in both of his own. "Did he tell you where he was?"

"He could only tell me that he was being forced to stay in a dark, musty-smelling room," Nora said, squinting her eyes in concentration as she tried to remember.

Noah and Layla looked at each other while Jen covered her mouth with a hand, her eyes wide.

"He must be in the chamber next to the Throne Room," Layla said. "Did he tell you whether he was okay?" she asked Nora.

"He said that the man kept pulling something out of him but that it's taking longer than he wanted, so I think he's tired," Nora replied.

Just then, Simmy, Aaron and Paul, who was leaning on Aaron for support, walked into the kitchen. After seeing the look on Jen's face, they stopped in their tracks.

"What?" Paul asked, looking from his wife to the young strangers in his kitchen. "What's wrong?"

"Noah's alive," Jen said, sobbing. "Nora's seen him."

Tears welled in Paul's eyes, and he quickly blinked them away. "Can you save him?" he asked Aaron, who he was still holding onto.

"We will do our best," Aaron said to him, guiding Paul to a bar stool to sit on, "but we will have to leave now. We do not have a moment to waste."

"Will you come back to us?" Nora asked. "Will we see you again?"

"I…" Noah began, "I don't know, but we'll try."

Appeased, Nora smiled, jumped away from her mother and took a step towards Noah, holding out her hand. "Good luck," she said.

Noah shook her hand and smiled. "Thank you."

"Ready?" Aaron called to him. Simmy had already used Ray to create a portal and was ready to teleport them to the Realm.

Noah jogged over to them. "Ready," he said as he stuck one foot through the portal.

"We will do our best to bring your son back to you," Aaron called to the Parkers, who were watching them. Jen was standing behind Nora, holding her close.

Noah felt queasy as his feet hit the ground. He released a

breath as the grunts he heard nearby told him the others had landed safely.

"Stay quiet," Aaron whispered to them suddenly, holding up a finger. "There is someone here." He pulled them into a nearby bush, trying to hide them all behind the branches as best as he could. Not that the bush provided much cover. The leaves were dead, and the small branches scratched Noah's cheeks as they waved their sharp talons near his eyes.

He tentatively pushed the twigs away from his face and peered past Layla's wild hair to see what was going on.

"Who is it?" Noah whispered to her.

Layla turned to him, her face pale, and pointed at two figures.

There, walking arm in arm, were Tick and Marian.

Chapter 38 - Nora

Nora rolled her shoulder, tensing as the skin pulled, but the pain had subsided, and the only sign she'd been hurt was the slightly pink, fresh layer of skin, which was hidden beneath her new fighting leathers.

Garvan had brought them in himself, much to Nora's chagrin. That meant they hadn't finished training for the day. Nora didn't know how her balcony hadn't been reduced to rubble with the amount of energy the two of them had fired at each other.

Stretching her neck, Nora stood to face Garvan once more, noticing that the amber flecks in his eyes, which he'd gained when he'd absorbed her life energy, were now gone, replaced by the usual deep blue which, as always, lacked any emotion.

His arrogant smirk was back too. Garvan slowly drifted his gaze from Nora's toes to her face, stopping when he reached her eyes. "If you used your water to fight as effectively as you do to heal yourself, you might actually stand a chance against your opponent," he drawled lazily, his grin widening when at the scowl on Nora's face.

"I don't need fighting advice from you."

"Clearly, you do. You were not taught how to utilise your unique gifts when my sister and uncle were teaching you.

How do you expect to understand your power if *I* do not teach you?"

Nora's eyes flickered in annoyance. He was right. She hated it when he was right. She needed to learn as much as possible, as quickly as possible, and thanks to the lacklustre training she'd received back on Earth, she was further behind than she would have liked.

Not waiting for her to reply, Garvan stepped forward, and instinctively, Nora took a step back.

Garvan lifted a dark eyebrow and took another step towards her.

Nora took another step back.

Smirking and tilting his head, Garvan continued to slowly step towards her, and Nora continued to take large steps back until she was right against the glass door leading to her bedroom.

Stiffening, Nora drew herself to her full height as Garvan took a final step towards her. He rested his hands on either side of her head and leaned in, his voice low as he whispered, "I like games of cat and mouse. I am happy to play instead of train if that is what you would prefer."

Clenching her jaw, Nora ignored the shiver that ran down her spine as Garvan's breath tickled her ear. She placed a hand on Garvan's leather-bound chest.

Leaning in, Nora looked up at Garvan through her lashes and opened her mouth to speak before blasting him away from her. "I'm not in the mood for games."

Garvan's eyes widened for a fraction of a second as Nora caught him off guard, and he fingered the new smoking hole which had appeared on the front of his black leather shirt.

A crooked grin slowly appeared as he absently played with

the burnt area. "Feisty. I like that about you."

Nora swallowed a gag. "I thought we were going to train."

"Stop repressing your emotions."

Nora looked at Garvan incredulously. "What?"

"Your emotions are the source of your power. It is called *life* energy for a reason. It is bound to your life. Your being. The more you repress yourself, the less you are going to be able to tap into that life energy when you need it."

"You're one to talk. You have zero feelings! If you can wield your powers without a single emotion, surely I can as well."

Garvan's eyes flickered, and, for the first time, Nora saw a flash of frustration cross his face.

"I am not void of emotions."

Nora snorted.

"Just because I do not choose to share them with you does not mean they are not there."

Rolling her eyes, Nora pushed away from the glass door and walked towards Garvan. "You wouldn't be destroying the Realm if you truly had a heart."

"I am *saving* the Realm," Garvan hissed, and Nora's heart skipped a beat. Whether this was due to fear or something else, she wasn't sure, so she pushed the reaction out of her mind and rolled her eyes.

"The fact you cannot see that goes to show how green you are when it comes to the Realm," Garvan added, taking a step towards Nora again. This time, instead of retreating, Nora took one towards him as well.

"You have two options. I can train you and teach you to wield your power in ways you never imagined, or you can continue to be wilfully ignorant of everything happening around you and continue relying on pathetic energy balls to fight your battles."

Nora didn't reply straight away, trying to figure out the catch.

Exhaling loudly through his nose, Garvan squeezed his eyes shut for a moment before turning on his heel. "Suit yourself."

Before he could take a step towards the door, and without realising what she was doing, Nora leapt forwards, gripping Garvan's wrist over the cuff of his shirt.

"Teach me," was all she said. He paused, then turned to look at her. "Teach me."

Chapter 39 - Noah

"What's Tick doing here?" Layla whispered. "I thought Nora created her. How is she alive in this timeline?"

Noah shrugged, watching Tick and Marian chatting and walking together, his chest tight.

"Actually," Layla went on, "how was Tick alive in the other timeline? Nora hadn't created her there yet either."

"Garvan is playing with time," Simmy whispered back, her voice strained. "He is making sure his allies are in these timelines before they should be."

"This is bad," Aaron said. "The Realm is already unstable. If he keeps pulling it apart like this, it is going to collapse completely."

"If he's trying to become the most powerful person in the universe, what use is pushing the Realm like this? If the Realm is gone, there will be no power left for him to rule with," Noah muttered to Aaron, keeping an eye on Tick and Marian to make sure they didn't see them.

"Because he is insane," Aaron replied under his breath. "Yet, there must be something we are missing."

Before Noah could reply, Simmy let out a shaky breath. Noah turned to her.

"I cannot believe Marian is working with Tick," Simmy hissed. "What could possess her to do such a thing?"

Noah saw Layla place an arm around her aunt and open her mouth to comfort her, but Aaron interrupted them with a "Shh!", waving a hand behind him to get their attention as he peered through the branches. "They are saying something."

"Garvan is almost ready for the final extraction," Marian said.

"Good," Tick replied. "He's been in a foul mood ever since he grabbed the boy. The sooner we're finished with him, the better."

"Why did he not just grab both twins?" Marian asked. "Why not become even more powerful? It is not like they were going to put up a fight."

"Something about wanting a backup." Tick waved the question off. "I dunno, really. The girl must be in reserve in case the boy doesn't provide enough life energy."

Marian shrugged. "It does not make much sense. If it were up to me, I would have grabbed them both and kept the other locked away here, so neither of them could escape."

Tick gave a loud laugh, tendrils of shadow floating away from her as she threw her head back. "Yeah, but you're ruthless."

Marian grinned.

"Speaking of ruthless," Tick continued, "how's everything going with your plan for Zion?"

"I have been keeping him busy, making sure he does not have time to check on Earth. He does not even know one of the twins is missing. Even *he* doesn't have eyes everywhere." Marian gave a low laugh while Tick cackled.

"I can't believe he hasn't realised you're working with us."

"My siblings were stupid not to take the chance when it was offered to them. There is only one way this will end, and it is with Garvan on top."

Noah clenched his fists as the two of them walked past, keeping them clenched until they were too far away to hear what they were saying anymore. Amber electricity sparked from his closed fists, and he felt Zion's life force threatening to spill over.

"Calm down, Noah." Aaron's warning whisper rang in his ears, and he felt Layla and Simmy each place a firm hand on his shoulders.

Taking a deep breath and releasing it, Noah watched the retreating backs of Tick and Marian, and vowed to prove them wrong. Garvan wasn't going to succeed. "We need to find the Noah from this timeline. Quickly."

"We know," Layla said gently, keeping a firm grip on his shoulder, "but we can't just rush in there without a plan. The boy will be killed in an instant."

"Pass me Arel's ring," Aaron said, holding out his hand. "We need to see what is going on."

Noah slid the large ring off his finger and handed it over, watching as Aaron slipped it on.

Faded images of Garvan flickered in and out of view, and Aaron grunted, frustrated, shaking his hand, trying to get the ring to work.

"What's going on?" Noah asked.

"The Arel in this timeline has sunk deeper into this petrification, so the ring is struggling to find a connection to him," Aaron replied.

"What does that mean?" Layla questioned, worry lacing her tone.

Aaron and Simmy looked at each other before turning to Noah and Layla. "You two need to stay here," Simmy said, her voice serious as she pulled her thick auburn hair into a high ponytail. "Aaron and I will go and investigate Garvan's temple to get an idea of what is going on, then we will come back for you."

"We should come with you. We're the Primary Guardians!" Noah insisted, moving to step out from behind the bush.

"You are *not* coming with us," Aaron said firmly, seeing the hungry look in Noah's eyes. He gripped Noah's wrist, pulling him back. "You need to stay here in case Tick and Marian return. We cannot have them walking in on us in the temple. If they come back, you will need to create a distraction."

Noah pulled out of Aaron's grip. "Fine," he grumbled and felt an electric flicker of energy behind his eyes.

Aaron shot him a look, then turned and clasped Simmy's hand. "Call out if you need us. Ray will be able to send a signal."

"We will," Layla said, waving to the two of them as they disappeared through the portal Aaron had created with his sapphire mandala.

"We should be helping them!" Noah burst out as soon as they disappeared, running his hands through his hair and pacing behind the bush.

Layla, who had grabbed Ray from Simmy before she had gone with Aaron, pulled her out of her pocket and placed Noah's hand on the amethyst.

Noah felt his breathing slow down and relaxed muscles in his face he hadn't realised were tense.

"We need to stay here and keep an eye out for Marian and Tick," Layla repeated gently, holding his finger in place.

"Aaron and Simmy are more equipped to handle an unbalanced Realm than we are, and Aaron's never led us astray before."

Sighing, Noah turned the hand Layla was holding over and clasped hers tightly. "You're right," he said. "I know you're right. I just... I feel so helpless. We're supposed to be the Primary Guardians, but every time we try to train, something comes up, and we're thrown in a new direction."

"You can't expect everything to flow smoothly," Layla said, a soft laugh escaping her lips. "For one, I don't think anything we've ever done has gone to plan, and two, how boring would life be if we could control every little aspect of it?"

Noah gave a small smile, released a long breath and rested his forehead against Layla's.

Layla gripped the hand that was holding hers tightly, silently supporting him.

"I feel like the energy Zion gave me is changing me," Noah admitted quietly after a few moments.

Layla squeezed his hand. "We'll figure it out."

The sound of approaching voices pulled the two of them out of their reverie, and they dropped to the ground. Noah pulled a few sharp branches aside so they could see the path in front of them.

Tick and Marian were approaching again, talking as they went.

"I wonder if the job's done yet," Tick said lazily, inspecting her clawed, shadowy, fingernails.

"Surely we would feel something if Garvan became as powerful as he said he would," Marian replied, shrugging. "Either way, we need to get back."

Tick stopped suddenly, placing an arm out in front of

Marian, and slowly looked around at their surroundings. "Something's not right."

Noah and Layla glanced at each other.

"Does she know we're here?" Layla mouthed to Noah.

Noah shrugged, his body tense.

Marian paused, looking around with Tick. "I cannot see anything." She pushed Tick's hand away from her with a finger. "Come, we need to go."

Taking one last sweeping look around the area, Tick nodded at Marian and followed her in the direction of the temple.

"We need to follow them," Noah whispered to Layla, "slow them down."

Layla nodded. She used Ray to coat them both in a shimmery camouflage.

As they walked, Noah marvelled at how his body adapted and changed to blend in with their surroundings.

"Hurry!" Layla hissed, pulling him forward.

Noah picked up his pace and plucked a few dead twigs from the bushes they passed, merging them into a sharp disk. He threw it into a tree near Marian and Tick, causing a large branch to fall in front of them.

The two jumped out of the way as it landed, and Noah and Layla quickly dove behind a withered-looking shrub. Even though he was sure their camouflage was working, Noah didn't fight the reflex to hide.

Tick grumbled. She used her sharp claws to cut the branch into smaller pieces, then threw them back into the brush.

They set off once again.

This time, Layla used Ray to ignite a spark in the dead leaves on the ground in front of Tick and Marian, forcing them to curse and extinguish it with their feet.

Stifling a laugh, Noah drew a large winding vine with his energy and flung it into their path, causing Marian to trip and Tick to catch her. "What is going on?" Tick exclaimed.

Layla let out a giggle, then froze as Tick's piercing eyes glared at the spot where she was standing.

"Who's there?" Tick called, taking a slow step towards them.

"I cannot see anyone," Marian said, brushing herself off.

"Someone's there, I'm sure of it!" Tick insisted, taking another step towards Noah and Layla.

As slowly as they could, Noah and Layla backed into the brush behind them, trying to make as little noise as possible.

Since they were walking backwards, Noah didn't see the tree root sticking out of the ground until it was too late. His foot caught, and he hit the dirt with a loud thud.

Tick immediately blasted a black energy ball where Noah fell, which Layla deflected, hitting it with the back of her hand.

"I KNEW IT!" Tick screamed, firing off blast after blast in the direction of the two of them. "I KNEW SOMEONE WAS THERE!"

Layla pulled Ray in front of her and ricocheted every blast Tick threw at them while Noah tried desperately to pull his foot free. He was so engrossed in what he was doing that he hadn't noticed Marian sneak up to him, her own body hidden from sight.

"Hurry and get out of here!" she hissed to Noah, causing Layla to stagger in shock, missing one of Tick's blasts. "Go!" Marian insisted, waving her hand over the root, causing it to shrivel up and allowing Noah to free his foot.

"Marian?" Noah exclaimed.

"Go!" she hissed again. "I will catch up to you."

Layla cast a wary look at Noah, who shrugged. Tick was gaining momentum now that Layla was distracted, so they needed to make a decision fast.

"Let's go," he said, taking Layla's hand as she repelled one final energy blast from Tick before stepping through a portal Marian had created.

They were transported to Aaron's treehouse. Noah, having just barely avoided one of Tick's attacks, swatted at the smoke coming off his pants as they steamed.

"What was that about?" Layla asked him as they climbed the ladder. She walked to the window, cautiously watching for anything suspicious.

"I don't know," Noah replied. "We should try and get in touch with Aaron and Simmy, though. Let them know what happened."

"What is wrong?" Aaron's voice cracked through Ray as Layla connected with him.

"We're at—" Noah stopped short at Layla's erratic waving.

"We've had to relocate," Layla jumped in. "Tick and Marian cornered us, but we managed to get away."

"Stay where you are," Aaron's crackly voice insisted. "We are almost done here, and then we will come find you."

The line disconnected.

"Why did you cut me off?" Noah asked.

"I didn't know who else was listening," Layla explained. "We can't risk being found here."

"What do we do now? Just wait?"

"Marian's bound to come to us," Layla said, although she sounded as if she wasn't sure whether that was a good thing or not. "Rest. I'll keep the first watch."

"Are you sure?" Noah stifled a yawn, but exhaustion overtook him. He stumbled over to the large, brown couch in the living room, and the last thing he saw before closing his eyes was Layla's concerned expression.

Chapter 40- Nora

"You are focusing too much."

"You just told me I wasn't focusing enough!"

"You are focusing on the wrong things."

Nora let out a groan of frustration as she unwrapped her legs from their lotus position and punched her numb thigh. "I've decided I don't want you to teach me anymore," she said and waved her hand dismissively towards the door. "Shoo."

Garvan raised a dark eyebrow. Ignoring her request, he gestured for her to fold herself back into her meditative sitting position.

Nora was very tempted not to, but her desire to learn overtook her frustrations, and she did as she was told.

"You are focusing too much on the outcome. You need to focus on the journey."

"Okay, Confucius."

Garvan tilted his head and looked directly at Nora, and she could have sworn he was holding back a sarcastic smile.

"There is so much power within you. It is bubbling right at the surface, and as soon as you tap into it, it is going to explode in ways you never dreamed possible."

"Bubbling potential." Nora inhaled through her nose and exhaled through her mouth slowly four times, then relaxed her shoulders, unclenched her jaw and closed her eyes. "I'm going to die if I have to sit like this every time I want to tap into my powers."

"Then get it right the first time, so you will be able to tap into it whenever you need to," came Garvan's unhelpful reply.

"Exploding powers," Nora muttered to herself, wriggling a little to get comfortable.

More steady breaths coursed in and out of her. She lost count of how many she'd taken as she drifted deeper within herself.

Nora could hear water bubbling. It was louder than the waterfall usually sounded, but she moved past it. Aware it was there, but also acknowledging it wasn't her final destination. Soon, an amber light began to glow brighter and brighter in front of her closed eyelids.

Instinctively, she began to force it away, but something told her to stop, to allow it to continue to glow.

Her eyes began to burn, and her body became uncomfortable, but still, she held focus on the light as it began to overtake her completely.

The more uncomfortable she became, the more she willed herself to stay focused. She pushed past the physical irritations. Just when she felt like she couldn't take it anymore, that she'd reached her limit, the light disappeared, and a warm tingling sensation tickled her from the tips of her toes to the top of her crown.

Slowly, she opened her eyes. She was seeing spots.

She blinked once. They were still there. Twice, the same thing. But, after the third blink, Nora realised it wasn't her vision that was spotty. Droplets of water, which had suspended themselves around her, were impeding her vision.

It had started to rain while she was in her meditation, yet she hadn't felt anything because she had subconsciously suspended the rain around her in mid-air.

Garvan, who hadn't moved while Nora was meditating, was dripping wet. His arms were folded over his chest, raindrops dripping from his hair and over his lips before landing on his arm and absorbing into his black leathers.

Nora shot him a wry grin, feeling her power as it pricked her arms, hands and fingertips.

Garvan raised his eyebrow before Nora flexed her hand, her palm facing upwards. A silent command to the droplets surrounding her to fly at Garvan, as sharp as needles.

The slight shift of Garvan's arm was the only movement he made as he brought his hand up to halt the attack. He managed to stop all of them, except for one.

Catching the trickle of blood dripping down his cheek, Garvan licked it off his finger, his eyes never leaving Nora's.

Nora let out a disgusted groan, the rain falling heavily around her now, and took a step back. Suddenly, Garvan was standing right in front of her, having teleported from his previous spot.

"Looks like I was right." His voice was low as he leant forwards, driving Nora backwards until her heel hit the brick wall which led to her chamber.

"You'll never hear those words come out of my mouth." Nora's own voice was huskier than she'd intended, and she turned her head to clear her throat.

Garvan caught her chin, forcing her to look him in the eye. "You are going to be unstoppable."

"You're not getting a drop of my life energy." Nora narrowed her eyes and lifted her chin defiantly.

Garvan grinned, his gaze dropping to her lips for a brief second, and Nora's heart gave an uncomfortable lurch, goose-bumps pimpling her skin. "You will have to stop me, then."

Nora exhaled in a short burst, the comment throwing her off guard, as Garvan lifted her chin even higher, dipping his face towards hers. His eyes bored into her own as his lips brushed softly against hers for the second time.

Her knees went weak again.

"I thought I told you to stop me," Garvan murmured against her lips, "or am I too distracting?" He let out a low laugh, which snapped Nora back to her senses, but before she could reply, his lips touched hers again, this time harder than before.

Nora could feel her power rushing to her head as the goosebumps on her arms intensified. But, instead of pushing him away, she lifted her hand and roughly grabbed Garvan's hair, pulling him into her more tightly. She wasn't going to give him the chance to control the situation.

If Garvan was surprised by her sudden enthusiasm, he didn't show it. Instead, he dropped his hands to her waist, gripping it tightly as she wrapped her other arm around his neck and bit his lip, forcing him to open his mouth.

Garvan's breathy chuckle melded with Nora's snarl as he lifted her effortlessly up and held her against the wall. She wrapped her legs around his hips, using him as support so she could pull him closer.

Nora shivered as Garvan ran his hands up her sides, feeling them clench as they reached just below her armpits, then run back down. He dug his fingers tightly into her ribs as if he was trying to stop his hands from roaming.

His hair was softer than Nora had been expecting, and she tangled her fingers through it briefly before moving to rest them on his chest.

Her lips were bruised, her breath was ragged, and she was certain she'd lost her mind, but her power was still within her. Besides that first sip, he hadn't taken a drop.

"If that is how you plan to stop me, I am going to attempt to take your life energy more often." Garvan's voice was more gravelly than normal, and Nora was pleased to see that his normally expressionless exterior was ruffled. His hair was out of place, his lips were just as bruised as hers, and his breathing was laboured.

He squeezed her one last time with rough fingers before lowering her unhooked feet back to the ground. Nora couldn't help but shiver at the cool air sweeping between them as he took a step back.

"You're not getting my life energy." The threat sounded empty, even to Nora. Garvan let out a breathless laugh.

"I can see that," he said, running a hand through his hair, messing it up even further. "That doesn't mean I will not try."

Suddenly, as if a switch was flipped, his demeanour turned cold once more. "As much as I enjoyed that, the Realm is my priority, and you are the best way to keep it safe."

Nora shivered again. This time it wasn't the cold air that bothered her. It was Garvan's cold exterior.

"Keep training," was all he said before turning on his heel and stalking back inside, wiping his feet on the doormat to stop from trekking water through the room.

It was only then that Nora realised it was still raining, and she stepped back into the downpour, willing it to cool her body down.

At that single thought, the water turned icy cold, and a bucket load dropped over her head.

Gasping for air, Nora wiped the now-drenched strands of hair out of her face, then threw her head back, enjoying the spattering of rain on her face for a while longer. After a few minutes, she opened the glass door to her bedroom, stripped off her leathers and left them in a wet pile on the floor. She then padded to the bathroom, turning on a hot shower.

She needed to get a grip on herself. Otherwise, she'd ruin everything and probably die in the process.

Stepping into the steaming stream of water, Nora let the heat soak into her chilled bones.

Garvan wasn't going to stop what he was doing, which meant it was time for a new strategy.

It was time to explore the temple.

Chapter 41 - Noah

"Are we going to take this Garvan back home?"

"We have no choice. We cannot keep him here."

"What about Noah? What's going to happen to him?"

"Zion knew the risks when he transferred his life energy, but keeping Noah alive is more important right now. Without Zion's energy, the Realm will drain everything out of him. All we can do is try to keep Zion's life energy from overflowing."

"What will happen if it overflows?"

"...Noah will become uncontrollable."

Noah's mind slipped in and out of consciousness before he realised the voices he could hear were right in front of him.

"What do you mean Noah will be uncontrollable?"

"Zion is a Celestial. He shouldered the burden of Earth's needs for an eternity until the Realm woke me, his brother, up and helped Zion create Simmy and the other Guardians as the Earth's needs grew. Can you imagine the power that runs through him? Can you imagine what even a *speck* of that power would do to a human? If Noah cannot learn to control this power… there is no telling what could happen."

The silence that followed Aaron's statement was deafening, and a shiver ran through Noah's spine.

Why would Zion risk giving him that energy?

"You are forgetting the most important thing."

A new voice had appeared.

"Marian?" Aaron growled. "What are you doing here?"

"I told the kids I would come see them shortly after I helped them escape from Tick," Marian said matter-of-factly. "I can only assume by the fact you are not locked up in a dark room somewhere that you are from an alternate timeline. The original one, perhaps?"

Aaron grunted in response.

Marian hummed, then continued talking. "Zion went from shouldering the Earth's needs by himself to dividing the tasks between the original twelve Guardians and you, Aaron. He then included Garvan and also had you create relics to channel the more potent of the Realm's pure energy, which cannot be controlled through our bodies themselves."

The room was silent, so Marian went on.

"Zion lost all of that support in an instant when Garvan petrified us siblings and forced Simmy to Earth. He even lost the support of you, Aaron, when he sent you to keep an eye on Garvan as a Shadow Being. So, all the energy that had been divided up was now forced back into Zion. He needed an outlet, and Noah needed energy. He is slipping and does not want you to know it."

"What does that have to do with the life energy he gave Noah?" Layla asked.

"Normally, he would never have done it," Aaron said slowly. "His life energy is pure Realm energy. It is far too much for a human to handle, regardless of whether that human had become a Guardian or not."

"Exactly," Marian said, "so, while you are all here trying to stop Garvan, Zion is alone with this energy coursing through him and is slipping more and more each day. He was probably aching to get rid of some of it in any way he could."

"Zion saved Noah," Simmy said defensively, folding her arms across her chest.

"Noah needed the energy, absolutely," Aaron said. "There is no denying that, but it was still a dangerous move, one that wasn't fully thought through. I wonder…" he trailed off.

"Wonder?" Noah asked, shifting in the bed to indicate he had woken.

"I wonder if Garvan planned this," Aaron said, glancing at Noah as he perched himself up on an elbow. "I wonder if Garvan is hoping to make Zion sloppy in his decisions. Maybe he is going to try to absorb Zion's power, too."

As soon as the words left Aaron's mouth, goosebumps sprouted along Noah's arms.

"What does he need Nora for, then?" Noah asked, feeling Zion's life energy start to tingle in his veins.

"Nora is powerful for an Earthling," Simmy answered. "The way the energy from the Realm works with her… she was even able to use it on Earth, something only Guardians can usually do. I imagine Garvan believes her to be the most powerful, more valuable twin."

"But now that Zion has transferred some of his life energy to you, Noah, Garvan has his pick of the two of you," Marian finished. "You need to get back to your timeline as soon as possible. You need to help Zion," she said, pointing to Aaron and Simmy. "And you two," she added, turning to Noah and Layla, "you need to keep Garvan from absorbing power from any of your duplicates in these alternate timelines."

"Did you capture the Garvan here?" Noah asked Aaron. He had almost forgotten why they had come to this timeline in the first place.

Aaron held up a small red stone and smirked. "I trapped him in here. I do not think this was the smartest duplicate. He did not even see us coming."

"And little Noah?" Noah asked.

"Home with his family," Simmy said. "I took him back myself."

"I am going to take Tick and use her to help me unpetrify my siblings here," Marian said. "I feel bad. I created a half portal and trapped her in one of the trees back there." Marian tried to hide her smile at the thought. "She is not a bad being. She just… has bad role models."

Marian pulled Aaron and Simmy into a hug, then patted Noah and Layla on their heads. "Do not let him get away with this."

"We won't," Layla replied before shooting Noah a look and a nod, handing Ray over so he could channel some more of Zion's life energy through her.

"Good luck," Marian said, and she stepped back.

Noah relaxed as the life energy flowed through his veins into Ray. With the smallest thought, he created a portal, and the group arrived back in the kitchen at Zion's palace with a small *pop*.

As soon as they arrived, Noah knew something was wrong. The palace was cold, and Zion's presence couldn't be felt anywhere.

"Guys," Layla said, waving them to a large window. "Look at this."

Noah, Simmy and Aaron walked over and gasped. Simmy's hand flew to her mouth.

Every blade of grass on the field outside was dead. The

trees had wilted, and the flowering shrubs had all turned into thorny bushes.

"Garvan must have come here. Zion should not have been trying to control all that power by himself! He left himself wide open for an attack!" Aaron cried furiously.

"Well, he's not by himself anymore," Noah said to him, placing a hand on Aaron's shoulder. "We're going to get him."

Chapter 42 - Noah

"Get… him?" Simmy replied, her eyebrows rising so high they were almost hidden in her hairline.

"What other choice do we have?" Noah shot back.

"*Not* jumping head-first into the lair of an evil mastermind?" suggested Simmy.

"We are not going on a rescue mission," Aaron said flatly.

"Why not?" Noah asked, incredulous. "That's what we've been doing in the other timelines. Why can't we do it here?"

"This is different," Layla interjected. "The other Realms are duplicates. While the people in them are very much alive, they're created based on the people living here. We don't know what will happen to the duplicate if one of us is hurt. The Realm's energies are all over the place. There's a good chance they'll die."

"So we just sit back and do nothing?" Noah argued, pushing himself back from the window, frustrated. "Let Garvan get hold of Zion's life energy and allow him to completely take over everything?"

"Of course not!" Layla replied hotly. The tone of her voice stopped Noah in his tracks, and he turned to her, wincing under her narrowed gaze.

"Garvan is not going to get hold of Zion's life energy," Aaron said calmly.

"How do you know?" asked Noah.

"Because, even in his worst state of mind, Zion would rather die than let Garvan get his hands on that power."

Silence fell over the room.

"Do you really think that will happen?" Layla asked softly.

Aaron paused before answering, rubbing the bridge of his nose with his thumb and forefinger. "No," he replied. "I don't… look, Zion is not in a great place at the moment, but that does not mean he is completely helpless. He just needs some support, so that is what we are going to provide for him."

"How?" Noah questioned.

"You two," Aaron said, pointing at Noah and Layla, "are going to check out the next timeline. Simmy and I are going to take on some of the load Zion's been carrying."

"It is time I take back some of my Guardian responsibilities," Simmy agreed.

"You are not a Primary Guardian now. Make sure you are not taking on more than you can handle," Aaron warned her gently. "But you can start to syphon some of the energy Zion has taken on board and link your life force with his, so he knows you are here to support him. I will do the same."

"Aye aye, captain!" Simmy saluted Aaron and turned on her heel, running to the Earth room to begin the process right away.

Aaron turned to Noah and Layla. "You two need to get to the next timeline. With Zion gone, we do not know how much time we have left or what Garvan has got planned for you, Noah. We cannot risk you being here."

271

"You're sure we can't help with Zion?" Noah pressed, anxious to be useful.

"You are. By going to the next timeline," Aaron persisted, giving them a crooked smile. "Now, go."

Nodding, Noah grabbed Layla's hand, gripped Ray in the other and created a portal.

With a familiar *pop*, they stepped through and landed in the new timeline.

"ARGH!" Layla screamed, and Noah felt a sharp pull on his arm as she launched the two of them onto the grass. A motorised scooter weaved past them honking its horn.

From the ground, Noah looked around and saw that their little town was completely overrun with people.

He'd never seen such a big crowd here before. Cars were backed up, the traffic was moving at a snail's pace, and people were riding bikes, scooters, and running in all directions. Even the sidewalks were packed, with pedestrians squeezed together on the path.

"Layla!" a familiar voice called out, and both Noah and Layla turned to see the Nora of this timeline running towards them.

"You need to be more careful. These people are going crazy trying to get a front-row seat for the speech."

Before either Noah or Layla could ask what she was talking about, Nora grabbed Layla's hand, helped her up and planted a soft kiss on her lips.

Noah's eyes widened, and his mouth dropped. Layla's eyes matched his own as they darted quickly to him.

"Noah!" Nora turned to him. "You should be watching out for her! What were you doing standing in the middle of the road?"

Noah's mouth opened and closed a few times. "Uhhh… um, well, we were, uh…"

"We were trying to get a good seat for the speech too, and we got pushed onto the road," Layla interjected for him, tentatively squeezing Nora's hand.

"You should have just waited for me. I told you I got front-row tickets. C'mon!" Turning on her heel, Nora ran off, pulling Layla behind her and leaving Noah to scramble up off the floor and stumble after the two girls.

Panting, he caught up to them as Nora stopped at a barricaded gate, just in time for Nora to hand him a ticket to present to the bouncers at the front of their town's showground.

The field was covered with people setting up picnic blankets and lawn chairs while a few hundred white plastic seats sat near the front of the stage, which only a select few had access to.

Grabbing for Noah, Nora turned to him. "We can't be getting lost now. Stay close."

Nodding dumbly, Noah let his sister grip his wrist and weave him and Layla through the thick crowd until they found their seats right in front of the centre of the stage.

"I told you I got us good seats," Nora said smugly.

"You sure did," Noah chuckled nervously. He leaned towards Layla as Nora turned to rummage through her backpack. "Did you happen to see anything that said what this speech is about?" he whispered to her.

"No," Layla whispered back, "but I don't think we'll have to wait long to find out." She pointed to the curtain right as a person stepped into view, and Noah recoiled in horror.

"What's wrong?" Nora asked him as she found the notebook

she'd been looking for.

"Nothing. Sorry," Noah said stiffly, not meeting his sister's eyes.

"Okay..." Nora replied slowly. She put her arm around Layla and began whispering in her ear.

Noah heard Layla's forced laugh as she chatted quietly to Nora, trying to steal glances at Noah every chance she got. She too had recoiled when the curtains opened.

"Isn't he the best?" Nora said. She cheered with the rest of the crowd, pulling her arm off Layla and jumping up and down.

Taking this chance to shift closer to Layla, Noah looked at her with wide eyes. "What is he doing here?"

"I don't know," Layla hissed in reply, "but it can't be good."

Rubbing his face in his hands, Noah turned back to the stage, where Garvan had taken hold of a microphone and was greeting the crowd.

"Thank you for that warm welcome," he said, smiling at his audience.

"He's undergone his rebirth in this timeline," Noah whispered to Layla.

"I can see that," Layla replied. "Do you think he has gotten hold of Noah from here?"

"Nora didn't seem surprised to see me when we arrived, so I doubt it."

"What are you two whispering about?" Nora asked, taking a break from cheering with the rest of the crowd.

"We were... um... we were just wondering..." Noah started.

"We were just wondering how long Garvan's going to stay in town," Layla chimed in, taking Nora's hand. "Do you know?"

"I'm not sure," Nora replied, placing her other hand over

the top of their enclosed ones. "I can ask Mum, though. She's offered him a stay at our place."

Noah choked on the breath he'd just taken. "What?" he spluttered. "Why would he be staying at our place?"

Nora gave him a weird look. "Where else would he be staying?"

Noah looked at Layla, who was trying to keep the surprise from her face as Nora talked to her.

Before he could press his sister for more answers, Noah was knocked to the ground by a man trying to push his way to the front of the stage. By the time he'd gotten up, Nora had turned away and was watching Garvan again.

"I'm going to see if I can find out more about why Garvan would be staying at my parents' house," Noah muttered to Layla, his shoulder throbbing where the man had hit it. "You stay here and listen to what Garvan's saying. Try and see what he has planned for this place."

"Right," Layla replied, "be careful." She leaned in to give him a kiss, but Noah pulled away quickly, giving her an apologetic look and nodding towards Nora.

Layla sighed and squeezed his hand instead. "See you soon."

"See you soon," Noah repeated, glancing at Nora to make sure she wouldn't notice him slip away.

Deciding to head straight for his house, Noah put his hands in his pockets, feeling Ray's warmth. He took a deep breath and released Zion's life energy, feeling it flow between the two of them.

He pulled Ray out, allowed her to expand to her proper size, and watched as her electricity sparked. He'd purposely forgotten to give Ray back to Layla. He knew what the power was doing to him and the pressure he was under to control it, but he also knew he absolutely wouldn't let Garvan get his hands on it.

A loud laugh pulled Noah from his reverie, and he looked around to see where it was coming from.

Horrified, he quickly dived behind the nearest tree as he saw Noah and Mia from this timeline slowly strolling towards the showgrounds.

"Why do you even want to go to this thing?" the other Noah asked. "You don't care about this stuff."

"Nora asked us to come," Mia replied, lightly punching his arm, "and we should be there to support her. She really believes he can make a difference."

Noah sighed, placed his arm around Mia's shoulders and kissed her on the lips. "You're too good, you know that?"

Mia laughed. "Too good for you, maybe!" She stuck out her tongue at him and began to run towards the showgrounds.

"Hey!" Noah said, feigning hurt and chasing after her. "That's mean!"

Waiting for them to run out of sight, Noah placed his face in his hands. *Are we going to be dating all our friends?* he asked himself. *Mia, this time?!*

As he slowly stepped back into the open, Noah hoped that Layla would realise the Noah showing up to meet her wasn't him. He figured she would because the other Noah was wearing khaki cargo pants and a black hoodie while he was still in his jeans and t-shirt.

As he walked along the main road, something kept catching his eye, so he sped up a little to see what it was. It wasn't anything he'd seen on this street in his own timeline.

It didn't take long for Noah to realise it was a large—very large—sign welcoming people to the town's top B&B,

renowned for hosting the best of the best. Not only that, the sign was right over his house!

Slowing down his normal walking pace, Noah looked at the offending sign in horror. *I guess this is why Garvan's staying at our place tonight.*

Running his hands over his face, Noah hesitantly walked around the back of the house and saw a fancy granny flat in the backyard, fully furnished, with a jacuzzi sitting near the front door.

He had to stifle a laugh as he took in the ridiculousness of it all and wondered how on Earth he was supposed to capture Garvan when he was sitting at the dining room table with him and his parents.

"Noah? What are you doing back?"

Turning around, Noah saw the Layla of this timeline, dressed in a yellow sundress and sandals, looking at him curiously. "Didn't you just go off with Mia?"

"Oh, well..." Noah fumbled for an explanation.

"Did you come back to help Josh and Max?"

Grateful she had given him the perfect excuse, Noah nodded his head wildly. "Yup," he said. "Yes, that's exactly what I'm doing back here. Mia... err, Mia went on ahead. I told her I'd meet her there."

"Okay..." Layla looked at him, unconvinced. "The boys are upstairs. Max is falling over his feet, as you can imagine, and Josh is completely oblivious, as always. Maybe the job will get done quicker with you there to help."

Not knowing what Layla was talking about in the slightest, Noah nodded and pointed in the direction of the house. "Great!" he said, exponentially more enthusiastically than he felt. "I'll help Max to stop... er, tripping over his feet, and maybe try and help Josh see… what's right in front of him…?"

"Okay," Layla said again, searching his face curiously. "Did you get changed?"

"No!" Noah replied more forcefully than he'd intended. "No," he said again, softly this time. He stepped towards the house. "I was wearing this before."

Layla took a step towards him.

"Well, you'd better go. You know Nora hates it when we're late."

Layla looked at the time, then looked at Noah once more, her eyes narrowing. "I'll see you at the showgrounds, then," she said slowly, turning on her heel and sauntering down the driveway.

Noah sighed and rubbed his eyes. This timeline was going to be tricky.

Opening the back door, the familiar creak settling Noah's nerves, he looked around the kitchen. His eyes landed on the clock hanging on the wall, and he groaned as he realised he didn't have much time before Layla got to the showgrounds, found the other Noah already there, and saw Nora kissing another Layla.

It was messy, but he hoped he would be able to get some more information from the boys and then escape to Simmy's with Layla safely in tow.

It sounded like a long shot even to him, but he had to try.

Squeezing his hands even tighter around Ray, Noah sent Layla the image of the other Layla heading towards the showgrounds.

He hoped she'd receive the message and come up with an excuse to leave.

Walking through the living room, Noah heard some muffled voices from above and the sound of something heavy hitting a wall. Taking this as a sign that Josh and Max were upstairs, he walked towards the noise.

Once he reached the landing, Noah quickly looked in the first three rooms before coming to his own bedroom, which was in the process of being rearranged.

"Max," Josh said patiently, "this is the third time you've bumped into the wall. What are you looking at?"

Noah peeked around the corner and was surprised to see Max's eyes brighten in embarrassment. His dark skin also seemed flushed. This was something that would have gone unnoticed by most people, but Noah, who'd seen the reaction many times before when his friend had been chasing Mia, recognised the implication behind it immediately. A grin spread across his face.

Now he understood what Layla had meant about Josh being oblivious as the redhead was looking at Max curiously.

"I—I, well…" Max took a deep breath. "I was looking at, ah… well…"

Noah waited a minute to see if Max would be able to put his feelings into words, but seeing him stumble over himself while Josh looked at him patiently tugged on his heartstrings, and he decided to step in.

"Knock knock," he said, lightly rapping his knuckles on the door.

"Noah!" Max said, breathing a sigh of relief as Josh turned away from him. "What are you doing 'ere, mate?"

"Mia let me come back and give you guys a hand," Noah replied. "What exactly am I giving you a hand with?"

"Your mum asked us to rearrange your room to create more space for the guests while they're here," Josh replied. Seeing

Noah's confused look, he continued. "While you're staying at Mia's house this week… because of all the guests who checked in for the speech…" he said slowly.

Noah chuckled and ran his hand nervously through his dirty blond hair. "Yes. Of course. Yup. I knew that. Show me what I can do."

"You can help me move this bedside table to the corner over here, then we've got to strip the bed and move it over here, too," Josh said. He lifted the table with Noah. "Max?" Josh called, turning towards Max, who had been looking at Josh with a giddy smile on his face.

"Yes?" Max replied too quickly, straightening up and averting his eyes.

"You okay?" Josh asked, placing the bedside table down in its new spot and walking over to Max, placing the back of his hand on his forehead. "You feel hot."

Max gave a breathy laugh and swiped away Josh's hand. "I'm fine," he replied, his voice an octave higher than usual. "What do you need help with?"

Not looking convinced, Josh took a step closer. "Are you sure?" he asked, raising his hand again.

"Yup!" Max laughed, launching himself onto the bed closest to him. "You know what? I'll take these sheets off and get some new ones."

Moving quicker than Noah had ever seen him, Max ripped the sheets off the bed and ran out of the room towards the laundry.

"He's been acting really weird lately. Have you noticed?" Josh asked Noah as they pushed the bed away from the wall, ready to move it beside the bedside table.

Noah laughed. "Only around you," he said softly.

"What?"

"I haven't noticed anything," Noah replied louder, picking up the bed and moving it across the room.

"Done," he said, brushing his hands.

"Let's go see if Max is alright," Josh said, worried.

"You first." Noah gestured towards the door.

Walking down the stairs behind Josh, Noah let his mind wander absently, so he didn't notice when Josh stopped abruptly and walked straight into him with an 'oomph'.

"Sorry…" Noah began, but when he looked up, he saw the reason why Josh had stopped in his tracks.

Standing at the base of the stairs with a ropeable Nora were two Laylas, the other Noah and Mia.

"What. Is. Going. On?" Nora said, stepping forward angrily.

Chapter 43 - Noah

N oah looked from the furious Nora and the two Laylas, the one from this timeline holding his Layla in a vice-like grip, to the other Noah, who was staring at him like he'd seen a ghost.

"Hey," his Layla said through a grimace, trying to tug free and wincing under the other Layla's grip.

Pushing past Josh, Noah stormed towards her, his eyes flashing angrily as she was pulled roughly away from him.

"Let her go," he growled. The tone of his voice surprised the other Layla enough for her to loosen her grip for a fraction of a second, giving Noah the chance to quickly tug Layla free and pull her behind him.

"Who are you?" Josh asked the two of them slowly as Max walked over to him and placed a gentle hand on his arm to make sure he was okay.

"You wouldn't believe us if we told you," Noah replied.

"Try us," Mia challenged, gripping the other Noah's hand so hard his fingers started to turn blue.

Noah shot Layla a look, and she shrugged, rubbing her sore wrist. "What do we have to lose?"

Trying to think of a way to explain the situation without sounding crazy, Noah pulled Ray out of his pocket and placed her on Layla's wrist, allowing soft blue healing energy to flow through her.

The others watched wordlessly as Noah and Ray worked, their mouths hanging open as the redness around Layla's wrist disappeared.

"Are you aliens?" the other Noah whispered.

"No, we're not aliens," Noah retorted, tucking Ray back into his pocket. "We're just from another timeline."

"Another… timeline..?" Nora repeated, her voice dubious. "And what, may I ask, are you doing here?"

"You're not going to believe us!" Noah insisted again. "Look, just let us go so we can do what we came here to do, and you can all move on with your lives."

"Nuh-uh. Not 'appening," Max said, putting a protective arm around Josh. "I can't believe I left you in there alone with him!"

"I'm fine," Josh insisted, patting Max's arm reassuringly. "Noah didn't do anything except help me move some furniture. We should let them explain."

Max looked at him incredulously for a moment before turning to the rest of his friends. "If Josh thinks we should hear what they 'ave to say, maybe we hear 'em out."

Nora scoffed. "Of course you'd say that. You're so in lo—"

"I AGREE!" said Noah from this timeline, cutting his sister off quickly and shooting her a glare. "Josh has a point. These guys have had the chance to hurt us, but they haven't."

"Speak for yourself!" the other Layla exclaimed furiously. "You're not the one who just walked in on your girlfriend kissing someone else!"

"I didn't *know* it was someone else!" Nora implored. "She deceived me!"

"I didn't *deceive* you!" Layla defended herself from behind Noah. "You never gave me a chance to explain!"

"You had ages to explain, and you weren't exactly pulling away from me!"

"Well, you kissed me right when we first arrived! You caught me off-guard!"

"How did you not know that wasn't me?" the Layla from this timeline injected, turning to her girlfriend. "As if I would ever wear what she's wearing."

"I thought you were being ironic!" Nora shot back. "And why are you on her side?!"

"Okay, OKAY!" Noah interrupted the argument, rubbing the bridge of his nose with his thumb and forefinger. "Enough. We're sorry. We didn't mean to make a mess of things. It's just... we're running out of time. My sister"—he nodded at Nora—"from our timeline is in serious danger, and we need to stop the Garvan of this timeline from absorbing the power he's here for, so we're not putting her in even more danger."

"Garvan?" Nora scoffed again. "Garvan is here on a peace mission. He's been helping people all over the world. He's helped bring clean water to third-world countries, and he's working to end world hunger!"

"We get it," the other Noah said to his sister, "he's a good guy, but what else do we know about him? What has he done before this? Everything he's doing could be a front, or he could be trying to make up for something he's done in the past." he turned to Noah and Layla. "How would you know if he was on track to 'absorbing' that power he needs?"

"Well," Layla glanced at Noah as she hesitated, "he would have captured either yourself or Nora."

"What?" the twins replied in unison.

"You two were born with some help from a place called the Realm of Intention—well, in our timeline you were—and some of that power resides in you guys here as well," Layla replied. "He needs to absorb that power to make himself stronger."

"Realm of Intention?" Nora asked, putting her hands on her hips. "What's a Realm of Intention?"

"Oh yeah," Noah said, scratching the back of his head. "We didn't cover that."

"It sounds complicated," Josh said, pulling out of Max's grip and walking towards Noah. "But I, for one, don't want to see my friends getting 'absorbed', so whatever it is you need to do, I'm with you."

Noah smiled at him and rapped his freckled arm with his knuckles affectionately. "Thank you."

Josh returned the smile and turned to Max. "What about you?"

Max had his arms folded and was tapping his foot on the floor, seemingly fighting within himself. "Fine," he relented, taking two big steps and placing his body protectively between Josh and Noah and Layla. "But only to make sure you two aren't up to no good."

"Understood," Noah replied, forcing the corners of his mouth down to stop from smiling. He knew there was nothing Josh could ask that Max would say no to. The amount of hoops Mia had made Max jump through in their timeline made many great memories.

"I need to keep an eye on you so you don't go after my girlfriend again," Layla from this timeline interjected, grabbing Nora's hand and eyeing her double. "I'm watching you."

"You have my word. I won't be kissing your girlfriend again," Layla said, almost laughing, before pulling Noah's face towards hers and kissing him smack-bang on the lips to emphasise her point.

"Oh, right. That's good then," the other Layla replied, pulling Nora towards her and doing the same.

Mia and the other Noah both sighed and walked towards Max and Josh. "I'm not really interested in having my boyfriend become bad guy goop, so I guess I'm in," Mia said.

"Yeah, and I'm not really interested in *becoming* bad guy goop, so I'll definitely come along," the other Noah added, standing behind his girlfriend.

"Well, what do we need to do?" Nora asked. "What's the plan?"

"The plan?" Noah drew the question out. "Well… I guess we find Garvan, and we… stop him… from absorbing you."

"Great," Max replied sarcastically. "Do you want me to whip out the anti-absorbing spray, or do you 'ave some out back?"

"I've got some out back," Noah quipped back without missing a beat.

Josh laughed and patted Max's hand. "Calm down."

Max grunted and puffed out his chest, absent-mindedly rubbing his hand where Josh had patted it.

"So we need to, what?" Nora asked, "kidnap Garvan?"

"Kidnap Garvan? That does not sound very pleasant."

The group froze, then turned slowly to the back door, where Garvan had let himself in.

"What are you doing here?" Nora squeaked.

"I am staying here, remember?" Garvan replied coolly, taking a step towards the group, who collectively stiffened.

"You're early."

"I finished my set and decided to come back to rest. Now,"—Garvan took another step forward—"what did we mean by 'kidnap Garvan?'"

The group each took a step back, all trying to keep the distance between themselves and Garvan at a maximum.

Noah held his arm out to keep Layla behind him. He felt Ray shudder, and Zion's life energy began to crackle from his fingertips.

Gripping Ray tightly, Noah felt her heat up under his touch. He pulled her out of his pocket, watching as his life energy ran through her embedded stones.

"We didn't mean to literally kidnap you," the other Noah chuckled nervously. "We meant to kidnap you to ask about the new projects you're working on, to see if we could help."

The group all nodded, giving unconvincing outbursts of 'yeah' and 'yup'.

Garvan took another step towards the group, eyeing them all suspiciously, before he stopped in his tracks, looking from the Layla and Noah in front of him to the Layla and Noah standing to the side.

The room held its breath as Garvan narrowed his eyes. "You're not from this timeline," he said, pointing to the Noah and Layla closest to him.

Layla gripped Noah's arm tightly, her fingernails digging into his skin.

Ray grew even warmer, and Noah clutched her tighter, holding her out for Layla to take as well.

"You are from the original timeline," Garvan continued, Ray catching his eye, "and by the look of those new gems, you have been to a few other timelines too."

Noah's breath caught in his throat, but he squared his

shoulders, refusing to back down.

Garvan put his hands up in surrender. "This belongs to you," he said, pulling a mandala out of his pocket.

The emeralds embedded in the relic twinkled as the light bounced off them.

Ray burned white-hot, but Noah didn't let go. The power of this timeline's mandala washed over him.

"Aaron from this timeline made this mandala for me before I descended to Earth," Garvan said, placing the mandala on the floor in front of him and taking a step back.

"Why are you saying it belongs to us?" Noah asked, narrowing his eyes in suspicion.

"What are you doing here if not to capture one of the twins?" Layla demanded. She looked at the rest of the group, who had been standing still in anticipation, watching the situation in front of them unfold.

"I was created to help my original, the Garvan from your timeline"—he nodded at Noah and Layla—"become more powerful. But I do not want to do that. I love the Earth. I want to see it flourish. Zion, Aaron, the Guardians and I have been working to heal the planet."

"How do we know you're not lying?" Josh asked, stepping away from the group while Max tried and failed to keep him where he was.

"Take a look for yourself," Garvan said, gesturing towards the mandala on the floor near his feet. "Emeralds are the symbol of truth and love. If I were being dishonest, this would not have an ounce of power."

Josh walked towards the mandala on the floor, looked back at his friends, and then bent to pick it up.

Before Noah and Layla could stop him, Josh's fingertip

brushed one of the emeralds, and blinding light exploded from it.

"Josh!" Max called, rushing forward to catch him as he stumbled. "What did you do to 'im?!" he demanded of Garvan, brushing stray red hairs from Josh's forehead.

Josh's eyes were wide as he looked from Max to Garvan and then to Noah and Layla standing to the side of the room. "Is that the place you're trying to protect?"

Garvan nodded.

"It's beautiful," Josh said breathlessly.

"It really is," Layla replied, stepping out from behind Noah. "Are you okay?" she asked Josh, walking over to him and crouching down.

Noah handed Ray over to her, and the familiar blue healing light ran from Ray, through Layla and into Josh.

"I'm fine," Josh replied, sitting up and smiling at the worried look on Max's face.

"That mandala is ready to be united with your own," Garvan said, gesturing to the relic lying on the floor where Josh had left it. "It has been jittery, and I had wondered if it meant you had arrived."

"Why are you helping them?" the other Noah asked.

Garvan hesitated. "I do not know," he admitted. "Maybe I am a defective duplicate."

"Maybe it's a trap," Mia said, her eyes narrowing, but Noah didn't think it was.

He walked towards the mandala and knelt down in front of it.

Ray gave a happy shudder as he placed her on top of it, and he visualised the two of them melding together.

The room filled with a rainbow of lights, oranges, purples,

greens and blues, as the two mandalas became one.

Once the lights dimmed, Noah picked Ray back up, her new emerald sparkling happily in its place amongst the other gemstones.

"What are you going to do now?" Garvan asked Noah.

"I don't know," Noah replied. "Do we just leave you here?" He turned to Layla. "Do we just leave him here?"

"I don't know if we can," she replied, nibbling on her thumbnail. "Aaron and Simmy are working so hard to help Zion right now. I think they would feel the need to come here themselves if we don't bring Garvan back with us, and that's time we don't have to spare."

Noah nodded at her and turned to Garvan. "Will you come with us?"

Garvan nodded. "It looks as though I will have to," he said, turning to the rest of the group and taking Arel's ring off his finger.

"How did you…?" Noah started to ask before realising that the ring must belong to the Arel of this timeline. He hadn't brought the other one with him.

"Find Simmy and let her know I have had to go to the original timeline," Garvan said to the others, handing the ring to Nora. "She will be able to keep you two safe," he added, gesturing to the other Nora and Noah, "and make sure you all stay together. You will be safer in numbers."

"Is there anything we can do to help?" Josh asked, standing up with Max's help.

"Plenty," Garvan replied. "Simmy will let you know more details, but there is always work to be done."

Josh smiled and placed his arm around Max's waist, causing a giddy smile spread across Max's face.

Noah placed Ray back in his pocket after creating a portal, letting her shrink back down, and held his hand out to Garvan and Layla. "Sorry for the confusion," he said, giving a guilty smile to the group.

"As you should be," Mia replied, but she returned the smile with a grin of her own.

"We'll try and keep your work afloat here," Nora said to Garvan, "so when you come back, you won't have to start from scratch again."

Garvan nodded. "Thank you."

"Alright then," Noah said, looking at Layla. "We need to move quickly if we're going to get to the next two timelines."

"Hopefully, we'll see you again," Layla said to the others. "Under different circumstances." Both she and Nora looked at the other Layla guiltily.

"I hope so as well," the other Layla replied, pulling Nora closer.

Noah watched as the others waved, then closed his eyes, allowing Zion's life energy to flow through him.

Stepping through the portal, the familiar *pop* told him they had arrived back in their own timeline.

They had landed on the brown training ground. "We need to get you to the Earth room," he said to Garvan, walking quickly towards the house. "You'll be safe there, and Aaron and Simmy will be able to continue their work with you under their watch."

"Lead the way," Garvan said, following Noah and walking in front of Layla.

The trio made quick work of the walk, reaching the Earth room and entering the rebirthing chamber.

"You'll need to stay in here for now," Noah said. "It'll stunt your powers, but you'll be comfortable."

"Not ideal, but understandable," Garvan replied, sitting down on the floor in the middle of the room.

"Do you need anything?" Layla asked, kneeling in front of him.

Garvan smiled. "I will be fine. I only hope this is over quickly, so I can get back to my own timeline and continue my work."

Layla squeezed his shoulder before standing back up and turning to Noah.

"We need to get to the next timeline," Noah said to her. "I don't want to waste any more time."

"I will be fine. Go," Garvan insisted, rearranging himself so he was sitting lotus-style and beginning to meditate.

Noah grabbed Layla's hand, walked out of the room and closed the door behind them.

"Shouldn't we see Aaron and Simmy first?" Layla asked. "Let them know we brought a Garvan back?"

"There's no time. We only have two timelines left, and I want to get to them as quickly as possible."

Noah could see Layla didn't agree with him, but she didn't argue. She just shot a worried look in Noah's direction as Zion's life energy crackled through his fingertips.

Noah took her hand, grasping Ray in the other, and created a new portal, the life energy burning as he concentrated.

With a *pop*, they arrived at their destination, and Noah opened his eyes at Layla's gasp of horror.

Looking at their surroundings, Noah clasped Ray and held Layla's hand in a vice-like grip, swallowing the lump that had formed in his throat.

They were in their little town, but it was unrecognisable.

The entire place was a wasteland.

Chapter 44 - Simmy

E ven though she had gone through her rebirth, Simmy's body was still becoming acquainted with living in the Realm again. She needed to relearn how to utilise its full potential, so much so that Layla had taken to sitting with her and going through the same meditations and breathing techniques that she, Simmy, had taught Layla on Earth.

"Best to start back at the basics," Layla had said when Simmy had expressed her frustrations over her stagnating powers. But Layla wasn't here to help now.

Taking a deep breath in through her nose, closing her eyes, and releasing it out through her mouth, Simmy prepared herself for the pure Realm energy she was about to take responsibility for when she syphoned it out of Zion.

Wringing her hands, Simmy wished Layla was here to help. She had been keeping a close eye on the dynamic between Layla and Noah as they explored their new Primary Guardianship and could see that Layla had taken a step back, giving Noah the impression he was the one in charge. This made no sense to Simmy. Natural connection to the Realm or not, Layla was the one who had been exposed to it from infancy.

Simmy herself had seen to that. Even though she had shielded her from the more advanced aspects of what she was capable of, Simmy knew Layla wasn't harnessing her new powers to their full potential.

She wasn't sure of the reason, but she was going to find out.

Light footsteps interrupted her thought process, and Simmy cracked an eye open to see Aaron walking towards her.

She frequently haunted this terrace. It was her favourite place to meditate, outside with the sun warming her skin, so Aaron would have had no trouble finding her.

Opening both of her brown eyes fully and tucking a long strand of thick auburn hair behind her ear, Simmy stood and brushed the dirt off her singlet and jean shorts before tilting her head in a silent question at the tight look on Aaron's face.

"Zion has made it difficult for anyone to syphon excess power from him," he said, moving towards the couch that was on the terrace and flopping backwards over the armrest onto it. He leaned his head back and threw his elbow over his face.

Simmy stepped over to the couch and perched next to Aaron's head, looking down at him. "How difficult are we talking?"

"I cannot even pinpoint where he is."

"Oh."

Aaron moved his arm slightly, so he was no longer covering his eyes, and tilted his head to look at Simmy. "Zion is gone. We know that much. And while every sign points to him being taken by Garvan, he may just be in hiding."

"So, has he added this extra security to stop Garvan from finding him or to stop Garvan from syphoning his power?"

295

"Both, most likely." Aaron groaned as he pulled his body into a sitting position. "This means we are back at square one, so you and I need to figure out another way to support Zion."

"Well, what was he doing before he disappeared?" Simmy asked, sliding off the arm of the couch and landing on a cushion next to Aaron.

"Holding the Realm together by its seams."

"Ah," Simmy mused. "I need to reconnect with the Realm more before I can help with that. The sooner my body adjusts to its energy again, the better."

Aaron hummed absently, and Simmy could see his mind whirring with ideas on what to do next. "I am worried that Zion will do something reckless."

"Like give Noah more of his life energy?" Simmy questioned quietly.

"Like to give Noah more of his life energy," Aaron affirmed.

Simmy stayed silent for a moment, her thoughts drifting through everything she had seen while they had journeyed to the alternate timelines. "The kids are pushing themselves hard. Harder than they should be. They have barely rested since jumping to that first timeline, and it is starting to take a toll on them."

"Time is not on our side," Aaron began but quickly changed tack after a stern look from Simmy. "But you are right," he amended quickly, raising his hand to block the sun which had begun to shine in his eyes. "They have been working themselves too hard. If they did not have the powers of the Primary Guardianship running through them, they would be completely burnt out."

"Noah is already unstable from everything that has happened."

Aaron shot Simmy a glance, which she brushed off. "Do not look at me like that. I know you have seen it too. I know you like him, I like him as well, but I am concerned that we have piled too much on him in too short a time. We have to remember that, out of all of the kids, he is the one who has had the least amount of exposure to the Realm and is now carrying the most power. It is a dangerous combination."

"He can handle it." Aaron didn't look Simmy in the eye. She turned her body, so he was forced to face her.

"He syphoned power from Layla before they even began timeline hopping. He is unstable."

"He can handle it!" Aaron reiterated, his voice hard.

Simmy narrowed her eyes and stood up, looking down at Aaron. "Just because you do not want to think of another solution to help the Realm, that does not mean Noah should take on more than he is capable of."

Aaron opened his mouth, but Simmy held up her hand to stop him. "I am going to continue my training, so I can help the kids when they get back. You should think of doing the same."

Without waiting for a reply, Simmy turned on her sandalled heel and stalked to her bedroom, determined to connect with the Realm even more deeply than she had in her previous life cycles.

Chapter 45 - Nora

A few hours after she and Garvan had finished training for the day, Nora slipped out of her bedroom and began exploring the temple, pressing small amber energy signatures on the walls with her finger as she walked to ensure she could find her way back.

Her own personal trail of breadcrumbs.

Berating herself for not doing this sooner, Nora forced down the fear of being locked in her old room again and focused on placing one foot in front of the other until she felt safe—well, as safe as she could—walking around the temple.

There must be a reason she hadn't seen Tick in a while, and Nora was certain it wasn't a pleasant one.

The more she walked, the less she recognised, and she realised she had severely underestimated how big the temple actually was. She didn't know how far her new room was from the Throne Room, and she had no idea how to find Tick. She was just walking blindly, hoping to run into a clue.

Nora, stop! she mentally berated herself. *You are becoming a powerful sorceress. Surely you can think of a way to find Tick that doesn't involve getting lost.*

Taking a deep breath, Nora brought her amber energy to her fingertips and thought of Tick, allowing the energy to ebb and flow from her until it snagged on something.

Clinging to that hint of a connection, Nora followed it down halls, through tapestry draped archways and past countless rooms until it finally came to an end in front of a dark room pulsing with black energy.

Nora shivered.

The room gave her the creeps, and every cell in her body was screaming for her to leave this place and head back to the comfort of her bed.

But she forced the feeling away and placed a shaking hand on the door handle, turning it softly until she heard it click open.

It was silent.

Too silent.

The energy pulsating around the room felt suffocating, and Nora uncapped the pouch of water she now carried at her hip and created a mask which she wrapped around her nose and mouth. The air in the room was too thick for her to pull water out of it, and she didn't trust that it wouldn't harm her.

As soon as she inhaled her first breath of fresh air, her head cleared. She hadn't even realised her ears had begun to ring.

Unease churned in Nora's gut as she took her first tentative step into the room.

Tubes with dark energy running through them were protruding from the walls, and strange, giant vials of fluorescent green liquid reached from the floor to the ceiling. Or was it gas? Nora couldn't tell.

Whatever it was, it was being funnelled into a large globe, which was levitating in the middle of the room. Nora took another step, unable to stop herself from trying to see what it was, and swallowed a yelp as she stepped out from behind one of the vials to see Tick and Garvan.

Quickly dropping to the floor, Nora crawled back behind the large vial, gripping her chest to steady her pounding heart.

They had almost seen her!

She tilted her head back and rested it on the glass behind her, but as soon as she touched it, the vial pulsed and zapped Nora with a shock so powerful that her water mask turned to steam.

Cursing under her breath, Nora opened her water pouch to create a new mask, but as she did, her eyes glanced at the reflection of the globe in the middle of the room. The pulse had shifted the mist enough for her to see what was inside.

"Abigail?" Nora whispered in horror. Her classmate from Earth was suspended helplessly inside the globe by her wrists. Her long brown hair was out of its signature braid and was floating behind her as her head lolled to one side.

Furious, Nora pushed herself out of her hiding spot and sprinted to the middle of the room. "Abigail!" She called out, covering her fist with water and punching a hole straight through Tick's chest as the Shadow Being teleported to her in an attempt to stop Nora getting closer.

Nora leapt into the air and smashed the same fist into the side of Garvan's head. The smug asshole hadn't even attempted to block her, and as his head snapped to the side, his eyes never left her face.

"What are you doing to her?" Nora demanded, flexing her palm. The water on her fist turned into thousands of tiny needles, all pointed at Garvan.

"It is a shame you had to see this," was all Garvan said, straightening himself and brushing Nora's needles away with a flick of his hand. Before Nora could so much as flinch, he pressed his thumb to her forehead.

Everything went black.

Chapter 46 - Noah

There wasn't a single light on in this timeline, and although exhaustion weighed him down, dread settled in Noah's stomach as he noticed the street around them was silent.

Normally at this time of night, there would be a few cars driving past, a porch light or two providing some dim light and a colony of bats flying overhead.

But there was nothing. Not even a mosquito buzzing.

A shiver ran up Noah's spine, and he reached his hand out to grab Ray, who Layla held out for him.

She was ice cold, and Noah knew they'd gotten here too late.

Turning to Layla, he saw her freckles stood out in stark contrast to her pale face. His voice catching in his throat, Noah whispered, "We didn't make it in time."

Layla shook as she gave a stiff nod, unable to speak through her clenched jaw.

"We need to go back to our timeline," Noah decided. "There's nothing we can do here."

Layla swallowed drily, her voice coming out hoarse. "Let's check whether Garvan got both twins."

"Why?" Noah snapped. This timeline made the life energy

coursing through him jumpy, and he didn't want to stay here any longer than he had to.

Ray sparked, and Noah let go of her, his hand smarting where she had zapped him.

"Because that's our job, Noah!" Layla shot back, pulling Ray away and tucking the relic into her pocket.

Turning on her heel, without waiting for Noah's response, Layla started off in the direction of the twins' house, throwing a glance behind her to check whether Noah was following.

He was.

The walk was short, but Noah used the time to force Zion's life energy to his feet. If it was going to wreak havoc within him, it might as well make itself useful.

He focused on Zion's energy flowing through him, and when he looked down at his shoes, Noah saw golden light shining out from the bottom of them.

A small smile formed on his lips, and Noah dug deeper within himself, urging his own life energy to meld with Zion's. The result was a single strand of amber weaved within the gold, lacing itself around his sneakers.

Stepping off the path onto the dead grass beside it, Noah took a deep breath and projected the energies from his feet into the earth.

Slowly, the grass began to shine as the melded life energy sunk through the soil, and when he lifted his foot up, a green shoe-shaped patch stared back at him.

A grin slowly spreading across his face, Noah moved along the grass, stepping in as many places as he could as quickly as he could, forgetting he was meant to be following Layla until he crashed into her.

"Why are you doing the foxtrot?" Layla asked drily as she

gripped Noah's elbow, steadying him.

"Look!" Noah said excitedly, pointing at the green patches where he'd stepped. "I brought the grass back to life!"

"How did you do that?"

"I combined my life energy with Zion's."

"So, your ability to work with earth can be used to help this timeline, too?"

Noah paused. "I hope so." He took hold of Layla's hand with his own and released some of Zion's life energy.

"Ouch," Layla winced, pulling her hand away.

"Sorry." Noah wriggled his fingers, the energy dissolving back into his hand.

"Is that what it feels like all the time?" Layla asked, rubbing her stinging fingers on her jeans.

"Most of the time." Noah shrugged as if it didn't bother him, ignoring Layla's narrowed eyes. "Oh, I didn't realise we were here."

Standing in front of the familiar house, Noah squinted to see if he could detect any movement inside. Nothing stirred.

"Let's see if anyone's home," Layla said, tugging on the sleeve of his shirt, careful not to touch his skin in case she got zapped again.

Walking behind her, Noah felt guilt settle in the pit of his stomach. If only they'd gotten to this timeline earlier.

Layla's loud knock on the front door snapped him out of his reverie, and he waited to see if anyone would answer.

There was some faint shuffling, the sound of slippered feet on carpet, before the door flung open. Jen Parker flung herself into Noah's arms, sobbing.

"Noah? Noah! Oh, Noah, you're back!" she cried into his t-shirt.

Meeting Layla's pitying gaze, Noah patted Jen on the head awkwardly. "I'm not Noah."

"What?" Jen's muffled voice replied. "Of course you are."

"I mean, I *am* Noah. I'm just not *your* Noah," he tried to explain. "I'm sorry to have to spring this on you, but I'm from another timeline."

"Another timeline? How is that possible?" Jen pulled herself away from Noah's chest and scrutinised him as she wiped tears from her eyes. "You do seem a little different," she sniffled. "Another timeline. So this has something to do with the Realm then," Jen responded, thinking out loud, and gave a grim smile at Noah's shocked look that she wasn't more freaked out about his explanation.

"So, Noah was the one who was taken?" Layla asked Jen gently.

"They were both taken," Jen replied, her voice thick. Her wavy, dirty blonde hair, which so resembled Nora's, was falling out of the haphazardly tied bun on top of her head, and her blue eyes were swollen from the shedding of many tears.

"Both of them!?" Noah and Layla exclaimed in unison, looking at each other in surprise. Regardless of how bad this timeline looked, they had expected at least one twin to be on Earth, like in all the other timelines.

"Who's at the door, Jen?" Paul Parker called from inside, his own slippered feet shuffling towards them.

He got to the door, saw Noah, and threw himself into his son's arms, calling "Noah!" as he did.

Thankfully, Noah had been expecting it, so he wasn't knocked off his feet when his dad hit his chest.

"It's not him, darling," Jen said to her husband from the

front step, wiping her nose as she sniffled.

"What do you mean it's not him?" Paul replied, his amber eyes searching Noah's own. "Of course it's him."

"It *is* him, but it's not him. Take a look at his face. You'll see what I mean," Jen explained.

Paul took a step back and looked intently at Noah. "There *is* something different about him…"

"What's wrong with my face?" Noah asked, suddenly self-conscious.

"There's nothing wrong with your face, dear," Jen said kindly. "You just seem a bit younger than our Noah."

"Come inside," Paul said to both Noah and Layla, moving aside so they could walk in. "You two look exhausted."

"Thank you," Layla replied, taking a step into the familiar house.

Once the four of them were all settled in the living room, cups of tea and lamingtons shared around, Layla turned to Jen and Paul. "How long have Noah and Nora been gone?"

"Almost a month now," Jen replied. Paul's hand shook as he lifted his cup of tea to his mouth, spilling the hot liquid down his dressing gown.

"And when did the town become… well… the way it is?" Layla played with the hem of her shirt as she fumbled over the question.

"Two, maybe three weeks ago," Jen said. "I took it as a sign that something had happened to my babies…" She pressed her face into her hands and sucked in a sharp breath.

Noah and Layla looked at each other somberly.

"Have you had any signs from them? Any contact at all?" Noah asked.

Paul shook his head, but Jen lifted her face, wiped her tears and stuck her hand into the pocket of her dressing gown. "I woke up with this beside my bed yesterday morning," she said, handing Noah a large opal.

"An opal," Layla breathed. "A symbol of hope."

"I want to believe it came from the twins," Jen said. "I've been clinging onto it, hoping I would receive some sign that they are okay, and now you've turned up—it can't be a coincidence."

Noah rolled the opal around in his fingers. The mandala of this timeline was no more, but this gemstone would still be able to help them.

"Take it," Jen said, leaning forward and closing his fingers around the stone. "It was never meant to stay with me."

Noah nodded wordlessly, taking Ray from Layla, who had immediately passed her over. He knelt down on the floor, placing Ray in front of him with the opal on top of her.

Visualising the two of them melding together, a kaleidoscope of colours exploded around the room, out of the windows and into the dark night. Noah released his and Zion's energy from his palm and squinted against the light the life energies emitted as they coursed through the gemstone, which melded into the relic.

Once the light had subsided, Noah picked Ray up. The smooth opal was now embedded within her.

"Look!" Paul breathed, calling the others over to the window overlooking the front yard.

The gloomy street was now bathed in the light of a full moon, which, until that point, had been hidden behind dark, stormy clouds.

Crickets started to chirp, and even a frog croaked in the distance.

"I wish we could stay and help more," Noah said to his parents, handing Ray back to Layla. "I want to help you get Noah and Nora back."

"You've helped us more than you could know," Jen assured him, and Paul nodded behind her. "Putting yourself in jeopardy will only make things worse."

"We need to go to the last timeline and see what state it's in before we make any rash moves," Layla reasoned, taking Noah's hand and leading him towards the front door. "Plus, we still need to catch up with Aaron and Simmy."

"But what if we—" Noah cut himself off at Layla's stern look and relented, reluctantly letting Layla lead him to the front of the house. "I'm sorry we couldn't do more for you, but know that we will do everything in our power to bring your kids back," Noah said to Jen and Paul as they followed the two of them to the door.

Jen and Paul nodded wordlessly and clutched each other. A bright emerald light escaped Ray as Layla created a portal.

"Be careful on your journey," Noah heard Paul say as they stepped through it.

Pop.

They were back on the brown training field.

Chapter 47 - Layla

"**N**OAH PARKER! LAYLA FORREST!"

Layla glanced at Noah as Aaron's voice bellowed from inside the palace.

"Yes?" Layla called back, scrunching her nose as she tried to think of what Aaron could be yelling at them about.

She didn't have to wait long to find out as Aaron came storming out the back door, pulling something behind him. Simmy followed in the rear, looking like she was trying to avoid touching whatever Aaron was dragging.

"Hello," the thing behind Aaron said when they stopped. Layla stepped to the side to see the Garvan from the third timeline tied up, calmly sliding along the ground as Aaron dragged him.

Aaron glared at them. "Well?"

Layla blinked. "Well?"

"Why did I find this Garvan sitting freely in the rebirthing chamber?!" Aaron demanded. "He could have escaped! He could have blown the whole place to dust!"

"He didn't, though, did he?" Layla asked, looking calmly from Aaron to Garvan to Simmy.

"No! But that does not mean he could not have!"

"He's a good Garvan," Noah said, stepping in. "We brought

him here to keep an eye on him, but he helped us, gave us the mandala from his timeline and didn't put up a fight. He's been working towards world peace in his timeline."

"World peace," Aaron muttered, rubbing the bridge of his nose. "Why did you not come and find me before leaving him there alone?"

"We needed to get to the next timeline," Layla replied, watching from the corner of her eye as Simmy loosened the ropes binding Garvan.

"He is harmless," Simmy said to Aaron as she finished. "You can feel that, can you not? You can feel his energy?"

"I still needed to know about it!" Aaron cried. "I thought the other Garvan had gotten free! I almost attacked him!"

"I will do whatever I can to help you on your quest," Garvan said smoothly, standing up and rubbing his wrists. "Thank you," he said to Simmy as she wound up the rope.

"We're going to need him," Layla said to Aaron, who was still looking at Garvan uneasily.

"Why?" Aaron asked.

"The timeline we've just come from... the Garvan there has taken both twins and the Earth has become a wasteland. He's completely upset the energetic balance," Layla explained.

"Idiot," Aaron muttered, rubbing the bridge of his nose again. "Obsessed with power."

"We only have one more timeline to check out," Noah added. "How did you two get along over here? Did you manage to take some of the strain off of Zion?"

Aaron and Simmy glanced at each other.

"It did not go according to plan," Simmy said slowly. "We believe Zion is shielding his power, so Garvan can't extract it.

Layla pulled Simmy into a one-armed hug, and Simmy

squeezed her waist in return.

"You'll come with us to the next timeline, then?" Noah prompted

"Well, I am not going to sit around here and do nothing," Aaron retorted, running his hands through his dark hair, messing it up.

"I will come too," Simmy added. "If Zion is keeping himself hidden, we need to figure out a way to stop Garvan as quickly as possible."

"Shall I stay here then?" Garvan, forgotten, asked from the sidelines.

Layla nodded apologetically over Simmy's head. "You're going to have to. We can't risk you being absorbed in another timeline."

"I will meditate in the rebirthing chamber until you return, then," he replied.

"I will take you back," Simmy said.

"I'll come too," Layla called, letting Simmy go and waving at the boys as the three of them walked inside the palace.

The girls walked in silence while Garvan hummed a light tune, holding his hands behind his back as Simmy and Layla fell into step behind him.

On the edge of her vision, Layla caught Simmy glancing at her, but as soon as Layla tried to catch her attention, Simmy would quickly snap her head back towards Garvan.

Raising an eyebrow as Simmy did this for a third time, Layla opened the door for Garvan to settle back into the Earth room's rebirthing chamber, watching as he sank down on the floor and slipped into meditation once more.

As soon as Simmy sealed Garvan inside the room with her red energy, Layla turned to her aunt with her hands on her hips. "What are you hiding from me?"

"I am not hiding anything from you!" Simmy rebutted. "What are *you* hiding from *me*?"

"I'm not hiding anything from you either!" Layla narrowed her eyes. "Why do you think I am?"

Simmy gave her an exasperated look. "If you think I have not noticed that you have taken a backseat in this whole Primary Guardianship, you are mistaken. You are *so* much more powerful than you are letting on. Why are you holding back?"

Layla's heart gave a pang of guilt as she looked at her aunt. "I wanted to give Noah a chance to take control of the Realm's powers without relying on me too much."

It was Simmy's turn to narrow her eyes. "That is it?"

Layla nodded.

"You are sure that is the only reason?"

Layla nodded again.

Simmy sighed. "Layla, there is more at stake than Noah's pride. The Realm, the Earth and everyone who lives there are counting on you—*both* of you—to give it your all. You are not helping him by holding yourself back, and you are certainly not helping yourself."

"He needed a push."

"Yes, but not from you."

Layla started to object, but Simmy raised a hand to stop her.

"The whole point of the two of you becoming Primary Guardians together was to be equals. If you are holding yourself back, you are creating an imbalance. I *know* you are just as strong as Noah, even with Zion's life energy flowing through him. Stop selling yourself short."

Grimacing, Layla glanced at Simmy. "When you put it that way..."

"What other way is there to put it?!" Simmy gripped Layla's wrists. "You are too important and too powerful to hold yourself back. You were not given this role to hide in the background."

"I'm not here to hide in the background," Layla affirmed.

Simmy nodded before dragging her out of the Earth room. "Now, let us see what this final timeline has in store for us."

Chapter 48 - Nora

Slowly, Nora's eyelids fluttered open, and she winced at the pounding in her head.

What happened?

Groaning, Nora rolled onto her side. She yelped as she fell onto the cold, hard floor.

It took a moment for her to remember everything, and then her body locked up. Her eyes adjusted to the darkness, and she looked around at her cell.

She was back.

He'd put her back.

Her breaths coming short and sharp now, Nora forced herself to sit up as she took in her surroundings.

There wasn't any space here. Nowhere to move. She was trapped.

Pushing herself to her feet, Nora ran towards the door. As she'd thought, the red sparks from the barrier grazed her skin as she pounded her fists against it relentlessly.

She couldn't scream. No one would hear her, and if they could, they wouldn't help her.

Stumbling back to the bed, Nora pushed herself up against the wall and curled into a ball.

She didn't know how long it took for her breathing to calm

down, but she focused solely on taking each breath in and releasing it as slowly as possible until her heart rate slowed.

When she was no longer at the risk of hyperventilating, Nora growled as images of what she'd seen flashed through her mind.

Garvan and Tick were holding Abigail hostage. She was suspended in that creepy sphere and was being pumped full of Realm knows what.

Inhaling one last, deep, breath, Nora forced herself to uncurl, her muscles groaning as they stretched, sore from how tightly she'd been clinging to her knees.

The weight at her hip told her she still had her flask attached, and she silently popped the lid, letting it hang next to the leather pouch.

Her fingers tingled, and she thought back to what Garvan had taught her in their last lesson about needing to harness her emotions.

Well, she was furious now!

With a curl of her fingers, the water in her flask pulled itself upwards, forming a ball as Nora contemplated the best way to break down the wall.

Walking back towards the barrier, Nora covered her hand with the water, pressed it to the red energy crackling over the door and let out a breath.

BOOM!

The door flew off its hinges, and the wooden frame cracked and splintered, the red barrier shattering as Nora's energy exploded through it.

"What do you think you're do—?!"

Tick's exclamation was cut short as Nora called her water back to her and flung it at Tick in one smooth movement, flicking her hands and instructing the water to become razor-sharp.

Wisps of shadow floated away from Tick's body and dissolved into the air as Nora attacked her relentlessly.

As soon as her water blades hit their marks, Nora would call them back to her before shooting another from her other hand.

Tick could barely keep up regenerating, let alone counter-attack. So, when Nora was knocked back by a surge of black energy, she whirled furiously towards the source, throwing one last blade of water in between Tick's sunken red eyes. She stormed angrily towards Garvan, who looked at her calmly as he dusted some dirt off his shoulder.

"I was wondering how long it would take you to break down my barrier," he said smoothly. There was a hint of humour in his voice, which made Nora's blood boil. She called her water back to her and flexed her hand, turning it into thousands of icy needles, all aimed at Garvan.

"Before you shish kebab me, do you want to hear my explanation?" He didn't look even slightly phased at the thought of being turned into an acupressure mat, so Nora didn't hesitate. She released the needles.

Garvan's eyebrows hit his hairline. He managed to stop a few of the needles with a wave of his hand, but Nora, who'd had enough of him blocking her attacks, released a strand of amber energy while he was distracted, shattering his shield and giving the rest of her needles an opening to puncture him.

He stumbled back a step and held out his arm to protect his face while the rest of the needles sliced his black fighting leathers to ribbons.

"I am not going to fight you, Nora."

"Then you're going to need to create a stronger shield." Nora seethed, her water flying back towards her. She flexed her hand once more, her needles materialising in the air, aimed at Garvan again.

"Abigail consented to everything we did to her. She wanted to work with the Realm."

Nora only hesitated for a split second, then growled, "And did you tell her exactly what she was agreeing to, or did you give her *just* enough information to entice her to accept?"

Garvan didn't reply.

"Well?!" Nora fumed. "Was it informed consent or not?"

When Garvan still didn't reply, Nora readied her needles to fly. "I didn't think so."

"Stop prattling on about things you know nothing about." Tick had regenerated herself and was now standing behind Garvan, her red eyes flashing as she stared Nora down.

Garvan held out a hand to stop Tick and stepped forward himself. "I have already told you that everything I am doing is to help the Realm. Why would this be any different?"

"Because everything you're doing is cruel, and the Realm is suffering because of it!"

"You know nothing of what the Realm feels. You have only known about its existence for a mere year, and you have been trapped here the majority of that time."

"Whose fault is that?" Nora muttered mutinously.

Garvan continued as if he hadn't heard her. "Abigail could be the first of many humans who are given a set path, who do not have to worry about the unknowns of life. If you work with us, we could create a new world. A new guidance. One where people are not always looking for answers. A place where they can see the light at the end of the tunnel."

"As great as that all sounds, at what cost?" Nora lowered her arm, her needles splashing helplessly to the ground before trickling back into her flask. "What's the cost people have to pay to live in that world?"

"I will become their Master. I will be Master of the Realm, and I will guide them." Garvan took another step towards her, his arm outstretched. "You can be by my side. You have the power to help people. More people than you could ever imagine. Your powers will be celebrated here instead of hidden away and ignored."

Nora looked from Garvan's offered hand to his face. His cold, blue eyes were thawed just enough for her to realise he truly believed that he was doing the right thing.

Her mouth pulled back into a sad smile. "I do want to help people, but I don't believe ruling over them is the right way to go about it."

Garvan's hand slowly lowered to his side. "You have time to change your mind. Tick," he called to the Shadow Being over his shoulder, "take Nora back to her new room. She will reside there while she thinks things through."

Shaking her head sadly, Nora flinched as Tick teleported in front of her, roughly digging her claws into her shoulder.

The last thing she saw before Tick whisked her away was Garvan walking towards the eleven Guardian siblings, black energy crackling from his fingertips.

Chapter 49 - Layla

A rriving in the final timeline, Noah, Aaron, Simmy and Layla landed in the Parkers' backyard. The sight before them sent a shiver down Layla's spine.

A hole had been blasted through the side of the house, and Tick's long sharp claws were slicing through everything within reach.

"Come out, come out, wherever you are," she sang as bricks crumbled beneath her ministrations.

Aaron quickly pushed the others behind a nearby bush and jumped in next to them, pulling out his mandala as he did so. "Stay behind me," he whispered. "Tick should not be alive in this timeline either. Nora has not had the chance to create her yet. This Tick has been based on the original, so she is a nasty piece of work."

Layla stared at Aaron's mandala. It had started off the size of his palm but had expanded as Aaron prepared to use it. The design seemed more intricate than before, the blue sapphires joined by a new deep blue stone.

"Lapis lazuli," Aaron whispered after catching Layla's stare.

"When did you get a chance to upgrade your mandala?" she asked, pulling Ray out of her pocket, her own new stones glinting in the sunlight shining through the leaves of the bush.

"Just after Zion stopped us from syphoning his life energy. I decided not to take any chances," Aaron replied. "We cannot let Garvan get hold of another twin, so I need to be on my A-game."

A light caught Layla's eye, and she saw Simmy crafting an energy ball in the palm of her hand, her moonstone mandala grasped in the other.

While Simmy's energy sparked, Layla's attention was drawn away yet again, and her heart lurched as she saw Noah and Nora from this timeline crouched over, running out of the kitchen Tick had reduced to rubble to hide behind a small tool shed in the backyard.

They looked like they were only ten years old.

"Did you see them?" she whispered to Noah, who looked where Layla was pointing and nodded.

"The twins are behind that shed, over in the corner of the yard," she heard Noah whisper to Aaron.

"Perfect," Aaron replied, producing his signature blue energy ball on the tip of his finger. He whistled sharply, and the ball flew from his fingertip straight through Tick's forehead while Simmy flexed her fingers and shot her energy ball through Tick's shadowy stomach.

Tick screamed at the sudden attacks and threw her arms out wildly in front of her, her viscous claws extending, slicing anything and everything in their path.

Aaron took this moment of chaos to raise his mandala and encased the twins in a shield. The translucent bubble lifted them off the ground just enough so they were floating, but not enough for Tick to see them from their hiding spot.

Distracted by what everyone else was doing, Layla almost missed Tick's swinging arms, and she winced, quickly pulling

Noah towards her as Tick's talons shot forward and sliced the leaves in front of their face, missing their noses by an inch.

Aaron grabbed Simmy and tucked her protectively under his arm, and then he crafted a shimmering blue shield around the group while weaving out of the way of Tick's wild attacks.

"Now's your chance, while she's distracted," Noah whispered to Layla. She nodded, her knuckles turning white as she gripped Ray tightly.

A large energy ball began to form from the sunstone in Ray's centre, emerald energy coursing through it.

Tick, the hole in her head still regenerating, was too busy running around slashing the Parker residence into debris to notice the shift in energy around her.

Once the energy ball had grown big enough, Noah placed a steadying hand on Layla's shoulder as Aaron released her from the shield. Jumping out from their hiding spot, Layla thrust Ray in front of her and shot her ball of energy right through Tick's chest.

Gasping and clawing at the hole that had been cut clean through her, Tick staggered backwards. Her red eyes flashed as her razor sharp fingers grew even longer, uselessly swiping in front of her.

Layla heard Noah let out a hiss of pain as the tip of Tick's claw scraped his cheek. Aaron had dissolved the shield, and Layla saw a drop of blood run towards Noah's chin. Aaron blasted Tick with relentless attacks, his fingertip creating endless balls of blue energy, which he fired at her so quickly her body couldn't regenerate.

While Aaron kept Tick occupied, Layla stepped aside as Simmy ran towards the twins. Puffing from using so much energy in her blast with Ray, Layla watched Simmy calm the twins down and push the shield they were encased in away from the action.

When the three of them were out of sight, Layla tuned back into the fight. She grinned when she heard Tick scream in agony as she became more hole than shadow, still fruitlessly clawing at everything around her. Layla brought her emerald life energy to her fingertips and joined Aaron in firing energy ball after energy ball at the Shadow Being.

Tick didn't stand a chance, and when she became nothing more than a furious scream and a few wisps of shadow, Aaron pulled a small bottle out of his jacket pocket, walked over to her, rounded her up inside and corked the top.

Layla and Noah leaned in close to the bottle as Aaron sealed it with his sapphire energy.

"What is that?" Noah asked Aaron as Layla continued to look at the bottle curiously.

"It is a confinement bottle," Aaron replied. "I am sure you recognise it."

"It looks like a genie's bottle," Layla answered, "but surely genies aren't real."

"They are as real as you or I," Aaron said seriously, "and they are not to be trifled with. Why do you think they had to be sealed away? Wishes are a dangerous thing, especially in the wrong hands."

Before Layla could ask anything more, Simmy pushed the twins over in their bubble shield. "Do you think we can release them now?"

Aaron made sure the confinement bottle was sealed tightly before nodding and waving his mandala over the bubble, popping it.

The twins stared at the group with wide eyes. "Who are

you?" little Nora asked. "Are you superheroes?"

Layla unsuccessfully tried to hold back a grin as she asked this, watching the young Noah nodding alongside her, clearly wondering the same thing.

"We just might be," Aaron answered with a wink, crouching down to their level. "Are you two alright?"

"We're okay," young Noah replied. "We're big and tough!" He emphasised his point by flexing his biceps.

"Whoa!" Aaron called out, raising his hands in surrender. "Look at that gun show!"

Young Noah giggled, flexing his muscles even more.

"Do you know where your parents are?" Simmy asked Nora gently as she knelt down beside Aaron.

"That shadow woman took them away before she came back for us," Nora replied.

Noah looked at Layla, his face grim. "They must be in the Realm."

"Garvan's temple, probably," she replied.

"Mum gave us this before she was taken, though. Told us to take it and hide," young Noah said, holding out the mandala of this timeline with stones of black onyx weaved through it.

"A symbol of personal strength," Layla mumbled, holding her hand out for the mandala.

"No!" young Noah yelled, pulling it back towards his chest. "Mum gave it to me to protect!"

Noah patted Aaron on the shoulder, gave him space to stand up and took his place, kneeling in front of his younger self. "Do you think I would be able to protect it for you from now on?"

"You look just like me!" young Noah exclaimed, his eyes wide as he pointed a finger at Noah's face. Layla hid a smile behind her hand at the accusation.

"Can I tell you a secret?" Noah whispered, leaning forward so just Layla and the twins could hear. "I *am* you. From the future!"

The twins gasped dramatically, each covering their mouth with a little hand.

"Where is future me?" young Nora demanded, looking around eagerly as if she were waiting for her to jump out from behind the bush.

Noah looked at her sadly. "She's in trouble, which is why I need your mandala, so I can go and rescue her."

Nora gasped again. "Give him the mandala, Noah! Right now!" She made a wild grab for it, trying to pull it out of his hands.

"No!" Noah yelled again, tugging it away from her. "Mum gave it to me to protect! What if we need it to get them back?"

Simmy, who was still kneeling on the floor with the twins, took one of their hands in each of hers. "I know someone who will be able to help you until your parents come back," she said kindly. "May we please borrow your mandala? I will take you to her."

Young Noah hesitated, but Nora stepped in front of him. "Yes!" she said. "You need to save me!"

Simmy smiled at Nora, sat her on her knee and looked at little Noah. "May I?" she asked, holding out her hand.

Young Noah looked from the mandala to Simmy and sighed, reluctantly holding it out for her.

"Thank you," Simmy said, passing the mandala to Noah, who mouthed '*thank you*' to her. He gave it to Layla, who already had Ray ready to merge.

"What's she going to do?" young Nora asked, attempting to

follow as Layla stood and walked a short distance away from the group, but Simmy held her back.

"You will see," she said, "but stay here for now. It is not safe for you over there."

Young Noah and Nora huffed, but they soon clung to Simmy as Layla began the melding process between Ray and the onyx mandala.

From the corner of her eye, Layla saw the twins using Simmy as a shield against the blinding lights, which forced the group to cover their eyes to wait out the long minutes until the process had finished.

Layla's energy crackled at her fingertips as she felt Ray become stronger, and she let it flow through her, Simmy's warning about not holding herself back anymore ringing in her ears.

After the light subsided, she walked back to the group. "Take a look," she said to the twins.

Nora reached her finger out to touch Ray, who was now scattered with a rainbow of gemstones, the black onyx taking its place next to the others. Layla pulled Ray just out of her reach. "Be careful," she said, "this is a very powerful relic."

Nora hesitated, her finger still outstretched, but then thought better of it and lowered her hand back down.

"You're going to use this to save our mum and dad?" the young Noah asked, peering out from underneath Simmy's arm.

"Absolutely," Layla replied, and Noah nodded at the young twins. "We'll do everything we can to save your parents," she added.

Simmy smiled at him and picked the twins up, one on each hip. "Come along, you two," she said to them. "You need to get somewhere safe before we can leave to help your parents. I will take you."

"We will be here when you get back," Aaron said to her.

Simmy placed the twins back on the ground and held their hands as they walked out onto the quiet street.

"Is she taking them to the Simmy of this timeline?" Noah asked as they watched the trio walk away.

"Yes," Aaron replied, watching them round the corner and disappear. "They will be safe there."

Layla stared at Ray and all her new gemstones, the black onyx sparkling in the light.

"She's heavier now," Layla noticed, holding Ray in the palm of her hand and lifting her up and down.

"I think the new gemstones enhance the power she already has within her," Noah replied.

Running her fingers over the stones, Layla took a deep breath before handing Ray to Noah. "I've had her long enough. You take her for a while." Taking his hand and placing Ray in it, Layla closed his fingers around the relic. "You need her support more than I do."

Noah gripped Ray tightly and let her retract down to pocket-size before pulling Layla towards him and giving her a kiss on the cheek. "Thank you," he whispered in her ear.

Layla felt her cheeks warm and playfully pushed him away.

Aaron, who Layla noticed had found the tree above him extremely interesting during this moment, looked back at the two of them. "Garvan will have realised that Tick is missing by now," he said, fiddling with the confinement bottle he'd strapped to his hip.

"We're going to be in for a battle," Layla agreed, sitting down cross-legged on the grass as they waited for Simmy to return.

"This is our last timeline," Noah said, playing with the leaves of the bush they'd hidden behind. "We need to make this quick. We need to capture the Garvan of this timeline and bring him back with us."

A hush fell that lasted some minutes as they silently considered the enormity of the task before them.

Soft steps made the group look over to the pathway, and Layla leapt up as Simmy appeared.

"Sorry!" Simmy panted as she jogged up to them. "The twins would not let me go."

"Let's go to the Realm," Aaron said as Simmy reached them. "There is no time to lose."

Noah ushered the group through the portal he created, which was crackling with Zion's golden life energy, and Layla saw Aaron turn to him with a strange expression on his face just as she was about to step through. "You did not use Ray to create that portal."

"What?" Noah replied, not yet noticing the others were staring at him.

"The portal," Aaron repeated, "you did not use Ray to create it."

"Oh," Noah said, looking at his hands, which were still sparking with Zion's life energy. "I guess I forgot."

Layla shared a look with Aaron and Simmy before entering the portal, and waited for the others to join her before taking in their surroundings.

"We're in the Throne Room," Noah said, "but none of the other Guardians are here, and there are no thrones."

Layla turned away as something caught her eye, and she broke away from the group, moving to check it out.

"Noah! Simmy! Aaron!" Layla called. What she found had

made her stomach lurch. "Over here!"

Jen and Paul Parker were inside the small, dark room hidden behind the Throne Room, looking worse for wear.

Jen's wavy, dirty-blonde hair was half-pulled out of her bun, and her clothes were torn and tattered. Paul's shirt was ripped through the middle, and there was dirt smeared all over his face.

It was clear they hadn't come without a fight.

Looking around the empty space they'd landed in, Layla tried to see if anyone was watching them as the others made their way over to her, but there didn't appear to be anyone else around.

Turning back to Jen and Paul, she took a step into the room and was instantly flung away. Landing roughly on her back, legs burning and spine aching from the impact, Layla groaned as she tried to sit up.

"What happened?" Noah asked as he ran to her side, placing a supportive hand behind her head.

"Barrier," Layla groaned, her head spinning.

Zap

Aaron had pressed his index finger against the doorway, red sparks flying out as he did so. "That is a strong barrier for holding two humans," he said, sucking on his sore finger.

"It is not for keeping the humans in," a cold voice said behind them. "It is for keeping unwanted guests out."

The group turned. Waltzing towards them was Garvan. He hadn't undergone his rebirth yet, although the old man was looking fit and healthy.

Almost too fit and healthy.

Ignoring the group, Garvan stalked over to the room. Layla saw Jen and Paul cower further into the corner the closer he got.

"What are you doing to them?" Simmy demanded, but Garvan knocked her to the floor with a flick of his hand.

"They stopped me from getting the twins," he said callously. "They need to make up for what I have lost."

Garvan raised both of his hands and placed his palms on the barrier, red sparks beginning to fly erratically around him.

Jen and Paul screamed and fell to their knees, their hands gripping their heads so tightly Layla was worried their fingers would leave a bruise on their skull.

"Stop it!" Layla cried, forcing herself towards Garvan to try to pull his hands away. Before she could get close enough, she was thrown back, landing roughly on her back again as an invisible force pushed her away.

Irritated, like someone would have been by a fly, Garvan glared down at Layla on the ground beside him and removed his hands from the barrier. The sparks subsided, and Jen and Paul collapsed to the ground in agony.

"Not only is this barrier good for keeping people out, it is also a nice energy source for me. I know this woman was created thanks to the Realm. Thankfully, she still has some power lingering within her," Garvan said, looking at his raw hands and smiling.

Layla began to call her energy forward to attack Garvan, but before she could, Aaron, who Layla saw rip himself out of a mild petrification spell which had been cast on him, whipped out his mandala and blasted Garvan away from the doorway.

The older man slid backwards, managing to stay on his feet with his arms crossed in front of his face for protection.

With another flick of his hand, Garvan's golden staff

appeared before him. He grabbed it, swinging it at Aaron, who threw his mandala in the air, quickly grabbing hold of it as it turned into a matching, silver staff, blocking Garvan's attack.

The lapis lazuli and sapphires embedded in Aaron's mandala glowed brighter every passing moment, and Layla realised Aaron was charging it up.

"I need to help him!" Noah called to Layla and Simmy, grabbing Ray from his pocket and gripping her tightly while she expanded.

"No!" Simmy called to him, grabbing his arm before he could attack and forcefully pulling him back to her.

Noah rounded on her furiously, and Layla flinched as she saw Zion's life energy crackling in his eyes.

Simmy quickly let go at Noah's look but latched back onto him a second later, determination etched into her face. "No!" she repeated. "*I* will help him. You and Layla need to break down that barrier and free the twins' parents."

Layla saw Noah hesitate. Stiffly jumping to her feet, she made the decision for him, grabbing Ray and pulling Noah towards the door. "C'mon, Noah," she said firmly. "We need to get them out of there."

Zion's golden energy continued to spark in Noah's eyes as he turned towards Layla, who was still trying to tug him towards the door. She glared back at him. "The sooner we break down this door, the sooner we can fight," she said.

Slowly, as if fighting an internal battle, Noah released his grip on Ray and took a deep breath, allowing Zion's life energy to flow through him and into Layla.

Layla gasped as her body tried to absorb the raw power, but she refused to falter as Noah continued to share the energy.

She could hear faint noises from the battle behind them, but Layla blocked them out, looking at the ragged figures of Jen and Paul Parker sprawled over the floor in the dimly lit room.

"Now, Noah!" Layla's voice sounded faint, even to her, as she gripped Ray tighter, releasing the life energy that had been flowing through them.

It felt like time slowed down as she watched their energy crackle towards the barrier, golden electricity meeting red as the two forces entwined.

Noah held his ground easily— he was used to Zion's life energy flowing through him by now—but Layla swayed as her knees buckled underneath her, and her grip began to loosen.

"Layla?" Noah called, his voice ringing in her ears.

"Keep going!" She gasped. "We can't stop yet."

"Layla!" Noah called again, turning towards her, but Layla forced herself up. Her green energy now melding with gold, creating a large crack in the barrier. "Keep going!" she demanded.

Noah nodded, forcing his own amber energy to mix with Layla's and Zion's, forcing the barrier to split even further. Layla took a deep breath and, groaning with effort, pushed everything she had into the barrier until, finally, it shattered.

Chapter 50 - Noah

Sparks of red, gold, amber and emerald exploded.

Layla dropped, her body falling forwards. Noah rushed to catch her, electricity still sparking from his fingers, making Layla flinch.

A low groan inside the room caught Noah's attention as he cradled Layla's head, and he looked over to see Jen and Paul Parker sluggishly push themselves up off the floor.

Catching Noah's eye, Paul stretched out his arm, silently begging Noah to come and help them.

He shifted Layla in his arms, then carried her gently to the bed in the corner of the room before running over to see his parents.

"Help us," Paul gasped. "That man… I don't know what he did… it was like he was sucking out our souls." He grabbed his chest as if to emphasise his point.

Noah flexed his hand and created a portal, Zion's life energy crackled from his fingertips once more. "I'm going to take you to the twins. You will be safe with them, so don't move from there until you are told you can."

Jen nodded, stiffly trying to stand, and Paul, properly seeing him for the first time, reached out and touched his cheek. "You look just like my Noah."

"I know," Noah replied softly, leaning into Paul's warm touch, reminding him of his own dad's.

Enjoying the affection for a moment, Noah took a deep breath. Then, he pulled back and bent to help Paul stand, slinging one of his arms over his shoulder before reaching down and doing the same with Jen. "I'll be back as soon as I can," he called to Layla, who was still slumped over on the bed.

Without waiting for a reply, Noah stepped through the portal and into Simmy's living room.

Portly Simmy, with her short auburn hair, looked up expectantly as he arrived.

"Thank goodness you are here," she breathed in relief, taking Jen from Noah and laying her down on the three-seater couch.

Noah staggered over to the armchair and sat Paul down, making sure he was comfortable before righting himself and walking back over to Simmy.

"I need to go back," Noah told her, looking around for the twins.

"Yes, go!" Simmy shooed him, her moonstone mandala already glowing a healing blue as she ran it over Jen's body. "The twins are playing upstairs. I will let them know their parents are here once I have healed them."

Noah bent and gave Simmy a quick peck on the cheek, then brought Zion's life energy back to his fingertips and created a new portal. "Thank you for helping."

"Of course," Simmy said. "We have known each other for a long time. I would do anything for them."

Stepping through the portal, Noah watched as the room disappeared around him, and with a *pop*, he was once again in the midst of the Guardians' Temple.

A loud explosion burst through his ears as soon as he arrived, and he turned to see Aaron and Simmy still battling Garvan, with no clear winner in sight.

Quickly running back to the room, Noah saw Layla trying to sit up. "Are you alright?" he asked, gingerly helping her up.

"I'm fine," she replied, holding her head but shaking off his help. "It's time to capture this guy."

Noah took Ray from his pocket, watched as she expanded to her full size and handed her to Layla. "You need her," he said, stopping her protest about them using Ray together. "I have Zion's life energy. It's about time I used it."

Turning towards the battle, Noah noticed Garvan was easily standing his ground against Aaron and Simmy, who's frustrated faces were scrunched up from the exertion of the fight.

Aaron and Garvan were sparring with their staff. Each advance one made was blocked by the other in a never-ending dance, while Simmy was using her mandala like an extension of her body. She tried to trap Garvan and knock him off his feet while dodging the energetic residue sparking from Garvan and Aaron's fight.

The air shifted beside Noah, and he saw Layla run forward to support Simmy, joining her in trying to trap Garvan. It didn't take long for the two of them to become completely in sync with one another. When one went low, the other went high, when one went left, the other went right.

Noah watched them for a minute, Zion's life energy rising to the surface of his skin as he waited to see how Garvan would respond.

He faltered in his steps for a fraction of a second before

regaining his ground and firing at the two girls.

Aaron hadn't wasted Garvan's moment of distraction, launching himself at his nephew, but Garvan quickly swapped his staff to his other hand and knocked Aaron back again.

Noah watched the scene in front of him for a moment longer, trying to decide on a course of action, before running in and supporting Aaron. Zion's life energy coursed through his veins, ready for a piece of the action.

"You have Zion's life energy, boy?" Garvan asked as soon as Noah reached them, amber and gold energy pulsing in the palm of his hand.

Noah ignored him, fusing the energy to form a single bolt of golden electricity, which he gripped like a spear.

Moving quickly, Noah lunged at Garvan, taking the older man by surprise. He felt Layla rush to his side, matching his movements step by step, weaving Ray, who was wearing Layla's energy like a blade, around her.

Sweat ran down Noah's temple. He forced himself to hold his ground as Garvan matched him blow for blow with ease. The group had captured Tick so easily, yet it was taking all four of them every ounce of power they had to merely knock Garvan off balance.

This duplicate was already so powerful. Noah shuddered to think how strong he would have become if he had absorbed either his or Nora's life energy.

Lunging forwards again, Noah aimed his lightning bolt at the hand that was holding Garvan's staff, but Garvan caught him with his other hand and bent his wrist back, forcing Noah to the ground. With a grunt of exertion, Noah ripped his hand out of Garvan's grip, barely registering that Garvan had hissed through his teeth in pain.

335

"Try that again, Noah!" Aaron called to him as he knocked a black energy ball away with his staff.

Noah lunged at Garvan once more while Simmy ran around and blasted him with her mandala from the back, and Layla weaved in to attack Garvan's other side.

Garvan was cornered with nowhere to go, which meant he had no choice but to block Noah's attack with his hand once again.

Garvan inhaled sharply as Zion's life energy burned him and quickly let go of Noah, giving Aaron, Simmy and Layla the chance to close in.

One more strike like that, and they would have him completely surrounded. They'd be able to capture him.

Noah forced more of Zion's life energy into the bolt of lightning he was still gripping, ignoring the piercing ache in his temples and readying himself for the next attack.

Noah roared as he jumped forward, but the wind was knocked out of him as he was thrown back, along with the rest of the group, by a strong gust that came out of nowhere.

Shielding his eyes and crouching on the floor with one knee raised, Noah squinted as he tried to find the source of the gale, then recoiled.

A new portal had opened.

Black electricity sparked from it, and Noah shivered in the wind, which turned icy as it forced its way out of the swirling abyss.

He was shaking, and the lightning bolt retracted back into Noah's palm as he attempted to protect his body from the sharp gale. Peering through his fingers, he watched in horror as a young man stepped through the portal.

Dressed in all black, just as he had been the last time Noah had seen him, the Garvan from his own timeline stared down at him before sneering and turning towards the older Garvan, who had moved in close to his creator.

"Sire," the older Garvan said, bowing so low his long grey hair brushed against the floor.

"Rise," Garvan said dismissively. "Did you get a twin?"

"I got the mother."

"Excellent," Garvan hissed, raising his hand and placing his thumb on the older Garvan's forehead. "That will do nicely."

The room exploded in black shadows. Dark electricity crackled, which forced Noah to raise his arms above his head to protect himself.

"NO!" he heard Aaron scream, and through the energy exploding from Garvan, Noah saw Aaron rushing forward, but it was too late. A final gust of wind knocked Aaron into Layla and Simmy, who were now sprawled on the floor, and pushed Noah back, sliding him away from the rest of the group.

When the wind died down, Noah lowered his arms and saw that Garvan was gone. Actually, both Garvans were gone.

"What was that?" he asked Aaron, who looked ashen.

"Garvan absorbed the duplicate," Aaron whispered, absently healing the large gash over his left eye.

"I thought he needed a twin's power," Layla said, staggering to her feet, half-carrying an exhausted Simmy with her.

"The Realm energy your mum has flowing through her must have been enough for now," Aaron replied. "The fact is, now that Garvan has absorbed power from this timeline, he has become even more powerful."

Noah rubbed his face with his hands, his arms stiff and aching. Even more powerful? They'd struggled to knock a duplicate off balance! How would they stand a chance against an even stronger Garvan?

Layla handed Ray back to Noah, who watched as she shrunk and then placed her in his pocket. "We need to get back," Layla said to the group, passing Simmy to Aaron and grabbing Noah's wrist. "We may not have much time before Garvan makes a move. We need to make ourselves stronger. We need more of Zion's life energy."

Aaron gripped Simmy and turned to Noah and Layla. "Noah," he said, "we need a portal."

"Right," Noah replied, dread settling in the pit of his stomach. He released the life energy to flow from his fingers once more and created a portal, waiting for the others to step through before he did so himself.

Chapter 51 - Noah

The group landed in Zion's kitchen. Aaron sat Simmy down on one of the bar stools and then got her a drink of water, which she gratefully accepted, while Noah and Layla each pulled a chair out from the kitchen table and slumped down, exhausted.

"What do we need to do? How do I connect with Zion to get more of his life energy?" Noah asked. He released a long breath out through his nose, his stomach churning.

Aaron walked over to him and placed his thumb on Noah's forehead like Garvan had done to his duplicate in the previous timeline. "You are going to have to absorb it through me. Since you already have his energy, he should not be able to hide from you."

"You're sure about this?" Noah asked hesitantly.

Aaron rocked back on his heels.

"Aaron?"

"Okay, look, this may not work. I am just going off a hunch."

Noah's head dropped back, and he groaned.

"But there is no reason it should *not* work," Aaron continued, holding his hands up defensively. "I will be linking you to Zion while keeping you grounded within the Realm. Zion is a Celestial," Aaron clarified, as Noah opened his mouth to ask why he needed to be grounded to the Realm, "and you have only been a Guardian for a short time. Too much of Zion's life energy will overwhelm you, so I will be here to stop that from happening."

Layla stood and positioned herself next to Aaron, placing her hand on Noah's shoulder. "I'm here too."

"Me too," Simmy said as she gingerly walked over to the group, placing her hand on Noah's other arm.

Taking a deep breath, Noah nodded. "Okay," he consented. "Let's do this."

Aaron pressed his thumb hard into Noah's forehead, and Noah closed his eyes, trying not to think of the uncomfortable pressure. There would surely be a bruise there tomorrow.

"Take a deep breath in," Aaron instructed him, and Noah filled his lungs.

Flickers of Zion sprang into Noah's mind. It looked like he was trapped in the same room he had been held in the first timeline they had travelled to. But, if that were the case, it would mean Zion was there willingly—that he could escape if he wanted to.

"Concentrate, Noah," Aaron called, his voice sounding faint, distant.

Noah could feel the light pressure of Simmy and Layla's hands on his arms, and he tried to push it out of his mind. He needed to focus solely on Zion.

Images flickered in and out. Zion was trying to tell Noah something, but the connection was too weak. All Noah noticed was that Zion looked exhausted. There were dark rings under his eyes, his toga was ripped, and the golden glow which usually emanated from him had dulled.

"Noah!" Aaron's voice was strained from the effort of

keeping Noah grounded as he egged him on to solidify the connection to Zion.

Finally, Noah connected fully. Zion was no longer flickering in and out, and it felt like Noah had been transported to the room itself.

Except Zion was talking, but no sound came out.

The connection wasn't perfect after all.

"I can't hear you," Noah shouted to him, hoping Zion would be able to hear him instead.

Zion stopped and looked at him with his large blue eyes, exhausted from the strain of holding the world on his shoulders. He sighed, resigning himself to something.

He walked towards Noah and placed his thumb on his forehead in the same place as Aaron's.

A jolt ran through Noah. His eyes widened, and his body stiffened as Zion transferred a larger portion of his life energy to him. Zion seemed to be handing over as much as he believed Noah could take, even though he looked reluctant to do so.

As the potent life energy coursed through his veins, Noah's body felt like it was burning up from the inside. He was screaming. He knew he was screaming, but he couldn't hear anything through the rush of blood in his ears.

His body couldn't take it.

Zion's life energy was going to consume him.

He wasn't strong enough to contain it.

Then, all of a sudden, Noah's knees buckled. The room began to fade, and everything around him turned black.

"Noah!" A voice called to him. "Don't you dare leave me, Noah!"

A small light began to flicker in the depths of Noah's mind

as the voice called to him, and the vision of a wild, red-haired girl appeared, holding her hand out to him.

"We're in this together," she said.

"Layla?" Noah reached out his hand to take hers.

"You weren't planning on giving up before you saw me again, were you?" Another voice called to him, taunting him, willing him to move forwards.

Another image appeared. This time there was a girl with wavy, dirty-blonde hair and amber eyes staring at him, holding out her hand for him to grab hold.

"Nora?" Noah croaked, reaching out his other hand for her to take.

"No sleeping on the job," Nora teased.

"Don't go slacking off now," Layla chipped in, and together they gripped Noah's hands, pulling him to his feet.

Noah's head cleared, and his vision focused. He was back in the room with Zion, whose thumb was still on his forehead, but he was also holding Noah steady with his other hand.

Electricity still coursed through him, but it no longer burned. Instead, Noah welcomed the energy, willing it to fuse with his own life force.

Zion was talking again, and Noah managed to catch a few jumbled words this time.

"… careful… plan… save Nora… twin."

He couldn't hear the whole message, but Noah had heard enough to know he needed to save Nora before Garvan could follow through with his plans.

"We'll save her," Noah said to Zion, patting the hand that was gripping his shoulder.

Zion shook his head and opened his mouth to speak again, but the room began to disappear as he was transported back to the palace.

Aaron knelt before him on his hands and knees, sweat dripping down his face. "Sorry," he panted, "I could not hold the connection any longer."

"It was long enough," Noah said, holding his hand out in front of him, watching as the gold and amber electricity sparked between his fingers. "Thank you." Noah gripped Aaron under his arm and helped him to his feet before resting his palm on Aaron's chest and sending healing blue energy through his body.

Aaron cracked his neck as the colour returned to his face. Flexing his hand and rubbing his shoulders, Aaron looked at Noah intently. "The transfer went well, by the look of things."

Noah cracked his back and jogged on the spot. He knew it was his body, but it felt like he had taken over someone much more powerful. "Yes, yes it did."

Layla took a step towards Noah as Simmy rushed forward to check over Aaron. "Are you okay?" Layla asked him.

Noah grinned. "Never felt better."

"I am going to take Aaron to the Earth room," Simmy called to Noah and Layla, guiding Aaron by the arm. "He has overexerted his body."

Noah waited until they had left, then swung his arms, stretched his hamstrings and jumped a few times, revelling in the newfound energy coursing through him. "I'm going to go and train for a little while," he said to Layla. "I need to get used to this new energy."

"I'll come with you," Layla said, making a move to grab Ray.

"No!" Noah exclaimed before backtracking at her suspicious look. "I mean, no," he said more gently. "I need some time to adjust. I want to see what I can do by myself."

Layla gave him a sceptical look but didn't argue with him. "I'll go and freshen up then," she said, slowly turning on her heel, walking slowly out of the kitchen.

Noah had a feeling that 'freshen up' meant 'discuss Noah's new energy at length with Aaron and Simmy', but he didn't want to argue with her. Not when he was getting exactly what he wanted; time alone to test out his new powers.

Noah waited for Layla's footsteps to recede, and then he stepped outside onto the field, bringing his life energy to the surface of his skin.

Garvan was getting more powerful by the day, and Noah knew he had to become as strong as possible if he wanted to save Nora and help the Realm.

The energy at his fingertips sparked, but he decided to take things slowly at first to test his limits. Noah walked over to the garden by the side of the field and saw a little sproutling that had freshly popped up through the ground.

Kneeling before it, Noah lightly touched one of its small leaves, and, as if time was on fast-forward, the sproutling shook and grew before his eyes, and would have kept on growing if Noah hadn't taken his fingers away.

Now, where the little plant had been before, there stood a small lemon tree. The veins in its leaves were tinted with amber and gold, and the small fruit it bore was also dyed with Noah's new energy signature.

Noah grinned to himself. He stood up and took his time walking around the entire garden, helping all of the little sproutlings to grow until there was a whole group full of small, tie-dyed trees.

He thought back to when he had practised this particular skill in the first timeline they'd gone to and how he'd been limited to helping flowers bloom. But now... now he could do so much more! If this is what he could do for a plant, imagine what he could do to help actual people.

Looking down at his hands, he released more energy and watched the electricity coursing through his fingers. For the first time, Noah revelled in the burning sensation running through his veins.

Pop!

A small portal appeared in the yard, and Marian's head poked out through it.

She looked awful.

Her long brown hair was tangled and messy. There were dark circles under her eyes, and her lips were chapped to the point of bleeding.

"Noah," she croaked. "Help... Nora... Danger."

Noah's stomach dropped, his head spun, and his throat thickened. His and Zion's melded life energy rumbled within him, sparking erratically.

A bright globe of light appeared before him, and without questioning, Noah reached out and grabbed it. Ray materialised in his hand, her warmth radiating through him.

"Take me to her," he said to Marian.

Nodding once, Marian's head disappeared, and the portal grew big enough for Noah to step through.

Without hesitation, Noah followed her through and felt the portal close behind him. There was a nagging in the pit of his stomach telling him he should have told Layla and the others where he was going, but he ignored it.

The only thing that mattered right now was Nora.

Chapter 52 - Aaron

"We cannot keep going like this! We need to be able to use our full powers!" Aaron ran his fingers through his dark hair, frustrated, while Simmy stood before him with her hands on her hips.

"Zion has not found a solution for a reaso—"

"Zion is overwhelmed and does not realise the extent to which our powers are capped!" Aaron interrupted, standing so quickly that Simmy had to take a step back. "Our fight with Garvan in the last timeline was pathetic. We should not have had that much trouble with him, regardless of whether he had absorbed Jen Parker's powers or not."

Aaron paused his rant as the door to the Earth room slammed open with a BANG, and Layla ran inside, her eyes wild.

"Ray's gone!" she puffed. "I was tuning her, then she started glowing and disappeared. I tried to find Noah to see if he knew where she went, but he's gone too!"

Aaron cursed before sending out a thin stream of energy throughout the palace to see if he could locate Noah.

Nothing.

Cursing again, Aaron had just whirled around to ask Layla for more details when Simmy came rushing out of the rebirthing chamber with Garvan from the third timeline.

"We need an extra power boost if we are going to get Noah back," she said, gesturing towards Garvan. "This Garvan has offered to give us his energy."

Aaron's stomach clenched. He didn't want to touch any of Garvan's power, regardless of whether he claimed he was good or not, but it looked like they didn't have a choice. Zion, being in the state he was in, couldn't release the hold he had on them, and they couldn't go into battle with the limited powers they had. "Fine."

Simmy and Garvan held out their hands for Aaron to clasp, the three of them forming a circle while Layla stood on and watched.

"Layla, you will need to create a shield around yourself, so you are not exposed to the transfer," Simmy called out to her niece, and Aaron saw her quickly encircle herself in a shield of flames, the warmth coming from it prickling his skin.

"I just wanted to say," Garvan began, and Aaron looked at him, "I am glad to be able to help you in this way. I never wanted my original to get my powers, so I am happy you two are instead."

Garvan squeezed Aaron's hand, and his heart thawed a little. "Thank you," he said, "for agreeing to help us."

Garvan nodded, then closed his eyes and took a deep breath. Aaron saw his life energy rush to their conjoined hands.

It started black as it left Garvan's body before shifting into Aaron's sapphire blue life energy as it entered his own.

The same was happening with Simmy. Garvan's life energy turned red as it flowed into her body.

Soon, the shield Layla created was reflecting black, sapphire and auburn light as Garvan's life energy transferred between hosts. Aaron breathed a sigh of relief as the cap on him shattered, and he finally felt like himself for the first time in what seemed like a lifetime.

Garvan's life energy flowing into Aaron slowed down, and his grip began to loosen. Aaron tried to wrench his hand away to curb the flow, realising he didn't want Garvan to give his life, but Garvan refused to stop. He gave every drop of his life energy to Aaron and Simmy, and as the last of it trickled into the two of them, the black, shimmering light surrounding Garvan dimmed, and he shot them both a grin as his body dissolved into the air, then he was gone.

Aaron's fist clenched the space where Garvan's hand had been, and he saw Simmy staring at the now-empty space next to her.

"He did not have to do that," she said. "We are going to stand a chance because of him."

Aaron didn't know why the duplicate's last act was one of rebellion, but before he had a chance to dwell on it, Layla's shield disappeared, and she walked over to Simmy, gripping her elbow. "What's the plan?"

"We need to see what is going on at the temple," Aaron replied, drawing a circle in the air with his finger and watching as it turned into a small mirror, showing the trio the eleven Guardian siblings.

Chapter 53 - Nora

Being locked in a fancier environment didn't make Nora's situation feel any less like being in a prison.

And no matter how many times Nora blasted the doors, pounded the walls or tried jumping off the balcony, she was always teleported straight back to the middle of the room.

Now, scratched, bruised and her energy depleted, Nora picked at the mediocre scraps of food Tick had shoved through her door earlier, nibbling on an almond and not bothering to pick up the dry crackers and cheese that that been haphazardly plonked onto the plate alongside the nuts.

None of this was enough to replenish her energy, but she had a feeling that was the point.

As she lifted the last almond to her lips, a strange current of energy coursed through Nora's veins. She jumped out of her chair, pushing the plate away from her, barely noticing as it crashed onto the floor from the table she had been sitting at.

Sprinting for the door, Nora was roughly flung back as soon as she reached it, and she groaned, her back aching where she'd landed on it.

The energy had felt so familiar. Familiar, yet different.

She needed to know what it was.

Was Garvan plotting another scheme?

She scoffed as she remembered him offering to let her rule by his side as he lorded over the Earth.

There was no chance in hell she would ever do that.

But still, a small part of her believed that Garvan truly thought he was saving the Realm, regardless of the barbaric way he was going about it.

Lifting her head off the ground, Nora saw someone—or something—walk past her door. She crawled over to it, peering under the crack to see if she could see anything.

Nothing.

Gritting her teeth, Nora sat back and waited.

There was nothing she could do while she was stuck in here, so she just had to hope the source of the energy would find its way to her.

And when it did, she would escape, whether she had taken Garvan down or not.

Chapter 54 - Noah

With a *pop*, the portal Noah had stepped through led him to the Throne Room. As usual, the eleven Guardian siblings were petrified, and Noah ran and ducked behind the pillar at the side of the room out of habit.

Scanning his surroundings, Noah looked for any sign of movement, but there was none.

"Marian?" Noah whispered. "Where are you?"

"Here," Marian croaked next to him, appearing out of nowhere, her projection flickering. "I cannot stay for long. I have used too much energy as it is."

"Where's Nora?" Noah asked urgently, not wanting to keep her in this form longer than he needed to.

"Garvan's chamber," Marian replied. "He said something about 'absorbing her energy' and took her with him."

Noah's blood turned to ice. "No. No! That's not going to happen!"

"You have to go, quickly!" Marian urged.

Scanning the room once more and finding it bare, Noah sprinted to the double doors that led out of the Throne Room. He pushed them open in haste, wincing as they slammed against the walls.

A part of him wanted to find Zion first and fight Garvan with him, but another part of him squashed that idea down as quickly as it had arisen.

There was no time.

As Noah made his way through the corridor, he noticed the temple was eerily quiet. Even Tick hadn't popped up at the racket he'd made. Noah had been expecting her to be patrolling the temple like she used to in his dreams back on Earth.

She must be keeping watch over Garvan, Noah told himself.

Deciding to keep a low profile nonetheless, Noah scanned the hall around him before running as fast as he could towards the next, thanking the Realm that the temple was the same in every timeline. Otherwise, he'd have had no idea where Garvan's chamber was.

Noah weaved his way through the temple's labyrinth-like halls before arriving in front of the chamber, looking around once more to make sure he was alone.

His heart stuttered. A small movement in the corner of his eye had caught his attention, but when he turned to see what it was, there was nothing there.

Taking a deep breath to calm himself down, Noah peered into the room from behind the door frame to try to see what was happening inside, but it was pitch black.

There wasn't any sign of movement. He couldn't hear anything either.

It was too still. Too quiet.

Fear gripped him like a vice. What if he was too late? What if Garvan had already absorbed Nora's life energy?

Noah stepped inside, pulling Ray from his pocket and holding her up to his face. "Give me light," he whispered, and her gemstones began to glow, illuminating the room in front of him.

It looked untouched. There wasn't any sign of a struggle.

A loud bang caused Noah to jump. The door he had just come through slammed shut behind him, and he turned wildly to see what had caused it.

He had expected it to be Garvan, or even Tick, but instead, floating before him was a wispy shadow.

It didn't look threatening, flickering in the light Ray projected, so Noah walked towards it.

There was something... familiar about it.

He held out his finger, reaching forward to touch the shadow which stretched towards Noah as if also reaching out a finger. As soon as they touched, Noah felt a tug in the pit of his stomach, and the shadow trembled as its body began to take shape.

With a jolt, Noah realised why this shadow felt so familiar. It was *his* shadow, the one that had been ripped from him when he'd first come to the Realm.

"Thanks," the Shadow Being hissed as his form completed, a wide, sharp-toothed grin forming on his face. "I needed your energy."

Tick appeared behind the new Shadow Being and cackled. "I told you it was worth waiting for your owner's life force before forming," she said to him. Then she turned to Noah and sneered, slowly looking him up and down. "Just as Garvan planned."

Noah's stomach churned as he whirled furiously towards Tick. "What do you mean *'Just as Garvan planned'*?"

Noah's Shadow Being cackled and cracked its neck. "Ahh, it feels so good to have a proper body." His voice was deeper

353

than Tick's, but it had the same scratchy tone to it. "Name's Tank," he said to Noah, holding out his clawed hand as if expecting Noah to shake it. When Noah didn't, he pulled his hand away and shrugged. "Rude."

Tick howled with laughter.

Noah's blood boiled as he watched the exchange. "Where's Nora?" he demanded.

"Nora…" Tick drawled, scratching her head, "Nora… that name doesn't ring a bell." She turned to Tank. "Do you know a Nora?"

Tank stretched his arms lazily. "You mean the girl Garvan's been playing with?"

Noah growled.

"Oh, right." Tick feigned recognition. "*That* Nora. Dunno."

"Well, this has been swell," Tank said, walking to the door and opening it, "but I've got places to be, people to scare. You know how it is."

Tick sniggered and followed Tank to the door, leaving Noah's blood boiling, Zion's life energy sparking from his fists as he gripped a burning-hot Ray.

Letting out a scream of frustration, Noah shot an energy blast at the Shadow Beings' retreating backs, but Tank had closed the door just in time, and the blast was deflected back at Noah.

Diving out of the way, Noah hit the floor with a thud, his elbow throbbing painfully where he landed.

"Tut, tut," a voice crooned as it entered the room, its owner walking straight through the closed door. "It is not nice to attack people while their backs are turned."

The air in the room became ice cold.

"Garvan," Noah hissed, goosebumps prickling his skin as

he stood.

"So noble of you to come to your sister's rescue." Garvan roamed his eyes over Noah, from his head to his feet. "And all by yourself, too."

Noah noticed that Garvan had grown older since the last time he'd seen him. His hair was slightly longer, and he'd removed his jacket and was just wearing his dress shirt with the sleeves rolled up, which he'd matched with dress pants and shiny business shoes, all of which were black.

"I love your outfit," Noah sneered. "Such a variety of colours."

Garvan let out a low chuckle but continued taking him in, slowly circling Noah as if checking out his prey.

Not taking his eyes off Garvan, Noah realised that this transformation was most likely due to the power he had absorbed from the Garvan of the last timeline. Noah knew that meant he was stronger than he had been before, which terrified him. Noah had been no match for Garvan when he had gone to find Abigail, and he had been with Layla and Arel then!

Zion's life energy zapped along Noah's fingertips as if to remind him he didn't have access to it last time, which eased Noah's doubts a smidgeon.

Garvan stopped circling Noah, apparently pleased with what he saw. He waved his hand, conjuring a flickering image of Marian in front of him.

"Help... Nora..." the image said in its crackly voice. "Help... Nora.."

Noah's heart lurched as he stared at the hologram. "Where's Nora?" he asked, cursing himself when his voice cracked.

Garvan laughed and waved the projection of Marian away.

"Where she has always been." His voice dropped as he added, "She has been very, very useful to me."

Noah clenched his jaw so hard it popped.

"But if you want to see her so badly…" Garvan clicked his fingers. Tick and Tank threw the door open and thrust Nora roughly into Garvan, who pulled her to him, holding her in place by her hair.

Noah called out when he saw her. Her face was bruised, there were scratches all over her arms and legs, and her clothes, the black leathers she was wearing, were ripped.

Nora snapped her teeth at Garvan once.

Garvan laughed and forced her to her knees in front of him on the floor, making sure to keep a firm grip on her hair. "She has been a lot of fun to have around here."

Noah watched helplessly as Garvan ran a finger down Nora's face, rested it under her chin and tilted it so she was forced to look up at him. Noah wanted to help her so badly, but he also knew if he attacked now, Nora would be in even more danger than she was already. So, with every fibre of his being, he willed himself to stay where he was.

Tick and Tank cackled as they watched the scene from the doorway. Tank was role-playing the events in front of them dramatically while Tick doubled over with laughter.

This hadn't gone unnoticed by Garvan, who rolled his eyes, letting go of Nora's hair and throwing her at Noah, who lurched forwards to catch her.

"I am not ready for you to fulfil your purpose just yet," Garvan said to Noah, waving his hand at the twins, encasing them in a black bubble. "Take them to the guest chambers," he instructed Tick and Tank, turning on his heel and opening a portal.

"Yes, sir!" Tick and Tank replied, instantly standing to attention.

"Make sure they are *well* looked after."

"Yes, sir!"

Looking Nora over one last time– the act making Noah's hairs stand on end– Garvan stepped through a black portal, disappearing with a *pop*.

Noah gently placed Nora down, then punched the bubble as hard as he could, but all that did was cause his knuckles to crack and his hand to throb painfully. He cradled it to his chest as Tick and Tank both gripped a side of the bubble and began pushing them roughly out of Garvan's chamber, Noah toppling over as they moved.

"What are you doing here?" Nora hissed to Noah, bumping her head on the side of the bubble as Tick and Tank not-so-accidentally hit the doorframe on their way out of the room.

"Marian came to me. She said you were in danger," Noah replied, clenching his jaw. "Now I see it was just a ploy to get me here as quickly as possible."

"Why didn't Layla come with you?" Nora asked, "or Aaron and Simmy, for that matter."

"I was by myself when the message came. I jumped through the portal straight away. There was no time to get the others."

Nora was silent for a minute.

"What's wrong?" Noah asked her.

"I…" She hesitated.

"What?" Noah pressed.

"We're here," Tick said, breaking into the twins' conversation as she and Tank threw them into a large bedroom.

"Home sweet home," Tank jeered, using one of his claws to pop the bubble.

Noah looked around the room. He'd thought that Garvan was being ironic when he said to take good care of them, but the room they were in was massive!

It was painted white, and there was gold trim on everything, including the couch and pillows on the bed.

Noah touched a cushion that was resting on the couch. It was real gold.

He looked at Nora, who was looking around the room with a sour expression on her face.

"There's no point trying to escape," Tick said to them as she and Tank sauntered out of the room. "The doorway's rigged. You'll just end up right back here. Although, you already know how it works, right Nora? You've been living here for a while now."

Nora just scowled.

"Any questions?" Tank asked, leaning against the doorframe lazily and looking at the twins.

Neither one of them made a sound.

"Alrighty then," Tank said, saluting them. "Enjoy your stay."

Turning on their shadowy heels, Tick and Tank closed the door behind them, leaving the twins in the guest chamber by themselves.

Chapter 55 - Nora

Looking around her room with Noah by her side, Nora let out a long breath through her nose and turned to him. He was staring at her.

"You don't look surprised to be here," he said.

"Here in this room or here with you?" Nora questioned, although she knew what he meant.

"I'm sure you're surprised I'm here, but last I saw, you were still confined to that little room near the Guardian siblings. When did you get an upgrade?"

Nora scoffed, but as she took in the finery surrounding her, she tilted her head to the side in resignation. "Garvan thought he could buy my loyalty with a nicer bedroom and proper training."

Noah raised an eyebrow. "*Proper* training? What do you mean by *proper* training?"

"I'm sure you're aware you are not using your powers to their full potential," Nora replied, looking at him from the corner of her eye before padding over to the large tan couch and plopping down on it. She felt the cushions shift underneath her as Noah jumped down next to her.

"I'm not? I know Zion's powers are difficult to manage sometimes, but I'm getting better."

Nora turned to him fully, her eyes wide. *"Zion's* power?" She shook her head. "I'll deal with that later. How were you taught to use your powers? What's your natural talent?"

"I connect easily with earth, so Aaron taught me how to make weapons from trees and stuff."

Nora's eyes narrowed. "Aaron told you that you had to make weapons from *trees and stuff* instead of just teaching you how to utilise the earth itself?"

Noah nodded.

"Noah, you are aware that earth is *everywhere,* right? You could be using everything around you to your advantage."

"That's not what Aaron said."

"I don't know why Aaron and Simmy haven't been training us properly, but they've been holding us back, and now that you have Zion's power—actually, why *do* you have Zion's power?"

"I was struggling to connect with the Realm properly. Zion syphoned some of his power to me, so I wouldn't take as long to recover after travelling to each timeline."

Nora inhaled loudly as she leaned back into the soft couch in thought.

"What?" Noah questioned her.

"Surely they could train you to rely on your own power instead of just palming Zion's off onto you."

"I was pretty beaten up, Nora. They helped me a lot!"

"Okay, okay." Nora raised her hands in surrender. "Did you adapt to it well? Has it been easy to manage?"

Noah opened his mouth to rebuke her but then closed it, turning to look out the large glass doors instead.

"I didn't think so," Nora muttered.

"What about you?" Noah fired back at her. "What have you

been doing?"

"Training. Trying to see if I can take these guys down from the inside."

"And did you find anything?"

"Nothing of substance. They have a girl from uni here, though. Abigail."

"I know Abigail."

"You do? Well, Garvan and Tick are holding her captive. I haven't been able to get back and help her yet. They confined me to this room when I found her."

"And you're still alive?!" Noah looked at her incredulously. It was Nora's turn to look away.

Noah placed a hand on her shoulder, turning her toward him. "What's actually happened here? Why are you in this room? Why is Garvan training you? What aren't you telling me?"

Nora sighed, standing up and stretching her back, contemplating how best to explain the situation to Noah. "Garvan wants me to be his—"

"Sorry-not-sorry to interrupt your little chat," a scratchy voice called from above. Nora and Noah jumped to attention, their backs touching as they scanned the room.

A portal appeared above them, black energy crackling from it, and out stepped Garvan, followed closely by Tick and Tank.

Tick was the one who had spoken.

The portal disappeared, and the three of them hovered in the air above the twins. Tick and Tank roughly grabbed Noah by his arms, forcing him to the other side of the room.

Garvan appeared directly beside Nora and grabbed her by her hair, pushing her down to her knees once more.

"Zion," Garvan whispered to her, "has ensured I have

everything I need without you. This is your last chance to accept my offer."

Nora heard Noah trying to fight off Tick and Tank. She allowed herself to glimpse over at him, just in time to see golden and amber energy spark at his fingertips as he roughly pushed Tick's head against the wall, blasting a hole through her temple as it connected with the hard surface.

Garvan's breath tickled her ear as he watched her, and Nora closed her eyes, feeling herself leaning into him slightly as she whispered, "I can't."

Garvan's breath hissed through his teeth, and his grip on her tightened to the point of pain.

"Disappointing. I have no use for you then, although it has been a pleasure," he said, raising his hand and creating a black blade over his fingers, the energy surrounding it sparking menacingly.

"No!" Noah called out, and Nora opened her eyes to see Tank pinning him to the ground, a furious Tick standing over them as her head regenerated.

The twins' eyes met, and Nora's heart lurched at the thought of what Noah would have to go through if he was left here by himself. Her blood pumping through her veins, Nora bucked against Garvan's grip. Water exploded from her pouch, forming hundreds of tiny needles, all aimed at Garvan.

She looked up again, just in time to see Noah's eyes widen as Garvan thrust his blade through Nora's back and out her chest.

A deathly gasp escaped Nora's lips, and her own eyes widened in shock.

Amber energy exploded from Nora's wound. She felt herself dissolve into nothingness.

Chapter 56 - Noah

"NO!" Noah screamed, pounding at Tank, his fist still covered with his and Zion's life energy, until he felt the Shadow Being's grip loosen.

Using that moment to escape, Noah shoved Tank off him with his foot before propelling himself up and launching himself at Garvan, who stopped Noah's advance with a flick of his hand. Noah slammed into his shield, breaking his nose in the process.

Blood streamed down Noah's face. He didn't even bother to heal himself, and he slipped down to the floor while Garvan slowly made his way towards him.

Everything he'd done.

This whole journey.

It had been to save Nora.

He'd had less than two hours with her, and now she was gone.

He had been so sure that he would be able to rescue Nora, save the Realm and go back to Earth to be with his family again. All of it, everything he had worked towards and everything he'd sacrificed, was for nothing.

"Brave, coming here all by yourself." Garvan circled him, his black dress shoes tapping on the marble floor as he walked, before stopping in front of him and tilting his face up to meet his eyes.

Noah stared at him blankly.

"I suspect that is why Zion gave you his life energy. He knew you would use it well."

Noah didn't even acknowledge he'd heard him.

"Nora had her uses, I will admit," Garvan went on, "but you are the one I need now."

Garvan gripped Noah's chin tightly with his thumb and forefinger and turned his head from side to side, inspecting him.

"You do not seem to be anything spectacular," Garvan said, tutting. "Nora had an enormous amount of natural talent, but you... you seem incredibly ordinary."

Noah felt the energy inside him flicker to life at the mention of Nora, but Garvan didn't seem to notice. He continued to tilt Noah's head from side to side until, finally having had enough, Noah ripped his face out of Garvan's hands.

Garvan raised an eyebrow and stood up straight. "Tank," Garvan called, clicking his fingers at the Shadow Being.

"Present." Tank instantly appeared next to Noah, bowing to Garvan.

"Tick," Garvan called, snapping his fingers once more.

"Yes, sir?" Tick asked, appearing beside Tank.

"Go and fetch our other guest. He must be dying for some fresh air."

Cackling, Tick and Tank bowed deeply before speeding out of the room.

Noah's body felt dirty after being handled by Garvan, but he resumed his blank stare as Garvan took him in from afar, his cold blue eyes boring through him.

Tick and Tank came bouncing back into the room, pulling Zion behind them, bound by a golden chain.

Noah started in shock and tried to catch Zion's eye, but the Celestial was staring at Garvan.

"Do you know why I have summoned you here, Father?" Garvan sneered as he said the final word.

"I have my theories," Zion replied. His voice was calm, softer than Noah was expecting, and there was pity etched on his face.

Garvan's face changed from a sneer to a look of fury as he walked over to Zion and leaned in uncomfortably close to his face. *"Stop looking at me like that!"* Garvan hissed. "I have accomplished more than you ever have! *I* am the reason the Realm will flourish!"

"The Realm is becoming more unstable by the minute because of what you have done," Zion replied, his deep voice resigned.

"The Realm is on the cusp of being reborn, and you have provided me with the last piece of the puzzle. Watch." Garvan stalked over to Noah and placed his thumb on his forehead, the same way Aaron had done, what felt like a lifetime ago, to transfer Zion's life energy to him.

Noah's entire body froze when Garvan touched him, and his forehead felt like it was on fire. He couldn't fight back, even if he'd wanted to.

Blood rushed through his ears, and Noah wanted to scream, writhe, anything! But he couldn't. It was like Garvan had petrified him, and for a terrifying moment, Noah thought that was what had happened.

And then he felt it.

He wasn't sure what it was at first, the tingling sensation

on his forehead, but then it changed, and it felt like his very soul was being pulled from his body.

Garvan gave a breathy laugh, and Noah saw his body begin to emit an amber and golden glow.

He's stealing my life energy from me! Noah realised.

Noah darted his eyes to Zion. Seeing the helpless look on his face, he realised Zion couldn't do anything.

He was bound and had given Noah most of his life energy in an attempt, Noah now understood, to stop Garvan from taking it exactly like this.

Fighting the hold Garvan had on him, Noah kicked and clawed at the mental barriers keeping him in place. He felt his fingers become raw and bloody as if he had been beating against a physical shield.

STOP! He wordlessly shouted to the abyss. *NO MORE!*

To Noah's surprise, his life energy stopped flowing out of him, like a tap had been turned off.

Garvan jolted as if someone had pushed him, but his thumb remained firmly on Noah's forehead. "Oh no you do not," Garvan muttered under his breath. "This rightly belongs to me!" He pushed his thumb even harder into Noah's forehead, trying to keep the connection as tight as possible.

Noah's mind stuttered, and the energy began to flow out of him again. He tried closing the gate once more, but it was useless. Garvan's will was too strong.

And now it was Zion's life energy slowly flowing out of him.

Garvan flicked his cold eyes to Noah's and sneered. "Your help is greatly appreciated."

Noah snapped, unfreezing enough to growl, "You killed my sister! I would never help you!"

Tears springing to his eyes, amber and gold energy exploded from Noah's pores, severing the connection Garvan had created. Garvan was pushed backwards, his shoes sliding along the tiled floor as he flung his arms up to protect his face.

Noah's forehead felt raw where Garvan had drawn the energy from him, but he ignored it, his amber eyes glowing and sparkling with energy as he stepped towards Garvan.

Garvan dropped his arms, looking Noah head-on furiously, daring him to come closer.

The energy stopped.

No, the energy hadn't stopped. It was pulling itself back into Noah. All the life energy Garvan had stolen from him was rushing back into his body so fast that Noah's head spun.

"Noah," he heard Zion call, "Noah, you do not need that energy back. You have enough within you already."

But Noah barely registered what he'd said.

The image of Nora being stabbed right in front of him flooded his mind, and his eyes glowed gold, his pupils disappearing.

"That energy is *mine!*" Garvan growled, making a move to disappear, but Noah quickly launched himself at Garvan, almost teleporting, and gripped his wrist, forcing him to stay put.

"YOU DARE TOUCH ME?!" Garvan bellowed, blasting black energy balls at Noah as he tried to pull his wrist free.

Noah didn't budge. He barely felt a thing.

He saw Garvan raise his other hand once more, a large black energy ball crackling in his palm.

"You asked for this," Garvan panted. He thrust the blast directly into Noah's heart.

367

But Zion's life energy had now completely surrounded Noah, covering his entire body in its protective shield.

Garvan's energy ball didn't make a dent.

As soon as the blast touched Noah's energy shield, it evaporated, and Garvan was thrown back. But, as Noah was still gripping his wrist, he was pulled forward once again, ricocheting back into place.

Garvan's eyes were wide as the last droplets of energy he'd stolen were sucked from his body and reabsorbed by Noah's.

"My energy could never be yours," Zion said softly, raising his hand and watching as Noah began to syphon more of his life energy out of him. As the energy flowed from Zion's fingers, colour returned to his face as if he was releasing a burden.

"STOP GIVING HIM MORE!" Garvan screeched, trying to pull his arm away from Noah fruitlessly.

Noah refused to budge, his golden eyes still boring into Garvan's face.

Zion ignored him.

"LET ME GO!" Garvan bellowed, tugging on his arm like a madman. "TICK! TANK! I ORDER YOU TO HELP ME!"

"We want to!" Tick called from afar. "Tank, where are you going? Tank?" Tank must have disappeared, as he didn't reply.

"Useless!" Garvan muttered, still trying to pull his arm away.

Noah had never felt more alive.

There were no blocks. Nothing stopped him from receiving the full extent of Zion's life energy, which his body greedily sucked out of the Celestial. Instead of burning him as it had done before, the energy replenished him.

When the flow stopped, Noah turned to Zion, his eyes returning to their natural amber, and saw the Celestial looking healthier than he had ever seen him.

He felt a tugging on his arm and let Garvan go without warning, watching as he fell to the floor.

Garvan landed gracelessly on his tailbone and wasted no time in scrambling to his feet, getting as far away from Noah as he could.

He threw a steely glare at his father before opening a dark portal and throwing himself through it. Tick managed to slide through with him just before it closed with a *pop*.

Noah watched them leave, not bothering to stop them. He was being urged to pick up Ray.

So he did.

He reached into his pocket and grabbed her, watching as Ray expanded to her full form, her gemstones crackling with power.

He held her to his chest and closed his eyes.

Ray exploded with heat. Noah could feel the burn, but it didn't hurt him.

"Noah!"

He could hear Zion in the background, but it was white noise.

Noah turned his face to the ceiling, and golden energy shot out of his eyes and mouth, engulfing the room in its glow. He released Ray from his grip as a burning pain stabbed through him, but it disappeared as quickly as it came.

The golden light changed to orange for the sunstone, green for the emerald, black for the onyx, deep blue for the lapis lazuli, purple for the amethyst, rainbow for the opal and sapphire blue for the sapphire, and continued to glow until all the colours of Ray's gems shot out of Noah like a beacon.

The light subsided, and Noah touched his chest. Ray had melded with him, and heat radiated into his fingers as he brushed them over the marks she had created.

A small *pop* caught Noah's attention, and he saw Zion disappear in a shroud of sapphire energy, but he barely registered it.

He walked out of Nora's chamber and made his way to the Throne Room, where the eleven Guardian siblings were being held.

One by one, he placed his thumb on their foreheads, sharing a tiny fraction of his life energy with them and watching as the petrification wore off.

Each of the Guardians stood unsteadily on their feet, looking at Noah as he passed them.

"Welcome to our temple," Arel said finally, stepping forward and gripping Noah's forearm in greeting.

Noah gripped Arel's arm back before turning to the large window they had been facing.

Noah had never looked at it before. It was only now he realised it was split into two views, one that showed the Earth and one that showed the Realm.

He walked over to them, placing a hand on each screen.

The Guardians followed, standing behind him.

Noah looked at the glass, his chest burning. "We have a lot of work to do."